PROLOGUE

"So what are you afraid of?"

His voice was deep and cold, all graveyard sounding and shit, and she didn't care. He lit up one of his own special smokes with a spark from his lighter, a momentary flicker of light showing off his rough face with the thin scars and deep set eyes reflecting the flame, then pitch black again. Only the silver rings on his hands gripping the wheel were visible as they drove down the dark road. Each one in the shape of a skull. Each and every one of them smiling.

She met him at the CubbyHole, a grungy little bar on the main strip here in Waverly, and he seemed nice enough. Bought her a few drinks, danced once to some old country song that was made before she was, and then she made him an offer he couldn't refuse.

She just smiled back at him in the dark of the car, passing street lights setting her face aglow in the soft autumn rain, and she took another hit on the blunt he passed her. He was a weird old dude, sexy in his own rough way, but he had good jokes and even better weed so if his conversation was kind of off it was no big deal. The three hundred dollars was kind of a good incentive too.

"Afraid of? Me? Not much this side of a Pit Bull with rabies." she grinned back in answer to his question and let her head fall back. Big man with a ponytail. Biker type. Sleeveless shirt showing off his well-toned arms and tattoos. More skulls there too. "I've seen a lot of strange shit in my nineteen years. Why you ask?"

"I always ask, and I bet you have." he said tapping those ringed fingers on the steering wheel while humming along with some classic rock tune. He had to be older than he looked if he was into this shit, she figured. "Makes for interesting conversation. Lightens the mood. I used to be afraid of things crawling under my bed as a kid. You?"

"The dark never bothered me." she said shifting her legs. "You care if I ask you something?"

"You ask me whatever you want, darlin'." he said bopping his head and casting glances at her twisting legs. Long and smooth like creamy butter in fishnet.

"Well, it's kinda personal and if you don't want to answer-"

He just laughed out loud in the darkness before answering.

"I don't get offended easy." he turned grinning at her like a smoky devil in the dark. "You don't have to worry about hurting my feelings, sweetheart."

"How'd you get the scars?" she asked.

"These little guys?" he said bringing up his hand to the right side of his face. "Some little bitch stripper in Kansas City. Pulled a knife on me." he smiled. "You into rough sex, babe?"

"As long as it's your ass getting beat and not mine." she laughed.

"I can deal with that." he grinned. "You know, my old man died right here on this parking lot when I was just a kid. Right by that drug store." he said pointing.

"That's completely fucked up." she said. "How'd he die? Heart attack?"

"Suicide by cop." the big man smiled over at her in the darkness. "Not a big prison fan."

"Who is?" she shot back.

"Don't talk much, do you?"

"Depends, I guess." she said looking out the window into the passing darkness. The motel wasn't far. All too familiar roads. Roads full of people going nowhere with their lives. She couldn't stomach working in one of those places again with time clocks and two weeks off a year. As soon as she saved up enough money from selling tail she was getting out to Los Angeles with her step-mom, her father's second wife, and she was going to help run her hair saloon. Legal shit where they would be their own bosses. None of this funky uniform wearing crap flipping burgers and smiling like a fucking maroon while telling people to "Have a nice day" or "Would you like fries with that?" shit. "I can talk about anything. Just not politics or religion. Neither one can save my ass."

"I hear you there, babe." he said and she eyed him over good again. He looked like he could be dangerous if he wanted to be. She had her butterfly knife tucked away for protection, a small canister of pepper spray, and one hit on her cell phone and Amos, the big bodyguard who worked for her pimp, would be all over him in seconds. He was always outside on the parking lot at the motel. "Gotta make a quick stop here at the drugstore and then we can get down to business."

"Stop for what?" she said not liking the detour. "I got condoms, baby. All sizes, brands and flavors. Just keep going. It's a few blocks down. The Blackstone Inn. I don't have all night for pit stops."

More laughter, deep and dark from where she couldn't see his face.

"Oh, I think you do." he said pulling into the near empty lot. "This is where it all started." he said smiling and taking a deep breath. "Long before the earth was completely populated, far away from the Promised Land. When the first morning star fell to the earth. The Spawning of one and another was conformed here. Right here." he said tapping his finger pointing to the center of the lot. "This is where my ancestors were born."

"What in the hell are you talking about?" Cherry said looking out around them. "You Native-American or something? This is a strip mall. Nothing special ever happened here, I can tell you that."

"Oh, you're wrong, but never mind about that. Just relax. I need a special brand of condom, I'm allergic to latex. So don't go making a fuss." he told her pulling the big black '67 Impala into the middle of four empty spaces so as nobody could park next to him. "What's your name anyway?" he asked her shifting the car into park and turning off the engine. "Just curious."

"I told you, Cherry." she said smacking her lips and pulling down the visor to check her face in the mirror. He stared at her and smiled wide and gave a soft deep laugh that chilled her.

"No, I mean your *real* name." he said and she turned on him, noticing his smile seemed illuminated there in the dark as he spoke to her. "What did your parents name you? It sure the hell wasn't Cherry."

"My real name doesn't matter." she said. "Could we just get what you need? I have other things to do tonight."

"My name is Alan." he told her touching her exposed thigh. "I'm a married man, you know."

"Yeah, you told me back at the bar." she said with no emotion. "I've dated lots of married men. Don't matter one way or the other."

"Kind of in a rush are you?" the big man asked taking the blunt back from her hand and taking a deep drag on it. From this angle, with the parking lot lights hitting his eyes, they seemed to glow red in tiny sparks at her. It was freaking creepy and she was ready to call the whole thing off.

"Always." she sighed. "Look, you paid me three hundred. Why don't you get what you need and you can have fun with me, okay?"

"You're name is Justine Rollins." the deep voice said and she stared hard into the shadows of the driver's seat to find his scarred face.

"How the fuck did you know that?" she asked with one hand reaching for the door handle. "If you're a fucking cop this shit is entrapment, you know that right?"

"Relax, baby girl." he said reaching out and brushing the dark hair out of her face to see her pale perfect skin shiver and sweat under the slight overdone makeup job. "I ain't no fucking cop. Not like your uncle, right?" he laughed softly.

"You know my uncle?" she squinted while waving away the blunt he offered her again.

"We've had some run ins." he smiled cranking down his window for the smoke to exit. "I don't believe you ever had anybody like me before, Justine. In fact, I'm sure of it."

"Look, you want me to praise you for all you can do in bed, get the condoms you need and take me to the motel." she said frustrated. "It will be the best sixty minutes of your life."

"I don't need that long." the man grinned leaning in closer.

"Wow." she said laughing softly. "Most men wouldn't want to admit that, Alan. But whatever turns you on. Can we get started?"

"Why don't you look and see what's in the back seat first." he said nodding back to the darkness behind them and Justine "Cherry" Rollins froze. She locked eyes with him, his smile almost drawing her attention away from the blood shot wild eyes, and glanced over her shoulder.

"What's back there?" she asked hearing something move on the seat straining under the weight as it shifted closer. "Hey, I'm not into threesomes, girls or guys, so if you got somebody else back there-"

"This is different." he promised. "Just take a peek."

Justine did turn and take a peek. Total darkness at first. The sound of slick movement and a slight hissing noise as if air were being released from a balloon. Her eyes widened as Alan brought out a cigarette lighter and held it not far from her face and flicked it to life. She jumped from the burst of flame so close to her face, and then her eyes adjusted and she saw what was stretched over the entire length of the back seat.

"Holy shit!" she jumped back and banged her head on the car's roof.

The big man with the ponytail laughed as the little flame went out.

"You fucker!" she said slapping him. "That shit's not funny. What is that, a snake? It's all white and shit."

4

"An albino python, yeah." he said. "Name's Moe. Cute little guy I picked up in Arizona."

"What does he eat, rats and mice?" she said keeping her distance.

"Mexicans and virgins." he grinned. "I don't think you have anything to worry about."

"Okay, now that you scared the shit out of me can we get down to business?" she asked. "As fun as all of this shit has been I am in this for the money, you know."

"Sure thing, we can do that."

Alan heard the sirens as he reached for the door handle. He looked up into the mirror and saw a chain of flashing lights coming down the road. He grinned in the dark while lighting up a smoke.

"How do you feel about having an audience?" he asked her.

"What?" she asked. "You mean the snake? God, I don't know."

"Well, maybe the snake. What about others?" he said still grinning.

"Look, you might have brought all of this up back at the bar." she said reaching for the door again. "I told you I'm not into group sex. Not much on being an exhibitionist either."

"Who's talking about sex?" Alan said reaching out with one strong arm and grabbing her throat. She struggled well. Strong for her size. Her right hand reached for something and he shot out his other hand and took the knife away, tossing it into the back with the snake. He snatched her purse and tossed it behind him out the open window.

Justine felt tears running down her face as her air was being cut off. She let her guard down. Her knife was gone along with her pepper spray and phone. She reached out with both hands and started to claw at the exposed flesh on the man's arms. She dug deep with her nails drawing blood in thin lines before her own fading black eyes.

He just laughed.

"More scars for my collection. I wonder if they will heal or stay like the others."

Five police cars pulled into the parking lot. They did a full circle around the Impala, bright spot lights from all cars shining directly on them, catching the girls panicked eyes and the man's bright smile.

"Showtime baby." Alan said and pulled her close like a long lost lover. One arm wrapped around her back as if they were simply at a drive-in movie, only his hand was firmly gripping her slim throat, and the other brought up a cannon of a gun. "Look's like Uncle Rollins is here to pay his respects."

She tried to speak but little came out that made sense. The lights were blinding and she heard numerous car doors clicking open as the cops got out and took their defensive positions. A big man with a star on his chest, even bigger than Alan, got out and lifted a bullhorn.

"We know that's you, Alan Woods." he said keeping behind the bright light and car door. "They gave you up at the Cubby Hole! You want to get out of that car and let that girl go now! If you don't this will end bad!"

"Got that right, Chief!" he hollered back and pulled the girl closer to his face and gave her a kiss on the cheek while letting his big revolver come up into view. "Guess what I got in here with me. Some sweet Cherry pie!" he laughed.

"You let her go or you're dead, Woods." the Chief said motioning for his men to get in position and take aim. "You get the chair for sure."

"Don't scare me any, boss." the man smiled. "She goes if I go. You don't want that, no sir."

"You let her go and we just take you to jail, Woods." the Chief promised. "No big deal for you. Familiar territory. But you hurt her or worse-"

"Justine says hello, Chief!" he screamed out the window and laughed.

The big cop let the bullhorn fall to his side. His men gave him a quizzical look, shifting between his blank expression and the wild one on the man's face in the car.

"You're a damn lie!" he called back without the horn.

"What's going on here?" Officer Lambert, a tall, broad-shouldered cop, asked from his left with his gun trained on the car. "Who the hell is Justine?"

"My niece." Rollins gulped finding it hard to breathe now. "Bastard has my brother's daughter."

"Shit." Lambert said and spit behind him before turning back and kneeling down. "What do we do? Your call."

"We was just gonna go up the road a piece and well, I was gonna get me a piece." Alan Woods laughed. "Her idea really. Little hanky-panky for pay, you know?"

"Bullshit, Woods!" Rollins called. "Let her go, she's just a kid!"

"Didn't know your little niece was selling ass, did you? Damn shame what's happened to the American family these days."

"Please, let her go." he said now with a weakened voice.

"Don't beg." Lambert said. "That's what he wants."

"That's not your fucking niece, it's mine." Rollins shot back.

"Actually, at the moment, she's mine." Alan Woods said and placed the gun up to her temple after finally letting her get some air. She screamed and he laughed as he heard guns cock all around. "Now, now, boys, let's not get all itchy!" he called out. "Shut those lights off or I kill her right now!"

"No way." Lambert said up to Rollins. "You take the lights off he can do whatever he wants to us. We're sitting ducks out here in the parking lights while he's in there in the dark."

"That's my niece, damn it!" he shouted down to the kneeling cop. "Turn off the fucking lights now!"

"Chief?" some skinny cop with a mustache asked from across the lot. Brunswick, the Chief thought his name was. Some rookie. "If we do that-"

"Turn them the fuck off!" he yelled into the bullhorn and the parking lot quickly faded into darkness as the spotlights clicked off. The flashing sirens gave little detail of what was happening in the car. Meanwhile they were clearly visible to him under the parking lot lights. "There! You have the upper hand! What do you want from us now? What will it take to get her out of that car safely, Woods? Tell me how to fix this!"

Alan Woods just shook his head and gave a most eerie grin and turned his head to look deep into the eyes of the young lady at his side. She was crying, and her heart was beating a mile a second. She was truly beautiful to him now. This was her in the purest form.

"Tell me what you're afraid of and I will let you go." he told her in a soft whisper like a lover would in the afterglow of sex. "Don't lie."

"I'm afraid to die." she managed between sobs and he wiped the tears running down her face along with the messy mascara. "I don't want to die, please I don't want to die."

"That's too easy, lover." he said tapping her forehead with the gun. "You can do better."

"Woods, what's it gonna be?" Rollins said edging closer.

"Talking it over now, Chief!" Alan yelled out to the big cop.

"We should really put those lights back on." Lambert suggested following him at a safe distance.

"Let me handle this." he warned back in a whisper.

"I don't know what you want me to say." Justine said watching the gun barrel move back and forth in front of her eyes. "Please, I just want to-"

"Tell me what you're truly afraid of." he said sparking the lighter to life and blinding her not only with the small flame but his red sparked eyes and glowing smile. "Must be something."

"Okay, fire." she said watching the flame dance in front of the man's crazed eyes. "I can't stand fire. It scares the shit out of me, okay."

"I like that one too." he said and smiled wide as he turned and pointed his gun back out the window. "Let's do this, boys!" he called out and began shooting. Chief Rollins was hit first. His right shoulder exploded into blood splatter and he sank to his knees, crying out in pain and trying desperately to get his gun with his left hand. He was a right-handed man and that bastard Woods knew it.

"Face your fear, babe." Alan Woods told the girl as she struggled to open the door. She pulled on the handle trying to escape and cried out as bullets shattered glass all around them. "Not getting away from this. Time to put on that show for me." Alan Woods grinned and tossed the lit lighter to the floor. She had time to scream, a beautiful wide mouthed scream accompanied by even wider eyes reflecting fire from the carpet, as Alan Woods continued to fire his own weapon at the cops all around him. "You're free, babe."

"Don't hit her!" Chief Rollins called bleeding from the cracked pavement. "Don't shoot my niece, damn it! Get her out!"

Lambert fired shots directly at the lower side of the driver's door where Woods was ducking down, his revolver and one hand only showing in the darkness as it fired, moving in fast and hoping to kill the man and drag the girl to safety. That was the plan and it was a good one. It might have worked if not for the explosion that came next.

A big ball of fire shot up in the passenger side of the car. A girl's screams echoed across the lot along with the *swoosh* of fire engulfing upholstery, glass and metal. Lambert made a mad dash for the other side of the car while the other cops froze in horror watching the madman laugh as he, the girl, and the car all went up in flames.

"Not quite well done yet!" the flaming man said still firing, and feeling that they had nothing to lose, the cops directly in front of the car shot through the wind shield striking the man dead on as he

8

continued to laugh and shoot wildly out at them. "You won't kill me here, boys. Not in the place of my ancestors. Not in the place where evil was born. You have no fucking idea!"

"Damn thing's locked tight." Lambert said tugging on the door while watching the girl continue to scream and burn. Her hair was gone and her flesh was peeling to black. "I can't get her. I just can't-"

"Get away from there!" some cop called watching the flames overtake the car while Officer Lambert finally turned to run. "Hurry before-"

A small explosion first. The glass blew and a cone of flames lashed out and struck the big cop sending him into a short fiery flight. He screamed in the night while flames covered his left arm and chest. A group of cops came charging out, a few taking off their jackets, and jumped on the fallen officer, beating the flames off him while dragging him away from the next explosion that came from under the hood.

"Nooooooo!" the fallen Chief screamed as a couple of cops dragged him away with his bleeding shoulder. "Justine! My little angel, no . . ." his voice failed him and the tears came.

They all heard the laughter over the flames eating away at the black vehicle. A deep steady flow of it still carrying through the night while the fire lit up the skies. It finally ended on the last little tremor that finished off the car. That would have been enough for all of them to remember from that night if not for what happened next. A distant sound of shrieks and cries that came from all around them in the night. Every cop stood petrified in place, hearing the ambulance and fire trucks heading their way, but that sound grew louder until finally the skies filled with dark flapping wings that flew in a circle high above the metal bon-fire they all bordered.

"What's happening?" Brunswick called out.

"Remember me." a weak and fiery voice came from inside the car and just then a shape emerged from the open window. Several cops took aim, expecting to see the flaming body of Alan Woods come tumbling out of the inferno, but instead a long flaming snake shot out and lay there twitching on the concrete. It wiggled about for several seconds and then went still, the fire having its way quickly with what was left of the body, and the cops let their guns and jaws both drop at the sight.

"What the hell was that doing in there?" the same cop spoke. "Some kind of snake?"

"What in the name of Mary and Moses?" another cop said as they all stared up at the strange spectacle of wings that now filled the night. Hundreds, maybe thousands of them. All dark ravens and blackbirds, crows and one cop would even say later over several beers that he swore he saw bats in there too, although it could have been a trick of the fire. But he didn't think so. A few of them swooped down pretty low and he got a good look at them. They stayed there for a few moments, hypnotic in their living whirlwind effect on the people below, and then they vanished, heading away like a dark swarm to the south over a bordering of pines behind the small strip mall. Nobody spoke anymore as the paramedics came to treat both Chief Rollins and Officer Lambert whose arm, chest and neck were burnt badly.

The bats would not make it into the official report. None of the birds would, with the strict encouragement of Chief Rollins later, and they all agreed. Nor would the fiery serpent or the madman's laughter that echoed long after his body should have been ashes and bone. Not one detail on any of it was ever written down. A psychopath was killed tonight, along with an innocent teenage girl who was not a prostitute by any report and that was the end of it. The entire town of Waverly was content believing these fabricated facts . . . for awhile.

ONE

It was the fifth night of October, a storm bringing Friday, when young Ryan heard the voices whispering from his bedroom vent. He lay there in the darkness covered by his football blankets listening to the approaching storm. Thunder rumbled and echoed throughout the night air while lightning flashed, but no rain yet. He could hear the wind chimes out on the back porch tingling in dance from the breeze. The glow-in-the-dark green hands on his clock told him it was just after one in the morning. They spoke again.

Softly they said, *"Can you hear us?"* and Ryan cringed back under the covers, the eleven-year old boy catching a scream in his throat while his small body froze up as the thunder rolled closer. Lightning flashed again casting long, strange shadows on the poster-covered walls and the vent came into view. It was flat against the wall with tiny dark slits cut into it leading into the black of the furnace below.

"Voices are coming from the furnace. From the basement." his young mind guessed and thought of calling for his mother. That would be option one. But, would she hear him? Most likely she was asleep with the television on. His sister, Amy, would not come and if she did she would make fun of him. She'd call him a crybaby and blame it on dreams and maybe she'd be right. Maybe he imagined it all. Maybe it was just the wind. Or maybe it was-

"Ryan? Can you hear us?"

"Shit!" he cried and tossed the blanket over his head and scooted back until his butt hit the wall where his bed met the corner of the room with blankets layered over him and his pillow gripped tightly as if some magical shield. "Who are you?"

Silence.

No movement in the darkness.

Then only thunder answered. He could hear soft rain pelting on the windows, the trees sighing from attacking winds, the house creaking like old bones and all the while young Ryan kept his eyes focused on the vent.

Option two. He could run. His mother's door was always unlocked. Ever since his father died she felt no reason to lock it. She had little need for privacy at night. But his mother's room was down the hall and around the corner. And of course he did have to go past the vent just to leave his room. There was another vent in the hall and yet another in the kitchen, and his mother's room as well.

"What if they follow me?" he thought. *"What if whatever is in there talking to me breaks out and grabs me just as I get to the door."*

Thunder boomed and shook the house and Ryan once more did his turtle impersonation under the covers. He waited until the shaking stopped, both his and the night skies, although his never completely went away, then he peeked out once more. The dinosaur on his desk grinned at him with tiny needle teeth, the football players and super-heroes on the wall seemed to scowl down at him from under their helmets and masks. Both Megan Fox and Jessica Alba grinned down at him from their dark beach posters where even their skimpy swimsuits didn't do much to make them less scary. And the vent seemed to be focused solely on him. Ryan made just enough room with one small hand to pull away some blanket and see. Something new started then. Something that almost made Ryan Woods piss his own pajamas.

A scratching sound. Some kind of struggled movement. Something *was* in there. Something that had to twist about and brush up against the metal hide of the duct. Ryan could hear the thin metal popping under its weight as it came closer, then silence for a moment with his eyes glued to the thin slats of the grate, and then something tried to move the vent open. Ryan's eyes widened as he saw the little lever in the middle move as if to make more room, regardless of how little it was, for whatever was in there to get out. Something wanted out of the vent. Something wanted into his room.

Then he saw two gleaming sparks of red. Eyes? One of them winked at him.

Ryan froze, unable to move.

Then it spoke.

"Ryan?" it whispered as the vent squeaked open perhaps a sliver of an inch. *"We see you."*

"Mooooooooooommmmmm!" Ryan cut loose over the thunder and winds. He repeated the phrase at least three more times before he heard his mothers footsteps and cursing, She entered, eyes squinting from the light as she clicked it on, his sister peering around her shoulder with a tired look of disgust on her face and the room took on a whole new scene. Everything was fine again. All was serene. Everything except for the vent only a few inches away from his mother's dangling robe. It still looked threatening even in the bright lights.

"What in the world, young man?" she asked scanning for any signs or trouble while Griffin, the smoky grey cat, slinked around her legs. "Griffin, get off me." she said pushing the cat away. "What's going on in here?"

"The vent." Ryan pointed while barely peeking out of his hideout. "There is something in the vent."

"What a goof." his sister sighed and turned back to her room. "Grow up."

"Amy. Enough. You've had your share of nightmares when you were younger." his mother scolded her as the door shut to soft laughter and the squeak of a bed. He watched his mother bend down closer for inspection while he came out from the blankets. "I don't see anything, Ryan. This is an old house, you know."

"Mom, don't!" he warned her letting his feet slide to the carpet. "Something was in there. I heard it. I *saw* it."

"What did you hear and see, Ryan?" his mother asked. He paused. How much could he tell her? What the hell could move in there with eyes that big, there wasn't room enough. What could whisper his name from inside the tiny confines of that vent? "I'm waiting."

"I heard something moving in there." he finally decided. "Then the vent was moving, you know, like it was trying to open up."

"Could be mice." his mother assumed staring at the vent without wanting to get too close. "Or just an over active imagination of an eleven-year-old boy who reads *way* too many creepy comics and watches too many scary movies."

"I'm not lying, mom." Ryan promised and they both jumped at the next clap of thunder.

His mother sighed and rose up again, closing her robe as she came over and knelt down to get face to face with him. "I'll have Mister Clark from next door take a look at it, okay? If that doesn't do it then I will just call an exterminator." she said and kissed him on the forehead. Normally that would have embarrassed him but tonight he needed the kiss. It was a touch of reality. "God, I hate mice." she said and started to close the door. "Get some sleep."

"Leave it open, please." he begged more than asked. His mother shook her head, left it standing open a good foot, and turned on the hall light before clicking his back off.

"It's just mice, Ryan. Maybe bugs. Maybe just a hole in the duct somewhere that's causing a draft to get in. Be a brave little man, okay?" she said and the floor gave way to squeaks as she walked away with Griffin close in tow.

"Mice don't talk." he fussed once she was out of earshot. "And bugs don't know my name." he said sitting back in his bed and listening to the rain grow harder while hitting the empty streets outside. "And the wind ain't got red eyes."

Ryan Woods did not sleep anymore that night and the vent remained silent.

TWO

Saturday morning and the storm was over. Ryan felt like a zombie as he approached the breakfast table. Amy started to make fun of him for his supposed nightmares but his mother cut her insults short and she decided to split. She snatched up her cell phone and car keys and headed out. Amy was sixteen after all and pretty much figured she ruled the world now that she had her driver's license. Ryan was happy to see her go.

"I'll call Mister Clark when I'm sure he's up." was all his mother had to say about the previous night. "I got the day off and have housework to do so go outside and play. And don't come tracking mud back in later. Stay out of the alley."

Ryan knew his mother well enough to know she wouldn't be doing any housework. She would put on some country music, open a bottle of Grey Goose, and maybe get lost in a Sue Grafton novel. Either way she wanted him outside and that was just fine by him. He wanted to be far away from the vent and whatever the hell was inside it.

The sun was out but the winds were chilled. Ryan barely got down the steps when he saw the fat boy on the black dirt bike ride up to his back fence, a chocolate rimmed smile on his pudgy face as always.

"Hell of a storm, huh?" Jeff Bates greeted him. His friend stood on the opposite side in the small alleyway that ran behind Ryan's house holding a half-eaten candy bar. "Wind was crazy last night, man."

"Seen worse." Ryan said to the blond haired boy who seemed the exact opposite to him. Where as Ryan was skinny with dark hair and eyes, Jeff was blond with blue eyes and twice as big with a whale belly from all that junk food his mother let him devour. At least that's what Ryan's mother said when she first saw Jeff. "We did okay. Any damage your guy's way?"

"Big ass Oak fell on my neighbor's garage." Jeff said smiling. "Lucky they were gone or that car they love so much would be scrap metal."

"I guess." Ryan shrugged. "Nothing bad here."

"My dad bought us a dog." his face lit with excitement. "Big ass Great Dane. Gray with black spots. Named it Thor, after the Norse God. He's the one with the hammer, you know?"

"I know who Thor is." Ryan rolled his eyes. "I collect comics, remember?"

"Yeah, right." Jeff said smacking himself in the head. "Anyways he's pretty bad ass looking but just kind of sits there and stares, you know. He don't do much. Kinda lazy. You wanna play some ball or what?"

Ryan opened the gate as Jeff was too big to climb the fence. His mother had seen big Jeff try to climb the fence once and was worried he would crush it before he got over it. And so they played some Wiffle-ball, but the vent was never far from Ryan's thoughts.

A half an hour went by. The sun rose up higher. The winds blew more, helping some hits and hindering a few others, and the boys played. Jeff talked more about the storm and how his father had good seats for the Rams this season, but Ryan kept seeing those red eyes winking at him and hearing the scratching noises. Jeff was beating Ryan by a score of nine to two, but Ryan didn't seem to care. The last pitch of the game was a weak throw on the outside and Jeff smashed it over Mister Clark's fence, which meant another homerun.

"Enough, man." Jeff waved to Ryan as he dropped the bat. "You've been pitching like a girl. And you're swinging at everything I throw at 'cha. What's going on, man?"

Ryan stared down his chubby friend while zipping up his jacket and then back at his own house.

"You keep a secret?" he asked keeping his eyes on the basement windows that were bordered by weeds and spider webs with nothing but darkness behind them.

"Sure I can as long as it's a good one." he said tugging down his blue and gold cap. "Please tell me it's about Anna Finch. She's only eleven and she's getting boobs already, man. Can you imagine what she will look like by the time high-school-"

"Not about her." Ryan smiled thinking of Anna. She was cute. She finally stopped wearing pigtails, and like Jeff said, her shirts were definitely poking out more. He liked everything about Anna. Her long red hair and hazel eyes. The way she tossed her head back when she laughed. He liked the freckles on her nose the best, but he wouldn't tell Jeff that. All Jeff seemed to care about was boobs and butts. "It's about my house."

"Your house?" Jeff said looking back as he leaned on the fence, the fence seeming to moan as he did so, and scratched his head as if deep in thought. "I don't see nothing wrong with it other than you live there." he smiled and clapped Ryan on the back. "What gives, man?"

"Promise you won't laugh?" Ryan said watching a couple of stray cats fiddle around behind some garbage cans across the alleyway. Something else was moving there in the grass that held the cat's attention but Ryan just figured it was the wind.

"I guess." Jeff said sounding as if he were losing interest already. "Spill it."

"I think it's haunted." Ryan said coldly and stared at the cats which were sniffing and licking fast food wrappers they managed to free from some trash bags. He waited for his friends response.

Jeff gave a short burst of laughter. Ryan glared at him but Jeff continued to giggle.

"You're nuts." Jeff said finally. "It's an old house, man, but nobody has died here that I ever heard of. I mean it's not exactly the type of place you would imagine ghosts and shit hanging out in, right? Haunted houses are like big old places next to cemeteries with creaky floorboards on the porch and statues of lions or gargoyles at the gate. You're old man didn't die here did he?"

Ryan tensed up. No, his father had not died here. He died miles away in a parking lot outside of a drug store inside a burning car. He died with some young teen girl. He died screaming and cursing at the cops who shot him full of holes while he set himself on fire. Sometimes people forgot that story. Ryan never did. His father had not been a good man.

"Sorry, man." Jeff said fumbling with his pockets backing away. "Sorry, I forgot that-"

"It's cool." Ryan grinned best as he could. "I heard some things coming from out of my vent. Voices and stuff."

"Man, that could be anything." Jeff said waving him away. "The wind from the storm, or maybe your sister was pulling a gag on you. She's pretty freakin' evil, you know. Remember all that stuff she used to do to us when we were little?"

If it had just been the voices Ryan might have eventually considered that. His sister did like to tease him. She had planted many a rubber spider in her day. She even did the whole boogeyman thing by hiding out in his closet on nights he had sleepovers years ago. She jumped out while he and Jeff and Marty Fitzgerald were all telling ghost stories while wearing a hockey mask. Marty actually pissed himself.

"Wasn't just voices." Ryan pointed out. "I heard things *moving* in there."

"Spiders? Mice?" Jeff guessed. "My dad found a snake in our basement once. I hate snakes, man. I mean the big ones, you know, like other countries have. This was just a garden snake but you should have seen my mom. I almost crapped myself the way she went flying up those steps, man. She almost completely creamed my cat and-"

"I saw eyes too." Ryan cut him off and Jeff grew quiet.

"Eyes?" he asked looking Ryan up and down. "You sure you just didn't dream it or imagine it. Maybe it was just the lightning flashing around in there."

"Red eyes." Ryan corrected his statement. "One of them blinked at me."

"No shitting way." Jeff grinned. "You're yanking my pecker."

"That's a really gross saying, Jeff." Ryan said. "And no, I'm not. I saw them. I heard whatever it was talking to me. It said my name, man. So what do you think?"

"Ryan, my man." Jeff said coming closer with that devilish grin. "I think you have a drinking problem." he laughed and clapped Ryan so hard it actually stung this time. "You didn't tell your mom about all of this did you?"

"Not about the eyes or voices, no way." he said wondering how long it would take before his mother had him at a shrink if he had. "But about something in there, yeah. She thinks it's mice too." Ryan said looking back at the dark basement windows. "Mister Clark is gonna come over later and take a look."

"The old dude next door?" Jeff said spying the house to the right of Ryan's. "Well he would know about ghosts. He's damn near one himself."

"That shit's not funny, Jeff." Ryan said as Jeff made his way out the gate to his bike.

"Hey, relax Ghost Whisperer." Jeff smiled saddling up on his skinny metal steed. "Just screwing with ya. Maybe he will find a snake or something. I told ya, unless somebody died in your house, it's not haunted. Who owned it before you?"

"I don't know." Ryan said with a shrug while watching the cats toy around the trashcans. "I wasn't even born when my folks moved in. Neither was my sister. My folks moved here about twenty years ago. No idea."

"Well find out from the old dude." Jeff said. "Maybe he can tell you. That would be your ghost. I'm out of here." he said shoving off with a heavy grunt. "Going to see Anna Finch. The hottest girl in Waverly."

"She will never be your girlfriend, man." Ryan laughed as the boy peddled away.

"I don't care. I just want to check out her boobs." Jeff laughed back and Ryan watched him go until he vanished around the corner. That was when he heard the garbage can lid fall and it spooked him into looking at the cats once more.

The two cats were making loud howling noises as they gave chase around the cans. Ryan pulled himself up on the fence and peered closer to the ground and saw movement. He let out a loud gasp as he saw dozens of mice running around trying to escape the cats.

"Jesus." Ryan breathed wondering if his house had any of these little rodents living in their basement. If they were than Griffin was not doing his job. "Freaking mice." Ryan said and headed for the swing in the corner of the yard. Noon was a few hours away. He decided he would wait for Mister Clark to come check out their house.

"Mice don't talk." he told himself swinging there in the chilly breeze. "They're not heavy enough to make all that noise." he deduced. "Wasn't no damn mouse." he decided and slowly swung back and forth on the rusted chains while staring at the basement window thinking of what Jeff had said about people dying in houses to haunt them.

He would ask Mister Clark. He had lived here for some time and he would know who lived here before they did and who died. Who had died and decided to stick around.

THREE

Mister Clark had come over about twelve-thirty. He had a big flashlight and some mousetraps. Ryan hated seeing this because it meant his mother had already decided what the problem was before hearing the full story or considering any other options.

Ryan hung back and waited for Mister Clark and his mother to talk. He would let his mother tell the story, hoping she wouldn't embarrass him too bad in front of the old man about the previous nights events, and then he would catch Mister Clark alone and ask his own questions.

"Nothing in the vents." the old man said with sparkling blue eyes behind rounded glasses and a witty smile. "No droppings or hairs that I could see anyways." he told Ryan's mother from the floor of Ryan's bedroom putting the vent back into place. "I'll take a peek in the basement and see what's going on down there if you don't mind."

"Please and thank you, John." his mother said slouching back into her chair where her magazines and wine waited along with Griffin. Ryan waited until Mister Clark was on the steps before he approached the old man.

"Mister Clark?" he called and watched the tall white haired man turn with the ever present smile. "Mind if I tag along with you?"

"Not at all." the old man sparked up. "Every worker should have an assistant."

Ryan followed closely while watching the tall, lanky man take careful strides around the piles of boxes and junk his mother had allowed to accumulate over the years. The old man's eyes glanced around the corners and then up along the ceiling beams searching for any signs of critters that might be lurking there while following the beam of his flashlight. Ryan didn't think he would find any mice.

"Your basement is more cluttered than mine." the old man noticed. "Anything this side of a Bengal tiger could be down here." he laughed to himself.

"I don't think it's mice." Ryan finally spoke up as the old man made his way to the furnace and started to probe around.

"Is that a fact?" he said while tapping and leaning his head to listen. "And what do you think it might have been, young Ryan?"

"Not sure, just not mice." Ryan said leaning into the washing machine while watching the old man snoop behind the furnace with his flashlight beam swaying back and forth. "I heard Jeff Bates dad found a snake in their basement."

"Yep. That can happen." Mister Clark said laying down a few traps and fixing them with tiny dabs of peanut butter he got from a small jar that Ryan hadn't noticed before. "But the Bates' have a walk-up basement from the outside and you don't. That boy probably leaves it open without thinking. I think he'd leave his head at home if it wasn't screwed on." he grinned back at Ryan. "No offense, of course. I know the boy's a friend of yours, but he's a few yards shy of a first down if you get my drift." he said turning and watching Ryan's expression in reaction to his trap setting. "Mice actually respond to peanut butter better than cheese. Has a stronger smell. Taste great too." he said smacking his lips and the boy laughed despite his eerie mood.

"Do you know who lived here before us?" Ryan asked straight out and the old man didn't seem to hear at first, then before Ryan could ask again, he stood and stretched and rubbed his short white hair and turned to face him.

"Yes, sir. That would have been the Thurber's." he said staring off as to recall their faces. "George and Mary, or maybe Marcie. I knew the husband better than the wife. Nice folks. He died of a heart attack I believe."

Ryan took a deep breath before he asked his next question.

"Did he die here?" Ryan asked nearly holding his breath.

"In this house? Oh no." Mister Clark said coming to the washer and dryer shining a beam in search of rodents while Ryan stepped aside. "He was playing golf. Waste of a good walk if you ask me, the whole damn game, excuse my French. They took him up to Saint Mary's. He died there next day. Damn shame because he was a decent man. Hell of a chess player too, pardon my French once more. His wife moved away. Why you asking, son?"

"I was just wondering if anybody ever died in this house?" Ryan asked with hopeful eyes and Mister Clark turned on him with lowered brows.

"Kind of a morbid subject for a boy your age, isn't it?" he asked. "Your friends been telling you tales, boy?"

"No, sir." Ryan shot back. "Just was wondering if, you know, maybe this house was . . . well you know, haunted?" he gulped and the old man's face lit up with amusement much like Jeff's had.

"Haunted?" Mister Clark smiled down and patted him on the head as if he were some silly dog. "Nonsense, boy. You *have* been hearing stories. I've lived here in Waverly for the past twenty four years and as far as I know nobody has ever died in this house, and even if they did that don't make a house haunted."

"So what does?" Ryan asked.

"Well, if you believe in that sort of thing, which I don't by the way, I would imagine it would have to be something very tragic. Take a lot more than just a body dying. If that was the case the whole blasted world would be haunted."

"Something tragic?" Ryan wondered thinking of his father and the parking lot. "Like what happened to my dad maybe?"

Ryan saw the old man's face change. A look of anger which quickly shifted into sympathy. He lowered himself to the boy's level and placed his aging spotted hands squarely on his narrow shoulders.

"You listen to me now, Ryan." he said with a shaky voice. "Your father did some bad things. I'm sure you know more than you want to about that. He is not, however, haunting this house. You understand me, son? He died years ago. Far from this house. That's the end."

"I heard they shot him and he was still alive." Ryan said thinking of the news stories. "I heard he was laughing and yelling and-"

"Ryan." Mister Clark said giving him a hard shake. "Those are just stories, son. You understand that some people are so bored and stupid . . ." the old man's voice trailed off and his eyes watered up. ". . . that they just have to make things up to entertain themselves, you see. You have to let that crap lay in the past where it belongs."

"I heard things, Mister Clark." Ryan said deciding it had to be said. "My mom doesn't believe me, but I *heard* things in my vent last night. It wasn't the wind either, or a mouse."

"And it wasn't your father either." the old man said patting him on the back much softer than Jeff would have. "I swear to you son, there are no ghosts in this house."

"But I saw-"

"Ryan, if you ever need me I'm right next door." the old man said standing up and wiping his eyes with a fresh handkerchief he produced from his back pocket. "No more ghost stories. I will check on these traps tomorrow and we will see what I caught, if anything. If all else fails I know a pretty decent exterminator who can help us out. God knows I can't stand mice. Little suckers scare the crap out of me." he winked.

"Yes, sir." Ryan said lowering his head.

"If it makes you feel better I can do some checking. About the house, I mean." the old man said."

"Really?" Ryan said voice returning to excitement. "You'd do that?"

"Yes, as a favor to you." the old man winked again. "But no more talk about your father. He didn't die here, you understand? I'll check and see on the family that lived here *before* the Thurber's. Maybe they were mad scientists or serial killers." he grinned and Ryan laughed with him despite the fact he knew better.

Whatever it was in this house Ryan knew for sure it wasn't a serial killer or a lab freak accident. And it was not something that could be caught with peanut butter.

FOUR

Night fell again.

The evening dinner came and went. Ryan watched his mother and Amy argue over how much she had spent on shoes, the lousy job she did on the laundry, and how much his mother disliked her new boyfriend. The one with the tattoos and pierced lower lip and motorcycle.

Ryan tried to stay up as late as possible. It was Saturday night after all. He cuddled up next to his mother and Griffin on the couch snacking on her popcorn while she flipped through news channels which all warned of more storms overnight.

"Jesus, it's going to be a wet and dreary autumn. Maybe even a wet Halloween." she commented and Ryan agreed while faking interest. "Getting pretty late, hon. You need to hit the hay."

"There's a pretty good movie supposed to come on after the news." Ryan tried and watched his mother crack a mischievous all knowing smile. "Something about space vampires taking over the world."

"That's the *last* thing you need to be watching, Mister." his mother said clicking off the set. "Why do you think you're having so many nightmares now?"

"So I'll watch something else." he tried. "Documentary Channel. Discovery. I'm just not tired."

"Ryan, no. You have to sleep." his mother said swatting him on the head with a magazine. "I'm right down the hall, my door is open if-"

"Can't I sleep in your room?" he said.

"You're a little old for that, hon." she said brushing his hair back. "Mister Clark said he found no trace of mice. No snakes, thank God. No nothing."

"He didn't say there *wasn't* anything either." Ryan said wondering if the old man would really investigate the history of the house or he was just shitting him like his mother did. "Mice are pretty smart, you know. If they heard him coming they would run hide I bet Even he said he was scared of them sometimes."

"If there are any mice Griffin will take care of them, won't you Griff?" she said stroking the smooth haired cat.

"That cat couldn't catch a cold." Ryan teased and his mother laughed with him.

24

"You're probably right." she agreed. "But if there are mice, then what, Ryan?" his mother said standing and tugging him up with her. "Are they going to break out of the vents and devour us. I admit I hate the little shits but they're mice, not cougars. That's no excuse for not sleeping in your own room. Leave the lights on if you want and no more horror movies."

So Ryan went to bed. He did leave the light on. Amy teased him once more until his mother yelled at her to shut up. She stormed off into her room with a slammed door and a warning from his mother that if she wanted to slam doors she could go out and get her own damn house and slam those doors. Typical mother-daughter moments he never grew tired of.

So he lay there still staring at the ceiling and, of course, the vent. It made no noises. No blinking eyes. No scratching sounds. Nothing. He listened to the thunder roll close, the winds pick up, and eventually the rain did fall. The vent remained silent.

FIVE

Ryan did dream.

He was in bed and the soft moon spilled across his covers while he lay there smelling cigarette smoke. Then a deep sigh and he turned and saw him sitting in the corner of darkness, that tiny orange glow dangling from his mouth and those eyes that seemed to have a light all of their own. Then he spoke in that cold deep voice of his.

"Sorry to wake you, boy." he said without really sounding as if he meant it. He cocked his head, that long mane of hair spilling over his shoulder, and he reached up to remove the butt and squash it out on a nearby table. *"I have to be going now. You won't understand this until later, but I have to go."*

"Where are you going?" Ryan asked sitting up and watching his father rise in the darkness, and there were shadows in that room with him, ones that moved around him, and he walked towards the bed in long slow strides.

"I have to go away. I guess you know I'm sick. I'm sure your mother told you that by now."

Ryan nodded cringing back. He had heard of the cancer. His mother told him it was bad. That the doctors could do nothing for him.

"I will see you again, just give me a while." his father smiled and leaned down to embrace him, and this was something his father had never done before. *"Relax boy, this won't hurt a bit."* he said and Ryan froze up as he watched his father's eyes begin to swirl in many colors and all at once he felt relaxed and sleepy as if floating away from the bed, the room, the entire town of Waverly. That smile remained as Ryan was laid back, paralyzed and unable to react or move or even speak. *"We will get together again real soon, boy. And we will have some fun."*

Ryan opened his eyes and his father was gone, so were all the shadows. Then he blinked and his room was gone, and now he was standing outside in the backyard. It was late and he could hear birds overhead in the trees that surrounded his yard and the cicada singing their odd little songs. He also smelled barbecue. This brought a smile to his face.

"Hello, young Ryan." came Mister Clark's voice. He stood there close to the driveway wearing a chef's hat and apron with a smoking grill in front of him. "Care for a bite?"

26

Ryan smiled and darted for the fence. The old man stood there tossing the tiny chunks of meat over as the flames leapt up and kissed them. He climbed over the vine covered fence while the old man reached into a dark chest and pulled out a fresh bottle of cream soda.

"Drink up." the old man said. "You're gonna need it to wash these little fellas down."

Ryan looked down at the grill, expecting to see hamburgers, hot dogs and maybe a few bratwursts like Mister Clark usually grilled, but instead felt his skin crawl as he saw what was there. Tiny little mice, tails and all, rolled about on the grill with fire licking at their fur. They let out screams as smoke poured from their whisker bordered mouths. Mister Clark just laughed at the horrid spectacle and poked them with his large fork. He got a good stab on a plump one and held it up for Ryan's inspection while it bled out onto the silver prongs.

"This one has some meat on it's bones." the old man grinned. "You want it?"

Ryan backed away and the old man just shrugged and lifted the squirming creature up to his own lips, opening wide and taking it down in one large gulp. Ryan felt the urge to throw up as he watched his neighbor chew and make the most pleasant face while finally sucking in the tail last.

"Magnifico!" he cheered making an "ok" sign with one hand while pulling the black stringy tail out with the other. "You don't eat the tails, boy."

Ryan backed away as he noticed more mice and some rather large rats as well, coming from all around them in the dark lawn. Mister Clark just stood there smiling and eating the grilled mice as the big rats made a circle around him. Their glowing red eyes were focused on the old man for now.

"I shouldn't have went down there, boy." he told Ryan as they moved in on him, teeth gnashing on the old man's legs as he stumbled back into the garage door. "In your basement. I guess I made them mad. You better watch out, Ryan. It's too late for me, but not for you. Run, boy, run!"

Mister Clark fell under the weight of the pack of rodents and Ryan watched as they began to tear away at his flesh and burrow their way into his old body. Ryan ran across the night grass towards the darkness of the alleyway with Mister Clark's screams echoing behind him. He made his way to the gate and was just about the enter the alleyway when he saw Jeff come peddling by at top speed.

"Jeff?" he called out, but his friend was not stopping, a look of deep panic on his chubby face while his fat legs cranked the dirt bike for all it was worth. "Jeff, what's wrong?"

"Run!" was all the boy said huffing hard as the bike swayed under his weight.

Ryan turned back to the direction Jeff had come from and saw the dark grounds of the alleyway moving on their own. Moving like black fluid. Like the alley had come alive into some form of dark water and then he saw why. It wasn't the ground at all.

They came in hundreds it seemed. Long, black slithering snakes overlapping each other as they all came towards Ryan. He didn't stand there for long. Ryan broke out from the gate and followed in the trail of Jeff who was nearly a good thirty yards away, almost to the end of the alley.

He looked back once, knowing he shouldn't because every time somebody pulled this stunt in the movies they would trip and fall, and saw they were gaining. Black snakes with bright glowing red eyes just like from the vent. Some were no bigger than his hand, others seemed to be as long as a car, thick as a tree stump, with gapping mouths like sharks.

"No!" he screamed as the alley was quickly turning into a lake of mud. Mud so thick and deep that not only was it making it harder to run, but it was dragging him down like quicksand. It didn't seem to be slowing the snakes down at all. "Jeff!" he called, but Jeff was turning the corner. A brief glimpse of his fat rump lifting off the seat and he was gone Swallowed up in the night.

"Ryan." one of the smaller snakes whispered as it slid up next to him chest deep in mud now. *"We want you. We need you, boy."*

Ryan screamed out just as a larger snake wrapped its cold scaly body around his throat and he woke up to yet another nightmare.

SIX

Ryan was awake, he was sure of it. He could feel the sweat running down his face and body, soaking his pajamas. He could feel the coolness of his sheets and see the lightning flashing through his window. He could hear the thunder growling far above and the rain assaulting the roof in hard spatter, but something was wrong. Something was different.

The lights were off. His light. The hall light. All of them.

"Power went out." he thought, but he could see the green numbers on his clock. It was just after one again. *"Mom must have came by and turned them off. Why would she do that to me?"* he thought, but it was a short thought because right away something else caught his attention. He wasn't sure at first so he remained still, his eyes trying desperately to focus in the dark.

Something on the ceiling was moving. A *bunch* of something's.

"Oh, God." he breathed and watched the wavy dark pattern going from the closet to just over his bed like some oil spill. It flowed like water only it wasn't. It couldn't have been a leak from the rain. Rain wasn't black. Rain didn't slither. "Please, no."

A flash of lightning and then it was real. Snakes. At least a dozen or more crawling across his ceiling from the open closet door to just above the center of the top of his bed. All about the size of his baseball bat or bigger. All black. And tiny red glowing eyes.

Ryan lay still and listened to his heart beating.

"I'm dreaming." he said out loud and could actually hear the things *hissing* as they crawled over each other in great lumps of living blackness. "Please, I'm dreaming, I'm dreaming." he said feeling tears streaming down over his cheeks along with the sweat. "It can't be real."

"Ryan? We're waiting for you, honey." a chilled woman's voice called out and Ryan peeked over the top of his covers to see his closet door creaking open even further. Standing there, dressed in a lacy white night gown with bloodstains, was an old woman. It was not his mother or sister, but there she stood with a big grin on her dry and decaying face with hollowed eyes. *"Give me a hug, Ryan."*

"You're not real!" he called out and dove back under the covers. Another flash of lightning and one of the smaller snakes dropped from the ceiling and landed on his legs with a heavy plop. Ryan opened his mouth to scream and nothing came out as he watched a few more drop and fall, one near his arm and the other close enough to his pillow that he could actually see the tiny tongue dart out a few times.

"*We're waiting, Ryan.*" the lady whispered and he felt her cold hand touch his leg under the sheet.

"Nooooooooooo!" Ryan screamed and tossed himself onto the floor, blankets and all, with some snakes coming with him. He rolled as if on fire, hoping not to get bit and finally freeing himself and made a mad dash for the door. "Mom! Amy!" he called bursting into the hallway. Somewhere in the kitchen lights came on and more cursing.

"Oh my God!" Amy cried out from her room. "What the hell do I have to do to get some sleep around this house?"

"Shut up, Amy!" his mother yelled kneeling down before Ryan. "Jesus, Ryan! You're sweating like crazy! What's going on in there!"

"Snakes!" he pointed back to the darkness of his room. "Somebody's in my closet too."

"What?" his mother said pushing him behind her, almost certain it was just another bad dream but taking no chances as she went to the kitchen and returned with a rather impressive butcher knife. "Stay here, Ryan! Amy, get the hell up!"

"Why?" she called back from her bed. "You need help killing ghosts?"

"Not ghosts." Ryan said holding tightly to his mother's leg. "Snakes! Bunches!"

"Ryan, honey, let go of me. I can't move." his mother said forcing him off while clicking on the hall light. "I don't see anything from here. You had a dream, Ryan."

"No way." he said. "I was awake. I swear. They fell on me and I rolled off. And there's a lady in my closet. Dead lady!"

"How the hell would a bunch of snakes get in this house?" his sister asked from a crack in the door. "You are completely psycho."

"Shut up, Amy! Help or go back to bed." his mother said creeping closer to the open door of his room. "Ryan, I don't see anything but your covers and . . ." she said squinting as she inched closer for the light switch. ". . . one of your belts, Ryan."

"It was a snake before."

"A freaking belt." Amy laughed and closed the door. "You need therapy, squirt."

"I'm going to use this belt on your butt if you don't shut up, Amy." his mother warned and Amy's bed squeaked as she went silent. "Ryan, there's nothing in here." she said clicking on the light and letting Ryan get a good look. Ryan did step in, noticing the closet door was closed again, and the snakes were gone. All of them. Not a trace on the ceiling either.

"I'm not lying." he said. "There was a woman in my closet. She touched me."

"Ryan, nobody is in here." she started. "You see? No snakes, no woman."

"I'm not lying." he told her.

"He's lying!" Amy called from the other room.

"You want your car privileges taken away, young lady?"

"Not really, no."

"How about returning those over-priced shoes you just bought?"

"I could do without that too."

"Then shut up!" his mother yelled and Ryan had to cover his ears. "Sorry. Ryan, you had a dream. Sometimes I have nightmares and when I wake up I still see and hear things."

"Did you turn off my lights?" Ryan asked as she headed for the hall once more.

"Your lights? No, why would I? Honey, there's nothing in there. No lady, no snakes. Just rain out there and bad dreams in here." she said tapping his head with one finger. "Okay. Tonight you can finish up with me, but only tonight."

Ryan followed his mother glancing back when a flash of lightning lit up his room. His belt was gone. He walked faster to catch up with his mother.

SEVEN

Ryan woke up alone. He could smell bacon and coffee and heard his mother humming as she made breakfast. There was rain but no thunder or lightning. The storm was past again. Ryan sat up and wondered just how much of last night was real and how much was a bad dream.

He also wondered how Mister Clark was doing.

"Feeling better, sweet-heart?" his mother asked working the eggs with one hand and sipping coffee with the other. Griffin, as usual, was close to her feet. The cat would patiently wait for a fresh bowl of milk or whatever treats his mother would spoil it with.

"I guess." Ryan said staring at the shriveled little strips of bacon on his plate that looked like tiny black snakes to him. "Not really hungry though." he said taking up the glass of apple juice instead. "Can I check the traps Mister Clark set downstairs? Might be dead mice in them."

"Ewwwww!" Amy called from the table. "I'm eating, please."

"Why don't we wait for Mister Clark." his mother suggested as the phone rang. "And let him do all of the touching please. Dead mice have germs you know?"

"He is a germ." Amy snickered.

Ryan wandered into the living room. He watched the rain streak down the window and after carefully setting his drink down he climbed up to the back of the couch and stared out. Mister Clark's blue Ford was still in the driveway. He turned to view the clock on the mantle and noticed it was already after nine. Mister Clark rarely missed church on Sunday.

He remembered the words Mister Clark spoke in his dream.

"I shouldn't have gone down there." he said. *"I made them mad. Too late for me."*

Ryan felt a chill run over him as his mother came into the room.

"Is Mister Clarks car still out there?" she asked as if reading his mind.

"Yep." Ryan shot back feeling like some bad news was on the way.

"That was Miss Fletcher on the phone. He was supposed to pick her up for church today. She said he didn't answer his phone this morning."

"He could be sleeping." Ryan tried but didn't believe.

32

"Not like him to miss church." his mother said starting to dial his number.

"Maybe he's sick?" Ryan suggested.

"Well, that's what I'm about to find out." she turned to her daughter. "Amy, run next door and see if Mister Clark answer's the door."

"God, mom, its like raining, right?" Amy said flipping her hair out of her eyes.

"Could you please just get dressed and run over, what the hell?" came the sterner voice and Amy just sighed and scooted the chair back.

"He's old, you know." she smirked passing her mother. "Maybe he's just tired and wants to be left alone. Wonder what that's like?"

"Stop being a smart ass and just go, would you?" she said listening to the fifth ring. "He's not answering. Damn."

"I'm going with her." Ryan said heading to get his shoes. He stopped when he got to the doorway. The closet door was still closed and the belt was gone. Then again, his bed was made too. It was obvious his mother had already been in here.

"You want me to hold your hand, squirt?" he sister teased passing by him pulling on a jacket.

"Wait for me!" Ryan called out dashing into the room and snatching his shoes.

"Damn, we're not going trick-or-treating." Amy said taking an umbrella from the closet. "Get a jacket on or mom will blame me when you catch a cold. Don't go stomping in any puddles either or I will kick your ass."

"Amy! Just go would you? God, you should have been born a mute."

"I should have been born an orphan." she said heading out. "Come on, runt."

Ryan tried to keep up with his sister but she had longer strides and started running once she got to the driveway. While she was bounding up the steps to Mister Clark's porch Ryan had just reached the driveway and was eyeing the house top to bottom. He looked down the drive to the garage where the Mister Clark in his dreams had met his grisly ending. There was no barbecue pit or pack of mice and rats there, just puddles and honeysuckle bushes blowing in the wind.

"You're gonna get all wet, goober." he sister called from under the cover of the porch. Ryan watched her ring the bell first and then start to knock. Nobody came. Ryan let his eyes drift up to the windows. The living room was dark as were the dining room windows. Mister Clark's house was set up pretty much the same as theirs was on the inside. The opposite side of the house he could not see would be the bedrooms. The back would be the kitchen and bathroom windows. Ryan couldn't see those and did not really want to go into the backyard and look in case any rodents from his dreams were waiting there for him. What he did notice was one of the basement windows near the back of the house. It was on.

"He's downstairs!" Ryan called over the wind to his sister.

"What?" Amy called back while still knocking.

"He's downstairs!" Ryan called again and took off down the driveway. He stayed close to the house, his eyes watching the windows above him remain dark, until he reached the lit basement window at the back corner of the house. He knelt down to a squatting position and peered into the glass. It was hard to see anything because it was that funny type of frosted glass they used for showers and stuff like that. You couldn't really see through it in detail, but you could see shapes and shadows. Ryan couldn't remember what it was called but knew the dentist office he went to had windows like that. "Mister Clark?" he called out and banged on the window three times.

Ryan wasn't sure but he thought he heard something. Then it sounded like somebody was coming closer. There was a shadow blocking the light from the single bulb. He could see a blurred figure above what he guessed might be some kind of work bench. Then more shadows. Lots of tiny ones. These shadows were small with . . . tails. They scurried about on the glass, nearly covering the entire window, and then . . . the light went out.

"Mister Clark?" Ryan said knocking again. Nothing. No more shadows or movement or sounds at all. "Mister Clark, are you okay in there?" he called out. Then Ryan felt a cold, wet hand grip his shoulder. He screamed.

"Hey Shrimp." his sister laughed. "You really are a scary ass lately." she said standing back up. "Come on, let's go. Nobody's answering."

"There was a light on. Then some shadows." Ryan pointed out tapping the funny thick glass. "I saw somebody moving."

"Well then he will answer the phone as easy as he can the door. Let's go, I'm getting soaked out here." Amy said starting for their own front porch. Ryan stood and viewed the basement window one more time. Cold and black, no movement now. He thought of telling Amy what he saw but knew she would not believe him.

He rounded the house to the front walk and stood there wondering how long it would take the old man to come up and answer the door. Nothing. No lights, no movement at either window or door. It was a dead house, and Ryan thought, it held maybe a dead man inside.

"I'm sorry we called you." he said. "Sorry you came over. Please be okay."

"Ryan Woods, get in this house!" his mother called from the front door. "You'll catch your death out there."

The boy ran and leapt over puddles as he made his way up the walk to the warm comfort of his home. At least for now.

EIGHT

Ryan had never been to a funeral before. This was his first. He didn't go to his fathers because his mother said he was too young. He had stayed with his Aunt Cheryl down in Joplin, Missouri. He wished he were there now with her floppy dogs, duck pond and spotted horse that nobody ever rode. He did not like it here at all.

Rows and rows of people crying. Even his mother was crying. Amy didn't cry but she looked sad enough to fit in. Those that weren't crying were stone-faced and grim. Ryan had no idea that Mister Clark had so many friends and relatives. Ryan didn't bawl like some of the ladies but he did feel a lump in his throat through the entire service. He wasn't sure if it was sorrow or guilt.

The pastor stood before them now, a tall man with gray hair and glasses much like Mister Clark himself, and began to speak. He spoke of how everyone was a sinner and all had to die. He said that Mister Clark had lived a full life for a man only sixty-seven. Ryan had always assumed the man was older. It must have been the solid white hair and shaky walk.

"From dust thou art, and unto dust thou shall return." the pastor said with little or no emotion in his voice. "He died in a good old age, full of days, riches and honor."

"Sixty-seven is a good old age?" Ryan thought listening to the sobs grow louder.

"To everything there is a season, and a time to every purpose under the heaven. A time to be born, and a time to die-"

"Heart-attack?" Ryan thought to himself while wishing he could peel himself out of the uncomfortable suit. That was the official cause of death. He was downstairs putting around by his tool bench and just dropped dead of a heart attack. *"Bullshit."* Ryan thought as he noticed the rows of people moving forward once the music started and folks were passing by the coffin one last time to pay their respects. *"It might have been a heart attack, but not the way they think."* Ryan thought remembering the shadows with tails. So many of them.

Ryan walked behind his mother and in front of his sister as he drew closer and closer to the casket. It was jet black and shiny, almost like a fancy new wax job on a car, and the lid was open to reveal silky white ruffles along the top. Fancy fixings for a death. Ryan felt the lump in his throat go from marble to golf ball size as he came closer and finally saw the man's body. A nice dark blue suit with a two-toned blue tie and white shirt. He actually looked very handsome. His gold wedding ring still intact glimmering under the florescent lights.

But he did not look like the Mister Clark that Ryan had seen last weekend. His hair was combed to one side and pure snow white as usual. His little white mustache trimmed neat, but his face looked waxed over. Pale and sickly, void of all happiness and life. Ryan thought he looked more sick than dead. The blue sparkling eyes shut in sleep pose, his glasses tucked neatly in his breast pocket. *"God."* Ryan thought while biting his lip and forcing himself not to smile. *"Do they think he's going to catch up on some light reading later?"*

His mother softly patted the edge of the coffin in passing, as if trying to say good-bye for the last time, and she made the sign of the cross. A single tear ran down her eye. Mister Clark was a Lutheran but his mother didn't care. She was always a devote Catholic even if she had not taken them to mass in over five years.

Ryan slowed some to look at Mister Clark's skin. He wanted to see if anything was wrong. The mortician's would have corrected anything by now, he knew this, but still he had to know if there were any signs of . . . bite marks or mice hair. It was a silly thought and rather disrespectful he knew, but he had to know. He saw nothing.

But what he heard was different.

"Coming for you." came the whisper and Ryan gasped out loud as he froze in place, his sister bumping into him from behind and his tiny eyes looked back at the old man's calm face.

"Keep moving you little goof." she whispered loud enough for him to hear. "There's a line back here, you know."

Ryan moved but looked back. The old man's face was silent and still, but that was his voice. Not the voices from the vent or the dreams he had. That was Mister Clark's voice. A warning from the dead. Ryan broke out of line and did a beeline for the bright red exit sign down the middle aisle. He could hear people whispering as he ran past. Some in comfort, others in shock. He heard his mother call his name once and then apologize to somebody in the front row for his rude departure. He didn't care what his mother or the others thought, he just kept running until he was out in the cool Autumn air.

His breath came at last when he was free of the funeral home. The sun was warm on his face and the winds quickly cooled him. He saw three men standing in a half circle in the parking lot smoking cigarettes. One waved and asked if he was okay, he nodded he was and turned away to walk to his mother's car. He craned his neck up to see a dark V of geese flying overhead, honking their departure as they vanished over a cluster of pines. He silently wished he could join them.

"They killed him." he finally said out loud to hear it for himself. "Whatever it was that was after me got him instead." The tears came freely now, flowing over his cheeks down to his stiff collar and choking tie. "I'm sorry." he said to nobody in particular. Mister Clark maybe, or God, or the dozens of crying people inside. "They won't get me too."

NINE

"Sorry about your friend." Jeff said from the fence. It was two days after the burial. There had been no bad dreams since Mister Clark died that Sunday morning and now it was Friday, just an hour after school, and Ryan sat wondering if whatever "it" or "they" were had gotten what they had come for with the death of his old friend. He did not know. "He was a nice old dude, you know."

"Yeah, he was." Ryan said sitting in the swing but not moving while letting his feet rest on the pole. Jeff had that look in his eye like he really wanted to get out and do something but Ryan wasn't taking the bait. Not today.

"Heart attack, huh?" he asked between bites of some nut-covered snack. "Lots of old guys go that way I guess. That or cancer. My grandfather had both. Tough deal."

"Which one got him?" Ryan asked only mildly interested. "Cancer or heart-attack?"

"Heart." Jeff said smacking his own chest and causing some fat to wobble there. "Cancer he got from smoking a pack a day. Heart-attack got him first though. My mom used to say that he ate like a grizzly bear. He did too."

"Probably the way you will go, Jeff." Ryan thought but did not say. "We didn't find anything in the basement." he did decide to say instead.

"What are you talking about?" Jeff said flipping his hat around so he could block out the sun better. "What's in your basement?"

"Remember last Saturday when you were over here and I told you about the haunting shit." Ryan said annoyed. Jeff was always like this and it got on Ryan's nerves. Unless it had to do with food or boobies Jeff Bates was sure to forget about it ten minutes later. "He came over to check."

"Oh, yeah. That shit." Jeff grinned. "Told you nothing was there. Not even mice, huh? You got an overactive imagination, man. Maybe one day you will be a horror book writer like Stephen King?"

"I know what I heard." Ryan said standing to come to the fence while viewing the trashcans again. He recalled the last time he stood here jawing with Jeff there were bunches of mice all around those cans tormenting the cats and driving them buggy. Now the mice were gone. So were the cats.

"So is Mister Clark." his mind said back and he got chills.

39

"You didn't hear shit." Jeff said leaning back and almost popping a wheelie on his bike. "Anyways, I'm really sorry about the old man. You wanna go up to Scooter's and get some comics or something."

"Mister Clark didn't die of a heart attack, Jeff." Ryan heard himself say.

"What?" the chubby boy said leaning in closer. "What are you talking about? That's what everybody else is saying. Even the police said that-"

"The cops don't know shit." Ryan cut him off. "I'm just saying I know he didn't."

"Ok, Doctor House, how the hell did he die?" Jeff grinned with crossed arms. "Tell me how you know so much?"

"I saw." he said blankly and let his eyes drift back nearly a week while kneeling by his basement window. "I saw him downstairs in his basement by the window and then there were these . . ."

Jeff was definitely paying attention now. His eyes wide, his arms dangling against the fence as he came closer to hear. It seemed neither boy was breathing and only the wind was alive around them.

"What?" Jeff continued for him. "There was what?" What'd you see?"

"Mice." Ryan said and cringed for saying it knowing what was coming next.

A burst of laughter. A loud hearty one at that. Jeff's eyes were actually tearing up.

"Mice?" he repeated. "You are as daffy as a duck. How the hell could mice kill a full grown man?"

"I just know what I saw." Ryan said defensively. "I didn't say they killed him. There might have been so many that it just gave him a heart attack. That's what I'm saying, dumb ass."

Jeff's face twisted up as he considered it and then leaned his bike against the fence as he wobbled around towards the gate to join his friend. Ryan stood to meet him halfway.

"Okay, that *might* be possible." Jeff said taking the lead as they started walking towards the driveway. "That would take a hell of a lot of mice to scare a full grown man like him. Damn Ryan, he was probably in one or two wars in his day. You think some mice are gonna scare him? Even if you're right, it's still a heart-attack he died of either way, right?"

"I guess." Ryan said nervously watching his fat friend head for Mister Clark's house. "Where are we going?"

"Show me." Jeff demanded as he went straight towards the basement window nearest the back steps. "This the one?"

"Yeah, it was Sunday morning and we came over because we couldn't get him to answer the phone. So my mom sent me and Amy to-" Ryan said now getting cut off by Jeff.

"You can't even see through this stuff." Jeff noticed kneeling down. "How could you tell what was going on, man?"

"There was a light on, and then a shadow of a man, then a whole bunch of damn shadows." Ryan said desperate for Jeff to believe. "Shadows with tails. Then the lights went out."

"Sounds like you actually saw him have the heart attack." Jeff figured lifting his finger to his pursed lips. "Like maybe he was trying to call the ambulance or something, fumbled and stumbled around something, then grabbed the light chain as he fell. That sounds possible."

"What about the mice?" Ryan pointed out.

"Well, did the police or paramedics say anything about mice?" Jeff asked. Ryan went silent. No they had not. If there had been as many mice as he had seen and the cops saw it they would have shut this place up. Exterminators would have been out here at the family's request.

"No. Guess not." Ryan said sounding momentarily defeated. "But they might have left."

"And gone where?" Jeff grinned again standing up and dusting off his already dirty jeans. "That many mice like you're talking about get into a house, no way are they leaving. They are there to stay."

"I know what I saw, man." Ryan said backing away from the dead man's house.

"I believe you saw something." Jeff said. "Just not a mouse plague is all. You said he found nothing in your house, right?"

"He came and looked around and set some traps." Ryan remembered while thinking of their little talk in the basement. Mister Clark had promised to look up more history on the house and see who lived here before the previous family. He probably never got the chance. "We found nothing in them."

"There you go." Jeff pointed out acting as if he was the presiding judge over this whole entire matter and it was now settled. "I told you about my basement. We get some creepy-crawlies every once in a while. Kill 'em and toss 'em out. That's all there is to it."

"I guess." Ryan said feeling only slightly safer back in his own yard.

"So you coming to Scooter's or what? I got soda money for the way home."

"Cool." Ryan said and went to get his bike to join his friend for the rest of an uneventful day.

"Anything to get away from here."

TEN

It stormed again that night. Jeff Bates wasn't afraid of storms like Ryan Woods. In fact they fascinated him. He liked it when the lightning struck down to earth in a blazed, jagged pattern while crackling across the night sky. He loved the way thunder belched and echoed long after the initial blast. He loved the way the wind would whip the treetops into a frenzy and scatter leaves and lawn chairs around the yard. He loved the rain too.

Jeff's thoughts stayed on the story Ryan had told earlier that day. The dozens of mice that gave old man Clark a heart attack. He didn't really *believe* it mind you, but he found it interesting. He began to wonder what strange hidden wonders his own basement held. Maybe some mice had decided to make a home of his basement. Perhaps another snake had taken refuge down under the steps. That one seemed to bother him, as he didn't care for snakes, at least not the big ones. The curiosity got the best of him.

He ate his mother's beef stew, talked football with his father, tried to play with Thor, who sat there like a giant horse with no energy, then Jeff gave up and decided he would go down and have a look around the basement. First he grabbed a root beer from the fridge.

"Where are you going, honey?" his mother caught him creeping through the kitchen.

"Just bored." he told her. "Gonna see if I can find anything to do downstairs."

"You don't play with those things anymore, Jeffery." his mother said and he cringed at his full name being spoken. He hated the long version of it. "It's dirty and cold down there."

"Just something to do is all." he whined knowing his mother would not want to argue this late.

"Stay away from my tool bench and that water heater." his father called from the living room while placing the television on mute. "Burn the skin off you, it will."

"Nice image, Robert!" his mother called back to his father "Honey, you have plenty of things up here to do."

"Just want to look around." Jeff sulked watching his mother's face shake and go blank as she finally caved. "You guys don't let me do anything."

"Well, go on down then." his mother said while turning back to the dishes. "Just look out for rusty nails and broken glass is all."

"God, mom, it ain't a freakin' construction sight." he said opening the door and feeling the cooler air wash over him as the darkness swept up to his eyes and nose. It didn't smell like mice.

"Don't crack wise, mister." she said without turning. "It's been a turtles age since your father has bothered to clean up down there. I just don't want you getting hurt."

Mercifully the phone rang and Jeff sighed with relief as his mother went to get it and he clicked on the lights and slid out of her view, closing the door behind him. He recognized the name "Glenda" and knew she was talking to Donny Schwartz's mom. She would be a while. That lady could outtalk a crack-head filibuster, as he had heard his father put it.

The basement was much cooler this time of year. Jeff himself had not been down in this dark and damp dungeon since last summer when he and his father were searching for items to sell for a yard sale. They found very little worth selling. No reason to come down here other than his father's work bench and tools and the washing and drying of clothes his mother did, this was just a place where old toys and junk came to rust and decay.

Every single stair creaked under his weight, the odor of mildew filled the damp air, sawdust and laundry detergent assaulted his senses, and the humming of the long crackling florescent lights broke the silence. It was just a typical unfinished basement. Stacks of boxes and wooden crates. A second fridge which held nothing but his dad's beer was pretty much empty now, thick layers of ice forming in the freezer section.

Jeff kept his eyes low to the ground to see if any mice were about. Of course there were none and had not been ever that he knew of. He saw nothing but paint stains and dust bunnies lurking along the walls edges. Some books on gardening and auto repair lined a slightly crooked wire bookshelf. Some old tools and a drill with sawdust for blood spilled at its base on the bench. His father would start a birdhouse and then begin a shelf and finish neither for weeks to come.

And then there was the furnace. A huge, hulking silver monster near the back northwest corner of the basement with long octopus arms jutting out in every direction. Right before that was the old toy chest and game closet. The game closet was basically just an open set of shelves with a curtain for a door full of board games and electronic toys that nobody in this house, or any other he could imagine, would ever play with again. Jeff set his soda on the floor as he eyed the toy chest for the first time in months.

"Nothing scary about this basement." he said walking to the toy chest. It was a nice sized thing, another of his father's projects that might have stretched over two years, made of wood with brass fixtures and blue paint with red trim. It was big and bright and looked to Jeff like what some midget clown's coffin would appear to be at a circus funeral.

Let's see what we got here?" he said taking hold of the large looped handle and tugged the lid up.

Layers of toys littered the interior. Stuffed stained animals that smelled like dead real ones, a few soldiers with broken arms or legs, three or two wheeled cars, sticky playing cards, cracked water pistols, decapitated action figures, a deflated soccer ball, and any other number of things that by all rights should have been thrown away. His mother kept saying she was going to come down here one day and sort through all of this crap and see what she could put on E-bay. Jeff had a feeling that the only thing that might even possibly sell on E-bay was the toy chest itself, and that was kinda iffy with the chipped paint and rusted hinges.

"Bunch of crap." he sighed and closed the lid now heading to the closet. He was only a few feet away when the purple curtain blocking his view of the games moved. It was just a slight movement, but enough to halt him in his tracks and raise some goose flesh on his neck and arms.

"Shit." he whispered. He was glad his mother was not here because he might have gotten a smack in the back of the head for that one. She abhorred cursing and let him know it on a daily basis. His father actually caught hell for it too, although minus the slap in the head. "What the hell?"

"Just a breeze." his young mind thought, but there was no breeze down here. The heat had not kicked on, if it had he would have noticed. He was standing close enough to the furnace after all. The upstairs door might have opened. That was a possibility. The walk out one was closed tight.

"Mom?" he called back over his shoulder with eyes watching the thick purple curtain, which remained still. "Dad? That you?"

Nothing. Soft rumbles of thunder. The wind was whistling though the bushes lining the house. Rain on the windows. The hum of lights. A slight drip somewhere. A small clock his father kept on the workbench ticking away the hours. Nothing alive. No creaks on the stairs sounding out approach. No indoor breeze. No mice.

"Screw it." Jeff decided thinking he was letting Ryan Woods and his haunted basements full of mice stories scare him enough for one day. He reached out bravely with one hand and ripped the curtain aside. No monsters here. No mice ready to devour his flesh or give him a heart attack like old man Clark.

"Just games." he grinned and stepped closer.

They were all here, most of them even older than he was, and in not so bad of shape. That was if they were your type of thing, which to Jeff they were not. Monopoly and Scrabble. Clue, Sorry, Candy Land and Payday. Twister and Trivia. All of the games his parents grew up with. None of them took batteries or plugged in or had bad ass sound effects. Just dice and cards and hours and hours of complete boredom. This was not the game closet of an eleven-year-old living in the twenty-first century It was a museum full of relics from the past.

Something moved then behind him. Something bumped against wood, a loud *thump* came from the toy chest, and Jeff spun about so fast he dropped the Uno cards he had just took hold of watching them spill across the gray concrete floor in bright colors. Then his eyes went back to the toy chest. The one big enough for a midget circus clown to be buried in . . . or him.

The lid crept open a few inches and Jeff backed closer to the closet a few inches as well.

"Mom." he said more than called. A reflex action of sorts, like blinking your eyes in the wind or sun, and he watched again as something bumped so hard this time that the whole toy chest moved away from the wall.

"Can't be nobody or nothing in there. I was just looking in there a second ago." his young mind raced while his feet refused to run. The lid creaked a few more inches and Jeff could see the skin of something pressing up against the lid. Black, slick skin, covered in tiny shining scales. It looked wet. It also looked big.

"Mom!" he cried out and then the lid flung completely open, the back slamming into the wall with a loud *thwack!* Jeff stumbled backwards into the closet as he watched the huge snake roll out, the body thicker than his own fat legs, the red glowing eyes set deep into the dark diamond shaped heard staring at him, and a little tongue darted out, flickering at him, teasing him.

"Honey, I'm on the phone!" his mother called from a world away. Jeff knew that just around the corner past the washer and dryer and his father's workbench were the steps. Just up those steps was his kitchen full of lemon cookies and chocolate milk and a mother who was probably trying to talk to a chatty woman and do the dishes all at the same time. Just beyond her was his father, probably sitting in his recliner with a cup of coffee and a Cheese Danish, watching cowboys and Indians and slowly falling asleep with the huge, boring Great Dane laying at his feet. The *real* world. A *safe* world. "What do you want, honey?"

"*I want to live!*" his mind screamed.

"Snake!" he managed to yell. The things head was huge. He recognized it from pictures and shows he had seen on television and the internet. It was an Anaconda sliding over the concrete at him now. A snake that should be miles away from his basement on this October night in Missouri. A world away from here.

"*What are you afraid of, fat boy?*" the huge serpent whispered and young Jeffery Bates decided he was losing his mind. It was talking to him.

"What?" his mother called and he could hear her heading in the opposite direction to get his father. What would his father do? Did he even own a gun? Would he be fast enough to help?

Jeff turned to climb up the flimsy shelves his father had built on the closet, wondering silently to himself if they would be able to hold his heavy weight, when he noticed it really didn't matter. The large black snake had not come alone. Dozens of tiny black snakes came at him from behind the board games in the closet like lightning fast shoestrings. He was quickly covered with them and had to let go. He had to run past the large thing that by all rights should be in a swamp or river somewhere thousands of miles away.

"Help me! Mom! Dad!" he said feeling them sliding down his shirt and over his belly and legs. A blast of thunder and then everything went black. Jeffery Bates screamed one more time as he ran off in no particular direction covered in snakes and tripped over something big.

"*Bye-bye, Jeffery.*" a voice said sounding full of liquids and dirt. A chortled laugh and then the young boy felt something powerful and wet wrap around his body, twisting him about like soft, warm taffy until he was completely in its cold embrace.

Jeff lived long enough to hear his mother clicking the light switch off and on. He lived long enough to hear his father's slippers leaping three steps at a time down the stairs to come and rescue him with the rattling chain collar of Thor in close tow. He lived long enough to feel his body being pulled into

the toy chest and the lid close over himself and the snake into the cold darkness within.

He did not, however, live long enough to hear his parents screams.

ELEVEN

Ryan found himself on the swing again. It was Saturday afternoon and the skies were still dotted with clouds. His mother had gotten a call from Sergeant Lambert. Ryan often heard he had been one of the cops to shoot his father. He had burn marks on his neck and his left arm. His left hand was kind of on the deformed side too. All from the explosion his father died in. He was kind of a friend of the family, at least his mother's, and had been one of the cops to find Mister Clark dead in his basement.

Now they had found Jeff Bates dead in his basement too.

The story he heard from his mother talking to Sergeant Lambert out on the sidewalk was that Jeff had gone down to the basement. His mother heard him call out something about snakes, she wasn't sure, but it sounded like snakes. The power went out and then screaming. Robert Bates, the father, had gone running downstairs with his giant dog behind him and found his son curled up inside an old toy chest. Dead. Face frozen over in fear. Heart stopped completely.

No snakes however.

"His hands were balled up so tight they had to pry them apart." Ryan had heard Lambert say from behind the bushes bordering the backyard. "Said he was scared to death. You imagine that?" the big, broad shouldered cop with the cool ass shades had told his mother while spitting on their front lawn. Ryan often thought the big cop had the *hots* for his mom. He had to admit she was pretty for a woman damn near forty. She was still slim from all her workouts at the gym. She had pretty dark hair that curled to her shoulders and brown eyes that sparkled in the sun and a great smile. Ryan remembered Jeff joking that he had a M.I. L.F for a mom, and then Ryan found out what it meant and gave Jeff a good head-whacking. It was the only time in history that he had ever beat Jeff without getting beat back.

"An eleven-year-old boy dead of a heart-attack." Lambert said shaking his head and lifting that withered looking hand to his mouth to place a toothpick to dangle there. "The mother, well she just lost it. She's up in Riverview for treatment and care. Nobody is sure for how long." he said and Ryan knew that meant the booby-hatch. "Don't make no damn sense. What the hell could scare a kid that bad that he would just up and die?"

Ryan knew what.

Whatever it was that killed Mister Clark in his basement. Whatever it was that whispered his

name through the vents and sent those snakes across the ceiling. Whatever it was that let him see that dead

woman in the nightgown in his closet.

"So why don't they kill me?" he asked himself sitting there barely moving across the little patch of

dirt under the swing. He found himself looking down the alleyway knowing that the dirt bike would never

be coming again. No more stories about boobies or football. No more wiffle ball games. No more Jeff

Bates period.

Ryan Woods wasn't just getting scared, he was getting angry.

"Why don't you kill me?" he called out hearing his own voice echo off the far house walls up and

down the alleyway. He heard no answer but a distant rumble of thunder.

TWELVE

A funeral for a friend on a rainy Monday morning.

Ryan's mother said he didn't have to go, but Ryan felt as if he did. In fact, he wanted to.

Jeff's mother wasn't there. Ryan heard whispers of how his mother still believed Jeff was alive and would not have anybody telling her otherwise. The father was there, sitting front row in a charcoal gray suit with a woman on either side of him, sisters maybe, comforting him while he sobbed quietly. Glenda Schwartz was there dressed in black, chattering to the unknown lady next to her a hundred miles a second, her son Donny sat next to her staring at the dark carpet with lifeless eyes. Marty Fitzgerald was three rows back looking as nervous as a mouse in a room full of starving cats. His bottom lip quivering, his eyes darting about the room seeking escape like maybe he would piss himself again as he did years ago.

And Anna Finch was there too. She sat quietly between her parents looking like the smallest and cutest angel dressed in black. Her mother pretty and sad all at once, her father still and quiet and probably wishing he were anywhere but here, and Anna with tiny beads of tears welling up in her eyes. He silently wished she would look over at him, even for a second, but her face remained straight forward.

The crowd was even bigger this time. Mister Clark had lived longer but a child's funeral brought in all walks of life. The crying was louder. The Minister was a large black man with more hair on his face than the top of his head. His own eyes were full of tears behind his squared off glasses.

"Suffer the little children to come unto me, and forbid them not, for of such is the Kingdom of God." he said holding out his massive robed arms. Ryan wondered just how much Jeff had suffered. Despite that they found him curled up in some toy chest, he had called out *"snakes"* before they found him. Hadn't it been snakes that were chasing him through the dark alley in Ryan's dreams. Even though he got away from his sight and Ryan was the one who was taken under, it seemed they eventually caught up with him. Ryan knew that Jeff had seen snakes in that basement of his even if his father did not. There were no bite marks on his body. But there were other types of snakes.

The kind that squeezed and squished you up like a wad of typing paper.

He did walk past the boys casket. He wanted to. His young friend laid out there looking like a complete stranger to him in a tan suit and dark shirt, his hair combed neatly with a part to the side. Ryan

51

barely recognized the boy without a chocolate smile on his face or a candy bar in his hand. There were no voices this time. No whispers. He caught the eyes of Jeff's father and nodded, the older man who looked sleep deprived and worn nodded back with a tiny grin that faded as fast as it had appeared. Ryan had the strange and strongest urge to run over and hug the man and apologize. He wasn't sure for what exactly. Maybe letting his son know of the things going on in his house as he had Mister Clark.

Ryan stood close to his mother, his sister Amy absent as she was somewhere out with Brandon, the tattooed, leather jacket wearing thug who had stolen her heart, and his mother worried a few more things. They watched the tiny white casket covered in flowers lower into the soft earth and Ryan paid special attention to the dirt. He saw that it was moving.

It was not snakes, as he had feared, but many long, fat earthworms that had come out to greet their new underground neighbor. Ryan watched them twitch and squirm as the casket finally reached its short and final destination. He also noticed that nobody else was seeing was he was seeing. If they had their would have been a stronger reaction than just the sobs and tears that flowed now.

These worms were all over the coffin. They ripped apart the flowers and left scratch marks all over the shiny white lid. Ryan walked in a daze as he drew closer feeling his mothers firm hand on his right shoulder as he dared to near the edge of the strange spectacle.

"He's mine." they seemed to call out to him and the softest laughter could be heard from down there somewhere under the dirt and soft rain. He blinked and saw the worms squirming in his direction. *"Soon, you will be too, boy."*

Ryan broke free of his mother's grasp and ran. Grave stones blurred past him as he ran as fast as his tight dress shoes would allow. He could hear his mother calling and giving chase. The rain mixing in with his tears as he ran over uneven soft ground, nearly losing his balance a few times, and he didn't stop until he reached the parking lane where his mom's car sat. He fell to the paved walk, not caring if his only good suit would be ruined by water or mud, and let loose with all the pain he was holding inside. If he hadn't told Jeff about the basement, and what happened to Mister Clark, maybe he would still be playing wiffle ball. Maybe he would still be chasing girls with big boobies and going to Scooter's for comics and soda and candy bars. Maybe he would still be alive.

Most definitely he would be.

He recalled nothing more of that day then being held by his mother while somebody else, possibly Sergeant Lambert, drove them home while he stared out the window at the falling leaves and rain.

THIRTEEN

Five nights had gone by and nothing happened. No bad dreams, no nightmares of things in closets or basements, no voices from vents. Nothing at all. Were the deaths of Mister Clark and Jeffery Bates enough, or was it just full for now, silently waiting for another meal to be offered up for sacrifice? Who would be next?

How much longer before it settled on its main course? Ryan Woods, well done, with a side order of his mom and sister. How much longer before the killing started again? Ryan decided he couldn't wait. He needed to find out some things about his father, and he knew just how to do it.

It was Saturday. The twentieth day of October, just over two weeks since Ryan first heard the voices from the vent, and already two friends were dead. Ryan knew he had to find out what was going on in his house before anymore people died. His mother did not allow the internet in the house. She felt Amy spent too much time on Facebook and was afraid he would get into porn, so it would be the library.

Ryan had talked his mother into taking him to the library and dropping him off while she went to visit poor Mrs. Bates up in Riverview. He had no idea why his mother wanted to visit the woman, other than the fact they were both mothers, because Ryan couldn't see anything being done for her. She was, as the big cop Lambert had said, lost to the world.

Ryan assured his mother that he could walk home on his own but she wouldn't hear of it. She told him she would only be two hours and to wait there for her return. This would give him very little time. He had to work fast and pray for good luck.

He really wasn't interested in any of the books regardless of what information they might have. He headed straight for the computers with his small notepad and pen and began his research. He wanted to start with what Mister Clark had thought of. He wanted to see who owned the house before his family and before the Thurber's. Maybe the answer lied there.

He was no genius but smart enough to find out what he needed to know without any help from the nosy librarians who kept casting odd glances at him. He assured Miss Bradsky, who was the nosiest of the nosy, that his mother was next door at the dentist and would return any second. He had to find out what he needed to know soon before they called his bluff.

It took him nearly half an hour before he came across anything helpful. It was a defunct paper that no longer sold in Waverly, Missouri. It dated back to the mid 1970's. *The Waverly Gazette.* The article was about a family that had lived there from 1964 until 1975. The *Woods* Family. Same name as him and his family. Before the Thurber's, who had lived there only about ten years, was another family called the Saunders. They only stayed five years. Young Ryan could find nothing odd on any of them. Then the family before them, with the same last name as his own, the Woods family. Janice Woods to be exact.

"Whoa." he breathed a bit too loud noticing some old man cast him a glare from a computer across the table. The Woods family was a family of four. It had been five but the father, Carl Woods, died in a confrontation with the police. "Sounds like my father." he breathed reading on. He left behind a wife and her three children. Two daughters and a son.

The youngest daughter, Sara, had died of a heart attack in the basement while playing with her dolls. A *heart-attack* at the age of eleven. "Shit." Ryan said and caught eyes with the old man again who only frowned at him and placed a single finger up to his lips. "Sorry." he told him and read on. Three weeks later the oldest daughter, Emily, had slipped and hit her head in the shower, knocked herself unconscious and drown. *"How freaking weird is that?"* Ryan thought scrolling the story down. The mother, Janice Woods, hung herself in the bedroom closet with an extension cord. That was only five days after the daughter.

"Which bedroom closet?" Ryan thought remembering the snakes and the woman who appeared to him. Could that have been her? He reached the final paragraph of the story. The son, Alan Woods, was the only survivor of the mess. He did not die but was sent to live with his Uncle and Aunt somewhere down in Oklahoma.

"Alan?" Ryan thought and felt his entire body go numb. His father's name had been Alan. The big man with the pony-tail and sleeveless shirts showing off his muscles and tattoos. "Dad lived there when he was a kid." he said in so soft a whisper that not even the old man noticed. "Then he met mom and moved back there. Why would he move back?"

Ryan checked the clock on the wall. He had maybe forty-five minutes before his mother got back. He wrote down his father's full name. Alan Charles Woods. He found out where he lived in Oklahoma, a small town called Watonga. He also discovered all of the trouble he caused down there. It seemed his father had liked to get into bar fights a lot. He did time in jail for stealing and selling drugs as a teen. He also had a nickname that the cops came to know him by. A name he earned for all of his night-time robberies of breaking into folks houses while they were sleeping.

"The Boogeyman." Ryan let out with a tiny gasp and stared hard at the picture of the man with the wild eyes and long black hair tied back in a ponytail. This all happened in the mid-eighties. Ryan figured it must have been at least another ten years before he met Ryan's mother since Amy had just turned sixteen. Did she know how wild he was? She had to have known. Ryan found out just sitting here in front of a computer in less than two hours.

Another note of interest. Uncle Owen and Aunt Clara, who Alan Woods had lived with until the age of sixteen, had both died in their home as well. Uncle Owen died of, surprise, a heart attack while stretched out under his old Plymouth one Saturday night in his garage. Aunt Clara died as the house burned down not a week later. Young Alan Charles Woods went into state care. Lucky state.

Ryan had just looked up information concerning his father's death when he saw his mothers face at the front desk speaking to Miss Bradsky. She pointed one of her long, bony fingers in his direction and his mother started for the computer room. He knew he would not have time to find out more. He would have to assume that what he already knew about his father's death was true or come back later on his own and find out more. But this much he did know and that was that somehow his father was involved.

"We need to go, Ryan." his mother snapped as he clicked off the page with his father's mug shot just in time before she rounded behind him. "I have to drop you off and do some shopping and run some other errands."

"Couldn't I wait here until you're done and you could come back and get me?" he tried.

"Ryan, I am tired." she sighed. "I don't want to go shopping and come back over here in traffic. Besides these folks are not getting paid to baby-sit. You can come back next week."

Ryan remained silent on the march to the car. *"Next week."* he thought as the cool winds blasted him once walking out the automatic doors. *"How many more people will be dead by next week?"*

Ryan knew that Mister Clark had said that a house could not be haunted unless somebody died there. What if he was wrong? What if that person was so evil and had lived there twice in their life that they had a *special connection* to the house. Would that make a difference?

"It has to be him. He's in our basement." Ryan thought following his mother towards the car.

"How the hell do I stop him?"

FOURTEEN

"You can drop me off here." Ryan said seeing Scooter's Comics & Candy Store up ahead. His mother let out a sigh of both frustration and surrender. "I promise I won't stay long."

"You better not, it's almost five. I want you home within the hour and I will call Amy to make sure you're there." she said as he climbed out. "No horror comics, Ryan. I mean that crap. We've seen enough scary things for one October, okay?"

"Okay." he said turning for the store and he actually agreed with her. She had no idea how much scary stuff had happened so far this October. She had no idea that her and Amy's life might very well be in danger along with his own. "See you later."

"Home within an hour." his mother called pulling away and Ryan gave her a short wave before ducking into the store.

"Hey, Mister Kelly." he called to the pudgy, balding black man behind the counter. The man's face lit up seeing the young child and he straightened himself up on his stool.

"Scooter to my friends, Ryan. You know that by now." the man called over to him. "How are you doing this fine autumn afternoon?"

"I'm okay." Ryan said eyeing the comic book aisle at the back of the store. Several other boys were in the store and two girls he could not completely see from where he stood. He knew both of the boys, Tony Pryor and Rick Campbell, but said nothing to him as the boys walked past with hands full of chips and soda. They were several years older than Ryan, freshman in high-school, so they pretty much ignored him. That was fine with Ryan, seeing as how he knew Tony both drank and smoked already, but he did miss having a best friend.

"We got some good comics in this week." Mister Kelly, a.k.a. Scooter, said while watching his little television set he kept behind the counter. Ryan could tell it was a western from the gunshots and noises the horses made when they galloped along. "Vampires and werewolves and aliens." he called out while the group of teens piled their snacks on the counter and began digging for their change. "All that stuff you like."

"Yep." Ryan said heading for the back. "Good to know."

58

There was a good selection and Ryan stood back and took them all in. Zombies and vampires were always a favorite. Invading aliens attacking small towns, werewolves and witches, serial killers and escaped mental patients. Ryan knew he promised his mother he wouldn't by any, but he could always just look. He did not notice the girls sneak up behind him.

"Hello Ryan Woods." came the soft pretty voice. Ryan jumped as he turned and the two girls giggled. "Sorry, didn't mean to scare you so bad."

Anna Finch. There she stood less than three feet away with those pretty hazel eyes and that bright red hair cascading down past her cherry Chap Stick lips. Her perky little boobs poking out from under her dark blue jacket. Donna Corrigan, a shorter girl with glasses and dark hair, stood to her left. They both looked like they just stepped out of a wet summer dream.

"No, it's cool. Just checking out the comics." he said and hoped she understood he wasn't here to look at the baby ones with talking ducks and mice. "You know, the horror ones. Graphic novels."

"Yeah, those are cool." Anna smiled and Ryan couldn't take his eyes of her freckled nose. He wanted to stand there and count them all day while she smiled but knew it would not happen in this lifetime. "So anyways, Donna's having a Halloween party next week. You want to come?"

"Ummm, yeah. I guess. Why not." he said looking over at short, bug-eyed but cute Donna who fiddled with her key chain. "I think Halloween's on a Wednesday this year?"

"Well, it's like next Friday at my Uncle's farm. Mark your calendar on the twenty-sixth for sure." Donna told him while popping her gum. "You don't have to wear a costume unless you just want to, but most of us will be. We will have music and food and paddleboat racing on my Uncle's."

"Great." Ryan said faking excitement while focusing back on Anna. "You will be there right?"

"Of course, silly." Anna said and crinkled her nose and Ryan thought he would fall on his ass it was so damn cute. "I have to have a dance partner, though. You can dance, right?"

"Yeah, sure, I guess." Ryan shrugged. "How do I get in touch with you?"

"Here." Anna said stepping up and taking hold of Ryan's arm. It shocked Ryan that Anna Finch would even lay hands on him, much less take his jacket sleeve and roll it up, produce an ink pen from thin air, and write her own phone number on his arm. She smiled the entire time she did it and so did Ryan. "There you go." she finished catching his eyes with her bright hazel ones. "Now don't call before noon or my mom will curse you out." she smiled and Ryan laughed with her. "And if you call after seven, my dad will kick your butt. Don't call on Sundays at all. They are both shitty about that." she said grinning and Ryan never thought he would get so excited hearing a young girl talk that way but he loved it. "I will give you the address when you call. Her uncle's farm, I mean. Just make sure you show up."

"And bring friends. It starts at six, but come whenever." Donna said with a bright hopeful smile. "His farm is out on route forty-one. You know where that is, right?"

"Yeah, sure. West Side of town." he said knowing of it but not having been out that way much. There was no reason for him to. It was all flat farmlands.

"North-West, you can't miss it. Big ass red, white and blue silo out front."

"So what are you going to be?" he asked Anna getting lost in her hazel eyes again. "You know, for the party?"

"Totally undecided." she grinned rolling her eyes. "Something scary, but sexy." she said shaking her little frame and Ryan thought he would pop a boner right there. "What about you? You're heavy into horror, so I hear."

"I'll figure something out. It will be a surprise."

"Good." she smiled eyeing him up and down. "I love surprises."

"Okay, I will call you soon." he said staring at the number with the little smile face for a zero in it.

"Okay, well, we have to go." she said. "Hope you find a good scary one." she said pointing to the comics. "If it's scary bring it to the party."

"You bet." Ryan smiled thinking how cool it was for her not only to curse like a boy but she liked scary comics as well. How wild was that? "See you at the party."

He turned back to the comics then and almost got lost in thought of what was going on in his life when he heard he soft voice call to him once more.

"Hey." she said then from the end of the aisle. He turned and she stood there alone, Donna already at the counter with her snacks, and she kind of waved for him to come closer. He returned the comic with the skulls and bugs to the rack and made his way down the aisle in a trance like state as he noticed her face had taken on a more serious look.

"What's up?" he asked her.

"I just wanted to say I was sorry about Jeff, you know?" she said and Ryan lowered his head with a frown. He had managed to forget about Jeff for a few precious moments and could have gone the rest of the week without thinking about it. "I mean he was kind of a jerk sometimes . . ." she said sounding like she might cry and looked away to compose herself. " . . . but I never wanted anything bad to happen to him like this. It's just messed up, you know?"

"Yeah, I know." Ryan tried smiling. "He liked you though."

She gave a short but loud burst of nervous laughter. "He didn't like me that much, just my boobs." she smiled and Ryan actually let his eyes drift there for a second, looking away when he noticed her noticing his stare and she smiled. "It's okay if you look. All the boys do these days. I get that a lot lately. My mom says I'm an early bloomer. I just wanted to let you know cuz I know you guys were cool and hung together."

"Yeah, I guess I'm gonna miss him. I guess a lot." Ryan said finding her eyes again. If they were adults, or even teens, this would be the part of the movie where he moved in and took hold of her and kissed her. But he was only eleven and had never kissed a girl yet. He had seen several nude photos from the Penthouse magazines that Jeff had sneaked out of his father's sock drawer, but that was it. And even as amazing and sexy as those women had been to look at, he still would rather look at Anna Finch and her pretty hazel eyes and freckled nose.

"Okay, well I have to go now." she said heading towards where Donna waited by the door. "Don't forget to call me, okay? You owe me a dance at the party."

"No problem." Ryan said and watched them walk out the door and kept watching them as they crossed the parking lot, the two of them talking and laughing as the sun shined on her red hair.

"Somebody has got it bad." Mister Kelly called from behind the counter and Ryan felt himself blush. "I don't blame you, Ryan. She's a real cutie. Treat her nice, you hear me?"

"She's just my friend, Mister Kelly." Ryan grinned and turned back for the comics.

"Sure she is for now." the big man said creaking back in on his stool still talking as Ryan vanished down the chip aisle towards the comics once more. "But soon you will both be in high-school, my boy. That is where the magic always starts. You wait and see."

Ryan liked the thought of him and Anna very much actually, but he had bigger fish to fry right now. He didn't want Anna to get hurt in any way so he could never tell her what was going on. Her and the rest of Waverly had no idea what truly happened to Jeff Bates or Mister Clark. He was hoping to get some ideas from some stories about how to deal with the problem. Maybe there was a way to get a house *un-haunted* somehow in one of these comics.

Ryan noticed a few things when he got back to the comics. First, the lights seemed a lot dimmer than they had been before. The store back here was bright a few moments ago. The air was cooler as well, as if a freezer door had been opened and frosty air had washed over the entire back of the store. Ryan stood there shivering while his eyes took in all the comics before him. That was when he noticed the next thing different. A lot more comics were lined up on the wall now, especially horror ones. Much more than before. He blinked his eyes and rubbed them to make sure he was not hallucinating. Where there had been only two rows of horror comics before now there were at least six. A few of them stood out from the rest for very specific and frightening reasons.

"What the shit?" he said. There was a comic called Basement Things. On the cover was a picture of an old man, who looked very much like Mister Clark, dressed up as a barbecue chef, hat and all, laying there in the driveway with mice all over his body. Ryan reached out with trembling hands and picked it up in order to make sure it was real. He thumbed through it quickly and saw the pages were mostly blank. A few pictures showed the old man on the basement floor while holding his chest with one hand and fighting off the legions of mice with the other. Ryan dropped the book and scanned the rest of the wall for more.

Another Basement Things comic caught his eye. This one had a little fat kid being squeezed to death by a large black snake while little snakes swarmed all over the floor. Ryan backed away and eyed them all over for anymore while not even realizing he was holding his breath the whole time. He finally let loose with a gasp for air when he saw the last comic there on the end of the shelf.

"No shitting way." he breathed taking in the picture. He reached out and grabbed it up from its place to get a better look. There was a young man dressed in a leather jacket and faded jeans with biker boots on. He had dark spiked hair and a dagger tat on his neck, and his lip was pierced. He was hung up in a large spider web spread out in the corner of a basement, hundreds of tiny spiders crawling all over him while one huge spider the size of a dog sat perched on the wall grinning.

A screaming teenage girl sat on the floor staring up at him with tears running down her face.

"Amy." he managed to choke out and let the comic fall to the floor and ran towards the front of the store. "Mister Kelly! Mister Kelly!"

"Ryan? What's wrong?" the big black man said leaping up from his chair so fast he spilled his coffee. "Shit, look what I did! What's wrong, son?"

"I need to use your phone." he said nearly out of breath as he gripped the counter. "Please can I use your phone?"

"Sure, son." the man said taking out his own cell phone. "Are you okay? What's the emergency? Are you hurt?"

"Please, I need to call my house." he said taking the cell. "Something bad might be going on there."

"What makes you say that?" the confused man asked nodding at the woman who walked in the store just then. Ryan recognized her too. It was Mrs. Edwards, the lady who worked here with Mister Kelly. "I mean, how do you know?"

"Just a feeling." Ryan said not wanting to tell him about the comics. He had two good reasons for this. One was that Mister Kelly wouldn't believe him, and the other was that if Ryan did tell him, Mister Kelly might just join the ranks of the dead. The phone rang seven times and nobody answered. Either his mother or Amy had must turned the answering machine off. "Nobody answers. I have to go." he said handing the phone back. "Thanks."

"Hold on, Ryan." the large black man said turning to grab his hat and coat. "You're way too excited to be running all the way home." he said turning to Mrs. Edwards who was headed back for the storeroom. "Tina. Mind the shop for me. I'll be back in a few. Let's go, boy."

Ryan was worried about getting Mister Kelly involved but he did think if he ran all the way home from here, which was a good dozen blocks, he would never make it in time. He just hoped there wouldn't be much traffic between here and his house. He hoped the comic cover had just been a trick played on him by the things in the basement. Whatever they were.

"Happening in the daylight now." he said out loud without thinking and Mister Kelly shot him an odd glance while starting up the car and pulling off the lot.

"What is?" he asked the boy.

"Nothing. Just talking to myself." he said. "Please drive faster, Mister Kelly. I think my sister might be in trouble."

"How do you know that, son?" Mister Kelly said eyeing the intersection and only doing a slow roll instead of a full stop, which made Ryan happy. "I mean if it's that serious maybe I should call the police. Those girls tell you something? I mean you're not going to sit there and tell me you're one of those folks that gets visions, are you? I've known you you're whole life pretty much and this is the first time I ever heard of it."

"Not like that." Ryan said. "Just got a gut feeling."

"Good enough." Mister Kelly said accelerating faster as he dug into his jacket pocket and handed Ryan the phone. "Why don't you keep trying your house while I drive."

"Thanks." Ryan said taking the phone and silently hoping that Mister Kelly would not die because of his kind actions today.

FIFTEEN

Amy and Brandon were entwined on the couch in the basement. Brandon lay on top of her shirtless and sweaty, one hand roaming under her shirt exploring her tender flesh while the other tugged on her jeans, all the while his tongue dancing with hers down here in the cool dark place they had retreated to so many times before.

Amy thought she heard the phone ring but didn't care. She knew her mother would be gone for awhile and hopefully Ryan with her. She let Brandon unsnap her bra and have his fun there with his mouth while she stared at the ceiling and enjoyed, what she thought in her young mind at least, made her a woman. It wasn't as bad as her mother had told her, the whole sex thing. Sure it hurt the first time but after that it was just him and her sharing their bodies. Brandon never lasted long enough for it to be a big deal. This was something she secretly hoped he could improve on in later years if they stayed together.

"Oh, you're so hot, babe." he told her while mauling over her breasts and she grinned knowing it was true while running her hands over his spiked hair. She was very hot for sixteen and more guys then just Brandon let her know it on a daily basis. She could never understand how her mother had given up sex now for five years.

"Just use a condom, Brandon." she insisted as he worked his way down to her jeans. He unsnapped them and made little cooing noises while unzipping them and tugging them down to reveal her pink and white cotton panties. "You like?"

"Me like." he said tossing her jeans to the floor and going to work on his own. "Got a condom right here, babe. It's got your name on it."

"My name's not Trojan." she grinned up at him while he stripped for her.

"Such a smart ass." he grinned back at her while ripping the packet open.

Something fell then in the far corner. A small stack of boxes. Amy let out a yelp while Brandon fell back on the couch with his jeans midway down to his knees.

"What the fuck?" he whispered. "Somebody's here."

"No way." Amy said covering herself with a throw pillow sitting up for a better look. "My mom is gone, dude."

"Your little fucking brother." Brandon said tugging his jeans back up and letting the condom fall to the floor. "Damn perv is watching us."

"Not him. He went to the library. We would have heard him come in the way he bumps around."

"So who the fuck is that back there then?" Brandon said zipping up and walking thug-style to the back corner of the basement. She watched his tattoos of skulls and daggers flex over his rippled arms as he strolled into the corner looking ready for a fight with the unseen intruder. "Your cat maybe?"

"Griffin is upstairs. Stop being such a scary ass." Amy said grinning now as she pulled out a pack of her mother's smokes and lit one. "Come on back, babe. I'm horny. It's just gravity. Ryan probably stacked them like that on purpose so they'd fall eventually."

"Something moved." Brandon said coming to a stand still as he watched yet another box topple over in the dark corner. "I think you got maybe a snake or a rat."

"Shit!" Amy said pulling her legs up on the couch and craning her neck to get a better view of where Brandon was while keeping her breasts hidden by the pillow. "Ryan said he was hearing shit. He said he saw a snake about a week ago. The little turd was actually telling the truth?"

"Well, have no fear, my lady." Brandon said flexing his muscles while reaching for a broom in the corner. "You're muscle man is here. Whatever the fuck is back there I will exterminate it's ass."

"Wooo-hooo, go Hercules." Amy teased taking another drag of her smoke while reaching for the near empty bottle of wine. "You know, you're gonna have to buy another bottle of wine for my mom or she's gonna start noticing all of this shit missing."

"You don't think your mom knows already that you're smoking and drinking?" Brandon laughed while poking at the boxes. He saw a nice sized spider scurry for the wall, but nothing more. "She probably knows we're screwing by now. She's not an idiot, Amy. Looks like some spiders is all babe. I fucking hate spiders. Always have since I was a kid."

"Poor baby." Amy mocked while noticing a few spiders herself crossing over the concrete floor. "Oh, gross. Get these fuckers, Brandon!" she screamed pointing at the little black creatures coming in her direction. "Hurry up!"

"Chill the hell out." Brandon said coming back over and swatting the things back to the wall and crushing them with the broom. "Not like they're poisonous or anything."

"Who cares. I still don't want them all over me." she said cringing. "Maybe we should do this another time, dude."

"No, no." Brandon panicked while turning back to the boxes. "Just let me check one more time and see what's over here and then we can get down to business."

This time Amy did hear the phone ring. She hoped up, skipping daintily with bare feet across the chilly basement floor, and headed up the steps.

"Hey, where you going?" Brandon asked smacking more boxes around.

"If I don't answer this time she will worry and head home. We do not want that." Amy called back reaching the kitchen. "Just get rid of the spiders and then come up here to my room. It's too freaking cold down there anyways." she said snatching up the phone after realizing the answering machine was not on. "Yello?"

"Amy, it's me. Don't talk, just listen." the small boy's voice said in panic.

"Ryan?" Amy said looking at the bright windows to the outside world and noticing she was standing here in just her panties. "Where are you? Where's mom?"

"Just listen?" he said louder. "Is Brandon there with you?"

"Nice try." she smiled slinking down into the kitchen chair. "You're not blackmailing me, little man. He stopped by, but now he's gone. So there. You can't prove otherwise."

"Amy, I don't care what you were doing, and please don't give me any details, but if he's there, you guys are in danger." Ryan said and his voice did sound more urgent than Amy had ever heard. "Get out of the house!"

***

Brandon had managed to kill a few more spiders but every time he did five or six more came from under the boxes. It got to be to where the whole floor seemed to be covered with them. Brandon backed away while sweeping himself a path with the broom.

"You got a serious problem down here, babe." Brandon said feeling afraid for the first time. "I think you got a whole nest of them."

He jumped and fell back into the wall as a few dropped from the ceiling above and landed on his bare back. He cried out while dropping the broom and turning about in circles while reaching to brush off the things that were now falling into his hair and on his legs.

"Shit! Shit!" he cried toppling into the couch. "Get the fuck off me!" he said watching the floor suddenly go black with them. They were everywhere. Climbing down the walls and over the pipes. He looked up and saw them scurrying along the beams overheard. Hundreds, maybe more. "What the fuck?" he breathed looking towards the stairwell that was blocked by a flowing black river of the spiders. "I can make it." Brandon told himself while crouching on the couch like a tiger ready to pounce. "All I have to do is make it to the stairs."

Just as the young man was ready to make a mad sprint for safety another shadow descended from the ceiling. This one was much bigger. Its bulbous body was black, about the size of the throw pillow and eight hairy legs jutting out at all angles. It glided softly to the smooth floor in front of him, the tiny spiders all running over its body while it stood there staring at him with glowing red eyes.

"Fuck with my daughter, you little punk." the spider-thing said.

"Fuck me." Brandon managed before the thing leapt at him and landed dead square in his chest.

***

"Are you outside you little pervert?" Amy grinned heading towards the window where Griffin sat twirling his tail. "You just want to see how we are dressed when we come running out of the house, don't you?"

"Amy, shut up!" Ryan yelled and Mister Kelly jumped in the seat next to him. "Just get out of the house! You're both in danger! Are you guys in the basement?"

"I'm not saying anymore, Ryan." she said heading back towards the basement door. "I am sixteen years old and mom pretty much knows that I have sex. She wanted to get me pills but-"

68

"Aw, Gross. I don't care about that." Ryan said rolling his eyes. "There is something in the basement. Something much worse than mice or snakes. Did you see any spiders while you were down there?"

"*You* put those there?" she accused standing at the foot of the steps now. "You little sneak. You scared the shit out of us. Where did you get them? I will tell mom big time if you even bring up that Brandon was-"

"Amy, I didn't put them there!" he yelled and he could tell that Mister Kelly was starting to get nervous as he sped up faster now. "I'm almost there. Mister Kelly is coming with me. Get out of the house!"

"Who is with you?" she asked and the phone started to break up. Static cut in over Ryan's voice until she only heard bits and pieces and then finally the phone went dead.

"Amy? Amy?" Ryan said and looked over at Mister Kelly who shared a silent stare only for a few seconds before he focused back on the road.

"Hold on tight, boy." he said slamming the gas down. "We're almost there."

***

Brandon felt the thing bite him. It hurt at first then his whole body seemed to go numb. He tried to move but could not, his legs and arms gone limp and useless. He tried to scream but when he opened his mouth only a soft cushion of air came out and then his mouth dropped shut again. He was paralyzed.

"You shouldn't be down here, boy." it said and Brandon's eyes grew wide. Was this fucking thing talking to him? What the hell had his shit been laced with that he was smoking?

The huge spider began to spray him with something sticky and white. *"Webbing!"* his mind screamed as he watched his body being coated with the thick strands and slowly he felt his body being lifted up into the air, dangling like some huge, near-naked housefly caught in a trap. *"God, no! Amy! Somebody! Please get down here and make it stop!"* his mind screamed but he could not act to save himself as his body began to sway back and forth in the webs as he was pulled higher.

The webbing wrapped its way around his throat nice and tight like a noose and Brandon could feel his breathing slowly being cut off. He was being killed by something that shouldn't even exist. His mouth formed an O as he tried one last scream but did nothing but make a short choking noise and then Brandon lost sight of everything and faded into black.

"Ryan?" Amy asked one more time before letting the phone drop to her side. Ryan was gone from the phone. "Brandon?" she called down the dark stairs. "You okay, babe?"

No answer at first. Then a shuffling of feet. Some more boxes moving about and then a muffled cry. Amy slowly stepped down the stairs one at a time while keeping her eyes to the open part of the stairwell for any movement. There was none.

"Hey, babe. You kill all the big, bad buggies for me?" she asked finally reaching the cool floor with her bare feet and she stood there shivering with little goose bumps on her naked legs, arms and breasts. "This shit is not funny, Brandon. If you jump out and scare me I swear I will kick your ass and it will be a long time before you get any of this kitty again." she threatened with a hopeful grin. Something moved. Something that sounded like metal being drug against concrete, a chain maybe. "Brandon just say something please!" she called out turning the phone back on and readying her fingers for 911. "Ryan is on his way home. Some guy is driving him so you need to clear out of here. Ryan might not talk but whoever is driving him home will see your bike out there, babe."

More movement and finally a loud smack of metal against the wall.

"Fuck this!" Amy said gathering her courage as she rounded the corner back to the couch. "You want to scare me, go ahead and scare me!"

Amy froze, eyes wide and mouth open, as the phone fell from her hand and cracked on the basement floor. Hanging before her was her boyfriend. Brandon had a chain around his neck, done up nice and tight, and had hung himself from one of the ceiling beams. His eyes wider than Amy's in both shock and fear, a trickle of blood running from his nose over his pierced lip. His nude body swung back and forth. Amy cut loose with a scream that lasted long past the knocking at the door above her.

SIXTEEN

When Amy wouldn't answer the door or phone, Ryan had used his key. Mister Kelly followed at a respectful distance until he heard the girl's screams from the basement. Ryan knew that Brandon was here upon seeing his motorcycle so he knew that is was going to be Brandon's body that he would find in the basement.

Mister Kelly beat him to Amy. He covered her with a towel he found draped over the dryer and held her while staring at the swinging young man and motioned for young Ryan to stay back and not look but Ryan had to see for himself. There were no webs or spiders, other than the ones that his sister told him about on the phone, but Ryan imagined that Brandon might have had a different tale to tell if he was still alive to tell it.

Mister Kelly, after checking the body and trying to lift it down, called the police and took Amy and Ryan upstairs. Amy was still crying and screaming when Sergeant Lambert and Chief Rollins showed up about five minutes later. Ryan stayed close to Amy who sat with a robe around her while rocking back and forth and sobbing. At least the screaming was done. Mister Kelly went inside with the police. They came back out and talked while they waited for the ambulance. Ryan overheard most of what they said.

Mister Kelly told the cops about Ryan wanting to go home for fearing his sister was in danger. Sergeant Lambert filled in Mister Kelly about Mister Clark, who he had not heard about, and Jeff Bates, which he did know about. Both friends of the family, and now this. A suicide of the girls boyfriend. The three grown men cast odd glances in Ryan's direction before continuing their conversation.

Ryan sat close to Amy but gave up on trying to touch her as she would go into hysterics every time he did. He heard Chief Rollins talking about how he had run-in's with Brandon before. He said Brandon was a "bad seed" and had been getting into fights and being drunk in public before. He also had numerous speeding tickets that the boy's father had gotten him cleared of. Chief Rollins seemed to think that Brandon was a punk who would have ended up in jail or the grave before thirty anyways and it was just a shame that such a nice young girl had to go through this. That last part Ryan agreed with.

Ryan didn't know Chief Rollins very well. The man made it a point to avoid his family. It was, after all, a fact that Alan Wood's last victim had been his niece. He had heard rumors that his father also

71

shot him that night. His father and the Chief's niece were sitting in a parked car and then his father set himself and her on fire while they had a shoot out. Why this should be Ryan's sin to bare he had no idea, but the Chief never spoke to him or his family ever. Sergeant Lambert had to do that.

Sergeant Lambert had called Ryan and Amy's mom. By the time she got home the paramedics had come and were taking Brandon's body out of the basement that sent Amy into a frenzy again upon seeing her boyfriend inside of a body bag. Ryan watched his mother take hold of Amy and cry some herself despite the fact he knew she couldn't stand the punk who had been dating and obviously having sex with her daughter. His mom's eyes found Ryan's sitting there by the porch and he just gave her a blank stare back. He knew when he got her alone it would be time to ask more questions about his father than she really wanted to hear. But it was long overdue.

"Ryan?" the deep voice from the unshaven cop came booming down at him drawing him out of his trance. "Can we talk, son?"

"Sure." he told Sergeant Lambert and they both walked out to the edge of the street away from the commotion that the neighbors had now come out onto their porches to witness. The darkening world was ablaze with flashing lights and droning engines now. Chatter filled the streets as folks tried to get closer to the house Ryan lived in and for the first time he now noticed it was marked off with that bright orange tape that read, "CRIME SCENE - - - DO NOT CROSS."

"Mister Kelly there tells me you knew this was going to happen somehow." he said looking doubtful. "That about right?"

"I don't know." he said looking over at Mister Kelly who was on the phone. Probably apologizing to Mrs. Edwards for being gone so long from the store. This whole night's event would be all over Waverly before morning even hit. "I mean I just got this feeling, you know, that she was in danger. He offered to drive me here and check and see."

"Mmmm-hmmm." the big cop grunted and spit past the sidewalk before turning back. "Seems like you and your sister had an interesting phone conversation on the way here?"

"I guess." Ryan struggled with his words. He didn't want to tell the cops. They wouldn't believe him. He also didn't want this big cop with the burnt hand who his mother liked so much to be the next body they pulled out of a basement from a heart attack or suicide either.

———

"Well, according to Mister Kelly, you weren't just worried about your sister. You were worried about Brandon too. You knew he was here?"

"He would come over sometimes." Ryan said looking over at his black motorcycle parked in the driveway. "If my mom wasn't home."

"Sure, I get that." he said and Ryan guessed he would. Maybe at some point in his life back when he was just a teen some mom didn't want the future cop around her daughter either. "But you knew they were in the basement and in danger? At least you guessed they were. You also said something about spiders?"

"Just what I felt I guess." Ryan lied thinking of the comic up at Scooter's. "My mom say's I read too many horror comics. I guess she's right."

"Yeah." the big cop said looking down at him and patting his head. Ryan hated it when folks did this but said nothing to the man with the shiny badge and the big ass gun strapped to his waist. "Sorry this had to happen around your sister, and at your house of all places. He could've just done this at home."

"You really think he killed himself?" Ryan asked. "You don't think somebody else could've maybe . . ."

"Murder?" the cop said shaking his big head. "Only other person was your sister. Nobody else in there but the two of them. So what makes you think it might be murder? You know something we don't know, son?"

Ryan shook his head staring at the street. He knew plenty. He knew that Mister Clark and Jeff Bates, and now Brandon Lowe, were all victims of something or somebody evil, possibly his dead father. He knew that the cops would never believe him. Neither would his mother or sister. He knew that he was going to have to find a way to make it stop or they would all be dead soon.

SEVENTEEN

Sunday went by in a blur. First, Aunt Cheryl came up early in the morning from Joplin, even before the sun had yet touched the sky, her little blue mini van rolling into the drive just before five. It was a brief visit. She never even made it into the house. A conversation on the porch, which was merely a sequel to the one she had with his mom on the phone only hours ago, and then Amy was gone. Flying south like the geese, or driving rather. Down with the duck pond, dogs and the spotted horse that nobody ever rode. She needed time away from the house of horrors. What a grand idea for them all.

Ryan waited until his mother was done slobbering all over Amy and then he crept up nice and quiet and embraced his sister. He was surprised at himself for this, feeling the stares of both his mother and aunt as he did so, but was even more surprised when she hugged him back.

"Take care of yourself." he said looking up at her lifeless eyes. Whatever spirit had been in there before, the one that teased and taunted him with a mischievous grin, was gone now. Perhaps dead.

"You too." she said with no added nickname like before. No Squirt or Runt or Booger, not even his own name. An empty voice void of emotion that had to practically be led out of the house by the hand as if some elderly senile thing that could not find her way down the sidewalk.

"I'll call you when we get there, Laura." his aunt promised and they were off.

Maybe, Ryan thought as he watched the tail lights fade around the corner, she would be safe there. Maybe.

Or maybe the house down in Joplin had a basement too. Ryan did not recall.

Ryan waited at the table for his mother with his little black notepad and pen. His mother stared out the window longer after Amy left than Ryan would have imagined, and when she did shuffle into the kitchen in her dangling bath robe she merely cast him an odd glance while pouring herself yet another cup of coffee.

"Little early for Breakfast, hon." she started to turn away. "Why don't you go back to bed."

"Not hungry. Not sleepy either." Ryan said listening to her sigh as she leaned into the wall by the phone. She looked ready to collapse.

"Hell of a night." she said mostly to herself.

74

"Can we talk?" Ryan asked.

"I'm not really in the mood for talk, Ryan." she said sipping loud. "It's been a long night, you know? Very long night, sweetie."

"I think we need to." he said hoping to find some sign of hope on her face when she did turn to face him there in the soft glow of the now rising sun. She didn't look like his mother anymore, at least the one he knew only a short few weeks ago, she appeared to be some confused stranger. She seemed to have aged with all of this. Her red rimmed eyes that carried dark circles, her stance and walk was staggering and her voice was weak and pained.

"I don't think I can explain any of this to you, Ryan." she said shaking her head and finding a chair across from him. "Don't ask me to because I don't think I can."

"Maybe I can explain it to you." he said and reached over to take his mothers hand. "But I guess you have to promise to keep an open mind."

"Honey, what are you talking about?" his mother asked with closed eyes that strained for comfort and a yawn that followed. "What could you know?"

"I need to know everything you know . . . about dad." he finished with holding his breath while waiting for his mother's red eyes to meet his.

"Jesus, Ryan. Don't you know enough from what you hear already?" she said and started to get up. Ryan shot both arms across the table and grabbed tightly onto her robe. "Ryan?"

"Mom, you have to listen to me, please." he said louder, but not quite a demand. He had to keep her attention without letting her think he had gone mad. "I found out some things about dad yesterday. Things maybe even you didn't know about."

"Is that what you wanted to go to the library?" she leaned back with her face taking on a harder glare. "To go snooping about your father's past? About all of the horrible things that he did. Ryan, I have told you everything you need to know about him. He was a horrible and evil man but now he's dead. Can't this just be left alone once and for all? How long do we have to live under the shadow of all the horrible things he did?"

"Did you know he used to live here?" Ryan asked.

"In Waverly? Sure, when he was a kid he lived somewhere over-"

"He lived *here*, mom." Ryan cut her off. "He lived in *this* house when he was a kid. I read it on the internet on some web site that had old newspaper articles on this town from way back. He lived here with his mom and sisters when he was a kid. His father was shot and killed here."

"Father? Sisters?" his mother's eyes narrowed staring past him out into the backyard. "He never said he had any sisters. I knew his father was dead, I didn't know how."

"They all died here, mom." Ryan continued. "His little sister died of a heart attack while playing in the basement. She was just eleven, mom."

"Honey, I can't explain why-" she began, but he cut her off.

"His other sister died not too long after in the shower." Ryan continued. "She slipped and hit her head and drown."

"Honey, as horrible as that is-"

"His mother hung herself in *my* closet!" Ryan shouted rising up from his chair. "I told you I saw someone in there that night. The lady in the white nightgown. That was his mom, my grandmother."

"Ryan!" Laura Woods said taking her child close to her in a tight embrace. "You can't be sure of what you saw that night. You were scared. You saw snakes too, remember? What if it's all made up, honey? What if the paper was wrong?"

"It wasn't." Ryan said feeling tears well up in his eyes. Not fear but frustration and anger. "Mister Clark is dead. Jeff was killed because I told him about it."

"No, Ryan, no."

"Now Brandon was down in our basement and he's dead and Amy is all messed up."

"It's not like that at all, Ryan." his mother cried. "Honey, Mister Clark was just old and had a bad heart. He died in his basement. Brandon might have been on drugs or something for all we know, honey."

"And Jeff?" Ryan asked pulling away and finding her eyes.

"Honey, I don't have all the answers." she said taking his face in her own warm hands. "I don't know why young people die or people take their own lives. But I do know that this has *nothing* to do with your father. He's dead and gone."

"The cops down in Oklahoma used to call him the Boogeyman." Ryan said and watched his mother's eyes glaze over in deep memory.

"I remember that." she admitted looking back at him with her best false smile. "He used to do a lot of night robberies. That was before I met him, honey. Hell, they used to call me Pixie in high school, didn't mean I could fly or grant wishes."

"Pixie's don't grant wishes." Ryan pointed out and snatched up his notepad. "The aunt and uncle he lived with down there died too. Heart attack and house fire."

"Ryan, those are all terrible things but just coincidences. Old men die of heart attacks every day."

"Especially when they are scared to death." Ryan said heading for the back door.

"Ryan, listen to me. We are going through some very bad times right now. I need you to be brave and stay on good terms with me." his mother said holding out her arms to her son. Ryan wanted to walk away because he knew she would never believe him about his father, her husband, but he did not. He walked to her and hugged her. It was a good hug, a real hug. The kind they used to give each other when he was younger before he parted for school and knew he wouldn't see her for hours. The kind she used to give him when he got tucked in at night. The kind that said it was her and him against whoever. "I love you, you know?"

"I love you too, mom." he told her and did mean it. He also knew he was in this alone now. There would never be a day when he could truly convince her of what was going on. She wouldn't believe it until it happened to her. That would be too late. Ryan could not let that happen.

"Wear a jacket, it's still cool out." his mother sniffled while taking her coffee towards her bedroom. "Don't leave the yard please."

"I won't." Ryan said shutting the door behind him and stepping to the soft ground below. He walked to the middle of the yard and did a slow turn in his private little world. There sat Mister Clark's house. Empty and cold. Blackened windows and leaf covered lawn that would have never been allowed if the old man were still alive. He kept a neat yard. Mowed and raked and shoveled through all seasons. Now it was just an abandoned four walls with a leaf covered roof and a dead heart inside.

The house to the other side was the Warner place. Kevin and Patrice. Fifty-something couple. He was balding and heavy, she was skinny with glasses. He worked at an office and she worked at a hospital. They both used to smile a lot. Then their son, Gary, a great quarterback for Waverly High, was killed in Iraq seven years ago. Blown to pieces on the side of some unknown desert road. They didn't smile so much anymore. Ryan used to hear Mister Warner sit on his back porch at night and sob heavy

while drinking his beer and his wife stopped coming over and having coffee and snacks with his mother.

Now she just waved over the fence and went inside the mostly dark house.

"Hey Brute!" Ryan called out to the big Boxer that lay there under the Warner's porch. Brute was

a slobbering thing that used to scare Ryan when he was younger, but now aged and worn, he was rarely a

threat to cats and squirrels anymore, much less kids. The big dog lifted up its head, eyes straining to see

the boy, and then let his chin drop back on his paws while staring lifelessly out at the yard. "I feel the same

way." he told the mostly hidden dog. This dog belonged to a broken family with problems of their own.

Ryan thought then that maybe everybody had his or her own personal Boogeyman to deal with in life.

"I need help." he said looking around at the empty alleyway. "But from where?"

It would not be from Mister Clark. Dead and gone and buried. Jeff was gone and his parents were

useless and best left alone to their private miseries. His mother would not listen to reason and his sister in a

little world all of her own for now. The cops were useless as well. Who was left?

Mister "Scooter" Kelly was a nice man. A big and strong man perhaps, but Ryan could not stand

the thought of the man getting killed over this. Sergeant Lambert was a big strong cop but he would feel

the same way his mother had. Hell, his mother would probably end up telling him everything he told her,

and the big cop would think he was going nuts. Who else did he have to turn to?

Ryan stood there in the cool morning air while the rising sun filled the yard listening to the birds

and the car horns while he slowly turned with eyes closed waiting for his answer. Who could help him

with an evil thing that might very well be his father living in his own house killing all of those who would

dare defy him?

A tiny smile crept across his face upon hearing the church bells ringing in the distance. He stood

still and listened again while they chimed out the hour. "Why not?" he said heading to get his bike.

EIGHTEEN

Something was different in the house.

Griffin, the family pet, noticed this even if those around him did not. He awoke from his nap on the back of the couch and sensed something strange right away. An odd smell from somewhere far away, accompanied by a sound. Somebody calling him? It didn't sound like the woman who held and feed him or the boy who moved about too quickly for Griffin's taste or even the girl who ignored him. This was a new voice.

Griffin leapt off the couch and padded his way into the tiled room where his food and water was. Nothing new here except the smell was stronger and so was the voice.

"Griffin." came the whisper that he could only hear. It was coming from the crack underneath the door that led downstairs into that large cold place he really did not care for. Sure, there were bugs to chase and plenty of box filled corners to explore, but if you stayed down there too long the fast boy or the mean girl would close the door and trap you there, away from the food and litter box, and he would have to wait for the woman to rescue him.

"What are you up to, Griff?" the lady above him asked. Griffin had no idea what she meant, he just liked her voice. She would scratch his head and rub his belly and more often then not fatten him with tasty little things from a can. "You smell those bad mice?"

Griffin made his way to the basement door. Whatever the new smell was it was coming from down there, along with the voice that sounded nothing like the others in the house. It was not mice.

"Here, kitty-kitty." the voice said at least trying to sound nice.

Griffin scratched at the door, peeking under with wide bright eyes to only see the steps as they descended into darkness. The woman came close and snatched the bright thing far out of his reach and twisted it, the door opening up to the coolness of the basement below.

"Go get' em, Griff." the woman said with encouragement and Griffin felt as if she wanted him to do something. He turned and looked up at her, she was waving him towards the dark steps with a wine bottle in one hand and a smoke in the other, and then he turned and looked down into the basement, the smell stronger now that the door was open and the voice spoke again.

"Come see daddy, Griff." the voice said trying hard to sound as nice as the woman did.

"Go on, Griff." Laura Woods said giving the cat a nudge with her slipper and Griffin reluctantly made his way down the steps, stopping half way to look back at his master. "Don't worry. I will leave the door open a crack for you, boy. Get those bad ol' mice."

Griffin crept down a few more stairs while studying his surroundings. Small rays of light broke through the windows casting shadows across the basement floor. It was all new and wondrous to the cat as if this were its first visit ever down here in this mischief-filled labyrinth. The smell was coming from further back in the basement, by the place where the woman sat and smoked while washing clothes and playing music. It was coming from the floor. A circle in the floor covered with a shiny plate of holes.

A drain.

Griffin reached the cold concrete floor, sniffed the air and scanned for movement, and then moved on in the direction that the whispering was coming from. The smell and the sound were both coming from the hole in the floor. Griffin had to see what it was. It might be somebody nice. They might have something for him to eat.

"Good kitty." the voice said lovingly as the cat drew closer in quick, short steps. *"Such a good kitty. Look in here, buddy. Right over here."*

Griffin stopped within a foot or so of the drain. He strained his neck up to see. Something was there, perhaps more bugs like on his last visit, and it was getting closer to the edge of the drain. Griffin reached out with both paws fast as lightning trying to seize whatever it was crawling around in there just below the plate. It seized him back.

"Got you, you little fuck!" the deeper voice cried out in triumph and Griffin let out a screeching howl that was cut short but something dark and wet coming out of the drain in strands of shining black ribbons that covered the cat's face and front legs while pulling him closer. *"Open wide. I'm coming in."*

NINETEEN

The big gold and blue digital sign in front of Patriot's Bank read it was now 7:37 and

57 degrees. It felt colder to Ryan while he peddled down Thrush Street past silent gas stations and

the black windows of Fix-It Shops, gift stores and fast food places. Nobody in Waverly opened before nine

on a Sunday. Nobody would stay open past six either. Part of the town's charm to some and pain in the ass

to others.

Saint Michael's was many blocks away. Ryan only hoped, as he dodged what little traffic there

was, that his mother had either gone back to sleep or got lost in some sappy paperback romance and would

not notice his absence.

He did not hurry as he did not want to be out of breath or sound any more crazy than he was sure

he already would. He stuck to the streets whenever possible and then took to the cracked and weeded

sidewalks whenever cars blew their horns coming by. He had not seen Waverly this early in the morning

for some time other than the route his school bus took, which was in the opposite direction and held little

scenery except for fields and small patches of woods.

This direction into the business district of town was quite different. Truman Road was lined with

all sorts of places Ryan didn't even know existed. Along with the normal dentists offices and tax places

and nail shops were corner bars with catchy little names like "The Cubby Hole" and "The Rust Bucket."

There was even one place that sat far back off the road across a gravel lot with dark mirrored windows and

a sign done up in purple in the shape of a woman's body called "Jiggler's." The glass door had bright

white letters that read out, "LIVE TOPLESS GIRLS!" Ryan thought how stupid it sounded. What did

folks want to see? *Dead* topless girls? Of course they're alive.

After about five blocks Ryan wasn't so alone on the streets anymore. People were out and among

the living. Some men were dressed nice in suits and ties while their wives and daughters wore dresses and

slacks, all walking to Church on a cool Sunday morning. Ryan could not remember the last time he had

been. Not since he was a child. More of a child than he was now. Not since his father was alive.

And that was when he saw it. The very place his father died. He and that teenage girl, the niece

of Chief Rollins. It was a strip mall. Nothing strange about it to the human eye but when Ryan slowed he felt something tingle inside his head, his chest even. He stopped the bike and sat there staring at the place where just five years ago his father had been burned alive in that inferno.

There wasn't much to the place, he thought, just a drug store on the corner, a nail saloon, a dry cleaners. Then it bent horseshoe and turned facing the road housing a barber shop, a mini post office, a travel agency, a Chinese food place and a shoe store. It bent again with a pizza place, an electronic store an arts and craft shop and a coffee house.

So why did he feel this way sitting here, like something was calling to him, not from the stores themselves, but the parking lot, the very place where his father died and burned alive? His tiny eyes scanned the lot over from side to side but could see not signs of the fire. Of course there would not be any. Of course they had repaved the lot since then and marked it with new lines and most people had moved on and forgotten what had happened here that night. But not everyone. He pushed away and felt better once the lot was out of his view.

A few people waved at him as they jogged by or went dragging in one direction or another while attempting to walk their huge dogs. Ryan waved back, recognizing some, but honestly not knowing who most of them were. Perhaps they just knew his mother. She was well liked in town by most folks who honestly knew her. Then there were the others who waved simply because they knew who his dad was too. They gave those waves with the sad eyes and the pitiful expressions as if to say, *"There goes that poor boy whose father was a killer. Damn shame, he will never live that down. He could move all the way to fucking Australia and the damn kangaroo's would feel sorry for his ass. Son of a psychopath. Son of the Boogeyman."*

He slowed as he saw a police cruiser coming towards him. He thought maybe it was Sergeant Lambert and waved, but then saw it was Chief Rollins inside. The man cast him a cold glare and Ryan let his arm drop to his side as he lowered his head and peddled on.

"That man will hate me for what my father did for the rest of his life."

The last thought caused Ryan to come to a skid on the sidewalk and when he did he heard the church bells again. Two blocks down to the left on Delaware Road. He could see the tall chapel, or steeple, or whatever it was called, from here. High and bright white with a pine green roof and gold, glowing cross on top for the entire town to see. Ryan hurried onward.

He hoped he would be able to talk to a real priest, not some young punk who had just made it out of the God Academy or whatever, and that this old man would be able to listen and understand what it was that Ryan had to say. There was something, or more likely somebody, in his house. Possessing it or haunting it. Controlling it from within. Maybe this priest could help him exercise it out, or whatever they called it. Getting it the hell out of his home was the bottom line.

It had been at least five years or more since Ryan had been down here to the church. He took note of the interesting changes. There was a Black Bridge Comics. Looked nice enough and surely had more to choose from then Mister Kelly's store. Ryan made a mental note that if he survived this he would ride back down here one day to get a better look. Maybe if he lived to be a teenager he could work there one day.

There was a new ice cream place called Flavor Freeze with dazzling pin ball machines and stand up arcade games and next to that was Madcap's, some sort of clothing store for teen girls with scantily dressed mannequins wearing tight leather things that made Ryan only imagine what wonders he had in store for him come high school. A sporting good store here, computers there, and a music store with skull posters plastered all over the windows called Blitzer's. A pizza parlor to one side of him and directly across from that a chicken wing hut. Yes, this would be a new playground for Ryan to check out if only he could live through the experience at hand.

He slowed his bike at the end of the buildings where on his side of the street there was a Quik-Stop Laundromat. At the corner, leaning up against the building with a cigarette dangling from his lips, was a skinny man dressed in dirty clothes with an unshaven face and a lost look in his eyes. Ryan ignored him while staring at the store on the opposite side. He didn't think Waverly would have such a place of business, but there it sat.

It was a dark little building with a deep purple awning hanging over its tinted windows. In blood red letters arched across that window was "MADAME BULVARIA - FORTUNETELLER" with a pair of bright red hands palmed in paint underneath. Across the black glass of the door in smaller blood colored letters it read. "PALMS READ---TAROT CARD READINGS---PRIVATE SÉANCE'S AVAILABLE."

Ryan knew enough about the occult from his comics and the movies he watched that these were scary and powerful people, these fortunetellers. Crystal balls and magic cards with drawings that depicted your fate as they laid them out before you. Ryan didn't need to know the future. He knew it was full of death and pain if something wasn't done. Right now he just needed to know how to stop it from happening.

He studied the small empty store a moment longer, his eyes barely seeing the shapes of things in the windows such as candles and statues. He would give the priest a try first. Madame Bulvaria would just have to be a last resort.

"The devil lives there." the old man said sneaking up behind him and Ryan jumped nearly falling of his bike. "Sorry, young fella. Didn't mean to scare ya none."

"What do you know about the devil?" Ryan asked.

"Plenty." the old man gave a quick laugh and Ryan noticed he was missing most of his teeth, not to mention he smelled like dog shit. "He roams about the world like a lion, seeking those who he can devour." he smiled his jack-o-lantern grin. "Name's Darby. And you are?"

"Ryan." he said back looking at the man's ripped and dirty jeans and smudged stains over his dulling red and black flannel shirt. His hair was greased back under a blue sock hat and his eyes were lined with blood vessels over dark circles. "Ryan Woods."

"Pleased to meet 'cha, Ryan Woods." the man said only giving a short wave with no attempted handshake and Ryan was happy of that fact. "Hey boy, you got any money on ya that you could spare an old war vet like me?"

"Which war was you in?" Ryan said looking the man up and down.

"Hell, pick one." he said stepping back a bit. "Don't matter t'me none. I just need some coffee."

Ryan dug into his pocket and came out with a quarter and held it out for the old man. He waited until the dry cracked hand with some grease and other questionable liquid stains was below his and dropped it into the palm without actually touching the man. "That's all I got, Mister Darby."

"The widows mite, eh?" the old man smiled, flipping the bright coin once in the air watching it sparkle, then palming it to pocket quick as a wink. "God bless ya, boy. Where you headed?"

"Church." Ryan said. "You want to come with?"

"Oh, I don't know." the skinny haggard man said looking over at the church only a good fifty yards away. "I don't think they like me. Funny thing, ain't it. The good Lord Jesus would sit down and break bread with me, but they won't let me sit in there. Not even the back."

"Maybe if you cleaned up a bit." Ryan said before thinking and the old man cast him a hard glare for a second, then smiled his wide, toothless grin again. "Maybe took a shower."

"The honesty of children." he said and headed back towards the alley. "You go churchin' boy. Pray for both of us and keep yer nose clean."

"I will, Mister Darby." Ryan promised and pushed off for the church.

He slowed as he passed the Church cemetery, his eyes watching the sidewalk for people while checking out the tombstones. Ryan hated graveyards and had seen quite enough of them for awhile. Even this one on the church property in broad daylight with no spiked fence or scary dead trees still seemed eerie to him somehow.

Plenty of cars here already. Ryan had forgotten how much earlier the Catholics got up before the Baptists and Lutherans. He guessed they liked first shot at the Lord, or maybe knew something the rest of them didn't, like maybe God was a morning person.

The good part was, unlike the others, their masses only lasted one hour, where the Lutheran's were good for about two or so and the Baptists could ramble on and on all day. So Ryan rode around the lot to the back of the church and waited for the crowds to leave. Then he would head in and find a man of God to help him fight something clearly not of God.

So he got off his bike and sat in the shadows watching the sun drift in and out of clouds. It was quiet here as he guessed a church parking lot should be. He could faintly here music and some singing. Then a thought came to mind, an image really. A pretty face bordered by red hair and covered in freckles. Ryan rolled up his jacket sleeve and was relieved to see the phone number on his skin was still there. He made a mental note to write it down first chance he got. His lips twitched into a grin as he ran his finger along the smiley face zero. He guessed even the darkest of days had to have some bright spots somewhere.

TWENTY

"God, how long has this shit been in here?" Laura Woods asked herself staring in the fridge. She had been drinking ever since Amy left. Not coffee either, no sir, that just wouldn't do it today, but good ol red wine. The kind with a Cherry taste to it. The tuna she was staring at looked like it had seen better days and she instantly decided that neither her or Ryan needed to test its mettle. "Griffin!" Laura Woods called down the basement steps. "Got a snack for you, baby."

She did a fancy little two-step over to the basement door, the wine already taking effect, and peeked down into the darkness. She was *not* going down there. Not today. Not for a long while. She might even have to do the clothes at the Laundromat for awhile. She hadn't actually seen the body hanging there, but had heard about it and knew her imagination would play tricks on her if she dared to journey into her basement anytime soon.

"Come on, boy." she said spying the set of glowing red eyes at the foot of the steps. That really gave her the creeps. *"Shouldn't they be green or yellow?"* her mind asked but then she reached in and snapped on the light and the darkness was swept away, leaving only the gray cat sitting there staring at her at the bottom of the stairs. "Get your little ass up here." she said. "It's freezing down there. I guess you didn't get any mice, did you boy?"

The cat merely strolled by her, heading into the comforts of the living room and taking its place back on the couch, and lay there waiting for her. Laura Woods did not disappoint. She stumbled in after him, a half bottle of wine to balance her, and plopped down in the favorite chair.

"Hell of a few weeks, Griff." she told the cat in between swallows. "Neighbor dies. Some little boy dies, my son's best fucking friend no less." she coughed focusing on her bottle. "My daughter is gone because her boyfriend kills himself and now my son might be losing it too. He's hearing things Griff. He's seeing things that aren't there." she said looking ready to pass out and the bottle landed safely on the coffee table before she fell back into the chair with a look of surrender spreading across her face. "I don't know what the hell to do."

Griffin stepped down from his place on the couch, sauntered slowly over to her chair with all the grace a cat should have, and leapt up daintily onto the arm of her recliner. She reached out clumsily at him trying to scratch his back or pet his head but the cat dodged her hand and made its way up across her lap

and onto her chest where he it laid and stared deeply into her reddened blurry eyes.

"Remember me, bitch?" Griffin said and leapt hard up to her shocked face while pressing its own

mouth to hers, muffling her screams and letting a thick strand of black goop slide down her throat.

TWENTY ONE

The bells did ring again and Ryan Woods waited while many worshippers filtered into the parking lot. He watched them with great fascination. Families that walked away holding hands and laughing. Children running about their parents legs begging for ice cream, teenagers quickly finding each other in numbers and sharing gossip. Grown men and women exchanging handshakes and hugs while talking sports, politics or new grandchildren.

These were normal families. They would go home and change from their fancy dressings and head out to parks or burger joints. They would wash their cars, rake their leaves, toss the ball around a little before a big dinner. They would lay in their beds after television and prayers and dream normal dreams under a watchful eye of God and they would wake up tomorrow and go to school and work and not once worry about what dwelled in their vents or basements.

"Lucky bastards." Ryan said and headed into the church. He didn't recall much about his last visit here since he had only been about five. He remembered it was big and that it felt chilly regardless of the time of day. Not much had changed.

Ryan entered the main doors, the large cross of Jesus standing tall at the back of the church, and he approached the little fountain. He knew it had a specific name but he had forgot, and he stopped and dipped his hand in the cool water. He had seen plenty of movies in his short life. He believed it went from forehead to chest, then left shoulder over to right. So he stood there in silence and made the sign of the cross, gave a slight bow, and headed over to the side aisle and began a slow walk up to the front of the church.

The stained glass windows to his right all depicted a certain stage of the existence of Christ. The first was his birth, with the stable and animals and three wise guys all circled around the baby Jesus in his manager. The second had him being baptized in the river, a dove floating overhead, the third had him healing the sick with his outstretched hand which almost seemed to be glowing. The fourth had him looking much worse, beaten and scarred while dragging his own cross up a hill surrounded by soldiers. The next of course had him nailed to it, outstretched hands and eyes turned up to heaven wearing his crown of thorns while those below mocked and pointed. Then the last had him risen up in the air, standing on a cloud while his disciples stood below holding out their hands to him and he gave them all the peace sign as he headed away to Heaven.

"He has to help me." Ryan said seeing the office door cracked enough to hear coughing and someone pecking away at a computer keyboard. Ryan crept up, raised his hand and knocked softly three times. The typing stopped and a chair creaked as heavy footsteps approached. Ryan thought of running back past the Jesus windows but before he could the door opened and a tall man with curly dark hair and a narrow face stood before him.

"Yes?" the soft but deeper voice came. "Are we lost, young man?"

"Ummmm, no." Ryan said unable to look away. This man looked more like a waiter than a priest to Ryan. He was tall, like Sergeant Lambert, but slimmer and looked too young. The priests he always saw in the movies looked to be in their sixties with no hair and glasses and tired voices with serious looks. This man actually smiled and his eyes sparkled. He had a rough jaw shadowed with an oncoming beard and a pointy nose like an elf. He was dressed entirely in black, both suit and shoes, with the only exceptions being the white collar and the silver cross dangling from around his neck. "I would like to speak to a priest. If that's okay." Ryan added.

"You are speaking to one." the man said leaning down while extending a hand with a small gold ring. "I am Father Thomas Leary. And you are?"

"Ryan Woods." the child said giving a brief but firm shake as the man led him into the office.

"Please, have a seat." the priest said waving in the direction of a chair that Ryan reluctantly took. It looked uncomfortable and fragile to him so he sat on its edge while watching the tall man round the desk. "Care for some butterscotch?" the priest asked sliding a glass dish in his direction. Ryan shook his head and the priest shrugged and took one for himself. "These little guys helped me quit smoking. Never smoke, son." he wagged a finger and Ryan nodded his approval. "Of course my dentist finds more cavities now then before, but it's a fair trade."

Ryan smiled politely, realizing there was a joke in there somewhere, and waited for the man to sit back in his squeaky chair. The priest leaned back and studied the boy carefully before speaking again. His voice almost sounded rehearsed.

"Ryan Woods?" he squinted. "Not Laura Woods son?"

"Yes, sir." Ryan said folding his hands in his lap. "We used to go here years ago."

"I remember your mother. Beautiful voice. How is she?" he asked.

"Okay, I guess." Ryan said trying to remember if he had ever heard his mother sing. "She's not why I'm here though. Well maybe a little bit, but not really."

"So what's going on, son?" Father Leary leaned forward. "What can God's house do for you today?"

"I . . ." he paused and looked the man over carefully. "How long have you been a Priest?"

"Me?" the priest grinned. "You want to know if I am qualified? If I have the experience?" he said and let a small laugh loose. "That's okay. I get that all of the time. I was called to the service of God when I was twenty-two. I just turned thirty-four this past March. So that's twelve years of service. I know the bible as well as anyone. I've dealt with all kinds of family problems. And I always route for Notre Dame. Good enough?"

"Sure, I mean, yes Sir." Ryan said sitting up straight. "It's just, well, what I have to tell you, you're not going to believe. I'm not sure why I came here. Out of options I guess."

"Too many people make God a last option, Ryan. Why don't you let me decide the belief part for myself." Father Leary said popping the candy in his mouth. "I consider myself to be fairly open minded. I've heard some crazy things over the years that have in fact turned out to be true. Try me."

Ryan Woods sat there staring at the man who looked like he should be teaching history in school, then the confines of the room around him. The crucifix on the wall, the picture of Mother Mary on the bookshelf with the praying hands close by. There was a photo of Father Leary when he was younger in a baseball uniform with two other men on either side of him, one muscular black guy and one skinny white guy, all three smiling in the bright sun. "You played baseball? What position?"

"Four years in high school. The Screaming Eagles." he turned towards the picture. "I played first base. You recognize the other guys in this picture?" he boasted while holding it out for Ryan's inspection. "They are kind of young in this photo so probably not."

"Sorry, not really." Ryan leaned forward and squinted. "Should I? Are they famous?"

"In their own right, yes." the priest said turning the photo to himself with a nostalgic smile present. "The skinny white guy is David Redmond. A writer. He was our catcher."

"Hey, I heard of him." Ryan's eyes lit up. "He's one of my mom's favorites. He writes horror stories, right?"

"Yes, he does quite well. Lives up in Chicago now. The African-American gentleman is Troy Parish. Sounds more like a place than a man's name, right? Best pitcher I ever saw. A very good homicide detective in Saint Louis now. One writes about monsters and the other one hunts them down. We all played ball in high school together. They were good friends. Still are."

"If he was so good how come he became a cop?" Ryan asked.

"He did what he was meant to do. We all do."

"Were you any good?" Ryan asked.

"Well, I'm sitting here, right?" the priest grinned. "Good enough for high school, I guess. Not much of a chance for the major leagues."

"I guess." Ryan leaned back. "Father . . . My house is . . . haunted." he said while letting his eyes find the carpet.

Father Leary leaned back with a loud squeak being the only noise in the room. Ryan looked up to see his eyes searching the ceiling, as if actually considering it, then they drifted down and found his. They did not look like they were convinced.

"And what makes you think this?"

"Because of everything that's been happening." Ryan started.

"And when you say *haunted*, are we talking about slamming doors, flickering lights and rattling chains? That kind of haunted?" he asked.

"No, this is more like voices from a vent, snakes in my closet and everybody I tell ends up dying, kind of haunting." Ryan said in one breath and held the stare of the priest to see his reaction. The man didn't move for several seconds.

"People are dying?" Father Leary asked. "Perhaps you should start from the beginning so I can better make sense of what your definition of haunted means."

"A few weeks ago I heard voices from the vent in my bedroom."

"Voices?" the priest asked. "Just voices speaking or speaking to you?"

"Speaking to me." Ryan said feeling goose bumps rising on his arms again.

"And this wasn't some joke that somebody else in the house was playing?" Father Leary asked with a doubtful grin. "I'm just asking."

"No, not at all." Ryan continued. "Then I heard things in there too. My mom thought it was mice so Mister Clark, our old neighbor, came over to check. The next day he died in his basement of a heart attack."

"I see. I'm very sorry to hear that." Father Leary said toying with a small glass paperweight with what appeared to be a scorpion inside. "There's more?"

"Then I told my best friend, Jeff. He died the next day after I told him in his basement. He was only my age." Ryan said feeling his eyes starting to well up and it angered him to fall apart in front of this strange man, priest or not. "Then last night my sister's boyfriend he . . . hung . . . he hung himself-"

"Ryan, Ryan." Father Leary said getting up and around the desk as fast as he could and taking hold of the boy. "Son, I am so sorry for all that you've been through."

"They all died because of me." Ryan said and he was sobbing now like a little girl and he hated it. Hated whatever the hell it was, father or not, that was in his basement making these things happen.

"No, son. It's not." Father Leary said lifting the boys face up and wiping his cheeks clean with a handkerchief. "Ryan, I am sorry for the tragedies that have happened, but they are not your fault. And there are simple explanations."

"No, there's something evil in my house. In my basement." Ryan said trying not to let too much snot and tears pour out on the man's shoulder as he leaned into him.

"Ryan, you said yourself that this Mister Clark was an old man. Old men have heart attacks." he said hugging the boy slightly tighter. "And while the death of your friend is tragic, sadly it does happen from time to time with no evidence as to why. And the young man dating your sister might have been depressed for a long time without your knowledge. He could have had mental problems or-"

"No!" Ryan said and forced himself back from the priest. "That's not it, don't you understand?"

"Ryan, please lower your voice and calm yourself." the priest said. "I want to understand what's going on with you. But everything you told me so far does not point towards your house. Your neighbor, so you said, died at *his* house, yes? And your friend died in *his* basement. Only your sister's boyfriend died in your house and that does not constitute a haunting, not that I believe in that sort of thing."

"So you don't believe its possible for a house to be haunted at all, no matter what?" Ryan asked wiping his own face clear and thinking about the trip he wasted here. "This was my last place to try for help. You were my last hope."

"I didn't say I wasn't going to help you, Ryan." Father Leary said. "After all, nothing is so firmly believed, as what we least know. You believe your house is haunted, right?"

"I'm not crazy." Ryan said defensively. "I'm not imagining what's going on either."

"Didn't say you were." the tall priest said rising up. "Have you spoken to your mother about all of this? Everything you told me?"

"I tried, she won't listen." Ryan said picturing his mother at home probably polishing off a bottle of cheap wine and playing records way too loud. "So a house can't be haunted at all?"

"Ryan, I am a man of the cloth." Father Leary tried to explain. "I believe that once a person dies, his or her soul either goes to Heaven or Hell. No coming back."

"What if you're wrong?" the boy asked and the priest studied him hard. "I mean Jesus brought people back. There was that Lazerine guy he rose from the dead."

"Lazarus." Father Leary corrected. "And that was not a self-resurrection. You are speaking of somebody coming back on their own, or having never left at all."

"I know who it is, Father Leary." Ryan woods said with a shaky voice. "At least I'm pretty sure I do. How much do you know about my father?"

Father Leary let his head dip, his face taking on a stone appearance, as he slowly walked towards the window at the back of his office. He stood there with arms folded behind his back while watching the trees sway in the breeze.

"Only what everybody else does I imagine." he finally said. "What I've read in the papers and seen on the news." he said and turned on the boy with a rather sharp, quizzical look. "You don't mean to tell me you believe your father is behind all of this?"

"I think so." Ryan said in a whisper. "He's the most evil person I ever knew."

"That may be so but he's dead as well." the priest pointed out. "Five years now, I believe."

"Do you think my father is in hell, Father Leary?" the boy asked.

"Ryan, that's really not for me to say. We don't get to judge who goes where or-"

"Come on, Father Leary!" the boy said in anger. "I thought it was your job to know these things. He had Chief Rollins niece in the car with him when he died, did you know that? He killed her. Don't you think that's good enough for Hell?"

"If your father died without confessing his sins, than yes, I believe he is in hell." Father Leary said. "But I do not see how this relates to your situation or the three deaths you've told me about."

"Because those people didn't die the way the police think they did." Ryan said standing ready to go. "Not of heart attacks or suicides. I can't make you believe that. But I think maybe me and my family and anybody else who knows are in danger."

"We are inclined to believe those we do not know, because they have never deceived us." Father Leary said with a polite nod, "That one's not mine. Samuel Johnson."

"Don't know him. Will you do me a favor?" Ryan asked.

"Name it, son."

"Will you come and bless my house?"

The priest smiled again despite the conversation he had just had and patted the boy on the back.

"Yes, of course I can do that." he said snatching another piece of butterscotch. "You have your mother call me and we will make arrangements to-"

"No, I mean now." Ryan said coming back to him and taking hold of his hand. "Today?"

"Well, I . . ." he said looking around and then reaching over for a few more wrapped candies. "I guess Father O'Brian could cover for me in noon mass if I make a call." he said. "He owes me a few favors from our softball days." He grinned at the boy. "This will help, you think? You're not trying to get me to do an exorcism are you? We don't do those."

"I know but you could say some prayers?" the boy lit up.

"Of course, every room." the priest promised.

"The basement too?" he asked almost holding his breath.

"If you like, yes. Why not?" Father Leary smiled at the boy. "Just let me make a call and collect my things. How did you get here, Ryan? Walk by chance?"

"I rode my bike." Ryan said back heading for the door. "I can always meet you there."

"Nonsense. I have a Jeep. We'll put her in the back and both go together."

94

"Father Leary?" he asked while the priest began dialing. "Are you going to bring lots of holy water too?"

"Ryan." the priest wagged a finger at him. "I will bring only enough for what we need to do. Regardless of what you may or may not believe, we are *not* dealing with vampires, right?"

"Yeah, right." Ryan said and closed the door. He headed off to the front of the church to get his bike and wait for Father Leary in the back parking lot. "I wish we were." he said finding his dirt bike where he had left it. "At least then I would know what I'm up against."

TWENTY TWO

Lost in both music and wine, Laura Woods did not hear the Jeep pull in her driveway. She had her head back in pillows listening to the best of Ricky Skaggs and Griffin in a furry puddle in her lap when the doorbell chimed. She lifted her head and noticed the tall shadow at the front porch.

She had been having the strangest dream. She had been somewhere dark and wet, not really scary, but lonely and cold. Then a burst of light and laughter and she felt herself flying. Flying high about this little town and as she looked down she could see fire and hear screaming and for some reason none of this bothered her. It all seemed to be right. Almost serene. Then the doorbell rang again.

"Who the hell on a Sunday?" she said forcing herself off the comfortable chair with Griffin falling to the floor just in time to watch the doorknob turn and see her son's face. Behind him a tall, good looking man who seemed quite familiar came in dressed in a leather jacket, blue jeans, and a priest's collar?

"Oh." she said embarrassed at her casual dress of sweat pants and extra baggy Aerosmith T-shirt. "Ryan, honey. You brought company without letting me know. How nice."

"I'm sorry to intrude on your weekend, Laura." the priest said stepping closer and extending his hand. "I'm Father Thomas Leary. It's been awhile. You have a very persistent son. He insisted that I come over and bless the house."

"Bless the-" she started and looked down at her son. "I thought you were in the backyard. You rode all the way down to Saint Michael's? Naughty boy." she said wagging a finger and Ryan gave her a quizzical glare.

"You wouldn't listen to me, so somebody had to." Ryan defended while staying close to the tall priest. His mother seemed off somehow, and it was more than just the wine.

"Ryan has told me everything that's been going on." Father Leary said and Ryan watched his mother sit back down to her place on the couch. "I am so sorry about what happened and what your daughter must be going through."

"She's down with my sister." his mother said taking a nice long drink. "She cries and stares at the walls is what I was told today. Life is a bitch I guess."

"Mom?" Ryan tried to approach her but the priest took hold of Ryan by the shoulders.

"Let her be." he said in a hushed tone.

"Hung himself in our basement." she said. "My son's having nightmares as it is and now some punk kid decides to off himself in our house. Now you want to bless it? Kind of late, *aren't you, Padre?*"

"Mom, stop." Ryan said wondering what was wrong with her voice. She sounded like she was getting sick or already was.

"It's never too late." Father Leary simply said and laid his things out on the coffee table. "But I do need your permission to continue."

"By all means." she said waving a hand around the room as she staggered to her feet. "Bless me too. Can you do that?"

"Of course." the priest said coming to her and then noticed her sly grin and he stopped.

"Bless me father, for I have sinned. And knowing me, I'll do it again." she said and laughed as she flopped back down in her place. "Sorry, that was just not right."

"Mom, you're drunk." Ryan said holding back tears of both anger and shame.

"You're damn right I am, but please . . ." she said struggling to her feet once more and snatching up her bottle in one hand and Griffin in the other. "Feel free to continue and bless everything you can." she said starting off towards her room. "You can skip my room. I may do something *a bit naughty in it later.*"

Ryan hung his head and remained silent while Father Leary turned off the music before going back to his things on the table.

"I'm sorry about that." he finally managed while watching the priest open his bible and place one of those long silky purple things around his neck that looked like a holy scarf. "She doesn't do that a lot."

"It's okay, Ryan. It's not for you to apologize. She's a grown woman. We all make our own decisions on how to deal with stress." he said standing and holding out a hand for Ryan to join him. "Most of us find the wrong ways to deal with life's troubles."

"What do we do now?" the boy asked.

"We pray." the priest said and began. "Peace be with this house and all who live here. Blessed be the name of the Lord." he said making the sign of the cross and Ryan saw the small vial of holy water in his right hand as he waved it also in the sign of the cross and sprinkled some water here and there, the coffee table and the rug, and Ryan's eyes watched in deep fascination as the water hit spots here and there but no scolding steam shot up like in the horror movies. Father Leary seemed to know what the boy was expecting and smiled as the moved from room to room repeating the same phrases about blessing the house and all those who came and left and lived and stayed and so on. Finally, they both came to the basement door.

"Saved the best for last." Father Leary smiled. "Shall we?"

"I'm scared." Ryan said as the priest opened the door.

"There is absolutely nothing wrong with that, Ryan." he said clicking on the switch. "Many brave men in the bible were scared, Ryan. Abraham was scared when God tested him to kill his son. Noah was afraid when the floodwaters came and covered the face of the earth. Joseph was afraid when he was thrown into the pit and sold into slavery. Moses was afraid in the wilderness for forty years. Daniel was afraid to be thrown to the lions. David was afraid when Saul hunted him down for years while he hid in caves. Even Jesus was afraid when he prayed at Gethsemane."

"They didn't have monsters in their basement." Ryan pointed out and Father Leary couldn't help but laugh as he led the boy down the creaking stairs.

"Here now." he said looking about as Ryan stayed close. "Nothing quite so creepy. In fact it looks much nicer than my basement."

"It's not about how it looks." Ryan pointed out as they rounded the corner and he saw where only the previous night Brandon Lowe had hung himself after facing down a pack of spiders that nobody could see but him. "It's about what is here."

"Very well." Father Leary said and held up the vial of holy water again as he began his passage. "Peace be with this house and all who live here. Blessed be the name of the Lord."

The lights flickered then and Father Leary paused, looked around and then down at Ryan who merely shrugged as he moved closer to the priest. "Told ya." he said up to the man.

"Ryan, if this is some kind of joke, I will not find it amusing." Father Leary said moving over to get a better look at the stairwell. "You don't have some little friend of yours up there playing with the-"

The lights flickered again. Only this time continuously and so fast that it hurt the eyes to focus.

"Enough, Ryan." the priest said now annoyed. "Joke's over."

"I swear I'm not doing this." Ryan said hugging up against the man and the priest was about to head for the steps when he noticed more changes. The concrete floor was now flooding over with blood. It was coming from the edges of the walls and from under the washing machine and sofa. He reached down and grabbed Ryan's hands to head for the steps and saw a waterfall of blood spilling down them. It was everywhere and they were trapped.

"What is this?" he said backing up against the wall with Ryan at his side. "What evil is in this house?" he said louder and reached up to grab his crucifix dangling from around his neck. He quickly pulled his hand away when he realized that it too was soaked in blood. "Jesus help us." he breathed feeling the room grow colder around him.

"You see it too?" the boy said lifting his feet away from the oncoming pools of blood.

"Yes, I see." he said moving towards the steps again. "We have to get out of here, you understand? Don't focus on the blood, just the steps. Please Holy Father, help your faithful servant." the priest said, and taking Ryan's hand, both he and the boy worked their way up the steps with the blood pouring down over their shoes. Father Leary could actually smell the coppery odor of it, feel the warm stickiness covering his socks and soaking through to his skin, but he held the boy's hand with one hand and the wooden rail with the other and worked their way up the steps in the flickering light.

"Made it." Ryan said rolling onto the kitchen door as the priest slammed the door shut behind them while panting for breath. "Now you believe me?"

"I believe." he said looking himself over first and then Ryan. The blood was gone. Nothing on their shoes or skin or even his crucifix. The smell and feel of it was gone too. He hesitated first and then turned, opening the door much to Ryan's warnings, and saw a dark stairwell with no signs of blood. "Very impressive." he said to no one in particular. "The devil is a crafty foe."

"It's not the devil." Ryan reminded him. "It's my father."

"You shouldn't be staying in this house." Father Leary said approaching the door to his mother's bedroom. He knocked first and leaned his head in to hear better. "Laura? Miss Woods? You need to get up, please. We have some urgent matters to discuss."

"She might be asleep." Ryan guessed.

"Passed out more likely." the priest said gently pushing the door open. He peeked his head inside and noticed the entire room was dark. "Laura." he barely whispered. "Please, you and your son need to get out of this house. You are in danger here." he said and reached for the light to click it to life, but nothing happened. The room remained black and now Father Leary realized it was very cold as well. He could actually see his own breath. "God save us."

"Maybe he will, maybe he won't." a strange voice came from under the covers. Father Leary forced the door open a bit more and stepped inside as he watched the movement on the bed. The blankets were in constant motion as something under them seemed to *squirm* and twist about beneath.

"Are you okay, Laura?" he asked taking a step in her direction.

"Never been better." her voice was cold and distant and seemed filled with liquid. *"Have you come to bless me?"*

"I think you need to get out of bed, Laura." Father Leary said reaching out to take hold of the blankets. Before he could, they were thrown away to reveal the naked woman who lay there before him, smiling up at him, entwined among the snakes and spiders that covered her whole body and the sheets around her, her eyes glowing fire red as they found his. "What in the name of..?"

"Why don't you get into bed, Thomas, and show me what kind of man you really are?" the woman said holding out her bare arms to him and he backed away stumbling into the door.

"Ryan, get out of the house!" he called back to the boy.

"Come on, Father." the temptress called to him. It was indeed the face and body of Laura Woods, but not her voice. The snakes, large and small, slinked around her nude body, caressing it, and the spiders hung loosely off her breasts and private areas, pulsating with life, their tiny red eyes glowing as brightly as hers. *"Let's sin a little."*

"Father, save me from this illusion of darkness." the priest said grabbing the crucifix once more and the thing that was pretending to be Laura Woods laughed at him while clapping her hands together. He then took out the vial of holy water and made the sign of the cross before stepping bravely forward and sprinkling it over the bed sheets. The snakes snapped back like whips, hissing as their skins burned and the Laura Woods she-thing sat up while removing all the creatures around her so that Father Leary could see her in all her naked glory.

"Come on now, Father. If you want to make me scream I can think of a better way." she said smiling and licking her lips while massaging her own breasts. He stood there watching the woman as she let one hand drift down between her legs. *"When's the last time you had a taste of this good stuff."* the thing grinned while the spiders and snakes retreated to the walls and floors around her.

"Laura, if you can hear me, I am taking your son away from this house." he told her finally getting a good grip on the door behind him again. "He will be fine with me. When you get the chance to leave-"

"My son belongs with me." her voice said only now sounding deeper like a man's. *"A boy's place is with his father. Wouldn't you agree . . . Father?"*

"Oh my God." Father Leary said and cast two more streams of holy water in the woman's direction. While the snakes and spiders hissed and burned on contact, moving away from the holy man before them, the lady with the deep voice who did indeed look like the nude Laura Woods simply sat there and smiled and licked her fingers dry.

"I think you faith is lacking somewhat, Padre." she giggled sounding somewhere in between the lady he knew and a man that had been dead for five years now. *"Maybe you better go and get a refill."*

"I will be back, Laura." he promised making a sign of the cross before leaving the room and closing the door. The laughter he left in there behind him was not his or hers or anything human at all. "We have to go, Ryan." he said guiding the boy away from the kitchen. "We will come back later."

"But my Mom is in there." Ryan said dragging his feet. "I won't leave her."

"You have to for now." he demanded grabbing up his things in the living room. "You heard most of what was going on in there. I will tell you what I saw when we are safely away. I can't do anything for your mother right now and neither can you."

"I can't leave her." Ryan said turning back and the priest reached down and seized the boy with both arms hard, turning him to face him with a jerk.

"Ryan! Listen to me!" he said and then softened his voice as he heard the thing in the bedroom laughing at him. "That is not your mother. You were right. Somehow your father is involved in all of this but I can't do this by myself. Nor can you. This demon, or whatever your father has bonded himself too, is too strong for you or me. We will come back, I promise. I need you to trust me."

"Okay." Ryan said taking the man's hand as they started for the door.

"Ryan, honey, don't leave me here all by myself." his mother called from the other room.

"Mom?" Ryan said looking back.

"No, Ryan. It's a trick. A lie." Father Leary said keeping a firm grip on the boy's shoulder. "He's trying to lure you back. We have to go."

They exited the house, leaving the mix of laughter and cries behind them, and drove away. Ryan kept looking back at his house with his mother somewhere trapped in there with the evil spirit that was his father somehow alive again.

"Any family in town?" the priest asked.

"No." the boy said still staring back at his home.

"You will stay with me." he decided. "At least until we get this mess cleared up. Maybe that aunt of yours in Joplin wouldn't mind having you for a visit as well."

"No." Ryan shot back. "I'm staying until this is over. It's about me, you know. He wants me."

"Why?" the priest asked. "What does your father possibly want with you?"

"I haven't figured that out yet." the boy finally said turning around in his seat. "Just does."

"If he wanted you dead, he could have done that already." Father Leary figured turning onto Thrush Street in busier traffic. "He wants you for a different reason. Any ideas?"

"I don't know why he wants me." he said staring out the window. "But he's not getting me."

"Amen to that." Father Leary finished.

102

TWENTY THREE

The day passed slowly for both priest and boy. They talked at the kitchen table for over an hour about everything that Ryan had been through. He told Father Leary everything while he sipped ice tea and the good Father sipped coffee. He told him of the dreams and the deaths in details as he knew them. He told him about all the history of his deceased father.

"I never heard of anything like this before." Father Leary confessed. "Much less faced anything of this nature. A true test of faith and I may have failed."

"I don't think you did." Ryan spoke up. "You're not dead. It, or my father, or whatever it is, couldn't hurt you. It tried to though."

"I couldn't free your mother, Ryan." Father Leary said leaning back and looking out the window. "She needed me to help her and I failed. My faith wavered, as the thing told me back there. I was afraid."

"Like you told me, all great people are afraid." Ryan pointed out. "Your writer friend is probably afraid, that's why he writes those scary stories I bet. And your detective friend probably faces bad guys all the time that he's afraid of."

"You're very wise for your years. It's just I think my faith needs to be stronger. It is, after all, faith not truth that keeps the world alive." Father Leary said. "I could hurt its little minions, but I couldn't hurt your father. I lacked the proper amount of faith to deal with it."

"It just did that so you would leave." Ryan pointed out. "I think it's scared of you and your faith somehow. That's why it wants you gone. Maybe it really does see you as a threat. Maybe you do just need a refill."

"You're a very perceptive boy." Father Leary said standing and collecting the glasses. "Speaking of refills, would you like anymore?"

"No." Ryan said. "So what do we do now?"

"I am going back tomorrow afternoon and getting your mother." he said. "And you are going to school."

"No, Father Leary." Ryan said angered standing. "I have to go with you. It's me that my father wants so-"

"And that is why you don't need to be anywhere near that house." Father Leary said coming down to the boy's level. "Don't you see that, Ryan? He's using your mother as bait to get you back in there with him. Then he will have both of you. Let me go and get her. You will be safer far away from that house."

"I guess." Ryan said looking the man over. He had seen the fear in the priest's eyes earlier. The doubt. The pain of losing a small battle. "Are you going to be okay? Will you be able to stop my father and whatever else is in that house all by yourself?"

"I won't be by myself." the priest smiled back pointing to his crucifix. "No man walks alone."

***

Father Leary had plenty of room at his house for visitors. Aside from the spacious living room in which he had with a very comfortable couch he himself had fallen asleep on many nights, he had three bedrooms upstairs. One was his, of course, the other an office and one spare bedroom.

He fixed up the spare room for Ryan. He put fresh linen on the bed, fresh towels and soap in the bathroom, and knelt down and prayed with the boy before wishing him a good night. Ryan looked the room over well. Despite the fact he was in a priest's home he still checked the closet and closed the vents as tight as he could. He left the light on in both his own room and the adjoining small bathroom. He waited until he knew Father Leary had gone downstairs before walking to the dresser and taking the small bronze cross and carrying it to the window sill, facing Jesus outward against the dark of night.

"Vampire or not, better safe than sorry." he said crawling into bed.

***

Father Leary fought the urge to smoke. If there was ever a time he desperately wanted a cigarette, it was now. It would not be a far trip to get them. He would not have to leave the property. He knew he still had a pack out in the garage tucked safely away in an old coffee can full of nails and screws. He opted for another piece of butterscotch instead and sat down next to the phone.

104

Despite the boy's strange story, he desperately wanted to call someone with more experience than himself. But who? Father O'Brian was a good man, had been a priest for close to forty years, but he would never believe this unless he went for himself. Did he really want that on his conscience? To draw another person into this madness? According to Ryan, everyone who had been involved in this was already dead. He himself was now in danger. He had faced the thing and it knew who and what he was.

"God help me." he said and took hold of the small white pages there by the phone, thumbing through until he came across the WOODS name. He scanned down and found Laura, made sure it was the right address, and picked up the phone.

It rang twice. Twice more and then somebody picked up. Dead silence.

"Laura Woods please?" he spoke as casually as he could, hoping to disguise his voice just a bit.

A tiny giggle. Something humming in the background, an old song he barely recognized, then it spoke to him. *"She's not here right now. Would you like to leave a message, Father?"*

"Laura, if you can hear me, I will be coming for you tomorrow." Father Leary said ignoring the laughter. "Keep your faith."

"You better keep your fucking hands off my boy, Padre." the deep voice warned. *"Or I will be coming for your ass. Don't go getting in family business now, holy-man."*

"I am not afraid of you, Mister Woods." the priest tried and felt his heart beat picking up. He was having a conversation with a dead man five years gone. "Your son is not coming back to that house."

"We know where you live." another voice now, not quite Alan's, nor Laura's, but sounding female somewhat. *"When we want him, we will take him. You get in the way . . ."* and then some laughter, very soft and girlish laughter, that made Father Leary's flesh goose up all over. *" . . . there will be so much pain for you. Torment like you've never known."*

"You do what you have to." the priest sounded off bravely. "But I'm coming for her tomorrow."

"Then we'll come for you tonight." several voices promised and the line went dead. Father Leary hung up and let loose with a deep exhaling relief. He waited until his body stopped shaking before he got to his feet and started to prepare.

First, he checked the doors. Three of them. Front, back and garage. All locked, not that he knew if that mattered. A locked door of wood and glass would not hold off whatever it was that he saw over at

Ryan's house. His windows were never unlocked or opened but he checked them all anyway. Finally, he went to his hall closet and got the blue shoebox. The one holding the gun that his brother Paul had bought for him two years ago. "Home protection", his brother had claimed when he handed the weapon to him along with plenty of ammo. "Just in case God is busy elsewhere."

Thomas Leary did not appreciate the sarcasm his brother injected along with the gift. His brother had not joined the priesthood as he had. He owned a bar somewhere in Philadelphia. Paul lived a little closer to the edge than Thomas would have cared to, but he knew the streets, and he worried about his brother. At this current moment in time Thomas Leary was glad he had the weapon with the boy sleeping upstairs. "Just in case." he said checking the gun.

He didn't know too much about guns, only what his brother told him. If he remembered correctly this was a Smith & Wesson 669 that carried twelve 9mm rounds. Or something like that. He picked up the stainless steel weapon and balanced the weight of it in his hand. It has been quite some time since he had fired it. Almost two years ago when Paul had given it to him they went to a target range over in Defiance where they also did some fishing. Thomas had hit the target five times out of twelve. Not very impressive. He prayed his aim would be better tonight.

He put on another pot of coffee, checked to make sure the gun was loaded, and sat himself at the kitchen table ready to sit guard for the night. He wondered what would come for him, how it worked exactly. According to Ryan, mice and rats had got Mister Clark. Snakes had taken care of that poor Bates boy and spiders killed Brandon Lowe. Would twelve shots be enough? He knew there were more clips in the closet, but would they even be enough?

The question that bothered him most of all was what if Laura Woods showed up here tonight? What if she was still under the influence and control of her dead husband or whatever evil was truly behind all of this? Would he have to fight her, shoot her . . . Kill her? Could he do that? Even to protect the boy?

"Anything but her." he said sipping his coffee while placing the gun within reach on the table. Not so close that he had to focus on it, but not so far away he couldn't get to it in time. He unwrapped yet another butterscotch popping it into his mouth while staring out the slightly parted kitchen curtains at the darkness barely illuminated by the soft glow of the porch light. He wished now that he had never moved to this town. He selfishly wished the Woods boy had never crept into his office with his wild story. He wished he had never given up smoking because he surely could use a few right now. But mostly he prayed

for the strength to deal with whatever might be making its way over to his house tonight.

TWENTY FOUR

The morning came with no demons visiting his door.

More than a few came in his the priest's dreams but those he could live with.

Father Thomas Leary did not go directly to the Woods house. He had to work up his courage first. He had to pray. He stopped by Saint Michaels and sat in the back. There were others here for morning mass and once that let out he went up and lit a few candles and prayed for strength. He prayed for courage. He prayed for the soul of Laura Woods, her son Ryan, and even his own.

He nodded to a few members of his congregation, avoiding small talk if at all possible, and made his way back to the Jeep. He was as ready as he was going to get. He had his holy-water which he blessed himself, his oldest bible which was given to him by his mother, and he even brought the gun. And of course, he had his faith. What else was there to add in a situation like this? An event, which by all standards, should not even be happening.

It was a short drive with little traffic and Father Leary felt himself growing cold as his Jeep pulled up in front of the Woods home. It seemed different somehow to him. The house looked paler and void of all beauty or love like a home should have. The paint seemed dull, the lawn looked dead under the amber leaves. The windows were dark and no movement there as the priest scanned them exiting the Jeep and digging for the key that Ryan had given him. He didn't recall locking the door when he left the other day but he was glad to have it regardless. He stood before the house frozen while thinking of what he was about to do and whom he was about to face.

"Where angels fear to tread." he said walking up the steps. The house seemed bigger now, huge and threatening. He opened the storm door, inserted the small gold key, and turned the knob to gain entry into the abode of the Boogeyman. At least that's what Ryan believed. He was starting to think it might just have been true. "Father be with me."

The living room was dark and very cold. Chilling, in fact. He could see his breath just like the other day in Laura's room. He stepped in, leaving the door open behind him, and stood there in the darkness taking in his surroundings while allowing his eyes to adjust. When they did he saw a living nightmare before him.

A group of snakes were on the couch. They were black and of various sizes. Some no bigger than a pencil darting about the cracks and edges of the cushions, while one of them about the size of a tree limb lay along the back, flicking its tongue out at him while watching him closely with crimson colored eyes.

"You here to perform an exorcism, Father?" the black serpent asked and Father Leary thought he might just piss himself for the first time in his life. The damned thing was talking to him.

"I am here to save a friend." he told the snake that made no attempt to move in his direction. It just stared him up and down.

"Good luck with that." it said and smiled.

There was a sound coming from down the hall. A splash, then a dripping, then another splash. Somebody was using the water. The bathtub, it sounded like. Laura Woods was down there, along with others no doubt.

He thought of calling out but liked better the thought of silence. He set his bag down, took out the vial of holy water in one hand, and pointed the gun to the floor with his right as he moved towards the hallway and then the thin line of light coming from under the bathroom door. Once there he stopped, took a deep breath, and rested his left hand with the vial on the door.

"Come on in." the woman's voice said sounding as if it was coming from underneath the water.

Father Leary slowly pushed the door open, taking in the sights before him as he did, all of them surely inside his mind and not real. At least that was what he was praying. The floor was covered with small snakes. None of them, thankfully, as big as the one on the couch. They writhed around on the floor in circles and over each other. Large spiders decorated the walls. Small ones jetted around with such speed he could barely detect them, bigger ones that looked like some mutant form of tarantula's covered the mirrors and shelves, their long, furry legs like thick, black fingers as they slowly made their way to the door where he stood. A few mice and even larger rats sat on the edge of the tub, one nearly as big as a housecat, where Laura Woods reached up with a devilish smile and stroked the things gray matted hair. The big rodent smiled at her first then back at him.

"Care to join us, Father." It said whipping its tail about while grinning at him.

"I've come to take you out of here, Laura." he told her ignoring the rat-thing while holding up the vial of holy water and undoing the top with the same hand. He let a bit spill on the floor in front of him and noticed that the small snakes, along with some worms thrown in for good measure, backed off as the water steamed off their silky skin on contact. "You need to leave this house. You need to come with me and be with your son."

"Why don't you bring him here instead?" she asked, and as she spoke, a dark red liquid of water and blood mix came from her mouth and spilled down over her exposed breasts. *"Bring me my boy, Father. He belongs here with . . . Us."*

"That boy will never step foot in this house again. Not as long as I have life in my body." Father Leary said and tossed another hit of holy water on the floor, sending the snakes, worms and a few mice scurrying back with tiny screams of their own.

"Then perhaps we will just have to get rid of that life in your body." she said and stood before him now, naked and soapy and smiling seductively. The water was blood red and Father Leary could see faces down there in that tub. Just under the surface of the murky water. Faces that could not possibly be there. He started to back away but grabbed onto his cross as the faces began speaking to him. He would not leave this woman today.

"Don't end up like me." the old man's face said with mice crawling over it. Father Leary knew from Ryan's description that this must have been the neighbor, Mister Clark. "Leave while you still have the chance, son."

"It's so cold in here." a boy's face came up next to his. This was Jeffery Bates. He did not know this boy either, but it had to be him. Small black snakes circled the boy's head and as he spoke they freely flowed in and out of his widening mouth. "I don't like being dead, Father."

"This is all an illusion." Father Leary said stepping into the bathroom, shaking the vial at the walls and watching the burning and hissing spiders fall to the floor. "These people are no longer here, Mister Woods. By whatever means you came back, it won't work for them. These were good people."

"Not all of us." Brandon Lowe said, his entire upper torso popping up from the tub. His body was covered with tattoos and spiders both. He smiled while reaching up and running his hands all over Laura Wood's nude legs. "I'm pretty damn bad myself, Padre." he said smacking the grown woman on her naked ass and they both laughed. "Ain't she just a M.I.L.F? You have any idea what that means, father? It means I fucked her daughter and now I'm going to fuck her."

"Sounds kinky, Father." the mother agreed kneeling down to join the dead teen in the tub while the other faces sank back under the bloody red waters. "You want to watch or maybe join in?"

"Still not real." Father Leary said lifting the gun up and aiming at the dead teen.

"You think you can kill somebody that's already dead, Father?" the teen smiled as he began licking on the face of Laura Woods while squeezing her breasts.

"I think I can end this illusion before me right now." he said and carefully aimed at the body of the teen. He squeezed off one shot, the bullet striking the doppelganger of Brandon Lowe in the chest and sending his body back against the wall. There was no blood, but the body itself began to fall apart in pieces as it crumbled into the water.

"Fuck you, Padre!" the thing yelled at him as its pale flesh turned into bugs and worms collapsing in a large heap into the tub. Laura Woods just sat there staring at what was left of her would-be lover while Father Leary took aim at the large talking rat that sat next to her.

"Same to you." Father Leary said watching the rat smile at him.

"Not a very holy attitude." the rat-thing said.

"You're next." he said and fired again. The fat rodent exploded and flew back against the shower wall in a heap of burning fur that fell and sunk to the bottom of the tub. Father Leary tucked the gun away in his waist band and came at her across the creatures spread out on the floor. "We're going now!"

"No! I like it here! Leave me be!" she said trying to push him away.

Father Leary was desperate. He knew he had to get her out of this house and away from whatever evil influences were here. He fell back, taking her with him onto the floor, and as her naked, wet body was pressed on top of his with her grinding on top of him, he forced her off him while snakes and mice covered his body. He crawled away from Laura Woods, who knelt by the tub smiling and giggling at his dilemma. He brushed the mice off and tossed the snakes into the tub while swatting at the falling spiders from the ceiling and walls. "Laura, you need to snap out of it!" he called to her while ridding himself of the creeping pests. "Your son needs you, woman! Your daughter needs you!"

"My . . . Son . . . Daughter?" she breathed and blinked while looking ready to pass out. "What's going on?"

"They need you, Laura." he said smashing the mice and spiders with his balled fists.

"Ryan?" she said sitting there trembling and Father Leary thought maybe he was getting through to her. Whatever it was that was in her was loosing its evil grip. He just had to get her out of this house.

"She's my bitch, Father." a voice said from all around him in the small room. "Get your own and leave my family alone."

"Go back to hell." Father Leary said taking hold of her and tossing the vial down and letting it break and burn on the snakes and mice there while reaching out with his free hand and tugging the dazed Laura Woods to her feet, "We have to go! Can you walk?"

"What's going on?" the woman said. Father Leary understood to her it was as if she were just waking up, perhaps from a bad dream, and here she was not only naked in his presence, but in a room full of spiders, snakes, mice, and somewhere the dead evil spirit of her long lost psychopath husband. Way too much information to process at once.

"Bad things." he said pulling her up. "We have to go."

He led her out the door, the creatures of nightmares close behind them along with the man's laughter. The hallways were also covered with them. The floor with snakes and mice, the walls with spiders and bugs, the air with buzzing flies. The living room was just around the corner.

"What in God's name is going on?" she cried out while holding his hand and trying to run and cover herself all at once. "What is all of this?"

"For now, just run!" he yelled back to her and led her towards the door. Only it was no longer open, and the huge snake that had conversed with him earlier was laid out and pressed tightly up against it, blocking their exit.

"Going somewhere, father?" it asked.

"Through you." he said and blasted away with the gun. A few shots missed hitting the floor and door, but most hit the snake, but still the large black mass of muscle kept coming. "Run, Laura!" he told her as the thing made it to his legs, it's tail whipping up and snapping the gun loose from the priest grasp as it began to wrap itself around him. "Get out while you can!"

"No, I won't leave you!" she screamed watching him fall to the floor as the slimy black mass of serpent encircled him almost completely with the speed and grace of a much smaller snake. Laura spotted the gun and knelt to snatch it up, brushing away the mice and spiders as she did, and took aim.

"Baby, you don't want to do that." the snake said in her dead husband's voice.

"Alan?" she asked as the huge snake squeezed tighter on the priest.

"I've come back for you and my family." it seemed to smile up at her.

"For God's sake, Laura, shoot." the priest breathed.

Laura Woods looked deep into the crimson eyes of the snake, remembered just how evil her husband had been, and pulled the trigger several times. Both her and Father Leary watched as the diamond shaped head exploded into a puddle of ebony ink and the body fell limp. Laura knelt her nude body down and helped the man loose from the coils just as the rest of the creatures made their way into the room.

"Not a problem really." one of the larger spiders seemed to say coming up along side them. *"I have so many soldiers. We will keep coming and I will get what I want, Padre."*

"We will be waiting." the priest said smashing the thing with a balled fist as he stood now. He took the small quilt that covered the back of the couch, placed it around Laura Woods, covering as much of her as he could, and led her out of the house. "The blue Jeep by the curb. Move!"

Father Leary reached the jeep just as Laura did, both of them grabbing the handles on opposite sides simultaneously, and the priest looked back and saw the gray cat sitting on the porch.

"We're not even close to being done yet." Griffin warned watching them enter the car.

"You won't have them, Woods." Father Leary said slamming the door and starting the Jeep.

As they pulled away from the cat and the house of horrors Father Leary looked back. He saw what he imagined nobody else would if they were walking by just now. A house full of hellish things. Spiders and snakes covered the entire frame of the place. They were all over the roof, the siding, and the windows inside and out. Father Leary was relieved that the road was clear so he could keep his steady pace of escape. He was not so relieved when he checked the rear view mirror a second time.

"Oh, God." he said seeing the huge black cloud rising over the Woods house behind them.

"What's wrong? What now?" the panicked woman asked next to him twisting about to see out her own window. When she did Father Leary caught a good glimpse of the woman's bare legs and found himself blushing as he checked the mirror again.

"Something's coming." he said accelerating. "A bunch of something's." he said glancing once more in the mirror. Black movement. A huge mass of feathered, flapping wings. They were gaining fast.

"Hold on tight!" he yelled just as the huge dark flock of ravens struck the truck like a living wave of air-born water.

"Shit!" Laura cried out as the Jeep was literally rocked on his shocks from the impact. "What are they? What's happening?" she cried and kept letting her bare breasts fall into view.

"Your husband is not quite done with us it seems." Father Leary said steering the Jeep carefully through the blackness that flew before him blocking his vision. He honked the horn as the truck slowed to keep from hitting anyone or anything. "I have a good idea they might not really be there at all, but considering the fact were are both pretty damned scared, it's working."

"Get us away from them!" she screamed covering her ears at both the shrieking of the ravenous birds and the soft laughter somewhere in the air from her dead husband.

"Dear Father, hear our prayer!" the priest began with a tribal yell while trying hard to find the edge of the road so he could pull over. "Save your servant, Lord! Place your loving hands around us and protect us from the spirits of darkness!"

"I think it's working." Laura said noticing now she could see the road again. There was another car close by in the other lane that had also stopped. Both Laura and Father Leary wondered to themselves without speaking if the person in the other car saw what they did or just stopped to watch them scream.

"Either that or we're just too far away. But I like your theory better. Father in Heaven deliver us!" he cried out again while watching the huge birds take to the air and make an upside down spiral cone of retreat as they followed each other up and away from the Jeep. "Thank you, God!"

First Laura noticed the woman in the car staring at them both and when she did she reached over and tapped the priest on the shoulder, who then turned and saw one Miss Gardener, a long-standing member of his congregation, staring at both him yelling to God and the naked woman next to him. It did not help matters when Laura smiled and waved at her, allowing the quilt to fall and flash a nice pair of tits at the silver-haired woman. A look of shock and disgust covered her face as she sped away in the opposite direction and Laura cut loose with nervous laughter, soon followed involuntarily by Father Leary.

"That will take some explaining next Sunday." the priest grinned with part embarrassment and part amusement. "That was Miss Gardner, the church Treasurer. Probably the most excitement she has seen in years."

"I'm so sorry I waved." Laura Woods said while covering herself. "Instinctive reaction. At least we are pretty sure she didn't see the birds." she smiled and the priest found himself giving a nervous laugh that ended up a pretty good one. His face quickly took on a more serious not soon after.

"We have to come up with some sort of plan to protect your son." he said finally making it to the end of the street. "He's the one really in danger here, Laura."

"Where's Ryan?" the naked woman asked next to him shivering from both the autumn chill and the events that had just transpired which he could not begin to explain. "My son?"

"He's fine." Father Leary said reaching down to click on the heater. "There, that should help some. I took him home with me last night. He's in school now. I told him I was coming for you today."

"I don't understand what's going on. Last thing I remember was you coming over to bless the house and I was kind of zonked." she said looking at him seeming even more embarrassed about the drinking than her current nudity. "And then I woke up and there you were and all of those . . . Things."

"It seems your son was right." Father Leary said trying to advert his eyes. "Your late husband evidently has found a way back from Hell. Seems he brought some friends with him. I'm not quite sure I understand it myself, except you and your son are in danger."

"Why especially Ryan?" she said trying to cover more of herself as she saw people in other cars beginning to notice her situation as they became more and more involved in traffic.

"I'm not sure. It seems your husband wants him specifically." he said. "Last night he seemed to take over or possess you. Temporarily anyway. Maybe he has the power to do the same thing to Ryan if he gets the chance. Neither one of you needs to go back to that house until this is over, if even then."

"Okay, but where will we stay?" she asked eyeing him with a bit of hope and curiosity.

"With me for the moment." he told her looking over and minding his eyes to focus only on her face, which seemed worn and frightened, as it should be. "The church has some clothing for a homeless drive we were doing. I'm sure we can find something to fit you."

"How will you explain this to people?" she asked scooting down in the seat as she saw the house coming into view.

"I won't for now." he said pulling into the garage. "You are having a family crisis if anyone asks and giving the current circumstances that's not exactly stretching the truth."

"I guess." she said as the Jeep pulled into the darkness of the garage. She felt vulnerable right now, more so that she was nude and this priest was so handsome. God, why did her knight in shining armor have to take a vow of celibacy? "You're kind to do this, Father Leary. I still don't fully understand what's happening to us, but thank you." she said looking over as his face came into view from the dome light.

"You're welcome, but thank your son." the priest said unlocking the door to the kitchen. "He's the one who convinced me to come over in the first place. Stay here for a moment. I'm going inside to get you a robe. Then I will head over to the church and get you some clothes."

"Thanks." she said sitting there in the dark shivering. The Jeep and garage were both plenty warm, but the voice that came out of that snake and then that spider . . . Jesus, that was Alan's voice. A man, regardless of how evil, that had been dead for five years. What the hell was he into that could have allowed him to do that. What dark magic arts had he fucking known that she didn't know about?

"Please, God, watch over my son." she said seeing Father Leary coming back with a long shaggy blue robe that looked three times too big for her.

"Here we are." he said sliding it through the window to her without casting a glance as her near nude frame. If he were not a priest, Laura Woods would have felt insulted. She had a damn nice body for a woman her age, and was sort of insulted priest or not. He could have at least stolen a glance, but she knew he was just showing her respect. This was something she was not accustomed to.

"Thank you." she said letting the itchy quilt slide off and then she squirmed about in the seat as she dressed herself in the robe that felt like a tent on her thin body. If this were any other kind of situation she would be laughing now. But it wasn't. She had just run naked out of a house of demonic creatures with a priest. She was sure there was a joke there somewhere, but it would be a long damn time before she got it.

"I feel compelled to tell you, Laura." he started with a serious tone once she stepped her bare feet out onto the cold concrete. "I do not keep alcohol or cigarettes in my house at any time, or allow it."

"You're just no fun at all." she tried with a grin but he wasn't biting. "Sorry. It's not a problem. The drinking needs to stop anyway and I can always find a substitute for the smoking I guess."

"Ever try butterscotch?" he grinned over while holding the door open. "It does wonders."

TWENTY FIVE

Mister Benjamin "Scooter to my friends" Kelly had decided not to go to church that chilled Sunday morning. It had been a long and restless night. Images of the Lowe boy hanging there in the Woods basement kept him up most of the night.

Instead he got up from his bed, which was not providing the sleep it used to when he was a married man, and staggered into the kitchen for his morning cup of Java. It wasn't so much seeing a dead boy that bothered him, hell he had seen dead bodies in his life, it was just the why and wherefore of it all. Back when he was younger and wilder he had played in a jazz band. He used to be a mean sax player in his day, and a slick dancer, hence the nickname "Scooter" from the way he used to move all over the floor. He and a few other brothers had stopped by a bar in Memphis for beers when a few locals decided they didn't like them messing with their women. Things got ugly fast.

Benjamin got his licks in, took a few more than he would have cared for, and when it was all said and done a buddy of his, the trombone player, Gerald "Big Bone" Turner, had beaten a young brother one too many times with a pool cue. The man died before the ambulance could get there and Gerald was sent up for twenty-five years. He died in prison with a shank in his gut in his third year. Benjamin Kelly stopped going to bars after that.

But the body still remained in his mind's eye. That young brother, just barely legal, lying there in a pool of his own blood dotted with spats of beer and his own teeth. His eyes rolled open and staring at the ceiling, lifeless, and he had been laughing moments ago until the fight broke out. Never even found out his name.

"Damn waste." he said thinking of the Lowe boy. He had heard Chief Rollins speak unkindly of the boy saying he was a thug and a criminal, but hell, Chief Rollins felt that way about most teenagers. Rollins would have hated Benjamin Kelly in his younger days too. "Still had time to turn himself around." he told himself rooting around in the fridge and found he really had no appetite. He missed Margie's cooking mostly on Sunday. She made some mean ass waffles and sausage. Then there was always that great wake up sex she used to provide that would make a man's toes curl. Nobody cooked or screwed like Margie did in the morning. Nobody before or since.

He stared down the phone and thought about calling her. It had been three years and maybe she had forgiven him. He smiled at this foolish, lonely thought and knew Margie would forgive him, but not forget. She would never trust him again and he did not blame her. The number would not be the same anymore. Chances are she had another man. Even if she didn't, Chicago was a hell of a long drive for waffles and sex no matter how good the two were together.

He noticed the Rams game would not start until noon, which gave him plenty of time to putt around in the garage. It eased his mind to work with his hands. Right now he needed his mind focused on anything other than last nights events so he slipped on his jacket and hat and stepped out into the cool morning air.

"Hey, Marley." Mister Kelly smiled as he saw the big Husky come trotting up the basement steps to follow him with its tongue rolled out in happy greeting. He reached down and scratched the big dog, which he had named affectionately after one of his favorite singers he and Margie used to dance the nights away too, and then fished out his keys to the garage door. "You want to hang with me for awhile, Marley?"

He heard another noise then as he stepped outside. A soft mewling from above. Benjamin Kelly backed away from the garage door and looked up to see a cat sitting on the roof staring down. He laughed at the sight.

"Well now, little fella." he said shielding his eyes and thinking the small critter looked familiar from somewhere. "You stuck up there, are you? Hate to tell you I'm a bit too tired to lug out the ladder and get you down." he said watching the cat walk about near the edge as if searching for a way down. "You're better off up there anyway." he said reaching down and patting Marley who had now noticed the cat and gave it a few low growls. "Marley here ain't partial to cats, not in this yard anyways." he said tipping his ball cap and headed into the darkness of the garage. Marley growled some more as the cat stared him down with red glowing eyes from its place above him.

The garage smelled of paint and smoke and the big man tossed the switch bringing three long florescent bulbs to life and headed over to his workbench. This used to be his escape from Margie whenever she got to nagging and bitching at him about fixing something or losing weight or taking her some place he rather not be. Now it was just a garage again.

"What to do, what to do?" the big black man asked viewing the mess before him. Here was a birdhouse in need of painting. There a tangled weed whacker cord. In the corner was a lawn mower engine that could use repair and blades in need of cleaning. Up on the wall hanging by two hooks was a bike with no chain and low tires. "Maybe we will start here." he told his canine companion as he sat on a creaky stool and dusted off a girly magazine while snatching a pack of smokes from out of his toolbox. Once one was lit he reached over and turned on a small radio on the shelf and let the sounds of the Blues fill the garage. "And we will work our way down from here."

Marley the dog took little notice of the flipping pages the lewd comments or the cigarette smoke. He wandered out of the dark confines of the garage and began to nose around the edges of the garage. There was something here. Something that his senses did not quite understand but detected anyway. There was something odd and new.

The dog knew smells. He knew rabbits by the garden and squirrels that would venture to and from the bird feeder. He knew cats especially, like the one on top of the garage, but this was not a cat. This smelled different to him. This almost smelled like his master only stronger and different somehow. If Marley were able to use human words to describe the smell, he would have used the word *dead*.

The big dog made its way to the back of the garage, whimpering in both fear and confusion, because this is where the smell was the strongest. He peeked around the corner noticing nothing different from his last journey here, same bare rose bushes, same short grass. Only now there was something strange. There, next to the dead bushes, was the cat. Only now it was a soft lump of black and gray fur and was not moving. It looked lifeless to Marley who approached with caution, nose working overtime, as he tried to determine if the cat was just playing games or truly dead.

"Marley?"

There was a voice. It seemed to be coming from somewhere near the cat.

"Here, boy."

The dog winced back, lowered itself to its haunches and stared at the cat. The voice was coming from within its body. It was a nice voice, a friendly one like his master in the garage, but clearly not his master's voice.

"Good doggie, Marley."

Marley cocked his head and tried to figure out why this voice was coming from a cat while his tail went into hyper-drive. It did sound like a nice voice but Marley did not want to go any closer because that smell was still there. The smell of rotting things. Dead flesh of some animal that he did not recognize. Not the cat. Whatever it was it sounded friendly but was not like his master.

"Come on, Marley." the voice said and now softly whistled for him. *"Come see me."*

Marley did inch closer despite the smell. The voice sounded the same way his masters did anytime he wanted to scratch his belly or give him a treat. This was something that Marley enjoyed. As the big dog scooted closer over the dirt he could detect a new smell now. This one was not so bad. If he possessed human dialogue he would have guessed it was a sweet smell. Rather like fresh honey.

"There's a god boy, Marley. Come closer. Such a good boy."

A few more whistles and Marley was had. He had forgotten all about the horrible dead smells which were mostly now covered up by the sweet oily scent of honeycomb and stuck his huge muzzle only inches from the body of the still cat. Something inside the cat was moving. *Lots* of something's. It's gray fur was bubbling all over as if ready to explode. Marley growled and started to back away but it was too late for escape.

"Gotcha!" something screamed and a thick, black living cloud full of tiny legs and wings shot out buzzing from Griffin's dead body and smothered the big dog's face.

***

"Nice." Benjamin Kelly said holding up the magazine to the light for a better view of the blonde leaning into the counter of the bar in the picture. "Not a bad ass for a white girl." he smiled staring at her tanned curves. "Could use a little more titty, but you can't have it all."

A yelp then. Loud and short, but sharp enough to catch his ears.

"Marley?" the big man said tossing the magazine and rising off the rickety stool. "What's wrong, boy?"

He ran out into the light of the morning, birds charming the world from bare branches overhead, and noticed Marley now seated in statue mode at the center of the yard simply staring at him.

"Hey, boy? You okay?" he asked kneeling to the damp grass and patting the space in front of him. "Come on over here. What's spooking my best buddy?"

Marley did come. Soft, slow and steady with eyes on the big man who was his master. His tail did not wag and his eyes narrowed down to a near slit. Benjamin took notice of this and rose up to full height, letting the cigarette fall to his feet, smashing it into the damp earth.

"What happened boy?" he said looking around the yard for any other sign of life. "Somebody teasing you out here?"

Marley did not respond to his master's voice or brief touch, instead he wandered past the big man and found himself a cool spot in the corner of the garage. The buzzing noises in his head were softer for now. Benjamin Kelly just shrugged his shoulders and returned to his workbench seating himself in front of the birdhouse and lighting himself another smoke.

"Hey, if you're okay, I'm okay." he said reaching for a small can of paint and a rather dry and brittle looking brush. "Wow, this shit needs cleaning bad. So what do you think?" he said turning to his four-legged friend. "Blue or red for the roof?"

"Fuck you." came a soft voice barely audible from the darkness and Benjamin Kelly grew still in his chair as his eyes rolled towards the door.

"Who the hell?" he said slamming the can down and leaping for the open door. "Who is out here?" he called looking around and rolling up his jacket sleeves preparing or a brawl. "You in my yard screwing with my dog, you better get ready for a beat down, jack!"

"Stay away from the boy." the soft yet deep voice warned and Mister Kelly realized the voice was coming from inside the garage. He turned, scanned the dark corners for any sign of an intruder, and then grabbed up the rake for extra defense and blocked the only exit.

"Who is that? What boy you talking about?" he asked looking from ceiling beams to paint stained floors for any movement. "Where the hell are you?" he asked. Only Marley sat there staring at him. "Somebody is screwing with us." he told the dog returning to his chair. "Punk probably ran off. Some help you were." he said turning his back on the dog and starting up his task again. He did not notice Marley rise up from his place on the cold concrete floor and head toward the doorway. "So what do you think? Let's do it up in red and give the birds a thrill."

The door slammed shut. Benjamin Kelly dropped the pain brush and turned his head just in time to see the large dog seated there before him.

"Somebody learned a new trick." he said. "Who taught you how to close a door?"

Marley sad there, eyes glazed over, breathing low, and then he began to growl.

"What's wrong, boy." Benjamin Kelly said rising up. "You sick? Not feeling well?"

Marley turned his head as if trying to understand his voice. In truth the buzzing was coming back and blocking out most of it anyway. That and the fact there was something in his belly that hurt and it was working its way up through his chest and getting closer to his throat. Marley's body started to shake all over and Mister Kelly backed away slowly watching with wide eyes as his own pet and best friend stared him down eye to eye and began to speak to him.

"You should have stayed away from my son." the dog said while going into convulsions.

"Stay the hell away from me." Mister Kelly breathed while backing to the wall searching for anything to use as a weapon. He found it quick enough. A large claw hooked hammer. He snagged it from the pegboard and raised it up in defense. "Come on, then! Whatever the hell you are."

"That won't be good enough." the dog seemed to smile and then its jaws opened wider. Wider than any dog or animal that he knew of should be able to open its mouth. The furry head tilted back until it was nothing more than rows and rows of teeth surrounding a snaking pink tongues that quickly vanished into the blackness of its own throat and made way for something much worse. *"Goodbye, Mister Kelly."*

The voice hissed and Benjamin Kelly saw something moving in that back throat. Tiny little shapes of yellow and brown with wings and legs and a buzzing sound that grew louder than the music on the radio.

"Sweet Lord, what the hell?" his voice drifted off while watching the cloud of bees vomit forth from what was once his dog. The garage filled fast with them, swarming all over and around the large man who swung at them with the hammer while trying to make his way towards the door. But the door was no longer visible. Nothing was. Just black moving air and the painful stings that came with them as they crawled over his body and attacked his face. "Get them off me!" he screamed and lunged in the direction where he prayed the doorway.

He missed it by about three feet. He found instead the hard wood wall and a ladder and some other tools with his hands that were now covered in both bees and welts rising up from their stings. He smashed the small window with his hammer, hoping they would leave or somebody would hear. Then he began to wipe his face and body free of them, only to have them come swarming right back. He tried to open his eyes but they were swelling shut on him and as he managed one more cry for help from anybody who might be outside at this hour, more bees found their way into his mouth and throat, causing him more pain than he would have imagined possible. His airflow was being cut off now and he could no longer stand.

Finally he fell to the floor, hands reaching for an exit, his mouth spitting bees. He did manage to pry open one eye and through all the buzzing blackness, he saw Marley sitting there unharmed and smiling.

"Gotcha!" the dog said and walked away.

TWENTY SIX

"Why won't he just kill me and get it over with?"

Ryan said on the edge of the cracked blacktop playground just under the backstop. He watched the traffic down on Carver Street where the backs of business's faced the side of Daniel Boone Middle School. He did not want to come here today, never did on a Monday, but Father Leary insisted.

The priest looked tired when Ryan came downstairs and he could tell the man had sat up all night. The smell of coffee lingered on the man's breath and his bible was laid out next to a very impressive looking gun. Ryan didn't know much about guns any more than the priest did, but that one looked like it could stop a buffalo in it's tracks. He was scared of something alight. Maybe he needed to be afraid. He had been helping Ryan now and he had been in the basement, exposed to the evil that lived there. He would most likely be next. Ryan wasn't sure if that big gun would be enough to stop whatever was dwelling in his basement. He was pretty sure it was not.

The sun did manage to squeeze a few rays of light past the cloud, but the chilled winds still kept everyone in jackets. Ryan could almost see Scooters from where he now sat. He wondered if Mister Kelly would be okay since he had also helped him. He also wondered what Father Leary would face when he got to his house this morning. Would it be his mother or something worse? But those thoughts were interrupted by a most unwelcome source.

"Hey, man." came the voice. Ryan turned and looked up to see the two boys standing over him. The Butler Brothers. Steven and Shaun. Steven was older and meaner, Shaun was pretty much all talk. Both of them were about as bright as a pile of rocks. Ryan was too tired to fight or run so he at there waiting for the latest torment or stupid comment. It was Steven who did the talking first. "I heard some dude hung himself in your basement? That shit true?"

"Yep." Ryan simply said watching the delivery trucks pull up behind the hardware store as it let out long, high pitched *beeps* in doing so. Ryan watched the fat man come out and start up some conversation with the bald trucker, their voices and laughter echoing up through the alleyway and trying to ignore the two boys casting shadows over him, one of them popping gum loudly.

"So what'd it look like?" Shaun asked. His voice was high and whiny like a girl.

"Looked like a guy hanging from the ceiling, I guess." Ryan said thinking about how much worse it must have been for Brandon before he died. Had he really hung himself, or was he forced to by something else. His father?

"How'd your sister take it?" Steven asked almost giggling. "She must have freaked out?"

"She's okay." Ryan said feeling the anger rising up in him. Steven Butler always knew which buttons to push.

"Did she go all nuts, like Jeff's mom did?" Steven pressed on.

"Hey, man. Lay off." Shaun tried but Steven shrugged him off.

"I said she was fine." Ryan said standing now. He was exactly the same height as Steven Butler, but perhaps a good twenty pounds lighter, and there was Shaun to contend with even if he was a pussy. These two had no intention of fighting fair.

"Really? Not what I heard." Steven grinned with a gap showing between his front teeth. "I heard you guys had to send her away. You know, one of those places with padded walls and soft music."

"Let's just go, man." Shaun tried again seeing Ryan's face redden.

"She's at my aunts. So you might want to shut the hell up, Butler." Ryan warned. "Keep talking and I will shut your mouth for you."

"That right?" Steven said stepping closer so much that they were damn near breathing on each other. "Sounds like Woods grew a pair since last week." he said back to his cowering brother who was a year younger and smaller in every way.

"You have no idea." Ryan said smiling right back and came up so close their chest were nearly touching. "Say anything else about my sister again, to me or anybody else, and I am kicking your ass."

"Big words." Steven Butler said and then laughed as he lunged forward and shoved Ryan hard, causing him to stumble back nearly loosing his balance. "You don't scare me, Woods. Just because you're some weird ass kid who had a killer for a father don't mean you're a bad ass. Right Shaun?"

"I guess." Shaun said remaining still.

"I bet you end up just like your dad." Steven grinned. "A freaking psycho."

"Let's find out." Ryan said stepping up in striking distance.

"Fine." Steven said raising his fist up in fighting stance. "Let's rock."

Ryan shot out with a hard punch but Steven easily grabbed his hand by the wrist, blocking the hit. He stood there grinning proudly of his fast reflexes while Ryan worked into a snarling face.

"That your best shot, Momma's boy?" he said twisting his arm. "I know girls that can hit harder than that."

"I'm not done." Ryan said and Steven felt something shift on Ryan's arm. Something under his jacket moved and squirmed and started to make its way to the opening in the sleeve.

"What the hell?" Steven said letting go of the boy once he saw the small animals come crawling over his own arms from inside the jacket. Black and gray fur covered things that opened their mouths wide to show off tiny sharp teeth. "Shit! Fucking rats, man!"

Ryan laughed while five or six more came tumbling out of his jacket and onto the black top below. The large rodents started after both boys who were running back towards the school with the small group of rats in close chase.

"You're a fucking nut job, Woods!" Steven called out as his little brother jetted past him. "I'm telling everybody I know about you! Telling them you're insane!"

"You better tell them!" Ryan called out and fell down to his knees feeling drained and dizzy.

"What the hell just happened?" he thought staring at his arms and then over to the rats that were now heading off into the streets bordering the school. *"How the hell did I do that? Did I do that? Where did they come from?"*

Ryan felt the world spinning and then everything went into a blur. Overhead another V of geese flew by, their fearless leader honking their way south, and Ryan stared at them as the world faded away.

"Take me with you." he thought and went off into his dreams.

TWENTY SEVEN

Ryan was not sure how he got back on Delaware Road. Last thing he remembered was getting into a fist fight with Steven Butler on the playground and the geese flying away overhead. Next thing he knew here he was standing on the sidewalk by the Flavor Freeze with a cool wind blowing in his face.

He turned to view his surroundings. Nobody in sight. Kind of odd for a Monday, if it was still Monday. A few parked cars but no moving ones, only the soft autumn breeze sending leaves scraping down the sidewalks. All of the stores still seemed to be closed as they had yesterday. Dark and cold inside with no movement of life. It was a ghost town. A *dead* town.

"Got to go see Father Leary." he said seeing the tall church steeple up ahead. He walked along at a rushed speed, wishing he had brought his bike, or remembered how the hell he got here in the first place, when he noticed a dark figure in the Flavor Freeze moving about by the pinball machines.

"Hey little bud." the tall thug called from the window that was now covered in webbing. "How's it hanging?" he said holding up the loose chain that hung from around his neck. Ryan froze as he watched Brandon Lowe crack a wide grimacing smile.

"You're dead." Ryan said backing away from the window which was filling up with tiny black spiders. "I saw you dead in my basement."

"Yeah, I was there dude." the young man continued to smile. "You need to stop letting people die, man. That shit is just not cool."

"I didn't kill you." Ryan protested watching the spiders make their way over the teen's body.

"You sure the hell did!" Brandon yelled and choked some as the spiders entered his mouth while he spoke. "You caused all of our deaths, dude. I was just about to nail your sister's ass too. Fucking bummer, man." he finished and then the spiders once again had their way with him. Ryan saw something much bigger, spider-like in appearance but not size, come up behind him and grab onto him with its huge furry mandibles and drag him away into the darkness while he screamed.

"Shit!" Ryan cried out and looked around for help. There was none to be had. The streets still empty of all life. Ryan crossed over to Black Bridge Comics and noticed the OPEN sign in the door. He hesitated for a moment then tugged the door and entered the dark warmth of the place.

A tiny bell rang out and Ryan's excited eyes scanned the place over, almost forgetting the second death of Brandon Lowe across the street, and then he saw who was behind the counter minding the store.

"Young Ryan Woods!" Mister Clark called out raising up a cup of coffee. "Can I help you find something, Ryan? Some horror comics? Creepy posters? A way to kill some more of your neighbor's perhaps?" he smiled and his teeth were all small and black.

"It's not my fault." Ryan said frozen in place. In his mind he wanted to run but he could not. This was a friend. Unlike Brandon, who he hated to see dead but never really cared for, this was somebody he truly loved like a grandfather. "Mister Clark, I had no idea. You have to believe me."

"Have to learn to take responsibility for your actions, young man." the old man smiled and Ryan noticed all the rats and mice now on the counter. He grinned while picking up a newspaper and swatted a few mice. "Blasted things follow me everywhere."

"You're not Mister Clark." Ryan accused finding the strength in his legs to back towards the door. "Not the real one that I knew."

"Ain't I now?" the old man kept right on grinning. "You got me killed, you little shit." he said and came out from around the counter. When he did Ryan could see his pants were tattered and ripped apart by the large rats that hung there feasting on his bleeding legs. "Just who the hell am I then? I look like a super-hero to you, boy? Rat-man, maybe? You want to be my partner? You could be mouse-boy. How'd that be?" he said and tilted his head back as if to observe the ceiling. He opened his mouth wide and reached in with his full hand. Ryan felt the urge to vomit as he watched the man pull out a string of mice all squirming and covered in the old man's blood and dropped them to the floor. "You can have these little fuckers. They was giving me indigestion anyways." he smiled his black pearls again.

Ryan turned and ran out of the comic shop. He felt safer for only a moment until he saw his one time best friend seated on his dirt bike in front of the music store, the one covered with the skull posters. Only now those posters were moving. Eyes winking, mouths opening and closing, and something else there too. Something black and slick in movement just behind the posters all over the glass.

"Snakes." Ryan said entranced as he walked down the street towards Jeff.

"Guess I should have believed you, man." Jeff said sitting there with a candy bar in one hand. "So how'd my funeral go?"

"It was pretty nice." Ryan found himself being quite casual with his dead best friend. He didn't seem scary like the others. The posters and the snakes were pretty bad, but they were behind the glass. At least for now. "Your father was there. He cried. Lots of people were there. I was."

"Yeah, I heard they dressed me up like a fucking nerd." he said as he guzzled on a soda and wiped his mouth on his arm. "What's that all about?"

"Sorry about that." Ryan heard himself apologizing. "Wish I could have done something. It was okay though. Your mom didn't show though."

"Yeah, I figure she will probably off herself being crazy and all." Jeff said tilting his head and placing his hand up in fake gun fashion and pretending to blow his brains out. "So I should see her pretty soon I guess."

"I guess that's something to look forward too." Ryan said wanting desperately to leave now. Jeff was getting a bit dark for his taste. "I guess I better go." he said heading towards the church and giving his friend a subtle wave. "I got things to do."

"Yeah, there's lots more to die." Jeff said and headed off in his own direction on his bike. "That fucking cop with the burns. Your priest friend. Your mom and sister. Maybe Anna Finch and her boobs. She could die and then she could be my girlfriend." Jeff laughed and Ryan refused to answer or turn around and see what form Jeff had taken. He kept walking as he heard his friend laughing while peddling away and finally his eyes caught sight of the Laundromat on the corner.

"Hello there, Ryan." the voice from the alleyway called out. Ryan noticed Mister Darby leaning there up against a Dumpster while lighting himself up a smoke. "And just how are we this fine day?"

"Kind of lost and confused." Ryan admitted while watching the man shamble over in his direction. "I don't know what's going on."

"Well, lucky for you I know all about that." he grinned his pumpkin smile between puffs. "Sides, you ain't lost. Yer right here on Delaware Road. Waverly, Missouri, yes sir. I believe the answers yer lookin' for are over there, son." he said pointing to Madame Bulvaria's little dark shop across the street. "I think maybe she can help ya. Better than that priest of yers can anyways."

"I don't know." Ryan said staring the place down which still had the purple awning and red letters done up over tinted glass. There was no movement there anymore than last time, but Ryan *sensed* something behind that dark glass waiting for him. Something not so nice. "Father Leary helped me get away from my house once, and he's going to get my mom back today . . . I think."

"This woman here knows things, son." the old man said coming closer and he smelled like sour piss and rotting food. Ryan had to struggle just to breathe with him this close. "You should go and see her, boy. I think she might have the answers you're looking for. I think she can help you." he said and coughed some as he dropped his cigarette and squashed it with a muddy shoe. "That's your best bet right there."

"Will you come with me?" Ryan asked not taking his eyes of the dark shop.

"She don't like me." the older man mumbled. "Don't particularly care for my aroma I reckon." he grinned down at the boy. "But you tell er Darby sent ya. She will understand."

Ryan started across the empty street, looking both ways regardless of the fact he knew no cars would be coming. He got almost all the way to the other side when he realized his pockets were empty.

"Hey, how am I gonna pay her for any-" he started to ask Darby as he turned but the old bum was gone. Nothing in the alleyway but a few cats sniffing around the Dumpster. The Laundromat was dark inside and vacant of life. Darby was gone with the wind, only his stench remaining behind.

The door was open and Ryan actually felt cooler as he stepped inside. A set of tiny wind-chimes announced his presence and Ryan could hear somebody far in the back moving about. Books were being opened and shut, soft whispers and even softer music in the background somewhere, so far away it was like a dream within a dream.

Ryan cast his tiny eyes around the mostly dark shop. Here was a statue of a cat's head in the window with blazing amber jewels for eyes and some Egyptian symbol carved on its ebony forehead. There on a stand covered with burgundy silk sat a clear crystal ball that sparkled with tiny flecks of baby blue and soft pink and emerald greens. On this wall were tiny carvings of figurines with elongated necks and hollow eyes, wooden and ceramic masks hung above them, mostly done up in bright paints with sinister grins stretched across their lifeless faces.

Ryan walked slow and cautious towards the back of the store where he soon heard the soft humming of a female voice. He strolled down the nearest aisle with shelves of bottles filled with strange colored liquids with specs of this and shards of bone and tiny floating dead things. He came out of the row of containers to see a rather plump woman with jet black hair and olive skin wrapped up snug in bright clothing of scarlet, violet and blue sitting behind yet another counter that held many wonders as well.

"Hello, little man." she smiled as her dark black lips parted. "Come where I can see you."

Ryan Woods stepped out onto the carpet before the glass counter. His young eyes took in the many sights here that put all of his comic books to shame. Tiny skulls of animals. Mummified hands and claws of beasts unknown. Decks of Tarot cards spread out in fan shapes to show off the colorful characters displayed on them in grotesque artwork. Odd shaped beads and multi-colored feathers. Ouija boards and zodiac sign statues and pentagrams with grinning goat heads in their centers.

"Sorry to bother you." Ryan heard himself say while still keeping his eyes on the display before him. "Mister Darby said maybe you could help me."

"Mister Darby is beyond even my help." she mused to herself while hooking a long bony finger at him with large hoops of bracelets clinking against each other as she did. "Come tell Madame Bulvaria what is your troubles, little man."

Ryan walked up to the counter, seeing a lizard with a bright blue tail scamper across the counter and out of sight behind a stack of old looking books at the far end. A large green parrot squawked something dirty from the corner and the big lady laughed. Ryan gave her a weak smile while eyeing the strange bird that whistled softly in time with the music coming from the unseen speakers above.

"I did not teach him to say that." she said smiling and at least her teeth were white and even.

"I've heard worse." he said and the bird squawked something about "bastards and pricks" and they both laughed again. "Wow, he really goes at it."

"He is showing off." the bright lady said. "Now tell me please what troubles a little man as cute as you on such a lovely day." she said and Ryan felt himself blush red hot.

"My dad is back from hell." he said simply. "He's trying to kill everyone I know. He wants me. I don't know why."

"A restless spirit?" she said raising her thick eyebrows that looked up close like two caterpillars trying to reach out to each other across her thick lined forehead. "Come back from the dead to claim his son?" she seemed to be consulting with herself on the matter now. "You have something that he wants, boy. Something he truly needs."

"What?" Ryan said backing away to meet her eyes and keep an eye on the lizard that had reappeared and the parrot which was eyeing him now like some large tasty snack.

"Life, silly boy." she said, her accent a bit thicker now than before. "He wants to inhabit your body. He wants to start over again and do the things he did before. He needs your body to come back and be more powerful than ever."

"What do I do?" Ryan said hypnotized by her eyes that he just realized were a bright hazel in contrast to her dark skin.

"You are his son, little man." she smiled down at him. "What he has, you have as well. You must take control of that which seeks to destroy you."

"I don't understand." Ryan said. "You mean I can do the same things he does, with the snakes, the rats, the spiders and stuff. I can control them? That's not right. If I could do that why are they killing my friends?"

"The slaves will obey their master." she wagged a long dark tipped finger at him. "And there can only be one master. And do not tell me, little man, what you can and can not do. You have already shown proof of your power. Think about the schoolyard."

Ryan's head popped up off the glass counter, his thoughts racing back to the fight he had with Steven Butler while his little brother stood aside and watched. *The rats.* Somehow they were there, right up his sleeve like a magician's card trick. Not only did they obey his wishes, but he had made them appear.

"You are your father's son." she smiled at him while shuffling a deck of cards in her hands now in a frenzied blur. "Blood of his blood, flesh of his flesh, and spirit of his spirit."

"Then I will end up just like him." Ryan said backing away with his eyes feeling the familiar sting of tears. "I will kill people too."

"Evil is a choice." the woman pointed out. "Even mighty Lucifer made a choice. You must make your choice. The power does not have to be for evil. Even the most vile creatures can serve a good purpose, provided their master encourages them to do so."

"Then I can stop him?"

"Only you." she sighed and laid the cards out on the table. "Would you care to know your future, young man?"

"I don't believe in that stuff." Ryan said knowing how silly it sounded considering everything he had been through in the past few weeks.

"Maybe, little man, it believes in you." she said and started flipping the cards over one at a time. Every single one of them was the Death Card. A figure that looked much like the hooded Grim Reaper holding its tall sickle standing atop a mountain of skulls. Madame Bulvaria gasped and quickly gathered the cards back together in her wide, plump hands. "Wrong deck, I am sorry." she lied. "A trick deck, no doubt."

"It means a whole lot of death ahead, don't it?" Ryan asked and the woman lowered her eyes first to the floor before finding his small doubtful ones with her hazel eyes.

"It could mean lots of things, young one." she said back. Just then the store started to grow darker. The candles blew out from cool winds that had come from the front door. A tingling set of wind chimes sounded out and Ryan could hear heavy footsteps coming down the aisle. "You must go quickly." the woman said struggling to her feet. "You must practice the dark gift you have, young man. Go and practice how to commune and control the dark beasts that are now at your father's command, for they shall be at your command as well if only you learn."

"What about you?" he asked and he could hear deep laughter behind him. Things were being smashed from off the shelves and walls and those heavy boots kept getting closer. "What's going to happen to you?"

"It is only a dream, Ryan." she pointed out. "You must go now. Run to the church, but be watchful of things in the night for he controls them."

"You better believe it bitch." Ryan heard his father's voice say. *"My son's too old for bedtime stories. You don't pay her no never mind, Ryan."* he heard his father say as he backed down an opposite aisle. *"Me and you sharing the same little body, now that's what father and son stuff is all about. I surely aim to show you that."*

"Run, little man!" the big gypsy lady screamed and Ryan turned and ran as he heard his father's laughter rise to an unholy level, the boots picked up speed, and the crashing of glass and wood sounded out as Ryan could hear the woman being attacked with blow after blow as he could see behind him the shadow of a large pony-tailed man beating on her behind the counter.

Ryan heard her screams but kept running with tears streaming over his face as the church grew closer and closer. He was almost there when the bells sounded out in the night. It was almost pitch black now except for the moon which hung up in the sky like a pale coin and the soft light coming from behind the stain glass windows of the church.

"It's too late for us, Ryan." a voice called from the darkness of the church cemetery. Ryan scanned the tombstones for the source of the voice and then saw the big black man coming towards him, his face and arms covered in tiny red bumps. At his feet was their cat Griffin, twisted and dying, crying out with bees covering his gray and black matted fur. "Don't let it keep happening." Mister Kelly warned while a small swarm of bees buzzed about his lumbering frame as he drew near. "You have the power to stop it, boy."

"Mister Kelly?" Ryan asked viewing the man up and down. "Is that you?"

"Scooter to my friends." the black man smiled and honey dripped out of his mouth, drawing more bees to his already scarred face. "Yeah, son, he got me too." he said lifting out his arms while the bees began to cover him completely now. "And he will keep getting everybody *until you give yourself up*." he said, the last part of it sounding more like the bees talking than him. More like his father.

"No!" Ryan said running past him towards the church. "It's not my fault! I don't want to die! There has to be another way!"

Ryan made it to the parking lot when the bells started again. This time much louder. So powerful that Ryan had to stop, fall to his knees, and hold his ears from the pain the ringing was causing. As he knelt there feeling ready to go into the blackness around him he looked up and saw the church itself being ripped apart by the shockwaves the bells were causing.

The great stone walls were cracking and crumbling apart before his eyes. The light had gone out of the windows and the stained glass shattered outward with such force that many tiny shards and fragments sprayed all around where Ryan knelt. He backed away, scuffling on his back like an injured turtle while still holding his ears as best he could, while looking up to see the great towering steeple begin its slow tilt over towards him from above.

"Somebody help me!" he screamed over the bells and watched the cross-tipped steeple do a free fall as it fell from its holding, the rushing wind before it forcing the breath from Ryan's small body, and as he felt himself grow cold and lost in its shadow the huge structure crashed into him. His final scream echoed in the black swirl of dirt and darkness and spinning cold air.

There was no pain. No anything but pitch cold black, and then a voice.

"Flesh of my flesh. Blood of my blood." his father's voice called from somewhere not so far away, yet distant enough he could not see or feel him. *"Spirit of my spirit."*

Soft laughter and then Ryan awoke from his nightmare with a rapid heartbeat, a gasp of deep breath, and a sigh of relief. He lay there in a bed that was not his own, or the good Father Leary's. There was soft light coming from an open window spattered with rain, unfamiliar voices from a brightly lit hallway, and a painting of two women picking apples in a field of trees.

"Doctor, he's awake." an older woman's voice called out from the doorway. A nurse?

"I'm in a freaking hospital." Ryan thought with another sigh and drifted back to sleep.

TWENTY EIGHT

Mister Leonard Darby woke up with a bad headache as usual from his hangover. He had spent the night in back of the Laundromat in between two large dumpsters to block the chilled winds on top of pieces of cardboard and under a car cover he found weeks ago and blocks away to keep the rain off him. Now it was mid-afternoon and he finally decided to do the vertical thing and get moving. He needed some lunch money soon.

He made his way down the alley towards Delaware Road where traffic was picking up for lunch hour. Lunch hour was a damn good time to beg for money. They were already there, they had their money ready, and most were pretty damn civil. He never asked for much. Some told him to get lost or get a job or go find a shelter. Sometimes folks were nice and those who knew him as a regular would toss him some change. It was enough for some breakfast down at Bella's Diner or he could save it for later for a few stiff drinks down at the Thunderbolt, a gritty red neck bar down by the train tracks on the south side of town. It was a long walk but they liked him there and nobody tried to give him shit or kick his ass afterwards like some of the bars around here in town.

Darby didn't make it to the street that afternoon though, at least not in a way he would have imagined. Instead, as he rounded the corner and caught sight of the small stream of cars and pedestrians, he noticed something odd. Something he had never seen in all the years he had been hanging around this part of town. Three large dogs all seated next to each other there at the edge of the alley. They all stared blankly at the far wall, as if waiting for some movie to start, and only when Darby grew closer did the one in the middle, a Husky, spark to life and move forward.

"Well, now." Darby said smiling his near toothless grin. "What have we here?" he said noticing the Great Dane, which was just named Thor not too many days ago unknown to him, and an old boxer called Brute, followed the Husky called Marley out to meet the old man in the middle of the trash littered alley. "If yer lookin' fer scraps I can tell ya, I'm fresh out boys. Even if I had 'em they would be fer me."

"We're looking for you, old man." Marley spoke up and Darby stood still fast, looking around the hidden places in the long alley that divided his way to Delaware Street. His old blurred eyes scanned the trashcans and broken pallets and skids for any sign of teenagers. They were the worst. Too many times

136

had he been awakened in the night to find himself getting an ass beating from a group of rowdy teen boys. Once they even filmed it and put it on the Internet, or so he heard.

"Who's here?" he called backing away without even looking at the dogs.

"We are." Marley said in Alan Wood's voice. *"Look at me, stew bum!"*

Darby did look. His breath caught in him as he stared down at the large black and white Husky that stood only a few feet directly in front of him. The big black and gray Great Dane flanked him to his left while the old brown Boxer shuffled over to his right blocking the way he had just come from. There was still a retreat up the alleyway straight behind him, but somehow Darby had the idea he could not outrun all three dogs today, or any day in the past twenty years or so, so he remained still for now. It was clearly their move.

"What the hell is this horse shit?" he said shaking his head to clear the cobwebs. "I'm either still dreaming or still drunk or this is a hell of a practical joke." he said with a nervous laugh. "You mutts got microphones on your collars?" he laughed, then noticed that Marley did not have a collar.

"No, sir." the Husky spoke again and this time Darby could see the mouth actually moving and forming the words. *"You're wide fucking awake, old timer. This is no joke. We got some business to discuss. Serious business."*

"This is freakin' nuts." Darby said reaching into his jacket pocket for his knife. It wasn't much of a weapon actually. A small carving knife he used to peel apples. It looked even smaller when he pulled it out and the dog laughed at him when he held it out in the light of day.

"You going to stop us with that?" the Husky asked coming closer. *"You even move to cut me or my brothers here and we will tear your throat out. You hear me? But first we will snack on your old shriveled nuts. You will feel pain for a long while before we finish you off."*

Darby put the knife away as the other two dogs growled, bearing teeth and moving in closer behind him. Every one of them looked big and bad enough to take him on their own. The three of them would turn him into meatloaf pretty damn fast, he imagined. So regardless of how insane all of this was, he decided to go along for the ride for now until he could see a means of escape.

"Okay, hell with it, it's gone now." he said holding out his hands in surrender while keeping his eyes focused on the street ahead. "I'm not trying nothing."

"You try to scream and we rip you up in shreds too." the Husky said following his watchful eyes to the street. *"We just got a favor to ask."*

Darby stood there paralyzed in the slight sunshine of a cool autumn afternoon. This was the kind of story you would laugh at if you heard it being told at the local pub. He could picture himself down there at the Thunderbolt telling Ike the bartender and Cliff and a few others who showed up tonight that he woke up this afternoon and found himself encircled by a trio of dogs. One of which was actually talking. No big deal, just wanted a favor is all. Yeah, that would go over well right before he ended up being permanently cut off from the bar forever.

"Favor?" he asked feeling stupid and scared as he stood here having a conversation with a talking Husky while his two buddies blocked his escape. "What would you want from me? "What in God's name are you?"

"There's a fortune telling bitch across the street." the big dog said nodding its head back in the direction of Delaware. *"She might help somebody that I don't want helped. I can't have that."*

"Madame Bulvaria?" Darby said looking out towards the open street a good thirty yards away.

"What do you want me to do about it?"

"I just need to borrow something from you for a minute or two." the dog grinned stepping closer.

"I ain't got nothing for you to borrow." the old man half grinned still scared out of his mind as he kept looking for a way to escape this nightmare. "Ain't got a pot to piss in or a window to throw it out of. Ain't got piss period."

"Oh, but you do, Darby." the dog said leaping up and knocking the man down on his back while pinning him to the ground while the other two dogs moved in to hold his arms down with their mouths and the sheer weight of their huge frames. *"I need to borrow your body."*

"What? No!" he said and then Marley's mouth was pressed tightly up against his as if the dog were trying to revive him with mouth-to-mouth resuscitation. There was a second of pain, a flash of light, and a series of memories that somehow he knew were not his own. Fires burning, people screaming, gunshots and then all was cold and dark and Mister Leonard Darby, a man who had failed at life and gave up way too early, felt tears running down his cheeks as he faded into another world. He had a feeling he would not be coming back anytime soon.

***

"A love potion, you say Mister Kessler?" Madame Bulvaria asked the man at the counter. He was a tall drink of water, barely any hair left, dressed in polyester slacks and an outdated shirt with a skinny cloth tie that she had not seen men wearing since the 1980's. He didn't need a love potion, he needed a fashion coordinator. "You have exhausted every other avenue with this woman?"

"Oh, yes." he grinned, his little fuzzy mustache twitching. "She's a school teacher, such a kind woman and so beautiful, but won't give me the time of day. I've tried polite conversation, sent her flowers twice, even left a note on her car."

"You may want to be a bit more careful." the gypsy woman warned with a smile. "People can get themselves fired for sexual harassment very easily these days."

"Yes, I guess that's true. I just can't seem to help myself. I know I'm losing my hair and my body has seen better days and-"

"I think I may have something that will at least . . . perk her interest." she said rummaging through the bottles on the shelf. She pulled out a tall blue bottle with clear liquid inside. She smiled bringing it back to the counter and setting it before him. "This is very strong so you only use a bit."

"Got it." the man said digging out his wallet. "Don't drink it all at once."

"No, silly man." she laughed and her earrings and looped bracelets clanged against each other as she did. "You do not drink this. You place little dabs behind your ears and on your neck. You make sure you get close enough to her for her to smell it, but not too close or too often. We don't want a fatal attraction, no?"

"No, of course not." he said picking up the container and looking the contents over carefully. "Looks like water." he said giving her a worried glance.

"It is clear, but it is so much more." she said. "Open the top and take a small whiff. Nothing too deep for too long, and keep it a few inches away from your nose. We can't have you falling in love with yourself." she laughed and he laughed with her. "That would be no good."

"Oh, my." he said drawing his head back after the first hint of aroma. "That is nice. Smells like some kind of exotic flower."

"Yes, there is that too." she said. "And so much more. I can not tell you all the contents, you understand?" she grinned and heard the tiny wind-chimes ring out the arrival of a new customer. "That would be bad for business."

"Of course." he said. "I don't imagine you have any cards or flowers to go with this?"

"This is not a gift shop, Mister Kessler." she said with her eyes narrowing when she recognized who the new patron was. The bum, Mister Darby, who hung out by the Laundromat and begged for coinage and smelled of foul dead things along with liquor. He carried what looked like a watering bucket with him in one hand. "There is a florist two blocks over. Perhaps you can go there, but from what you told me that venture has already failed."

"I guess, but maybe with this stuff on my neck and behind my ears like you said, it might help add a little extra *zoommfff!!*" he said grinning as he shot out his arms. "You think?"

"You do whatever you think is best." she said watching Darby stop midway down the aisle and stop to nose about some hanging bags of herbs. "That will be twenty-one fifty."

"For one bottle of this?" he asked holding the small bottle up with wide eyes. "For a tiny bottle of cologne?"

"You either want this woman or you do not." Madame Bulvaria said still watching the drunken bum. "Love has a price here, Mister Kessler."

"Fine." the balding man said slipping her two tens and a five. "I don't suppose there is a money back guarantee on this stuff."

"Of course. If there are no results within, let's say, two weeks please come back and-"

Madame Bulvaria never got to finish her refund promise because Mister Kessler's head was yanked backwards by the bum with one hand as another came around with a small knife and slit the man's throat right in front of her. Mister Kessler's eyes went wide, his mouth opened to make a small inaudible remark as his tall frame slid down in a quivering heap in front of the counter. She screamed as the bum smiled at her with a wicked gleam in his eye as he lifted the knife up and licked the fresh blood off the blade.

"Well now, it's just you and me." Darby said stepping forward after reaching down and lifting up the watering bucket. He started to pour the contents there in front of the counter and Madame Bulvaria

could tell from the look and stench that it was gasoline he was pouring out, not water. *"I'm afraid after the dream that Ryan had I have to eliminate any help he might get."*

"I don't understand what you're talking about." the big woman said nearly falling off her stool as he rounded the counter with his little sharp knife. "Who is Ryan? What are doing with that gasoline? I have customers coming, you won't get away with this!"

"He dreamed about you, see, and in that dream, you helped him." the bum smiled and Madame Bulvaria knew this was not the same voice the bum had from the many times she passed him on the street. Same smell as before, same stance and clothing, but the face was different, more twisted and sinister, and that voice, something from the grave or beyond.

"What evil thing are you?" she finally managed while backing towards the phone. Next to the phone was a letter opener done up in the shape of an ancient scimitar sword. It wasn't exactly sharp edged, but she thought it might prove to be defensive enough for this little man and whatever it was inside him now. "Why do you possess this man you now inhabit?"

"Clever girl." the old man smiled with Alan's Woods grin setting the bucket down. *"I've come to remove a threat. You may not understand what this is about but you will die all the same."*

She snatched up the letter opener as he took a few more steps nearer, just as he raised up the carving knife to attack, and made an attack of her own.

"Back to hell with you, unknown demon!" she called out and sliced at the old man's face. He staggered backwards lifting one aged hand up to see the blood from the mark she made across the tender and weak flesh of his face. He smiled at the sight of it.

"Not my body to worry about." he said raising the knife again. *"Go ahead and kill the old beggar. I have many eyes around here. Many little friends I can send for."* he said and knelt as quick as the old man's body would allow and made a fast cut across the woman's large belly. She squealed out as the bright fabric gave way to let blood flow from her fresh wound. He swung a few more times, each time striking either her torso or her heavy thick arms she used to block with.

"Get away from me! You will not be the end of me!" she screamed and charged him using her full weight and the little man, possessed or not, went tumbling backwards from her sheer mass. The thing that was once a bum simply shook off the assault and smiled up at her and laughed.

141

"I will be the end of all there is." the old man grinned tossing the remains at her dress and the carpeted floor. He watched her turn for the phone while balancing her huge wounded body as he rolled over to one side and furiously dug for the lighter.

"Please, please help me!" she screamed into the phone as the lighter sparked to life. "He killed a man already. Please help." she sounded out of breath and strength and Alan Woods, inside the fragile and weak-hearted old Leonard Darby, just gave a grin as he tossed the old lighter down to the soaked carpet of gasoline at her feet.

"Burn, baby, burn." he said to her while watching her huge frame light up in flames. *"And me without my marshmallows."*

He watched the fire swoop across the carpet and up the big woman's bright dress engulfing her completely in a matter of seconds. She screamed with much pain into the phone which dropped from her hands and was consumed along with her. *"Come on, boy! Hurry!"* he called and Marley came charging up to the old man, and much as before, gave him a deep kiss to transfer the man back into his canine body.

"There we are, all done with you Mister Darby." the dog told the old man who screamed as the flames also began to cover him as well. *"Thanks for the favor."* he finished and the two burning humans together made beautiful screams to the dog's ears as it ran back out of the shop.

It would go and sit across the street with its two other canine brethren and watch the fire until help arrived. The entire place would be consumed by then of course. Both parties dead and out of the way. Then they would go together to pay a visit to another man who seemed to be in the way. He lived close.

"Only a few more left to go." the dog said watching the building billow out black clouds of smoke. *"Then it will just be me and him. Me and my boy."*

Alan Woods actually felt his pseudo tail wagging at the excitement of it all.

TWENTY NINE

Two steaming cups of coffee on the table, an open bible, a rather large gun on the table, and then sirens in the distance.

"Sounds like a fire-engine." the priest said standing and moving along with his fresh mug of coffee through the living room to the open window viewing the street. "Not the church, thank God." he said watching the bright red truck fly by soon to be followed by an ambulance. Laura Woods watched as he made a sign of the cross over his chest before turning back to her. He looked different now that he had changed into jeans and a black sweater and sneakers. More like a blue collar worker than a white collar priest. "Looks like one of the little shops up the street caught fire. I pray everyone is okay." he said looking the woman's blank face over. She was distant, eyes staring deep into the wall, through it in fact, lost in thought. "Laura?"

"We were in the middle of getting a divorce." she told him. "Alan and I were. Things weren't working out, they had been bad for a while."

"His doing?" Father Leary said leaning into the wall with crossed arms.

"He drank too much for my taste, more than when we dated, and he just seemed to get in such dark moods. Strange, dark moods that came up from nowhere."

"From what I heard about his past I guess we know why." he said back.

"I guess I knew he was cheating and he pretty much ignored me and Amy, but he always had an attraction to Ryan."

"Do you mean that he . . . made moves on Ryan in any sort of way? That he tried to-"

"No, no, not like that." she shook her head and blinked with a deep sigh. "He spoke to him more, hung out with him whenever he could, wanted to know everything about him."

"Why do you think that is?"

"Alan found out he was dying of cancer. His company doctor told him a few months before he died. The funny part is, if you want to call it that, is that he didn't even seem to care. He just said it was no big deal. It was like he was expecting it."

"Maybe he knew he could come back even then." the priest sighed himself.

143

"How can this be happening?" she asked as he sunk back into his chair. She leaned back as he did and they stared at each other across the table. She waited for an answer that he didn't have. He noticed how striking she looked fully dressed as well, although the clothing was not her own or very flattering. The jeans were a bit too big, the shirt also hung on her like a scarecrow's garment, but she was a pretty woman and kept her beauty despite what they had just been through. She was the prettiest woman he had known in years. "How can Alan be back from the dead?"

"I wish I knew." he said watching her pop yet another butterscotch into her mouth. "Hope you don't mind the clothes. That was about all they had that would fit."

"Not really my style, but better than a towel." she smiled with some subtle embarrassment while stretching the oversized shirt out in front of her.

"Van Halen?" Father Leary said finally getting a good look at the shirt. "I saw them in concert once. Back in the early eighties."

"You did?" Laura grinned with surprise letting the shirt pop back into place.

"I wasn't *born* a priest, Laura." he laughed at her expression. "I used to go to rock concerts, drink beer and Jack Daniel's, smoke weed . . ." he said pausing to see her eyes go big as pie plates again. " . . . and some other things I can't tell you about. But I got the calling. I chose God over those things and haven't regretted it since."

"I hope you and God are as close as you make it seem." she said. "There are too many things going on I don't understand."

"This is new territory for me as well, Laura. The bible gives examples of demon possession and evil spirits, but nothing like this. Not on this level. Your husband evidently found a way back from hell somehow. Either that or some demon is doing a very fine job of impersonating him. But I do believe its him, and so does your son."

"Why?" she asked. "Why does he want my son?"

"Like I said before, I believe he wants to take him over. He wants to do to him what he did to you back at your house, only permanently. He wants to continue doing the horrible things he did when he was alive. Your son said he was the Boogeyman. As silly as that sounds it may be quite accurate in a way."

"So you believe he was more than just a man when he was alive?" she asked.

"It's possible from what I have seen." Father Leary said shaking his head. "Trust me I would have laughed at all of this only a few days ago, but now I don't know. All I know is that he wants your son and that he has to be stopped. I think I made a mistake taking Ryan to school though. I think we should go and get him and the three of us need to find a safer place to be until we can decide what to do next."

"I agree. If he could take me over who's to say he couldn't take over somebody up at school." Laura pointed out and spit the butterscotch out into her coffee. "Okay, no offense, but this candy thing isn't working. May I please have a cigarette? Just one?" she asked with pouting lips and Father Leary broke a grin as he rose up from his chair. "I'll smoke it outside."

"I suppose one wouldn't kill you." he said heading for the garage. "Just so happens I still have a pack left out here. You smoke one, outside of course, then we get Ryan."

"Thank you so much." she said standing to follow him. "Just a few quick puffs. I probably need to call the market and tell them I won't be coming in today."

"If you have any vacation time now would be the time to use it." he said opening the garage door and clicking on the lights. "We have no idea how long this will take us." He said noticing he had forgotten to close the garage door and a cool breeze chilled his body as he walked past the Jeep to the workbench where the rusted Maxwell House can sat. The voice spoke out before his hand found the pack of smokes.

"You left the door up, Padre." the husky said from the side of the Jeep. *"Kinda careless of you."*

"Marley?" the priest said recognizing Benjamin Kelly's dog, and then corrected himself. "Alan?"

Father Leary stood still for a brief second, his hand in mid-reach for the coffee can and his head turned to see the dog lying there by the back tire. *"You try anything and my boys will rip that bitch inside to pieces."* the dog warned. Father Leary's eyes shifted back to the pegboard, a nice sized rubber mallet hung there along side a long screwdriver and monkey wrench.

"You're here to do that anyway, aren't you Alan?" he said to the dog snatching up the mallet.

"Smart man." the dog said rising up. *"So its Alan now? First name basis and all? Guess you're a believer? That won't save your ass."*

"What's going on?" Laura said edging closer. "Who are you talking to?"

"Stay in there Laura!" Father Leary said. "Don't move!"

"Not sure I like you giving my wife orders, Padre." the dog said.

145

"Where's Ben Kelly? This is his dog you're inside of now. What did you do?" the priest asked.

"Sometimes a dog is not a man's best friend." the dog actually smiled at him. "He should have stayed the hell away from my boy. Same goes for you."

"I know what you want." The priest said bracing himself for the dog's attack. "You won't get your son. Not unless you go through me first."

"Yeah, so you said back at the house." the dog said. "As long as life is in your body, or some brave-ass shit like that. Well, sounds good to me." the dog backed up and leaned its head out in the direction of the yard. "Take em both! Now!"

Glass shattered and Thor, a huge Great Dane that had once belonged to Jeffery Bates and his grieving family, came leaping through the kitchen window where Laura Woods stood waiting for her cigarette. She screamed and moved back towards the counter as the large dog skidded across the linoleum floor. It looked like a small horse to her.

"Grab the gun!" Father Leary yelled striking out at the husky leaping up at him. A glancing blow to the beasts shoulder, a loud yelp, and then the dog had him back up against the wall. "Take more than you have to stop me, Woods." the priest said shoving the dog back.

"Let's find out." the dog said stepping back a few paces and Father Leary saw another dog enter the garage. A large brown Boxer growling as it ran up the opposite side of the Jeep. "Hope you know how to multi-task, Father." the Husky said coming at him again, while Brute the Boxer went after his legs.

***

"Father Leary!" Laura called out as the huge Great Dane came at her. She did not realize the trouble the priest was having until she ran past the open doorway and saw him trying to strangle a huge Husky while a Boxer had a strong grip on his right leg trying to pull him off balance. She was about to help him when the Great Dane slammed into her sending her body rebounding off the dishes on the counter and then to the floor.

Plates shattered and silverware and broken glass rained down on her as the monstrous dog rounded the table both growling and slobbering as it moved in for the kill. Father Leary had cried out about the gun but it was too late. Everything was happening too fast. The dog had placed itself between her and the weapon. Her hand shot out and found a steak knife, not much of a weapon perhaps, but lunged out at the dog as it moved in over her. The big animal cried out in pain as she sliced its snout, backed up a few paces, then attacked her legs. It bit deep. Laura shrieked feeling the blood flowing already and leaned up trying to slice the dog again. She couldn't reach it. Every time she leaned up to strike the big dog, it would drag her legs and cause her to fall back again. Laura grabbed up plates and broken glass and starting tossing them at the thing's head. It finally let go and moved back some, licking fresh blood from its chops while Laura pulled herself over to the edge of the table. The gun was up there somewhere. She hoped the safety was off.

"Please God." she said reaching for the chair to brace herself. "Save me so I can save my son."

She stood, the pain stinging her as she did, and saw the weapon on the opposite side of the table. She would have to make it to the other side. "Shit." she breathed watching the dog prepare to leap for her. "Here goes nothing."

***

Father Leary's left arm was bleeding from where Marley, also now Alan Woods, had bit him. His right leg was not in great shape either from the Boxer. He tried not to think about what was happening to Laura Woods in his kitchen. He heard the window break, her screams and a dog growling, but no gunshot. Either she never got to the gun or never had a chance to use it. He might soon be joining her.

"Off!" he cried out forcing the grinning Husky onto the Boxer that had his leg. He struck down with the mallet repeatedly not really sure which dog he was hitting but happy to hear the sounds of pain coming from one of them. "You won't have him!"

"*I'll have you all.*" the man's voice swore as the Husky leapt up onto the hood of his Jeep.

"No!" the priest yelled and slammed the mallet a few more times down again on the aging Boxer that lay still at his feet. More blood spilled onto the concrete floor and the priest felt bad that he had to kill this dog that was probably acting against its own will but he had little choice. "Your turn." he breathed up at the dog on the hood. "Come on, let's finish this."

147

"You look tired, Padre." the Husky teased. *"You're bleeding. Better get that looked at."*

"As soon as I'm done with you." the priest grinned and heard Laura scream as a shot was fired. "Laura!" he called out and headed for the door. The big Husky leapt out and brought him down to the blood soaked floor.

"We're not done yet." the dog grinned down as it opened its mouth to reveal many teeth. Father Leary held the big dog by its furry throat trying to force the mouth and those shark looking teeth away from him but the mouth just kept getting closer.

"Laura!" he called out hoping she had finished off whatever dog was attacking her with that gunshot still echoing in his ears. "A little help please!"

***

Laura did manage to grab hold of the gun, but Thor had managed to bite into her arm as she did, causing her to fire the gun. She shot the wall, shattering a nice picture of Father Leary in his younger days standing along side perhaps his brother and father on a riverbank, each proudly displaying a nice size fish of some kind dangling from their hands. She used her free hand to punch the Great Dane in the head while trying to bring her bleeding arm around for good aim at the dog's body.

"Get off me, Marmaduke." she said rolling across the table, watching the thing's eyes seemingly glow with dark swirls of green. They both rolled off the table onto the floor, luckily the dog hit first and took most of the broken glass in it's hide instead of hers, and she took the momentary distraction to switch hands with the gun. Thor saw this and let go of her arm in an attempt to escape. Laura was not having it. The single gunshot exploded the dog's head away from anything normal looking and a good deal of it's blood and bone fragments hit her solid in the face.

She back peddled away on bleeding palms gasping for air never taking her eyes off the dog while spitting debris from her mouth and lips. It was dead, but then again so was her husband. Maybe it could come back to life like he did. She snatched up the gun and took aim again just in case it stirred and pulled a Jason number on her, coming back to life at the last minute. It did not. Whatever evil had been inside the dog was gone now. Nothing now but flesh, blood and bones. Big ass bones.

"Laura!" the priests voice again.

"Oh shit!" she breathed and started to rise up to help him but the combined pain in her legs and arms dropped her to the floor again wincing in agony. "Shit!"

***

"Your faith is wavering again, father." the dog breathed on him still inching closer with those shark teeth. *"Maybe you're in the wrong profession."*

"Never." the priest said trying his best to press the big dog back off his chest. The damned thing seemed to be getting heavier. Maybe, he thought, since one or two of the dogs are gone all the strength has returned to him. He wasn't sure how it worked or if he wanted to know, but he knew if he didn't do something quickly he was going to die.

His eyes scanned for weapons. The rubber mallet was too far out of reach. The only gun he owned was in there with Laura. He heard the gun go off again, but still no Laura. Maybe she was wounded too bad to help him. He did notice something when he looked up over his head on the lower shelf just behind him. A small red dot on a charger. A *drill* charger. But could he reach it with one free hand while holding off the widening mouth descending on him with the other? He didn't think so, but it was his only chance.

"Hey, you worthless fuck!" came a voice from the kitchen door. Both man and possessed beast turned their heads in the direction of the light shining out on them. It was Laura, bloody and worn, and laying flat on her belly with hair in her eyes, but she had the gun.

"Bitch survived. What do ya know about that." the Husky said.

Father Leary moved fast. He pushed off with one hand and grabbed the drill, switched the damn thing on, and brought it back right into that large gapping mouth. The dog part of the thing howled in pain and somewhere deep inside that black wet throat past all of those teeth, he thought maybe he heard Alan Woods scream a bit too. That was nice. But it wasn't enough.

"Die fucker!" the dog said diving down for his throat now that the two hand grip had been released, but another shot rang out and most of Marley's head exploded into kibbles and bits all over the

149

garage floor. Father Leary sighed relief while toppling the body off him and grabbed his heart while taking slow deep breaths.

"You okay?" the wounded woman asked letting the gun fall from her hands.

"No, but I will live." he said back. "You?"

"I think an ambulance sounds good." she said mostly into the floor. "Damn thing bit me a few times."

"Me too." he breathed back.

"Think there are any more?" she asked trying to prop herself up against the wall.

"If so I think they would have moved on us by now." he said coming up to a sitting position. "We really should get to the ER"

"Who's driving?" she smiled trying to study herself while rising up.

"I'm all for that ambulance-calling thing." he said pointing towards the phone there at the entrance way by the kitchen door. "Give it a shot."

"What do I tell them?" she asked stretching out while slithering up against the wall like a snake finally taking hold of the receiver while making sounds of obvious pain and discomfort.

"Anything but the truth." he told her. "And that we might need rabies shots."

"You're going to need more than that." the voice of Alan Woods called from outside the garage door. Laura jerked the gun in the direction of the open door and Father Leary waved at her to drop her aim.

"Don't waste any bullets on that." the priest said seeing the large crow sitting atop his mailbox just outside at the edge of his sidewalk. "He'd just switch bodies again. That thing can't hurt us."

"I'll find something else that can, Padre, you bet on that shit." the crow said and flew away.

"Bastard." Laura managed to breathe. "He's going to keep coming."

"They say fear has many eyes and can see underground. I guess it can see from the skies as well now. Call the ambulance." Father Leary said coming towards her slowly leaning against first the tool bench and then the Jeep. "Then call the school and check on your son."

THIRTY

When Ryan Woods awoke again it was Tuesday morning and people he mostly knew surrounded him. Seated to his left was his mother, the worn tired look still on her face, and now her arm and leg were bandaged. She smiled weakly and took his hand. Standing over her with his own arm and leg bandaged as well was Father Leary. Over at the foot of the bed was a doctor and nurse he didn't recognize and then by the doorway was Sergeant Lambert with his big arms crossed and his shades still on despite the fact he was indoors.

"Hey, baby." his mother said squeezing his hand. " I heard you had quite a rough day yesterday."

"Looks like I'm not the only one." he said feeling the dryness of his throat as he spoke. "What happened to you two?"

"Long story for another day." Father Leary said and when they made eye contact Ryan could see the good priest rolling his eyes back in the direction of the trio at the end of the bed. Ryan understood this to be a hint that perhaps it was best they did not speak of what the three of them shared in front of anymore strangers. Ryan nodded in silent agreement. "We will be fine. What can't be cured must be endured. All patched up now. You're the main concern."

"You have way too many quotes." Ryan smiled weakly.

"How are we feeling, Ryan?" the skinny doctor with the pencil thin mustache asked coming up to him with the smiling nurse with blonde hair and breasts the size of fresh cantaloupe. Ryan found his stare glued there as the doctor continued. "My name is Doctor Keaton. From what we understand you had an altercation at school and then passed out. Any of this sound familiar to you?"

"I remember the fight." Ryan said thinking of the Butler Boys. "Steven Butler was talking crap about Amy so I guess I lost my temper. We fought some, it was only a few punches, then they ran away, then everything started spinning."

"You're going to be fine, Ryan." the doctor promised with a pat on the shoulder. "Just passed out is all. All of your tests came back fine. Now if you all will excuse me, I have rounds to make. Ryan, you take care of yourself."

"Ryan? I hate to bother you under the current circumstances but I need a few details."

It was Sergeant Lambert who spoke in his deep voice of authority. Ryan noticed no bandages or wounds on him and assumed he was still ignorant to what was happening.

"Sure, go ahead." he whispered and the nurse took a pitcher of cold water and filled a plastic see-through cup nearly to the brim before handing it to him. He took little sips and stole glances of her exposed cleavage while the big cop continued.

"Now, Steven Butler and his brother Shaun said you had some *rats* or mice or something with you and that's why they ran away." the big Sergeant smiled and both he and the nurse laughed. Ryan shifted his gaze over to both his mother and Father Leary. They did not laugh. They did manage a pair of phony smiles on their faces.

"Well, I guess he would make up anything to get out of losing a fight." Ryan suggested. "Even with his little brother there who wasn't much help. They ran off and made up some story I guess. I didn't see any rats or mice."

"That's what I thought." Sergeant Lambert said reaching down and patting the boys' legs. "Guy lost to you and wanted to cover it up. No problem. I get that. Glad you're feeling better. I have to go and check on that fire they had out on Delaware yesterday, see if it's getting handled properly." he said tipping his hat to Laura. "I'll see you later, Laura. Take care of each other."

"We will Wes, thanks." his mother said watching the big lawman saunter out of the room and Ryan thought that was the first time he had heard Sergeant Lambert's first name. Wes, as in Wesley. Plus the fact if came from his mother made him wonder if his earlier thoughts about her having feelings for him were true or not. It was kind of a shame because if Thomas Leary were not a priest he thought he would be perfect for his mother.

"I'll go and get the slugger's paperwork in order." the healthy nurse smiled and followed the big Sergeant out the door.

"Looks like you have some girl's attention." his mother grinned patting his arm.

"God, mom, she's like twenty years older than me." Ryan said eyeing the nurse as she rounded the corner. His mother and Father Leary laughed at the misunderstanding.

"No, silly." she said patting his exposed arm once more. "You have a phone number on your arm. I am assuming it's some young lady your own age."

"Oh." he said nearly forgetting the other afternoon in Mister Kelly's store. It seemed like an entire lifetime ago. Back when the big black man was still alive. "Yeah, Anna Finch."

"Pretty name." Father Leary chimed in.

"Pretty girl." Ryan added. "She gave me her number. She invited me to a Halloween party at her friends uncle's farm." his face went blank as his eyes dropped. "Supposed to be a bunch of kids there. Music and food. Normal stuff."

"You can still go." his mother said. "If you want."

"Not sure that's a good idea." he said up to them both. "More people might get hurt if I go. I'm afraid to even call her now. What if something . . . you know . . . happens because she knows me? I dreamed that Mister Kelly died. Is that true?"

He watched his mother lower her head as Father Leary knelt down next to him.

"Sergeant Lambert just told us." the priest said while placing his big hand on his shoulder and giving it a squeeze. "Neighbor woman found him in the garage. He was . . ."

"Stung by bees." Ryan said and felt his own throat swelling again. "In freaking October."

"They're saying it's a stroke. Why do you say bees?"

"Just something I saw in my dreams. I think he was afraid of them."

"It's not your fault, Ryan." the priest said. "None of this is."

His mother leaned in, brushed his hair back, and kissed him softly on the forehead. She stood, obviously still in pain from the involuntary noises she made, and headed for the door.

"I'm going to see about that paperwork, and maybe some pain pills for me and Father Leary, then we are taking you out of here." she said. "Be right back."

"Don't worry about the party, Ryan." Father Leary said seating himself down in the chair his mother had vacated. "There will be others. Anna Finch isn't going anywhere."

"So what happened to you guys?" Ryan said looking the priest up and down.

"Your father sent dogs after us yesterday." Father Leary said after making sure they were alone. "He was in possession of one of them. Mister Kelly's dog. Nearly got us too. Lucky I had a gun and your mom knew how to use it."

"So you believe it's my father now?" Ryan asked with hopeful eyes.

"Hard to deny what you see and hear." he said leaning in. "We have to figure something out fast."

"I think I have." Ryan said also peeking to make sure nobody was in the hallway. "I had a dream. You know that occult shop on Delaware? Madame Bulvaria's?"

"Oh, yes." the priest said with a sly grin. "Most of my congregation has been trying to get rid of that place for the past two years since it moved in. What about it?"

"The lady there, she was in my dream." the boy said taking his hand. "She told me I am my father's son. She said I could control them the same way he can. She said I have the same gift he does."

"Ryan, this was just a dream, son." the priest pointed out. "I think if you had any of these powers you would have known by now that-"

"What Sergeant Lambert said happened at the school, what the Butler brothers said, it happened."

"What?" Father Leary said looking deep into the boys fearing eyes. "The rats? Really?"

"They just came out of my sleeves." he said. "I didn't even know I was doing it. I was mad and they just came out from nowhere."

"My God." the priest breathed. "You have what he has. No small wonder he wants you. Not just your living body but your if your abilities were matched with his own there would be no stopping him."

"What fire was Sergeant Lambert talking about?" Ryan said trying to force the images of the rats from his mind. "He said it was on Delaware."

"Yes, we heard those fire trucks this morning." Father Leary said and they both stared at each other in silence. "I'm guessing your father found out she helped you, even if it was just in your dreams."

"One more person dead." Ryan said. "She told me I had to practice with what I had. I had to get better if I was going to face him."

"We're getting you out of here and back to my house." Father Leary said standing. "I'm not sure how your mother will take this news."

"Doesn't matter." Ryan said sitting up anxious to leave. "It's all we have. I have to face him."

"You will not be facing him alone." the priest promised. "I won't argue with you on that."

"Me either." Ryan half way grinned up at the man. "I need you there in case I screw it all up."

THIRTY ONE

Ryan knew the three dead dogs. At least he was pretty sure he did.

He helped Father Leary move the dogs bodies from the house to the back of his Jeep. The first one was Brute. He had just seen the Boxer the other day sleeping under the Wagner's porch. The Great Dane had to be Thor, Jeff's dog, from the description his dead friend had given him. And he knew for a fact that Mister Kelly had a Husky. His father had summoned them to attack Father Leary and his mother. He had failed. But there was still loss of life. They might have just been dogs but they were three more innocent lives his father was responsible for sacrificing.

After they were loaded the man and boy headed back into the house where the priest took to the task of boarding up the window Thor had broken on his way in. His mother sat on the couch considering the story he had told her on the way over while drinking coffee and finishing off a bag of butterscotch.

"How can you be like him?" she asked. "He's a monster and you're my son."

"I'm his son too, mom." Ryan said back. "What will you do with the dogs?" Ryan turned and asked the priest who was nailing some plywood over the window after he had cleared the shattered remains of glass away. "Just curious. You gonna bury them?"

"I know a man who owns a junkyard out by Miller Road. He will let me bury them there." Father Leary said banging away. "What I'd like to know is how are you going to find out if this power is really yours or not and if you can control it. I mean it's not like I can coach you or there's a book on the subject."

"Might have been one at Madame Bulvaria's." Ryan guessed thinking of how the place looked when they drove past it not long ago. Burnt to the ground, only the framework remained. Nothing left but bricks and blood. Sergeant Lambert was there and as Father Leary slowed while they passed the big cop waved them to a stop and told him what he knew so far. He was quite a gossip for a man.

"Fire Chief says it was started in the back by gasoline." he told the trio leaning on the Jeep while a few men shifted around in the rubble behind him. "Found our fortune teller's body and two other bodies yet unidentified. Both male. Not sure what happened but it's definitely on purpose. Maybe an arson."

"Or the Boogeyman got them." Ryan thought to himself thinking of the car fire his father had died in years ago. He seemed to like fire a hell of a lot.

Ryan stopped listening and looked the other way past his mother to the Laundromat. Mister Darby was nowhere to be seen. He was almost certain one of those two men had been him. Two birds with one stone in his father's favor. Three including the stranger Ryan did not know about lying in there like life-sized charcoal on the floor. All because of that dream. His father didn't want any outside help. That was why she was dead, and why he tried to kill his mom and Father Leary with the dogs. He wanted this fight just between the two of them. Father versus son.

"Well, we will have to depend on you learning for yourself." Father Leary said shocking him back into the present tense. "I have my gun, but Lord knows your father can find plenty more dogs to send after us. Or something worse. I'll be out of clips before he's done."

"Ryan? Father Leary?" his mother called from the living room and her voice sounded desperate and afraid. Father Leary came down the ladder as fast as his legs would allow and then he followed Ryan to the living room.

"What's wrong, mom?" the boy asked following his mothers' stare to the front window. She pointed and Ryan saw the dozens of spiders crawling about there searching for a way inside. Big ones like tarantulas you saw in the horror movies. "Oh, man."

"Now's your chance, Ryan." the priest said coming up behind him. "Let's see what you can do."

"What are you talking about?" his mother said jumping up and blocking the way of her son. "We have to get in that Jeep and get the hell out of here! They're all over!"

"And where we would go, Laura?" he asked her taking Ryan closer to the window that had doubled in spider count. "Where in the world would we run and hide from spiders and snakes and bees? From dogs or rats or God knows what else he can control?"

"Don't worry." Ryan said walking slow and steady to the window. "I'm not afraid."

"You should be, boy." the voice came from outside and Ryan saw the large crow perched there on the porch railing. "I won't stop coming for you."

"Maybe you won't . . ." Ryan said parting the drapes and placing both hands on the glass that was nearly black with the army of arachnids. " . . . but they will. Leave us alone." he whispered and felt a tingling sensation in his hands. More spiders crawled around and over each other and the big crow on the railing just laughed. Ryan ignored it and his mother's pleas to come away from the window. "I said leave us be!" he yelled and the window shook so violently that all three in the house thought for a fleeting

moment the pane would burst and spiders might come flowing in over the boy.

Instead the spiders began to depart. Almost unnoticeable at first, then the day shone through as

more cleared away, some actually falling off while other's scurried away. Ryan smiled at them as they all

darted off in different directions across the lawn, then over at the crow.

"Not even close to my level, son." his father seemed to grin with the beak of the dark bird. *"So*

much I can teach you, boy. So much if you just let me show you the way."

"Get lost." he told his father and shut the curtains on him. He sighed with relief and plopped

down on the couch, looking over at the astounded priest and his mother. "Nothing to it." he grinned.

"You did it." his mother barely said aloud. "My God, you made those things leave. They listened

to you."

"Obeyed is a better word." Father Leary said approaching the window. He peeked out the curtain

and saw only a few large spiders scattering across the open street headed for the sewer opening. The large

crow was gone. "You have the ability to make them obey you, Ryan."

"Yeah, maybe to leave us alone." he said. "But can I make them attack him?"

"One step at a time." the priest said rubbing the boy's head and this time he didn't mind so much.

"My son controls monsters." his mother said in near shock as she returned to her coffee. "How

the hell is that possible?"

"They're not monsters, mom. They're just animals like anything else." he said and turned back to

Father Leary. "That gypsy woman in my dreams said evil was a choice. She said I could get them to not

do evil and do good if I tried hard enough."

"Well, I don't pretend to understand any of this, Ryan." Father Leary said seating himself next to

him. "But she was right about that choice part. Your father, no matter what he has done, was not born evil,

he chose to be evil. He embraced it."

"I don't want to be evil." Ryan said thinking of the dead woman burned in her little store. "And I

don't want him taking me over. I'm afraid to fight him, Father Leary. But I will anyway."

"And like I told you, Ryan, you won't be alone." the priest said taking his hand. He was both

surprised and happy to feel his other hand taken by his mother.

"You're my son." she said over to him with tired eyes and a weak grin. "No matter what you are and what you can do, that never changes, Ryan."

"I think we need a new game plan." Father Leary said with a thoughtful look of a man who had just had a revelation of sorts. Maybe his faith would get them through this after all.

"What do you mean?" Ryan asked. "I thought we had one. I can control what he can control. I might be even to stop him with his own creatures."

"That may be true but thus far we have been playing defense. We still are." he said standing and turning to them both. "He's been the attacker all along. We need a good offense. I think it's time we took the fight to him."

"How?" Ryan asked as they all sat in semi-circle there on couch and chairs. "We don't know where he is. He could be possessing anybody or anything."

"In spirit form perhaps." Father Leary pointed out. "But his body is a different story. I'm not sure it will help but you never know. Laura, you went to your husband's funeral, yes?"

"Yes." she said still casting nervous glances at the window. "I was about the only one."

"Where is your husband buried at?" he asked. "Maybe if we could get a hold of the body we could-"

"He wasn't buried." she interrupted. "The fire pretty much took care of that." she pointed out. "There wasn't much left after the explosion."

"Cremated then. Great. Where are his ashes?" he asked and her face went pale.

"Oh, God." she breathed looking at him and then Ryan with tears forming in her eyes.

"Don't tell me somebody else got them." the priest said with a worried look and Ryan sat up now also curious. This was a little detail he had never known either. "A distant relative maybe?"

"No. I got them." she said with the blank expression of regret.

"So where did you put them, mom?" Ryan chimed in now for the good Father.

She turned with a half wrinkled grin of a cat who had just been caught with the canary in its mouth, leaning back and cutting lose with a deep sigh that sounded out defeat for them all.

"I was pissed at him." she said. "You have to understand he was a bastard and got caught with that girl. So I just-"

"You what?" Ryan asked impatiently.

"Laura, where are they?" Father Leary cut in again.

"I took them down in the basement and I . . . poured them into the floor drain." she said and let her head fall into her hands. "Sorry."

"Not your fault." Father Leary said sighing as he rose up to pace about the room. "We will just have to come up with something else."

"We're screwed." Ryan said letting his own head fall with hers.

"No, we are not." Father Leary said looking the boy in the eye. "We still have you. We need to see exactly how strong this power of yours is. I think I know the right place to try it out."

THIRTY TWO

Nightfall with a bright moon and no rain.

A bird could fly much better without rain. From this height Alan Woods could see much of the small town he was born in, shit-hole that it was, and it was sort of beautiful from up here in the night skies. The tall pines that seemed to run almost all around the border of it, the narrow creek that zigzagged its way through the center, the train tracks that cut north to south. Hundreds of tiny orange and yellow porch lights all lit up from one end to the next as unsuspecting potential victims laid in beds with visions of sugarplums, whatever the hell they were, danced in their worthless, empty heads.

He felt like a god, a weak and tired god, but still a god all the same. How many men could say they soared through the night skies without man-made aid of some kind? How many men could see the moon and the stars quite the way he was seeing them now on a cushion of air currents with the wind in his feathered face?

Alan Woods was tired and needed to feed. He fed off fear and it was time for a meal. He also needed a new body. Animal ones were fine but they were not enough. They seemed to weaken too fast. He needed a new host, a fresh shell to inhabit. He preferred a big, strong one so as he could finish the task at hand. The only thing was they had to either be willing or weak of will. Weak, like the old bum Darby or perhaps drunk like his bitch of a wife. He had tried Sergeant Lambert, the big goofy cop who had tried to save the girl in the car with him all those years ago, but evidently the big cop had a strong will.

He had approached him at the burnt store in the body of an alley cat after the priest, his bitch of a wife and his son had pulled away in that blue Jeep. The cop reached down and petted him and he licked on the cops hand and that should have been enough to start a transfer of sorts. It didn't work. Either the big bubba bastard was a solid Christian or just strong willed. Either way he would have to find another soul to take soon. This bird, cat and dog thing was getting old fast.

The boy he killed earlier, Jeff Bates, had a father. He thought most certainly he would have been weak and depressed from not only from his son's death but the fact his wife was in some nuthouse. But

160

alas, the man had taken to going to church even more now and praying at home even more. His faith was too strong. Alan couldn't even stand to be near him.

His wife Laura, lush that she had been and might be again one day, would not be drinking anything as long as that bastard priest was around her and her boy. No help there. But he did have another idea.

The big raven that housed the dark soul of Alan Woods came to a rest in a small tree in front of a house at the end of a dead end street. A proper life statement for the man who lived there as far as he was concerned. He sat and waited, really no other choice in the matter, and within a few minutes which seemed like hours he saw the big man through the kitchen window come in and sit at the table with his coffee and paper. Perhaps he was working the nightshift. Alan thought so because the big fucking goon had his uniform on.

"How do I get in there to you." he said from the naked branch. The windows were all closed. The doors. It was autumn so of course they were. How long would he have to wait until the big badge-wearing bastard came out? Maybe he wasn't going anywhere tonight. Maybe he just got off on walking around in his uniform. The man had no life, after all.

Alan wondered in his small bird brain if he flew fast enough at top speed, whatever top speed for a crow was, would he be able to break through the window or would he break his little stupid hollow boned neck? It was a risk he was not willing to take. If this host body died his soul would be released. He would be able to float about in spirit form for a bit, how long he was not sure, but if he could not find another host quick enough, he would fade away and go back somewhere not so nice. Somewhere where pain was a constant thing.

He did not want this.

"Get off your fat ass and go to work." he said shivering from the cool night winds. If the dropping temperatures were effecting him, he was indeed getting weak. He thought about flying over to the nearest liquor store and seeing if he could inhabit some half-wit when something down below on the sidewalk moved and actually made his tiny heart flutter. *"Well now, who do we have here?"*

He watched the dull orange cat slink its way up to the porch. It took its sweet ass time doing so but finally managed to creep up the steps and with wide, wild eyes get lost in the show the moths were putting on around the porch light. The large crow that was Alan Woods came loose from the limb and went into a nosedive with wings spread wide as he glided down towards the cat, trying not to make any noise at all. No flapping of wings. No shrieks of attack. The cat did notice him as he got within several feet of it, but it was too late. All he needed was contact.

Once the switch had occurred the cat chased the big bird off the porch and watched it take flight back into the dark skies. It turned to the door, ignoring the moths in the night dance now that a human inhabited its body, and began to meow. Softly at first, then louder and more in tones of a howling.

"Okay, okay." the voice came from behind the door and the cat sat there looking dainty and non-threatening as the footsteps came closer and finally the door gave way to the indoor light of the house. "I thought you would never get back, Sherlock." Chief Rollins said down to the cat as he stood aside and let the little pet dart in out of the cold. "You glad to be home, boy?"

"You have no idea." the cat that was now Alan Woods whispered to itself as it headed for the couch to lay down, eyeing the cop with a grin as he watched the big man head back to the table. He would wait until the man was a bit more tired, and then he would make him the most powerful weapon yet. The Chief of Police, with a badge and a gun. *"This should be fun."* he said resting his new little face on his paws. All he had to do was wait.

THIRTY THREE

"Here we are." Father Leary called out to both mother and child as the blue Jeep made its way down the narrow road along side the tall wooden fence covered with signs. Miller Road. "Tubbman's Junkyard. We can kill two birds with one stone here."

"Two birds?" Laura asked from the passenger seat while Ryan sat quietly in the back with his eyes reading the signs as they passed by. "Keep out, bastards!" one read and Ryan let loose with a laugh. "Will shoot trespassers! Will shoot again if I miss!" on another. "What do you mean by that?"

"Well, first I have a place to bury these dogs and second we can put your son's abilities to the test out here without having to worry about an audience." he said pulling the Jeep up to the gate. The gate was actually two fences that rolled together on a small metal track topped off with barbed wire and two larger signs also covered each gate. The first read, "No smoking unless you're the owner." The priest laughed. "He does have a way with getting the point across. He's quite a colorful character."

The second sign was the one that worried Ryan a bit more. "Beware of man-eating dogs." He cast a worried glance up to the rear-view mirror where Father Leary met his gaze.

"Don't worry about it." The priest said honking his horn. "I'm sure it's just an exaggeration. Besides, nothing you can't handle, right?"

Ryan shrugged his shoulders. He had no real idea of what he could handle. But just because he could scare a few spiders off a window didn't mean he could turn an angry pack of junkyard dogs away. And there would be no pane of glass to separate them in here.

"Maybe he's not here." Laura said straining to see past the slates of the fence covered in metal and wooden signs. "Perhaps he went home for the evening."

"This is home." Father Leary said honking again. "He lives in a little shack on the south side of the junkyard. He knows we're here." he said pointing to the top of the fence. Laura saw two cameras pointed directly at the jeep. "He's just deciding if he feels guilty enough to get up out of his chair at ten o'clock at night to let a priest in."

"And what do you think he will decide?" Laura asked. Before the good father could answer the gates clicked and rambled back to their own sides, making just enough room for the jeep to enter. Father

163

Leary drove in and no sooner had he made it past them they rattled their way closed again. "Okay, never mind." she smiled over at him. "Perks of the job I guess."

"Not so much perks as guilt." he said pulling over to a bare spot within the mountains of car parts and old appliances. "Tubbs used to be an usher at our church until I caught him making off with a great deal of the collection. I guess I shouldn't be telling you that, I don't want you to judge him on it. But I kept the cops at bay as long as he returned the money. He stopped coming to church but I guess he still feels like he owes me now and again."

"So what do we do now?" Ryan asked sleepy eyed from the backseat.

"Let me talk to him for a minute and then we will get down to business." Father Leary said seeing the large man coming his way riding in a rusted out red golf cart with a crooked white roof. "Be right back. Best if you both stay here. Tubbs is not partial to late night company."

"What about the dogs?" Ryan asked with eyes darting about the moon-cast shadows of junk and debris. "How many are there?"

"Let me worry about the dogs." he said getting out and waving to the fat man in a teepee sized black t-shirt and gray sweat pants. He wore a dirty ball cap on his balding red head and food stains covered his shirt. Tubbs was always a bit of a slob even in his church going days. The fat man did not wave back. "Tubbs. It's been awhile, my friend."

"Many moons." the fat man said stopping the cart about ten yards shy of the Jeep. He puffed on what was left of the stubby cigar hanging out of his mouth "What in blazes are you doing out here this late, Father? Man has to sleep, you know."

"You weren't sleeping." Father Leary smiled coming up and shaking a reluctant hand. "You were sitting in there watching one of those old black and white monster movies."

The fat man grinned like a kid with his hand caught in the cookie jar. He shook his head and leaned back in the seat causing it to cry out in a metal shriek. "You know it. Some big damn Japanese bug thing fighting off aliens." he grinned. "Just getting to the good part too so lets make this short and not so social if you don't mind. What can you do me out of tonight?"

"I have a few bodies I need to bury." Father Leary said. He liked the shocked expression that quickly shifted over into yet another childish grin.

"See, now you're shitting me." he laughed and coughed something black up and spit it over to the opposite side of the cart. "Gonna get that looked at one day."

"The day you give up drinking and smoking is the day I give up on God." Father Leary said.

"The day after never." the fat man agreed. "So tell me what's really going on. What bodies?" he said casting eyes over to the jeep. "And what's with the late night outing?"

"The bodies are just three dead dogs." he admitted. "The woman and her boy are just staying with me for awhile. Domestic problems. Husband is a real bastard, if you get my drift."

"Oh, yeah." he said tossing what was left of the cigar to the ground. "You watch your holy ass with that one." he warned. "You know those abusive husbands have got no problems with popping a priest one right in the head if they stand between them and their women."

"I will be careful." he said looking around. "Where would be a good place to get rid of the dogs?"

"Over on the northwest corner as far as you can get." he said pointing to a crooked narrow lane that ran between tall stacks of car parts and empty shells of stoves and fridge's. "Not much up that way 'cept weeds and burned out vehicles that nobody will ever want. Make sure you bury em nice and deep so my pooches don't go digging them up."

"Speaking of the terrible trio, just where might they be?" the priest said backing away as Tubbs started up his cart again to circle back for his little humble home. "I would hate to have a run in with them."

"Well, Boris is up in the shack with me." he said scanning around the darkness in the light of the few poles he did have illuminating the yard. "As for Lugosi and Chaney, I haven't the foggiest. Out there somewhere lurking in the darkness."

"So if we should happen to come across them?" he asked. "Any ideas?"

"Well, you must be pretty good at praying by now." the fat man laughed. "I hope you wasn't expecting me to help you bury those critters?"

"I have the boy for that." Father Leary said hooking a thumb back at the Jeep.

"Lucky boy." Tubbs smiled and gave a wave. "Don't worry none. They're nice dogs once you get to know them." he laughed and drove off with one shaky hand on the wheel.

"Thank you." Father Leary said watching the shadows as he headed back for the jeep.

"So? What did he say?" Laura asked.

"He said bury them deep."

"What about the dogs?" Ryan asked looking out the window at the surrounding darkness.

"They're nice dogs." Father Leary said keeping his eyes on the path but feeling the two sets of eyes staring holes in his head. "Really they are." he grinned and kept right on driving deeper into the heart of the place. The northwest side would be far up to his left. Maybe the dogs were asleep. Maybe they were busy chasing rabbits far on the south side of the yard. Maybe they were headed home to see their master for some late night dinner.

"And maybe the Pope is an atheist." Father Leary thought keeping his eyes on the edges of the path for any movement. He wasn't just worried about them being normal junkyard dogs. He was worried about them being *Alan's* junkyard dogs. He had been bitten several times by dogs recently, been bandaged and received shots, and that was quite enough for him. He didn't tell Tubbs he had the gun on him. Tubbs might not let him come in the yard. But he had little choice. For whatever reason he felt he had been chosen to protect this family and that was exactly what he was going to do, no matter what.

THRITY FOUR

Alan Woods was a patient man. At the moment he was a patient cat.

He watched Chief Rollins mull around in the kitchen after having his late supper. He mumbled to himself a lot. The man was a straight out mental case with a badge. Alan wandered about the house in feline form and noticed the pictures. A wife, a son perhaps, a picture of his niece that Alan had burned up along with himself five years ago. She was younger in the picture with a ponytail and no make up but Alan could still tell it was her.

Obviously the wife and kid were either dead or gone because they sure as hell didn't live here. The aging cop's bed was only made up for one. There were no signs of teenagers or women living in the house that Alan could deduce from his short tour. No video games, no younger men's taste in music, no woman's clothing. Just the big cop, his horrible TV dinners, and more than a few bottles of Jack. Hell, if Alan had known the man was this lonely and liked to drink he would have come over more often.

He waited. He lay there on the couch like a normal cat would and watched the man toss back glass after glass of the good stuff. He mumbled some things about Vera, he guessed that was the cute little brunette in the photo who looked to be about forty-something now, and flicked through the cable channels at rocket speed. It was dizzying and annoying, both his channel surfing and the depressing little blurts of agony he had every two minutes about how he "fucked up" with his wife and never got to see "My Boy" anymore. But this was good too. Drunks were easier to take over. Like Darby and his wife when she was hitting the sauce just the other day. And being Rollins was depressed and tired he would not have to wait long. Just thirty minutes after he started drinking, Chief Rollins was fast asleep, or passed out, in the big brown recliner under the soft glow of the lamp.

The cat which was Alan Woods smiled.

"Bout fucking time." Alan said leaping down and with stealthy steps made his way to the big cops chair. He carefully crawled out on the man's gut, the badge glimmering in his cat eyes, and crept oh so quietly up to the unshaven stink of the man's face. Rollins was in a deep snore and the smell of his rubber chicken dinner mixed with the booze was nothing too pleasant. *"Jesus, you smell as bad as you look."* Alan said and closed his eyes as he pressed his own little lips up against the slightly ajar mouth of the big

cop. *"This ever gets out that I kissed a damn cop on the lips, I will never live it down. Oh well, here we go, pard."*

***

Alan still felt the effect of the booze, although he sensed he could deal with it a bit better than Chief Rollins could, and straightened himself up from his place in the chair. He found the bathroom and did some personal inventory on his looks. Hair needed combing, face was unshaven, and he smelled like yesterday's garbage. This would just not do for the Chief of Police.

He took a shower, nice and hot, much better than the bath he had while possessing his wife's body the other day, and enjoyed the moment. He whistled softly to himself while shaving, still not liking the man's face that he shot at five years ago, and was careful not to nick himself.

"Not quite as handsome as I'm used to." he laughed at the face he was peering out of in the mirror back at him. *"But you do what you can.."*

The thought of that night crept into his memory again and being inside this cops body he couldn't help but be curious. He wondered how he missed it taking the shower. Just wasn't thinking about it, he guessed. Too caught up in the scent of fresh soap and shampoo. Alan Woods let the hand of Chief Rollins drift over to his right shoulder and feel for it. Yep, it was there.

A little circular scar where Alan had shot this body five years ago. Bullet must have gone straight through. Alan had been aiming for the heart, but hey, things were going on around him and he was distracted. Got to give him a break for that one. Besides, because of that near miss, now he had a fun body to go cruising around the town in. Not just any body, the freaking Chief of Police. A man who could most likely do any damn thing he wanted to.

"And what will you do tonight, Chief?" he asked the older face in the mirror as he wiped away the last of the shaving cream and took a nice long swallow of the green mouthwash. Couldn't have ol' Rollins smelling like the back of a bar. That would never do. *"Have us some fun."*

He hated the fact that he could not disguise his voice. No matter whom he inhabited the voice thing just would fade in and out uncontrollably. There might be times he would sound like Rollins, but

168

more often than not, he would sound like some dead thing at the bottom of a well. Nothing he could do about that. Oh well, he thought while polishing the badge, small potatoes. Work with what you got.

The memories were there too. Bit and pieces of everything Rollins was or had been or ever wanted to be were floating around his in skull now too. It had happened with the bum, Darby. He felt that man's loneliness and regrets of his drinking. Saw all the things he wanted to do with his life, like fucking running a farm or teaching at a college. It was sad and hilarious all at once. Rollins little mind assortment was really no different.

Rollins had grown up hard, just like his father, and wanted to be the best damn cop on the beat since Clint Eastwood. He was doing okay until the night his niece was killed on his watch, by Woods of course, and then finding out she was a prostitute to boot. It put a strain on his marriage. He had never forgiven himself for letting Justine "Cherry" Rollins die. Too bad for him.

"Time to take a drive." he said finding everything he needed right there at the night table by Rollin's lonely and cold bed. Keys to the patrol car, nice big gun, even bigger and better than the one the Priest had at his home. Wouldn't they be surprised? He slipped on the dark jacket with his badge shining brightly there in the full-length mirror and he had himself a nice long laugh. *"Who the hell would believe I'd ever be standing here in this get up?"* he said turning to view himself at all angles.

He did a proud strut for the door while thinking of the fun that was about to begin. So much fun. He would kill the priest first. That would be a great joy. The bastard wouldn't even see it coming. He would just walk right up to him with a smile and a wink and then just blow his holy brains all over the walls.

Laura would be different. Maybe with Laura he would drag things out a bit. After all, it had been five long, lonely, dark years since he had a nice piece of tail. He'd get that ass and then if she didn't want to cooperate after that . . . well, her brains could join the Father's on the wall.

No huge loss.

Then would come Ryan. He would surrender this old, fat worthless fucking cop's body as soon as he had the boy. With his son's obvious growing powers added to his own, he would really shake this town up. There would be nobody left to stand in his way. The killing could go on forever. Well, at least another sixty or seventy years.

A man could have a lot of fun getting into trouble in seventy years. And then Ryan could grow older and he could have yet another son. Another person to take over the family business. Things could stay fun for a very long time yet.

He smiled while reaching down and scooping up the cat as he walked out the door.

"Here we go, puss." he said dropping the cat to the porch while watching it run off into the night. *"Let's go do what we do best."* he said observing the animal start to chase something there by the edge of the yard into the darkness of the trees and vanish from sight. *"Let's go hunting."*

THIRTY FIVE

The ground was as damp as Father Leary had hoped for. The rainy nights softened up the earth but despite this he had worked up quite a sweat digging the hole which had to be deep and wide enough to accommodate all three dogs. He was starting to think he was being too generous in their funeral arrangements and wished he had just opted to call animal control to come get them. But of course this would mean explaining certain things like bullet holes in their heads.

"You should really be trying to do your thing instead of helping me, Ryan." the priest said to the boy standing there holding the flashlight. "As much as I appreciate the help, this is not why I brought you out here."

"We have time." the boy said glancing up at the hazy moon slipping in and out of passing clouds.

"I'm scared of all of this." Laura said standing near the foot of the grave. She had, much to her obvious disapproval, drug the three furry corpses over to the edge of the hole. "What if he can't control this *gift* we seem to think he has? What if he passes out again like last time?"

"Then it's better we find out here and not in the presence of your husband." Father Leary said slamming the shovel down and standing up to stretch his back. "Jesus." he breathed while mopping his forehead dry. "It's been awhile since I've done physical labor like this."

"How's you leg and arm?" Laura knelt down asking.

"Doing well I guess." he said feeling the leg giving a bit. "Your arm?"

"Not too bad. Got some pain killers if you need them?" she said shaking the bottle at him.

"I'm good, thanks." he grinned back and then over to Ryan. "So what do you think?"

"I think it's deep enough." Ryan said moving away from the dog corpses.

"I agree." the priest said lifting himself out of the hole with a groan. "It's not like any relatives are going to show up later and complain. Let's get these pups buried." he said grabbing hold of the large Husky as Laura knelt down to help him. "Ryan?" he called to the boy who turned and placed the priest in the beam of the flashlight. "Let your mother hold that while I finish up here. You need to be seeing if you can call these things and control them once they show up."

"Yeah, okay." Ryan answered and turned to walk away.

"Honey, don't go too far." his mother said helping the priest slide the Boxer's body over to the fresh grave. "Right there is good enough."

"I think it's going to have to be." Ryan said noticing the two shadows doing a slow trot around the corner and come to a stop once they noticed him. "I hope you brought your gun, Father Leary."

"What's going on?" the priest said looking up from where he was lowering the huge Great Dane.

"We have company." Ryan called back watching the two junkyard dogs, both big German Shepherds, walking in unison in his direction. "Lugosi and Chaney, I presume."

"You can control them Ryan." Father Leary said taking out the gun that was tucked in his belt. "If your father can do it, so can you. At least that's the theory we're working under."

"Ryan, don't." his mother said starting for him but Father Leary took hold of her arm.

"No, Laura. Let him try." he said prying the shovel loose from the ground and handing it to her for a weapon. "If he fails we will fight. Only if he fails."

"That's my son you're asking to-" she began but Father Leary cut her off.

"He has to prove what he can do." the priest said cocking the gun. "Trust me, if they get too close I will kill them both. Let him try first. Let's see what he can do."

"Nice doggies." Ryan said as they both started a low growl while inching forward.

"Reach out to them, Ryan." Father Leary said lifting the gun up slightly. "Like you did with the spiders. You're not their friend, you're their *master*."

Ryan closed his eyes and lifted his hands the way he did back at the priest's home. He felt the familiar tingling sensation, as if his legs had fallen asleep, run through his body, and when he opened his eyes the dogs were not alone.

"My Lord in Heaven." he heard Father Leary gasp from behind him and saw the ground covered in rats and mice. Hundreds of them were emerging from the piles of junk. They came within a few feet of him, lined up in rows like tiny furry soldiers. The two dogs were sitting still in place like statues, soft growls deep from within their throats, but they did not come after him. They sat there waiting for him to move. Other creatures of the night came out as well and Ryan stood both amazed and slightly frightened as he watched them all gather around them in semi-circle where he stood with outstretched arms like some tiny priest preaching before an unholy congregation.

Snakes of all sizes slithered up to become a part of the dark congregation. Cats, both wild and domesticated, slinked around the high corners of junk piles, all kinds of spiders, every creeping kind of bug that he could imagine, roaches and beetles, worms and night crawlers, crickets and fireflies. Birds of every dark shade, ravens and crows and black birds and starlings were now circling overhead in the skies with bats and owls joining in. The sky grew thick with them so much you could barely see the clouds or the shy moon. Ryan felt frozen in place, felt his adrenaline rushing through his body, as he stood not just before these creatures but over them in command as their Lord and Master.

"My baby." Laura Woods said clapping hands to her mouth with tears running down her cheeks. She fell involuntarily into Father Leary's arms who held her tight while making the sign of the cross for the both of them, all three of them in fact. "What is he?"

"He is their king." Father Leary said in awe as the flying things of the air lowered themselves and took roost on any available surface for a perch. "He is their leader." he said noticing the creatures on the ground lining up as if waiting to be addressed by this small general before them. "He is their very blood." he said noticing now even more animals lined up on the opposite side of the fence that bordered the junkyard. More dogs and cats. Raccoons and foxes. Bigger rats. Lord only knew what else was out there that he could control if it had time to get here. "He is what his father was before him. He is . . . The Boogeyman."

"Awesome." Ryan breathed to himself letting his arms slowly settle to his side.

"They are yours, Ryan." Father Leary said soft as only Ryan could hear while lowering his gun.

"And I am theirs too." Ryan said sounding so grown to both adults standing behind him. "But they obey him too. My dad. They can't help it." the boy said looking back at the priest.

"There can be only one master." Father Leary said while letting his eyes scan the creatures that surrounded him in the darkness. He knew he could live three or four more lifetimes and never see such a dark and miraculous spectacle such as this. Animals, that by all rights should be trying to kill each other, standing side by side as brothers. Dogs, cats, birds of all species, insects of every kind, snakes and spiders, rats and mice, rodents and reptiles and amphibians such as frogs and toads, and every mammal that lived in the area, were all under this boy's dark command. "That's what this is all about. You have to be that one and only master."

Ryan stood so still for that moment listening to the priests voice while staring out at his huge audience. All eyes were on him. All glowing in brilliant shades of red, green and yellow. All waiting for the little master to speak directly to them and tell them what to do next.

"Okay." Ryan finally managed after a deep breath and a shiver running the length of his body. "I guess we better get ready." he said looking out at the masses before him. "We're going to war."

THIRTY SIX

A nice quiet drive in Waverly. A town this size didn't have much traffic after midnight and that was just fine with Alan Woods, a.k.a. Chief Rollins, as he wasn't in the mood for much conversation. He patrolled the streets, keeping the radio off so as he didn't have to make contact or answer any calls, and kept his eyes open for the priest's Jeep. No luck.

He passed by fast food places where drive-through windows were open in case they wanted late night snacks. Nothing. He did have fun with one pimpled-faced boy at the burger joint, causing him to see cockroaches all over the windows and floor which sent him screaming out into the night. Cheap fucking thrills but better than nothing and it did give him a bit of a boost.

He passed by motels and diners where they might be hiding. Nada. He did manage to stir up some old duff having late night coffee and pie. He let him see his dead wife outside dying of a heart attack all over again. It took a long time for the waitress and cook to calm him down. Never the less, it fed him well.

Maybe, he thought, they ditched the Jeep. Maybe they were staying at a friends house. Laura had to have more than a few at the market. But Alan didn't think the priest would allow any more innocents to be placed in danger. They were hiding somewhere, just the three of them, and Alan would find them. He had many friends too. Dark ones. All he had to do was pick up on their fears.

After about an hour of this he decided to head on over to the good Father's place. He hoped to find some lights on when he pulled up, but the house looked dark and deserted. They might be asleep inside or simply waiting. But would they be waiting for him disguised as a cop?

"Damn." he mumbled passing by a good three houses before parking. *"Don't tell me they picked tonight to wise up and move on."*

He got out of the car and looked around. Just a narrow street full of porch lights. Small town folk had gone to bed early. Besides, who would dare question the Chief of Police as to what he was doing out this late? Nobody in this little burg. He strolled casually down the sidewalk until reaching the priests house. The very place he had been in the body of the Husky. Oh well, if at first you don't succeed, just keep coming until you get the bastard. That was his motto.

175

He noticed the boarded window and thought of gaining access that way. He thought better of it since if they were gone he didn't want them noticing anything different when they came back. That and some nosy neighbor calling the cops who may not recognize who he was. He didn't need another standoff right now with the cops. The last one went rather badly. He wanted his visit to be a surprise to all concerned so he headed around the back of the house which was suitably dark for his forced entry. No lights on anywhere inside. They were either gone or asleep. Either way it did not matter. The man had to come home sooner or later and he was betting sooner.

The back door gave way considerably easy from the man's weight and Alan waited a few moments standing still in the darkness to see if a voice or gunshot would ring out. Or perhaps an alarm. Nothing. Just the warm flow of the furnace and the darkness welcoming him in. His eyes quickly adjusted and he stepped across the holy man's threshold for the second time and made his way to the kitchen. No life signs.

"Nobody here but us undead." the man laughed and drew his own weapon as he headed upstairs. He made a quick search of the rooms, actually took a much needed piss due to the cop's overloaded bladder, and made his way back downstairs.

"Won't you be surprised to see me." he said smiling while heading towards the garage. He remembered the casual conversation the priest and Laura were having before he and his canine brethren attacked them. Something about cigarettes. It only took a few seconds to find the single pack of Marlboro's along with the lighter tucked neatly beside them in the coffee can.

"Mind if I make myself at home?" he said flopping down on the couch and propping his large boots on the coffee table. He tore back the cellophane, pulled out a smoke and lit her up with the lighter, taking a long, deep drag that he blew out into a tiny circle that floated towards the ceiling. *"Life is good, but the after life is sooooooo much better."* he laughed cocking the gun and setting it beside him. He would wait here like the predator waited on its prey. No need to hunt. They would eventually come to him.

THIRTY SEVEN

Ryan Woods had seen and heard some creepy things in the past few weeks, but the one at the Junkyard had topped them all. It was a nightmare come to life. It was a part of who he was.

Just watching those creatures step aside, parting a way for him and his mother and Father Leary like the Red Sea as they left, was something he would remember for the rest of his life, regardless of how long or short that might be. Apparently Mister Tubbman hadn't noticed the grand gathering because when they honked to get back out he just opened and shut the gates for them with only a barely audible muttering of a "G'night" and then a "C'ya later, Father" from the speakers.

"We're going somewhere safe for tonight." Father Leary said as they drove away and left the freak show behind them. "Maybe we will stay there until this is all over."

"Nobody's house please." Laura said from her dark place in the passenger seat while fidgeting with butterscotch wrappers. "I don't want anyone else getting involved."

"Of course not." the priest said heading for the service road which Ryan knew would lead to the highway. "I know a little motel outside of town where we sometimes do interventions for people with drug or alcohol problems. We should be safe there."

"You okay?" Laura asked back and Ryan just nodded still feeling a tiny bit of that tingle running through his body. He wondered silently to himself if any of those animals would follow them to this motel. He could detect nothing in the dark skies behind them.

"I'm fine." Ryan said wondering if that was the correct word to use. "As much as I can be anyway." he finished with a weak smile and his mother reached back in the darkness and touched hands briefly with his. "We will be okay, mom." he assured her, not really sure if this was the truth or not.

The drive to the motel was short and quiet. Some little place sitting far off the road at a truck stop along side a brightly lit 24 hour gas station and a diner. The Maverick Inn. It was done up in cowboy décor with wagon wheels leaning against the faded stone walls in between patches of tall weeds and a big blinking blue boot for a logo. The priest went in, chatted with the skinny old man with the hillbilly beard behind the counter, and came back out walking slow and tired with a room key. Number thirteen. How appropriate. The unluckiest number of all.

"You two take the beds." Father Leary said as they stepped into the room. "I got dibs on the chair."

"You need sleep as much as we do." Ryan heard his mother say as he found a stiff padded chair by the window and parted the thick drapes just enough to look across the parking lot to the highway.

"I think after every thing we've been through you can call me Thomas." the priest said finding a chair for himself while laying the gun on the nightstand next to him.

"I guess I can do that." his mother said seating herself on one of the beds. "Thomas. You know my husband was going to die anyway." she said staring out the window past her son. "Cancer."

"It was terminal?" Thomas Leary asked.

"That's what we were told. I hate to admit it, but I was almost relieved when I heard the news." she said casting shameful eyes his way for only the briefest second. "I figured it wouldn't be long and he would be gone for good. That must seem horrible to you."

"No, not really." the priest shook his head leaning back. "I've met a few people like that. I didn't wish them dead but when I saw their obituary notice, I didn't exactly feel too bad either. This may be important to us. He knew he was dying so he got himself killed by those cops."

"And that girl, Rollin's niece?" Laura added.

"That may have just been bad timing. She was in the wrong place at the wrong time. Or just to get one last shot in at the police, Rollins especially. He wanted to die, but why there?"

Ryan heard, but said nothing. He sat there wondering if his father really could find them out here. He was sure he was out looking now, in one form or another, searching for them. Seeking to kill Father Leary and probably his mother while taking his body over for his own evil purposes. Maybe he had even been there at the junkyard in disguise watching and studying them, sizing him up. Maybe he had followed them here as well.

He sat there watching the cars enter and exit the gas station. The little diner was completely out of sight and the motel grounds were pretty much dark and silent. Three other cars, one of which probably belonged to the old man behind the counter, sat close to a row of dumpsters on the edge of the lot. That was all. Ryan stared the dumpsters down and focused, squinting his eyes and trying to *feel* if anything was inside or around them. He picked up on many living things. Bugs mostly and a few mice. Three of those things were slightly bigger than the rest in there scavenging for late night snacks. Those were the ones he called to in his mind.

He watched them emerge from the shadows. Two of them wobbled across the parking lot towards their room while one flapped its big black wings and came over and landed on the top of Father Leary's Jeep. A crow that eyed him with some suspicion and a bit of respect. The two possum's were slower in getting there. Once they were they cuddled up close to each other right underneath the window Ryan grinned down at them. They would have to be enough for now.

"Okay, we will sleep in shifts." Father Leary told his mother. "And I have the first one. I will wake you in a few hours." he said leaning back and finding the remote. "I'll keep the television on mute so as not to disturb you."

"I don't think anything could disturb me more than I am right now." Laura said. "And I'm not sure how much sleep I will get tonight anyway. Not after everything I've seen today."

"You need to try, Laura." Father Leary said clicking past channels until finally settling on a news station. "I will wait awhile and go over to that diner and see if they have anything editable for us to eat."

"What's wrong, honey?" Laura said noticing the look on Ryan's face as he was peering out into the darkness. "Anything out there we should know about?"

"Nope." Ryan smiled while eyeing his new friends. "Just making sure we got some help looking out for the night. You got a pen on you?"

"Pen?" his mother said turning towards the small desk there and started rifling through the drawers. She came out with some sticky note pads and a worn pencil. "Will this do?"

"Thanks." he said and extended his arm out while copying the number down before him in the dim light of the room. He even wrote her name the same as she did with a heart above the letter I.

"You really like her, don't you?" his mother asked looking at him with eyes that knew he was growing up so fast. Almost a teenager now. He would be driving soon and of course dating. Moving away for college. If they all lived through this nightmare, that was.

"I gotta have something to look forward to." he said turning back to the window.

"I promise you will." his mother said stroking his hair softly from behind.

"You mean you *hope*." Ryan corrected her feeling cold staring out into the darkness.

"They say hope is the only thing stronger than fear, Ryan." the father said from his chair.

"Way too many quotes." Ryan said and closed his eyes against the world.

THIRTY EIGHT

Alan Woods was his old self again, at least for the moment.

He had his own body back. The long, thick shank of a black mane like a lion hanging over his back done up in a ponytail, the muscled tanned arms covered in tattoo's, the stubble covered face with the deep set eyes. It was all him the way he liked best. Best of all he was seated behind the wheel of his black beauty again. His Impala was once again roaring up and down the main streets of this shit hole little town. It brought a grin to his face.

It was summer again, he could tell from the open window allowing the warm night breeze to blast his hair back behind him, and the town seemed as young and alive as he was. Def Leopard was blasting across the radio, the fuzzy black dice were swinging from the rear-view mirror, and the girl seated next to him was wearing a cut off sleeveless shirt with a leather skirt and studded bracelets with bangs hanging over her forehead. It was the eighties again.

"Faster, baby, faster!" came her excited voice. He looked over and saw the pretty little red head smiling at him. "Make this mother-fucker scream!"

"You got it, darlin'." he grinned and slammed the pedal down while the streetlights and small buildings got lost in the blur. He remembered the carrot-topped bitch from years ago. One of his first after he came of age actually. Tara or Kara or some damn thing. Fucking cheerleader. She was afraid of spiders big time. A tasty little meal to be sure. "Hold onto your cute little ass."

"Why did you have to do it, baby?" she called to him over the roar of both the engine and the night winds. Alan looked over and saw her sitting there, spiders crawling across decaying flesh, a smile still on her face. "I really liked you."

"It's who I am, sweetness." he said laughing while focusing back on the road. "It's what I do. Why does the hawk kill the field mouse? It has to feed, darlin'."

"We loved you." came another voice. A pretty blonde with blue eyes and ponytail dressed in a bikini. Jackie something. She was afraid of the water. He promised to teach her how to swim. That was a good one. Once he got her out to Cherokee Lake he showed her how deadly water could really be.

"Never asked for your love." he told her grinning again. "I just needed your fears."

"I wasn't ready to die!" she screamed at him and pounded on his right arm while he laughed. She had changed form too. Bloated and blue from all the years of being underwater before they finally found her tied up down there with chains and rocks which he noticed were now secured tightly around her ankles soaking into the rugs of his car.

"Hey, you're making a mess of my ride, bitch." he said smiling. "You never really did learn how to swim very well did you?"

"Fucker!" she said and vanished from view, only to be replaced by a pretty light skinned black girl with braids, a perfect body and a tattoo of a skull on her arm.

"Old white bastard!" she screamed at him. Sydney Taylor. A sexy stripper he met in Kansas City. She was a tough little fighter. Almost got away, had to give her credit for that one. Her pretty brown eyes glared at him from across the seat. "I trusted you!"

"Your first and last mistake." Alan sighed. "You actually gave me a few scars, babe." he said bringing his hand up to his face. They never did heal like the rest. Must have been from the strong emotions the bitch had at the moment she struck him while they were struggling. "But you lost anyway."

"Left my mark on your punk ass." she said starting to wither away right before his eyes.

"That you did, baby-girl." he said back watching her shrivel up to a ripe old age past any human life expectancy. It was her greatest fear. Growing old. She went from twenty-one to three hundred in a matter of minutes. Damn good fighter though. Full of passion. "Too bad it wasn't enough." he finished and the next time he looked over there was nothing but ashes on the seat which quickly vanished into the night winds. "None of you were."

"What about me, Alan?" came the all too familiar voice and Alan hesitated to turn and see who he knew was seated there. His wife. The one he had chosen to spend his life with. Not because he loved her, although there was some of that, but because he needed to continue the bloodline. He needed a little wild child. Laura used to be that woman and that was enough to give him first a daughter, who would be no use to him at all because this particular family trait only passed through the male members of the family, and then at long last . . . A son.

"What about you?" he told the younger version of Laura back in her tight faded jeans and no bra days of youth. "You made your choices and I made mine."

"Why didn't you kill me, you worthless fuck?" she snarled at him.

"I needed you to birth me a son so I could carry on with my work." he simply said back.

"Why can't you kill me now?" the phantom girl grinned over at him quizzically.

"Don't flatter yourself." he said to her. "I will finish your ass when I no longer need you. Only reason you're alive now is because my son needs you alive."

"I still don't scare easy." she whispered over to him.

"Don't over estimate yourself, darlin'." Alan grinned bringing the car to a screeching halt that nearly threw the young version of Laura Woods through the window. "You're not the little spitfire you used to be. You got things to consider these days. Things you could lose. Like your bitch of a daughter. Like your son. These are fears you can't escape."

"We'll see." she said making a move for the door to escape.

"Yes, we will." Alan said slashing out with a large hunting knife and striking Laura right in the throat, her body falling forward as blood spilled out over her smooth young skin. He knew it was not really his wife, that he was dreaming somewhere back in the house of Father Leary, but it felt good all the same. It just felt so right. "You won't get off that easy in real time darlin'." he told the fading copy of his dying wife. "You will suffer worse than all the others combined. And the most fun part is . . . our precious little son will be the one to kill you."

THIRTY NINE

The doorbell brought Alan Woods away from past pleasures of causing others pain.

The bright rays of sunlight stung his eyes and for a second he forgot he was occupying the body of an older man. Some damn near retired cop with arthritis in his back and sore legs and what seemed to be an ulcer brewing, not to mention a bum ticker. Then he moved and it all came rushing back to him. He had made a bad choice in his rush for a human host. He would not make that mistake again.

The doorbell rang again, this time followed by a series of knocks, and the framework of Chief Rollins rose up to its full six-five frame. Rollins was a big sucker at least and he did have a gun. Maybe whoever was at the door would be a suitable replacement. Or at least have fresh fears to feed off of. That would be a nice way to start off a Wednesday morning. If not they could just be another victim. What was one more life anyways? He was on a roll after all.

"Chief Rollins?" came the whiny voice of the man on the opposite side of the door. "You in there, Chief?"

Woods in his now Chief Rollins form shambled over to the door and leaned down to peer out the peek hole. On the other side was a scrawny man with a bushy mustache and the nose of a hawk. He wore a badge on his chest. *"Fucking cops."* he muttered to himself as he undid the locks. *"Always around when you don't need them."*

"Hey, Chief." the cop said as the door swung open to even more sunlight. His badge read BRUNSWICK. He looked familiar, like maybe another one of these bozos from the night he took a baptism by fire on the parking lot of that drug store, and the big cop stood back to allow him entry. The part of him that was Rollins knew him well enough. Bit of a shy man, stayed to himself when he wasn't trying to pal around with the bigger and badder cops, and loved baseball. Chief Rollins little memories served him well. "Thought that was your car outside. What're you doing here?"

"Thought I saw-" he started and faked a nice long cough as the skinny cop's eyes widened at the unusual sound of his voice. *"Sorry, I must be coming down with something. Thought I saw an intruder breaking in-"* he finished again with another few fake coughs and cleared his throat as he watched the hick cop dig a few cough drops out of his pockets.

"Hope you ain't got strep throat. My niece just got over that shit and it's horribly painful."

"I'll be fine." the man who appeared to be Chief Rollins said unwrapping the medicine and popping it into his mouth. He smiled down at the smaller cop and shot out a huge hand in greeting. *"Good to see you, Brunswick."*

The skinny cop gave him an odd glare, questioned the motive as if not used to contact with his superior officer perhaps, and then reluctantly reached out and gave a firm handshake. The big man let his smile fade away once he realized he could not swap up with the man before him. Nothing happened. Not so much as a tingle. Either he was a man of God or he had a strong will. Oh well, perhaps he would provide an interesting breakfast. Only one way to find out.

"I think he went-" The large cop coughed again on purpose. The longer he talked the more he sounded straight from the grave. That would not do. *"Downstairs. In the basement."* he said waving his arm in the direction of the basement door just outside the kitchen.

"You don't think we should wait for backup?" the nervous cop said glancing from the door back to the big man.

"You're it." The doppelganger of Rollins said patting him on the shoulder. Maybe this cop was a little Barney Fife Chicken-shit after all. He could work with that well enough. *"After you, partner."* he finished with a strong set of coughs.

"You should really get that looked at." Brunswick said strolling over to the door with his hand falling to his side near his gun. "You sound like death warmed over."

Alan Woods let one of his own smiles cross over the older man's face he now gazed out of as he came up close behind the younger cop. He had no idea how right he was. He watched him try the knob, pull it open and flick on the light giving view to the gray wooden steps descending down to the same color concrete floor.

"Anybody's down there you best come on up." he said with some tone of authority. Not really enough to scare anybody, especially the man standing behind him. Alan Woods thought of just shoving the man down the steps then, but it would rob him of his snack. The skinny fuck might break his neck on the way down and then there would be no playtime. Instead he just gave the younger cop his space and let him do his thing. "Was there just one?" he asked turning back to look up at his fake boss.

"All I saw." he pointed down the steps. *"Let's go round 'em up."*

Brunswick gave a weak smile and headed down the steps, his gun now drawn and his steps more cautious while Alan Woods in his older shell just followed nonchalantly, knowing the only danger down here was himself. Brunswick called out a few more times before reaching the floor and crouched down with gun aimed out at the room scanning from left to right. What a little pro the prick was trying to be.

"Last chance before we come in! You don't want that, believe me." he warned to the empty basement. "Maybe he went out another way. A window?" he said back to his pseudo commander.

"Possible." Alan agreed strolling by him. *"Let's check anyways, shall we."* More coughing and a few sniffs for good measure.

"Sure." Brunswick said sliding around a few shelves and heading towards the back area where Alan could see the good father's weight bench and exercise equipment set up. "I just really hate basements. I ever tell you that, Chief?"

"No." The big cop said letting his grin spread wide. *"Why is that, pray tell?"*

"Kind of embarrassing really." the skinny cop said while poking around. "Just some shit from my childhood."

"We all have those." Woods slash Rollins said back. *"Something bad happen?"*

"Yeah, my father happened." the cop smiled back feeling more relaxed as he rounded the last corner of the basement. A washer and dryer sat before him with empty plastic baskets and detergent bottles. "There's nothing here, Chief. You're boy got away. Can't believe he got away with too much. I don't think Father Leary had much to take in the first place. Not his way."

"Yeah, he's my hero." Rollins said impatiently watching the young cop holster his weapon. *"Finish your story, please."*

The look he got back was a mix of confusion and embarrassment. Brunswick twitched that big shaggy soup strainer of his a bit, then fidgeted with his feet while staring at the floor. There was more to the story and the monster that stood before him knew it, could *smell* it. Perhaps he just needs a bit of coaxing.

"Nothing to be ashamed of, Brunswick." he said coughing some more. *"What about your old man?"*

"He was no saint, that's for sure." he began and Alan Woods remained still while listening for a weakness in the man's very fiber of his speech and movements. "He used to beat me some, shove me in a closet whenever he felt like I was being bad or maybe he just wanted to get pissy drunk and didn't feel like babysitting me much. I just got a touch of claustrophobia is all."

"Interesting." the big cop remarked while reaching out with his mind and starting to just nibble at the image of that closet. Dark and small with a few coats smelling of wool and leather and maybe even mothballs. The walls closing in on a child in the dark and the deep fear of what just might be in there with him. *"How long did the bastard do this?"*

"Longer than I want to remember." Brunswick continued. "They didn't make closets then like they do now. They were not the kind that you can just walk into. Pretty small spaces."

"I do recall." the big cop smiled as he reached out with his twisted mind and grabbed a hold of the skinny cop's thoughts. *"Must have been hell."*

"It was. It was so bad I just-" his voice trailed off and he realized he was standing in pitch black surroundings. Just that fast the lights went out. "What the shit?" he said reaching out and finding a wall close by. "Hey, Chief, you there? We blow a fuse or what?"

Alan Woods laughed then but it was not his own laugh, nor was it of the old cop Rollins. It was the deep and drunk laugh of one Norman Brunswick, cab driver, alcoholic, and father of the skinny cop standing before him. In the cops mind he thought he was trapped in a small closet back in the little brick house in Harmony, Oklahoma so many years ago.

"Who's that?" Brunswick asked while finding the coats hanging before him. "What is this shit? How the hell did I get in here? Chief? You out there?" he asked reaching for his gun, but it was gone. Nothing there but pockets.

"I'm here, boy." came his father's voice and the skinny cop froze. "You ain't coming out of there til I fucking say so unless you want more of this strap."

"This ain't possible." Brunswick whispered to himself. His hands rumbled with the coat hanging before him in the dark. It was heavy and smelt of leather and cheap after-shave and sweat. He recognized it instantly from all of those days, over all of those years, of being locked in this very closet. It was his father's bomber jacket he wore while driving his taxi. "Dad? How the hell did you-"

"Little pussy is what you are." he heard his father call out and now that his eyes had adjusted to the dark he looked down and saw the tiny sliver of light coming in from under the door, and the two large shadows that must have belonged to his father's boots standing just outside. "Puss, puss."

"Stay away." He said backing further into the closet using the coat as a shield. "I'll be good."

"Just like your mother." his father chuckled and Brunswick could actually hear his father snapping the black leather belt along with his torments. "Never know when to shut up."

The skinny cop could actually *feel* the welts rising up on his legs and backside. They were fresh and stung like hell. He had just got them spilling Kool-Aid on his dad's carpeting on the stairs. He tried so hard not to spill any, but that fucking cat Misty ran past him and startled him and the bright purple liquid streamed all over the lime green shag. He heard the cursing only seconds later as he ran for his room. His tiny hands tried to close and hold the door against his father's entry, but to no avail. After that there was just pain.

"Stop crying in there you soft little bitch!" the monster that was his father roared. His mind couldn't comprehend it. His father had died years ago on a bar room floor with a hand clutching his heart and a bottle of whiskey in his hand. He got off easy. "You want some more?"

"No, daddy." he heard his voice call out sounding like he did back when he was just a skinny boy with glasses and knobby knees and pale skin from staying inside so much. He could feel the warm tears running over his cheeks in the darkness. "I'm so sorry."

"Yer always fucking sorry, you candy ass!" the door shook and Brunswick felt the shirt sliding off him as his shoulders narrowed and his chest started to shrink. His pants were now too big for him as he could feel his body going back to the size it had been many years ago when he was just eight or nine. He stood there shivering and naked in the dark as the door was quickly being ripped to pieces.

"No! Stay away from me! Mom!" he cried out, but his mother was dead too. Dead and gone and rotting out there in Cedar Hills Cemetery for all the worms and maggots to feed on, as his father had so eloquently put it. She died of cancer when he was only six and that's when his father took to drinking, dating whores and beating his son's little pale ass.

"Mommy's not here." came the deeper voice now and the door was showing light as large claws came ripping through taking chunks of wood with each hit. Soon all that was left was the large shadowy figure standing before him with the bright red eyes glowing down at him and that leather belt dangling from his right hand. "It's just daddy now."

Alan Woods watched as the naked child that was once Brunswick fell to his knees as the phantom father lifted the belt up and began his assault. With each smack of leather on warm skin a tingle of joy shot through the bigger cops body. It was like a drug to him. The fear, pain and terror of never ending torment. The blood, sweat and tears sending a rush through his body. It only lasted a moment, the younger boys heart giving out far too soon for his taste, but it did wake him up.

"Better than coffee." the big cop grinned down at the fully dressed Brunswick who now lay curled before him in a ball, a look of horror frozen on his dead face. He gave the cop a swift kick before turning away and walking back upstairs with a bit of pep in his steps. *"Thanks for the cough drops, asshole."*

Now that he had had his morning nourishment he headed outdoors. They would most likely find the skinny cop sooner or later, deduce that yet another resident of Waverly had died of a heart attack and rack their tiny minds trying to figure it all out. Let them, he thought stepping out onto the porch and watching the school bus stop just as the corner with a group of tiny jacket wearing children waiting, he had bigger fish to fry. He watched the bus pull away and a smile crept over his face once more.

"There's an idea." He smiled heading for the patrol car. *"Let's go to school and see what's on the menu for lunch."*

FORTY

Ryan Woods stood still as his mind reached out to the world around him that with his eyes closed and arms outstretched he might have looked like a tiny scarecrow to those passing by. He could feel everything around him, his mother close by the Dumpster still nursing her second cup of coffee and the fear in her as to what she was witnessing. Father Leary far over to his right on the edge of the motel parking lot with arms crossed and curious eyes on him. He could hear the morning traffic, those coming and going from the gas station and diner, and of course his little servants of darkness all around him in the weeds, the nearby woods and alleyways and those flying in the morning air.

He woke early, his mom shaking him free of a dream that was neither sweet nor sour, and he smelled the diner breakfast along with the adults coffee. He ate like a starving dog, downing two eggs with cheese biscuits, three sausage links and cold orange juice. Then Father Leary suggested he try something new. The idea sounded good to Ryan and knew he needed to be outside to try it. Better reception, he told the tall priest, and he actually got a smile on that one. He stood there focusing as best he could while hoping nobody would think he was too nutty, not that he cared at this point, and thought first of the dream he had just left behind.

He had been in a field, far and wide and covered in the greenest grass, and the skies were deep blue as summer often promised. Children were there all laughing and playing without a care in the world, as they should be. No Boogeyman, no dead bodies piling up in basements, just childhood and all of its deep-rooted innocence.

"Play with us." a soft voice called from behind him and he turned to see her smile. Anna Finch in all her budding glory with pretty sparkling eyes and bright red hair and nice boobies pressing up against a gold sweater. She took his hand, a slight tingle coming up his arm from her gentle touch as her tiny fingers entwined about his own, and she led him towards the towering old barn where others were running and playing.

A chilled wind came from the south then, blowing straight through him, and he turned his head in that direction while still walking with Anna towards her friends. He could see a tall metal weather vane with a rooster spinning lazily in the breeze, a shabby scarecrow with a sagging potato sack for a head and a thin line of gray clouds on the horizon. A distant threat, but coming all the same. Something flew past him then, above him actually, and he could see the shadow of large wings and feel the wind grow even colder, and then it was gone. An omen of bad things yet to come. Things he would not be able to avoid.

"Time to play." Anna said with her nose crinkling the way he loved so much and the far away storm was all but forgotten. He leaned in close to her as they walked, smelling sweet strawberries on her lips and rose scented perfume. That was when his mom shook him awake.

Now he stood here concentrating. His eyes were closed and the sound of traffic and gas pump conversations faded away as he saw blue skies come before him and the gentle wind carrying his weightless body. He was *flying.* He blinked and looked down, seeing the town he lived in all his life below him. Waverly was down there. Far below with tiny cars rolling around like metallic ants. Houses and trees dotted the waves of amber grain. He was not really flying of course, but he was looking through the eyes of one of those who served him. He was looking down at Waverly through the eyes of a bird. A rather large one at that. A hawk of some kind. He was looking for his father.

"Lower." he said in a whisper while focusing on his feathered friend he spiritually occupied and the bird descended to a height where he could make out more detail. He could see where they were now, the ballpark and his school, and then even the church. "There. Fly down there and check on Father Leary's house." he told the hawk and felt his stomach drop as if riding a roller coaster that had just taken a dip on the biggest hill as the bird took a nose dive and headed for the house with the boarded windows and the two cop cars outside.

One of them was leaving the house. A tall cop with a slow saunter about him. He knew who it was from the sunglasses and broad shoulders. Chief Rollins.

"Cops are at your house." he said over to Father Leary with eyes still closed focusing on the hawk landing of a rooftop. "One of them is leaving. Chief Rollins. They must be looking for us too."

"Or maybe it's him." he heard his mother say. "He might be there looking for us."

"It would make sense to be a cop." Father Leary thought out loud. "Nobody would bother you and you would have a gun at your disposal. I'm glad we didn't go back there. Can you follow Rollins, Ryan? See where he's headed?"

"I can try." Ryan said squinting harder and getting the hawk to take flight.

"Follow him." Father Leary whispered to the boy. "But keep your distance and stay above him."

"I will tell the bird that, it's not really me doing this." Ryan tried to explain. "We're kinda working together."

The hawk did as it was commanded, lifting both itself and the weightless specter dwelling inside its head into the air once more, eyes focused down on the patrol car that sailed along the narrow tree bordered road below. Ryan lifted his own eyes up, the bird following suit, and saw the school bus that the cop was following.

"He's looking for me." Ryan said to the two adults. "He's following a school bus. He's going up to my school."

"So are we." the priest said heading for the jeep.

"How do we know Ryan's ready for this?" Laura said taking hold of her son as he appeared to weave a bit on his feet while coming out of the trance. "He's barely practiced using this shit. He could get himself killed."

Father Leary turned on her, the worried look of a frightened mother causing him to tone his built up anger down while shifting gazes between her and her son. "We have to try now, Laura. If you husband gets inside that school just think of how many children can get hurt. Can you live with whatever he might do while he's there? We face off against him *now*!"

"He's right, mom." Ryan said up to his mother. "I'm not afraid. "Not that much anyways."

"Call your cop friend. Call Sergeant Lambert. Tell him to meet us up there." the priest said heading for the jeep.

"And tell him what?" Laura said following after him letting her coffee fall to the ground. "That his boss is a killer. That Chief Rollins is dangerous."

"Tell him to be ready for anything. Tell him those kids are in danger."

"But won't he try to contact Rollins? Then what?" Ryan pointed out.

"You're right." he said unlocking the doors for them. "We need the element of surprise on our side. Forget Lambert. Let's hope we get to him before he can do any real harm."

"Bastard has caused us so much grief in life." Laura said heading towards the jeep with Ryan in tow. "And now even in death."

"So let's end it." Father Leary said letting his hand reach up and caress the silver cross dangling from his rearview mirror while the others got in. "Please be with us."

FORTY ONE

"All of God's little children lined up in a row. So many sins to conceive and oats to sow." the possessed cop grinned still sitting in his patrol car watching the young laughing and smiling faces walking into the front doors of Daniel Boone Middle School. He didn't spot his own son among them but it was hard to tell. All of the little shits looked alike.

He stepped out into the cool October air, adjusting his belt and sunglasses while tossing a friendly wave at a few curious children who happened to glance his way, and began a soft steady stroll for the doors. Some old bitch with curly silver hair dressed in a blue blouse with beige slacks stood sentry at the door with a whistle around her neck and a stern look on her face.

The part of him that was still Chief Rollins knew her. Beverly Turner. Assistant Principal and history teacher. She used to have a thing for Rollins long ago. Nothing ever came of it outside a few movie dates. How nice. She liked reality television and unicorns, from what he could recall through the old cop, and Alan Woods wanted to vomit on her pretty shoes but instead he just kept right on grinning as he drew up closer to her one step at a time. He nodded politely as he finally stood before her on the even platform of the stairwell before the double glass doors.

"Chief Rollins? It has been some time." she said with a polite smile, her voice with a bit more bass then he cared for. "What a very pleasant surprise. What brings you up to our fine school this morning?"

"Business." he said and faked a cough with a good clearing. *"Allergies."* he apologized.

"Sounds a bit worse than that." she said with genuine concern. "You may have the croup or worse."

"Might be right." he said and let loose with a deep cough. In his mind he silently promised himself this would be the last time he would ever need to make an excuse for his voice. After he got his boy he would sound just like him. Until then, who gave a fuck. He glanced over at the tall woman who nearly came up to his height and smiled again. *"Been looking for the Woods boy. He here today?"*

"Odd you should mention that." she answered. "We heard he was in the hospital after what happened to him the other day, but he never came back. Perhaps he is more ill than we thought."

194

"Checked the hospital. We haven't been able to locate him or his mother." Woods slash Rollins said to the woman. *"Sure would appreciate your help."*

"Any way that I can, Paul." she said turning to open the door for him. "Let's get in out of the autumn chill."

"Might help if I had her number. Cell phone that is, we tried her home phone." he finished with a short series of cough while bracing himself against the wall. Beverly turned to help him but he waved her away and felt his eyes watering as he caught sight of her own concerned blue ones. *"Happens every spring and fall."* he faked his best grin.

"I don't recall you having many allergies." she said leading the way to the corner office. The big lumbering cop just followed silently, tired of the fake coughing, and let his eyes fall over the paintings covering the hallway from floor to ceiling. All Halloween pictures painted by the students. Fat swollen pumpkins on picket fences or porches, black cats with their backs arched, witches flying past the golden moon, funny ghosts haunting cemeteries. Each one done up with the child's signature printed out in the corner. It only took half the hall before he found his son's.

"Very nice." Rollins/Woods said standing in front of the one with the haunted house. It was all black save for a few yellow windows with a purple night sky as a backdrop. A silver moon and peppering of stars, a dead leafless tree holding an owl on its longest naked branch, and far in the bottom corner, which could only be from its placement a basement window, were a set of bright red eyes peering out into the darkness of the autumn night. *"Very nice indeed, boy. That me, I wonder?"*

"Excuse me?" Beverly Turner said turning to a stop.

"Ryan Woods." the big cop simply stated while ripping the picture off the wall and folding it neatly as he continued down the hall. *"Worried about him."*

"I see." the snooty woman said giving him a bit of an odd glance for his theft of the drawing. "Let's get you that cell number and then you will have to excuse me, I have work to do."

He faked yet another smile at her, tired of talking and more so of coughing. He stood there patiently as she went through her files and with a subtle nudge only he was capable of, peeked inside her frail little mind just to see what was hiding there. It was common stuff for a lady of her stature and age as far as he was concerned. She didn't like bugs or slimy creepy things. Hated snakes and mice. Bad storms were something she could do without but she endured them. There was something else though. Something

deeper and much more . . . personal.

She had been attacked years ago. College years, he thought. Some teacher had forced himself on

her. She fought well, avoided rape, but still had that fear in there. It was something that tasted so sweet to

him but not strong enough to pursue right now, not when he was so close to his ultimate goal. Once he had

his boy under control maybe some day he might look up Beverly Turner again and she could relive her

little nightmare. With a different ending of course.

"Here it is, Paul." she smiled turning away from the cabinet with the file in her hand. "Cell

number is right here." she said sliding him a sticky note and a pen. "You will have to copy it, I can't let the

file leave the office."

"Sure." he grinned jotting the number down and feeling her eyes on him as he did so and smiled

all the more for it. The old bitch still had a thing for Rollins. How sweet and very pathetic of a life she

must have to have the hots for this old codger drunk with a badge.

"You see your boy much these days?" she asked and when he lifted his gaze up to hers she

seemed to regret the question immediately. The large cop watched her eyes want to pull away but decided

to have a bit of fun with her instead.

"Not much. Bitch of a mother won't let me." he laughed and she laughed with him only because

she felt she had no choice. It was a short but haunting laugh that came out of this man she had known

know for nearly twelve years and she didn't like it. He gave a polite nod to her and strolled out the door,

making a left instead of a right for the exit. He did not intend to leave just yet.

"Paul?" Beverly Turner said getting up from behind her desk and rushing towards the door.

"Chief Rollins? Might I ask where you are going?"

"Gonna have a look around, Bev." he said waving the picture his son had drawn at her while

heading for the steps leading downstairs to where he knew was a cafeteria. He could already smell the grub

cooking up from here. *"Never know where a young boy might be hiding at."*

He left her standing there in the hall, not caring what she thought, and bounded down the steps

two at a time, surprised the old cops legs had it in them. Once at the bottom he spied the cafeteria at once

off to his left. He stepped into the entryway, his boots clicking on the hard checkered tiles and spied the large lunch lady in the back preparing the morning meals for the children. She kept going back and forth to a cigarette she had burning there on the counter while bopping around to some fifties music.

"Not exactly what I had in mind." he said looking her over. She was squat lady with lots of weight on her and looked to be even older than Rollins. Not exactly first choice for a suitable replacement. A sound from behind him then and he turned to see a tall, lanky fellow with short cropped black hair dressed in faded blue jeans and a gray dress shirt pushing a mop bucket into the men's restroom. *"Janitor Jim."* he mused and followed the tall man into the urine scented darkness.

"Hey, Chief." the tall man said and he had a crooked grin on his face and stood rather awkward by his bucket while waiting for a response. The large cop stood still, letting the brain he now possessed tingle a bit and then realized he knew this young man. Charles "Chip" Douglas. Twenty-nine years old with the intellect on the nine side, if that. He was retarded. Oh well, that would just have to do in a pinch. Better than a fat old lunch lady with a bad smoking habit.

"Hey, ya Chipster." he said and the tall dummy grinned at him while swishing the mop around in dirty water. *"How're the turds floating today?"*

More laughter, almost to the point of annoyance, and then a response in child mannerisms.

"Same I g-guess, Chief." he grinned while twisting his nervous hands on the mop handle. "A t-turd is just a t-t-turd, I guess."

"Sure you're right." Rollins said strolling up to the urinal. *"Mind if I take a squirt?"*

More giggling like a stupid little school girl and then, "S-sure, that's w-what it's f-for, right? Are you s-sick or something, C-Chief? Y-you sound like y-you might b-be."

"Nothing serious." he said taking a piss and glad to do so, it had been awhile. *"Say there, Chippy, have you seen the Woods boy around lately? You know, Ryan Woods? Been looking for him."*

"R-Ryan hasn't b-been in for awhile." he said still standing at attention while the big cop shook himself, zipped up and headed over to the sink. "He g-got sick the other d-day and then w-went home I guess. R-Ryan is a n-nice kid."

"Is that right, Chip?" the big cop said turning fast, so fast that the tall skinny janitor jumped back and nearly hit the wall, and then began shaking the water free of his large hands. *"Is Ryan really a nice kid? You like Ryan?"*

"He's n-nicer to me than m-most kids, yeah." the large child-man said backing to the wall. He didn't like the look in Chief Rollins eyes. He had heard some stories about the man being mean but up until now Chief Rollins was always nice to Chip. Chips father played cards with him and used to go fishing with him in the summers.

"Awwwwww, Chippy, are the other kids mean to you?" the big cop said mocking a face of pity and sorrow and Chip knew that face. This cop was making fun of him now. But why?

"S-Sometimes." he said sliding across with his back to the wall towards the urinals.

"Poor Chippy-Whippy." the cop said sniffing and faking tears and Chip just stared at him in disbelief.

"I h-have to get b-back to work now, C-Chief." he said and let out a yelp as Rollins shot out and gripped his wrist so hard it hurt bad.

"D-Do you h-have t-to right n-now?" the cop laughed and Chip Douglas looked both angry and ready to cry all at once.

"W-Why are you m-making fun of-"

"Because I can, you soft minded fuck." Rollins said and shoved the boyish man back against the urinals so hard he fell off his feet. *"I need to borrow you for awhile, Dopey."* he grinned kneeling down next to the shaking man. *"You may not be the sharpest tool in the shed but you look like a pretty fair trade for now."* he said wiping the sweat from his forehead. *"Don't worry, it won't hurt much."*

Charles "Chip" Douglas sat there shocked and scared as the large man grabbed out with rough hands and seized his head, leaning down over him as if they were about to kiss. Chip had time to let out a short yell of protest, smelled the alcohol and mouthwash flood over him with a darkness that carried so many fears and memories of his past. Flashes of images from his youth filled his head. The boys who teased him at camp. The girls who made fun of him in school. The mean football coach who lived next door who fondled him in that place where his mother told him nobody should ever touch him. All of the soft whispers and giggles from every child he ever knew came rushing at him and while it was overwhelming him with panic and terror, the cop above him who held fast to his face with those strong large hands just let out a clear and utter sound of joy as something both liquid and smoke and dark as sin itself floated out of the cops mouth and into that of the slow-witted janitor.

198

"Yessssssss!" the big cop said and let loose, falling to the floor like a limp rag doll while the once dull eyes of Chip Douglas lit up with a brand new fire of energy and life. *"M-Much b-better."* he said noticing the stuttering problem was still there. *"S-shit! I j-just can't catch a f-fucking b-break."*

The tall janitor that now housed Alan Woods stood and drug the limp body of Chief Rollins into the nearest stall. He propped him up on the toilet and stood back while patting down his own pockets. House keys, chewing gum, vending machine change, and oh yes, a pocketknife. How very handy. Every boy should have one.

"G-Good-bye you s-son of a b-bitch. Say hello t-to Cherry f-for me." he said and sliced the Chief's throat from ear to ear in a bright crimson grin. He dug the paper with the phone number on it, along with the cell phone and the picture his son had drawn of Halloween, out of the dead cops' pockets and headed for the cafeteria. It was time for a phone call, along with some conversation with the lunch lady.

FORTY TWO

"Almost there." Father Leary said seeing the dark roof of the school. He could feel a lump rising up in his throat, his heart rate quicken. His last two encounters with this "Alan Woods" creature had not gone so well. Both ended with his own retreat. He could no longer do that. "You ready for this, Ryan?" he asked glimpsing at the boy in the back seat through the rearview mirror.

"Yes." Ryan said coldly. He sat motionless while also viewing the school loom larger over them as they neared. He knew his father was in there. He could feel goose bumps rising on his flesh, could feel ice water trickling down his spine. He was in there waiting. The man who had killed his friends and would kill more unless Ryan could use whatever it was he had to stop him.

"I'm still not sure about this, Thomas." Laura said trying to search for an answer on the priest's face. If there was anything at all there it was the same doubt she felt now. "He's still so new at all of this stuff. He's still learning. We don't even know if he can-"

"We don't have a choice, Laura." the priest cut in. "Ryan's the only one who can confront your husband. You and I can't do anything against him. The police can't stop him. He's in another body at all times. We would be killing an innocent person."

"He's going to be doing that anyway, isn't he?" she stated staring at the old school.

Laura Woods cell phone cut her off this time. A high pitched chime that rang out one of her favorite country tunes, doing it really no justice, and she answered it with hopes it would be no more bad news. She was wrong.

"Hello d-darling." the familiar voice came. It was Alan. *"How's my f-favorite b-bitch doing this morning?"* He said with a laugh and she felt a chill run through her. Still deep and low, only it sounded as if he were talking to her from the bottom of a well, and he was stuttering for some reason.

"Why are you doing this?" she asked and both priest and boy cast concerned looks at her. "What have we ever done to you, Alan? How are you even here now?"

"Whoa there, way t-too many q-questions, darlin'." he laughed again and took a deep breath followed by a few short coughs. He was smoking. *"I just came b-back to see my b-boy is all. We have b-business to discuss."*

"I think *we* have business to discuss." she growled at him and he laughed. "You've hurt enough people in life, you have to come back to do more to us now?"

"Hang it up, Laura." Father Leary told her pulling into the parking lot of the school. "Don't give him any attention right now."

"This is who I am." Alan said coughing some more. *"Ryan is t-the same as me, b-bitch. You ain't seen hurt yet, b-but it's coming. I know you're j-just outside. I can f-feel my b-boy with you. I'm d-down on the lower level in the c-cafeteria. Making nice with the lunch lady and some b-boy who wandered in here so you t-two p-play nice. You and that half-assed p-priest b-better stay out of my way."*

"We'll see about that, you bastard!" she yelled and Father Leary snatched the phone away from her as he heard the hellish laughter echoing and snapped the phone shut.

"That's just what he wants." he warned her. "You upset and afraid."

"Well he got it." she said looking back at her son who seemed far too relaxed to be getting ready to do whatever it was he and his dead father were getting ready to get into. "I'm afraid for my son. I'm not ready to let anything bad happen to him."

"Neither am I." he said parking the car close. "What did he say?"

"He's in the cafeteria, lower level." she said letting Ryan out with her and then casting worrisome look over the hood of the jeep at the priest. "He said he has the lunch lady and some boy with him. He has hostages, Thomas."

"Still taking prisoners." the priest said thinking back to the story of Chief Rollin's niece on that parking lot years ago. "Coward that he is."

"And he kept stuttering for some reason." she said perplexed as the three of them moved towards the school in a row with Ryan in the middle.

"Stuttering?" Ryan's eyes went wide and he knew what that meant. He could picture the man clearly in his mind's eye. "Our day janitor stutters. Chip. He's a nice guy, Father Leary, kinda retarded, but most of the kids like him."

"That mean's he's switched bodies again." Father Leary said sighing and lifting hands to his face with his eyes closed. "Which means something bad has probably happened to Chief Rollins."

"How many more?" Laura said with shaking voice as they neared the concrete steps.

"Let's try for zero." Father Leary said taking Ryan's hands as they entered the dark doors. "Be ready for anything. Try not to pay attention to any mind tricks. He will make us see things to frighten us. Illusions of people or things that aren't real. Focus on him, Ryan."

"I'm ready." Ryan said taking a deep breath and walking slowly sandwiched between the two adults towards the staircase which he knew led downstairs to the cafeteria. He could feel the temperature drop as they descended, could feel the presence of his father somewhere down there and the evil that swirled about him like a thick fog.

"You have your gun on you?" Laura asked over to the priest.

"Not in here, not with these children around." he said. "He might trick me into killing somebody innocent. I won't take that chance."

The lower level of the school took on a much more sinister appearance than the above brightly lit halls. Darkness with flickering florescent lights. Shadows moving along the edges of the walls, slithering and scurrying about as if living things in the shapes of large spiders and snakes that no human eye had ever seen. Ryan stayed close to the priest and his mother as they walked down the center of the hall that led to a slightly brighter cafeteria.

"Don't be afraid." the priest said. "He feeds on fear it seems."

"He *is* fear." Ryan corrected.

Inside a thin mist swirled over the beige tiled floor in between the long rows of lime colored tables. At the far end a voice rang out from the darkness of the kitchen. Three shadows were huddled together in the flickering lights, the one in the middle, the tallest one, seemed to have glowing eyes of red.

"Well now, h-here w-w all are." the tall skinny janitor chimed. *"T-together at last. How's everyone d-doing, this f-fine morning?"*

Ryan stood there between his mother and the priest taking in the sight of the large man-child that had once been his friend standing on the opposite side of the counter in the food serving area of the kitchen. It was the same man, but the look on his face was different. Chip liked to smile, but not in a sinister way. That grin belonged to his father alone.

To his right seated on a stool was Harriet "H-bomb" Henderson, the lunch lady. The kids called her H-Bomb not just because of her short and stout frame but her booming and commanding voice. She

202

didn't look too tough at the moment with the lanky janitor having one arm draped over her shoulder as if they were on some date.

On his left was a boy. Sniffling and wet faced with short blond hair and glasses and a knife pressed up to his pale, bobbing throat. Ryan recognized him right away. It was Marty Fitzgerald. The kid who had spent the night at his house a few years ago. The one Amy had made piss himself. Ryan wondered if Marty was making water again and couldn't blame him with that silver blade pressed up to his throat.

"Let them go, Woods." the priest said moving forward. "This has nothing to do with them."

"Got n-nothing to d-do with you either, p-padre." the janitor smirked giving the boy a shake. *"This is b-between me and my b-boy and the b-bitch I married."*

"Where's Rollins?" the priest asked stepping closer.

"I finally g-got him to smile. Of course it's across his throat, b-but we do what we c-can." the janitor laughed and hugged the plump lunch lady closer to him. *"He's lying in a p-puddle of p-piss in the bathroom where he b-belongs. A fitting end to a worthless man. He seemed d-depressed anyways so I did him a f-favor."*

"It doesn't matter what you do here, Alan." Laura said coming up alongside the priest. "You're not getting my son."

"Our son, b-bitch." the thin janitor said as his eyes took on a brighter glow and the mist began to rise up around the trio before him. *"He has a lot m-more of me in him than he d-does of you. Let's f-find out how b-brave you really are. Let's see w-what you're all r-really afraid of."*

"Stay focused." Father Leary said as the room went dark despite the sunlight coming in through the small windows. "Whatever you see is not real. It can only harm you if you believe."

"You're a coward, Alan!" Amanda screamed as the priest took her hand. "You afraid to face me one on one?"

"I've already had you, b-bitch." came the laughter from somewhere in the darkening fog. *"And I w-will have you again. B-but first I get my b-boy."*

"Ryan." Father Leary said feeling the young man come up beside him and place his hands on his. "Deal with your father."

Ryan stepped past his mother and the priest into the swirling dark mist and stay focused on those two burning orbs of red. This was his father. The Boogeyman. A creature in human form that lived and fed on the fears of others. A thing that had killed his friends and others for years since Alan Woods was born. A creature that helped create him.

"Dad?" he said in a whisper.

"I told you I would see you again. Look at my boy." Ryan heard his father's voice, but this time there was no stuttering and it was not coming from around him, but somehow *inside* him. *"Ready to make that rite of passage, are we?"*

"What are you-" Ryan began to speak but Alan Woods cut him off.

"We don't have to talk out loud like the rest of these dolts, boy." his father said inside his head. Ryan could feel both the tingling and the smile creeping across his father's face beyond the thick fog. *"We're not like them, Ryan. We can speak with our minds, son. We are better. You come from a long line of greatness."*

"Nothing great about killing people." Ryan shot back with his own thoughts as he drew closer, those eyes being brighter but not painful to look at. Swirling now in circles, almost comforting. *"You killed my friends. Mister Clark. Jeff. Mister Kelly. Brandon. All of the others."*

"You don't fault the lion for killing the antelope, boy, or the fox for killing the rabbit. It's how they survive, by feeding on the weak. Ain't you ever heard that only the strong survive? If they would have been strong, I couldn't have touched them. But they were afraid, and all I did was have myself a meal. How can you hate me for that? That's nature, boy. That's the way of the world. You let me show you the way and as father and son we can do any damn thing we want."

*"No, that's the way of **your** world, not mine."* Ryan thought almost on top of him by now. *"You're not attacking me because you need me. You don't want to be with me. You want to be **inside** me. You want to go on doing what you are doing now through me. That's not gonna happen."*

"Smart boy." his father said and somewhere in his mind he could actually hear the laughter of the older man before him still inhabiting the body of the slow janitor. *"But right now you best be worrying about your mom and your holy buddy. I think they got problems of their own."*

More laughter, from inside his mind and echoing through the cafeteria.

***

"So what are you afraid of?"

It was her husbands' voice without the stutter. It didn't seem to be coming from in front of her but inside her head. The only thing around her now as the swirling mist and those bright eyes glaring at her from a seemingly long distance. Father Thomas Leary's hand has slipped away, or pulled away, ripped from hers, and now she stood here alone, without friend or son at her side.

"Ryan? Thomas?" she called hearing her own voice echo off the walls she knew was there but could not see. "Anyone at all?"

"Nobody here but us, babe, just the way you like it."

"You won't get him, Alan." Laura promised. "He will stop you. You have no idea what he can do now."

"Sweetheart, you have no idea what we can both do. I will have him, and live in that scrawny little hide of his for many years. I will travel the world feeding off the weak and simple-minded like the idiot I'm inside of right now, and Rollins and your slut daughter's boyfriend. But first I will have some fun with you."

"Give it your best shot you son of a bitch." she said balling up her fists and moving towards the glowing set of eyes. "If you're such a bad ass, why do you need that woman and child to protect you?"

"Always have an escape route." he laughed softly. *"But this is about you and me now. You remember the days when you used to care about me. When you needed me, darlin'."*

"Many years ago, before I knew what you really were." she grimaced letting her fingers reach out and find the smooth table tops for balance in the mist.

"You have no idea what I really am. But you did enjoy having me around, right? For those long nights of rolling around in sheets and grass. Fast drives down the strip in my car, showing off your bad boy to your little whore cheerleading friends."

"I was young and dumb. I'm not a teenager anymore."

"Used to love having me around for fixing an' repairing things, carrying things . . . killing those nasty little bugs you were always so afraid of . . ."

Laura heard them. Tiny little clicking noises from the floor. She saw them coming, dark shapes of all sizes in the mist below. She held her breath and backed away seeing the spiders, some as small as her thumbnail zipping about and others as big as her hand coming slower but seeming to sense where she was. Centipedes were snaking around table legs while roaches and other bugs she didn't know the names of were now coming at her from all directions.

"Shit!" she cried out and leapt up onto the table. "Get them away you coward. Fight me yourself!"

"I am. I think they like you." he laughed inside her head. *"Be careful, darling. They bite."*

Laura kicked several large ones away as she balanced herself and kept moving backwards as the bugs pursued her. She yelped like a pup while swatting the things off her jeans and leaping from table to table, while the bugs followed in hot pursuit.

"Stop this you bastard!" she screamed reaching the last table and turning to see the entire floor covered in them, tiny and large insects and arachnids all making their way up the table legs while crawling over each other to get to their latest fresh meal. "Make it stop!"

Her hands couldn't move fast enough to keep them all off of her. She swung ferociously, sending large palm sized spiders sailing through the fog into the walls. She was smacking centipedes and roaches and ants bigger than she had ever seen flying off one direction and then another, but they kept coming in black swarms all the time, eventually making their way up her jeans and shirt. His deep laughter sounded from all around the room as she screamed. She could feel their legs on her skin as they made their way up her body, under her clothing, and her hands couldn't keep up with them as she watched her entire body go black. Then the biting began. Laura Woods screamed louder than she ever had before.

Alan Woods laughed louder than he had in years.

"Mom." she heard the small voice in the back of her mind call out. *"It's not real. Not this time. Focus on my voice, mom. They are not real."*

Laura froze as she felt the seemingly thousands of bugs traveling the length of her body now, crawling across her bare arms, her breasts, tiny legs across her throat and up to her face. She pressed her lips together tight and eyes followed suit as they covered her completely. She dare not scream any longer or they would invade her mouth as well.

206

"They're not here, Mom." Ryan's voice tickled inside her head again. *"Just focus on me. Listen to my voice."* he said softly and Laura Woods squinted her eyes and saw him there, just past the fog and the collection of bugs scampering across the floor. *"Think about something good, Mom. Think about Amy and me. About us all being together again. You can make them go away. Think about something good."*

And she did. Despite the things she felt crawling on her skin she focused on her young son's voice, his smile, the way his eyes lit up whenever she told a joke, his booming laughter. She pictured Amy young and happy and following her around the house singing and dancing before she got older into her rebellious teen years. She pictured the three of them on the couch late at night watching scary movies and jumping and laughing every time something happened on the screen, and falling into each others arms and teasing each other. She felt their love and her love for them.

"I love you, Ryan." she heard herself say as she sank to her knees on the table and felt the bugs falling off her, withering away in small groups. Then she felt his smaller hand reach for hers, squeeze tightly on her fingers, and she opened her eyes again.

"Good thoughts?" he asked with his mouth this time instead of his mind.

"The best." she said pulling him close and hugging him to her. Her eyes scanned the thick fog around them and she drew in a deep breath as she let him go. "Where's Thomas?"

***

"What are you afraid of?"

Thomas Leary stood alone. He felt Laura's hand being ripped away from his, heard her scream, and then she was gone. Ryan as well. Now he stood here in the swirling mist with those two glowing eyes that seemed to be drifting further away from him, almost too far to be in this school cafeteria, and he could feel the thing's presence in his mind as it spoke. Some form of telepathy. He had heard some priests in the past discuss this as a means of communication for angels and demons both.

"Nothing you have will scare me, demon." Father Thomas Leary bravely stated. "You're a coward, Woods. Hiding here in a school full of children, holding that woman and boy hostage, killing Rollins and taking over this young man's body."

"Guilty as charged." came the laughter. *"You were warned to stay out of the way, Padre. Now let's see how brave you are underneath that cross and collar."*

"You've lost your edge, Woods." The priest said taking long strides towards where he knew Alan Woods was in the kitchen. "You surprised me the first time. I know what to expect now. You and your parlor tricks."

"Brave words, holy man." the demon laughed. *"But you can't hide anything from me. I can reach inside that tiny, limited mind of yours and see all of your regrets, pains and fears. From your meaningless birth to this very moment in time, son. All of your darkest shameful secrets are mine."*

"Give it your best shot, monster." Father Leary said reaching up and taking hold of his crucifix while still heading in the general direction of the eyes. He took perhaps a dozen or more steps before he heard the splashing beneath him and felt the dampness around his shoes. He stopped and looked down to see about a half-inch of water running across the floor around him.

"Watch your step, Padre." Woods voice tickled his brain. *"Kinda slippery down here and Rain Man here forgot to put out the wet floor signs. You never did care for the water much, did you?"*

"That the best you got, Woods?" Thomas Leary said. "Where's Laura and Ryan?"

"In a safe, dark place." he laughed and behind that laughter Thomas Leary heard even more giggles from other dark things as he had on the phone days earlier. Woods did not travel alone. Whatever he was, he had company. He prayed Ryan was ready for that. *"You sweet on my wife there, Padre? Isn't that a sin for a collar wearing bastard like you to have the hots for a drunken slut like my wife?"*

"I care for her and your son and you won't hurt either one of them." he threatened getting closer still to where he could make out all of their shapes in the mist. "That's a promise."

"I seem to recall a day at the lake, how bout you preacher man?" the voice whispered and Thomas Leary could feel the warm summer breeze and smell the suntan lotion all around him. It was his childhood memories Woods was drawing on now, he could feel sand underneath his bare feet despite the fact he knew he was still wearing sneakers. *"You and your friends at Lincoln Lake. Hot dogs and pretty girls and rock n roll. I do believe you were about ten or so."*

"I got past it." he said picking up the pace scanning through the fog looking for those glowing eyes. "I was only a child then, you can't do better than that?"

"And here I thought it was a sin to lie. Childhood is when fear is at it's strongest, padre. That's the place where fear is born." Alan Woods softly chuckled as the water rushed in and Father Thomas Leary could feel it rising up to his shins now, cool and swift like a running river. He looked down and saw the ground beneath him, full of mud and weeds and tiny fish darting past his feet. He really did feel as if he were back at that Lake. *"You remember what happened that day, son? When you went out on that big inner tube with your buds? Got to staring at those pretty girls and . . . Oops, lost your grip."*

He could see the waves moving in on him, hear his friends screaming at him as he went under. The water was waist high now, the current pulling him back and under, his footing slipping as he reached out for support. The walls seemed further away then before, the tables and chairs all knocked down from the water which now was quickly rising to chest level.

"You never did learn how to swim, did you preacher?" Woods laughed as the priest slipped and went under momentarily. He was only submerged for a few seconds, but he saw things under there that should not have been. At first it was just the darkness and the water, then the tiny fish and weeds and rocks on the bottom of the muddy lake, then there was more. Skulls mixed in with those rocks, faces of people long gone, his father's eyes peering at him from that dark muddy floor. The body of his mentor, Father Hoffman, dressed in holy robes, floating with arms outstretched, his crucifix swirling above him as his body sunk lower and lower out of sight.

"This isn't real!" he screamed once he broke the surface gasping for air.

"Feels real to me." Woods replied. *"You really should have died that day you know. Would have been better for everyone. You haven't made a difference here. You know you're lonely and can never have anyone. Stop struggling and just give in. You still have Heaven to look forward to."*

"I'm not done with you." Father Leary said spitting out water while flailing his arms about. Through the fog he could see the shore of the man made beach. It was maybe twenty yards away, miles to a man who could not swim. But none the less he started a weak attempt at dog paddling in that direction. He was doing a fair job of it until the hands reached up from the black depths and started to pull him under.

"What's going on?" he called out struggling to free himself from their grasp. He could see them then, his dad and Father Hoffman, and many more. The old man, Mister Clark, the boy Jeffery Bates. Mister Kelly and that young thug that Laura's daughter was dating. Some old bum and a lady from the palm reading place down the street from the church. Even Chief Rollins and his pretty niece who died years ago and some skinny cop with a push broom mustache. They were all trying to drag him down there into the black water to join them on the victims list. "Let me go!" he cried out feeling himself weakening at the overwhelming strength of their number.

"Father Leary?" came the boys voice and the Priest heard it just faintly as if coming from far away on the shores. *"You have to ignore them, Father. They are not real. You know this. The water's not real. None of it is this time."*

Father Leary closed his eyes, the hands still tugging at him, but not as many now, the water still surrounding him though, the water still very much a threat as he sank under. Then the boy's voice again, Ryan Woods, but inside his head now.

"You can breathe. There's nothing there. Think of something good. Think of the times you were happy, not the lake or the water, something else. Anything else before it's too late."

He thought back to the day he got his calling. The day he decided to become a priest. He thought of his acceptance into the church. The bright day with his parents sitting there front row as he knelt before the altar of God accepting his first communion. The large wooden cross, the tiny flickering candles, the Mother Mary statue in the corner, the smiling Father Hoffman standing above him. He felt at peace as those rays of sunlight streamed in through stain glass windows over his narrow frame while kneeling there in the presence of the Lord.

***

"Thank you." the priest said opening his eyes and finding himself on all fours. Only one set of hands remained on him now, those of Ryan Woods. Soon another joined them as Laura Woods helped him to his feet. The fog had almost cleared away along with the illusions. "You lose, Woods."

"I d-don't understand w-what happened." came the shaky voice of the janitor, Chip Douglas, who knelt there trembling at the door to the kitchen. "W-here am I? Why d-did I do b-bad things?"

"It's not your fault, son." Thomas Leary said kneeling next to him while Laura moved over to help the lunch lady who was also crying and trembling as much as Chip was. "You were not in control."

"I killed someb-body, I know I d-did." the tall man whimpered and fell into the priest's chest to sob. "He m-made me do it. I did b-bad things."

"I'm so sorry." Father Leary said looking over at Laura who held the plump little woman who shook at the sight of this janitor she thought she knew so well, now backing away from him.

"He was going to kill us." the lunch lady mumbled while back paddling across the floor. "Why did you do this, Chip? What did we do to you?"

"S-so s-sorry." the janitor said still shaking. "I d-didn't mean t-to do it."

"Stay still." Father Leary said holding him tighter. "How can I make him understand?"

"Where's Marty?" Ryan asked stepping between the kneeling adults. He saw the back door to the kitchen wide open and took off in a mad dash in that direction despite the warning yells from both his mother and Father Leary. "Marty?" he called running up the steps to the parking lot of the school. "Dad?" he called again this time knowing full well what had happened. His father had found another weak soul to possess. Now he had a boy, an innocent child, as his new evil puppet. "Damn you." Ryan heard himself say as Father Leary joined him.

"Your mom is going to stay with them both for a minute. I'm not sure what we are going to tell them, or how much of what just happened they will understand."

"None of it, I guess." the boy spat back scanning the edges of the parking lot and play ground.

"Did you see which way he went?"

Ryan just lowered and shook his head.

"No. He must have taken off while I was bringing you out of your trance." Ryan said back as they both headed towards the car. They never made it.

"Stop right there!" came the booming voice of Deputy Lambert. The big cop with the scars and burn marks had his gun drawn, right on Father Leary. He had two other cops standing to his left and right, both had their guns out as well. "Nobody moves until we straighten this shit out!"

"Deputy, the man you are looking for is getting away." Father Leary told him.

"Really? All I know is that Chief Rollins is dead downstairs in the boy's room with his throat slit and we found Officer Brunswick dead on your basement floor, Father. Heart attack."

"Jesus, no." Father Leary said letting his hands remain up. "Not again."

"I guess it's time we tell him what's going on, Thomas." Laura said from the top of the stairs. "Miss Turner is with the others. She want's to know what's going on too."

"Laura?" Lambert said spinning in her direction but letting his gun lower at the sight of the woman he cared for so much. "Why are you here? Why are any of you here? What is going on?"

"You won't believe us." Father Leary warned him letting his arms drop as Lambert instructed his fellow officers to do the same with their weapons. "Not in a million years."

"Try me." the big cop said moving closer. "And make it good."

"It's Alan, Wes." Laura started. "He's the one doing this."

The big cops eyes narrowed in confusion and then almost laughed looking back and forth between her and the priest and the boy. His tone was serious but the smile remained.

"Alan? *Your* Alan?" he sighed and shook his large head. "Laura, Alan is dead. Has been for quite some time. I was there, remember?" he said pointing out his war wounds.

"We know how this sounds, Deputy, but it's true." Father Leary continued. "You only killed a part of the man that night. The physical part. What remains is much worse."

"This is nuts." the big cop smiled and turned to his two grinning cops on either side of him. "You here this, boys? We have a zombie on the loose. Maybe we should put out an A.P.B. on the Boogeyman."

"Maybe you should." Ryan Woods spoke up. "Because that's what you're dealing with."

FORTY THREE

Marty Fitzgerald had run until his tiny legs could take no more. Alan Woods was actually in control of course. This boy was merely a tiny meat and bone puppet. He scanned his frail mind and knew where the boy lived, only seven blocks away, but would not go there. That would be the first place they would look. Alan was tired right now. He needed some rest. He had done way too much soul jumping in one day. The cop, the janitor, the boy now. He needed rest before another battle with the holy trilogy back there.

He headed for the ballpark. Past that would be the woods and a creek. At the end of that creek was a place to hide away from the prying eyes of his son and his gift of sensing his presence, a place to hide away from the visions of the animals he now had under his control. He knew a place this boy Marty Fitzgerald went to when he felt alone and scared. Now it would serve him as well.

Apple Green Drive was a narrow paved road that led to the park. Tall gray trees with naked witch finger branches covered the path as he walked while cautiously keeping his eyes open for any cops that might be out looking for him. There was only one old man there at the edge of the dugout, walking his little shitty mutt for the afternoon. Marty smiled and waved as the man threw him a curious glance along with the return wave. He sensed the boy he now housed knew this old man.

"You look familiar, boy. Don't I know you? Marty something or another? Shouldn't you be in school?" the old codger said returning a pipe to his mouth. Marty smiled wider as he stopped by the fence to get a good feel of this man's fears. Maybe he could use an afternoon snack. The priest and his ex-wife were tasty but he needed a boost right now. Something to tide him over while he planned his next move.

"Sick day." he said with his distorted adult voice and the man's eyes went as wide as open windows and actually took a few steps back while palming his pipe. *"And I doubt if you really know me."*

"Sounds pretty bad alright." he said and Alan reached out as only he truly could and grasped the old man's mind with soft invisible fingers The old man had many fears.

He saw flashes of news reports across many T.V. stations. News stories of elderly people being taken advantage of through various scams and schemes. His generation being ignored and shoved away into nursing homes. Younger and stronger punks and thugs that constantly robbed them in the streets. It was this last one that sent a joyful jolt through his heart and he met the old man's curious glare with one of his own. He knew his greatest fear and it was a feast fit for a king. "You okay, son?"

"Just worried about you." he told the narrow framed man whose dog was now growling. Behind the old man in the soft dirt of the ball field three figures rose up from the ground in swirls of mud and leaves. Images Alan plucked from the old man's mind. They took on the shapes and form of everything the old man feared.

"Rocky, what's wrong?" the old man said turning to see what it was that had gotten his dog's attention. He assumed it was possibly a rabbit or stray cat passing through the field, only to see three young boys in baggy jeans and over-sized T-shirts headed his way.

"Hey, gramps." the middle one said. He was a tall, white boy with shades and a backward cap. Snake tattoos ran up and down his arms and he carried a shiny switchblade. "You got some spare cash?"

"Yeah old man, can you help a brother out?" the shorter but more muscular black teen with a sleeveless shirt on asked casting his widest smile while running his hand over his cornrows. He had a skull tattoo on one shoulder and a pair of guns inked on his other. "We need to get some brews, you know what I'm saying? Hotter than a motherfucker out here."

"I don't really have anything on me." he said turning to the boy for help who was still smiling. "You little shit, did you set this up?" he said and Alan enjoyed the look of anger mixed with fear. "No good worthless bastards, all of you."

"Come on, poppy." the Latino teen said coming around to the old man's left. A tall skinny boy with a Yankee Jersey. He had slick black hair and dark eyes. "Old man like you must be loaded, right?" he smiled over his pencil thin mustache and flashy gold chains. "Give us some of those social security funds. Help out the less fortunate, you know?"

"Why don't you all get some jobs."

Alan stood there in the body of the child grinning at the old man's stereotypical illusions of how he saw all young teens. Mean and vicious without conscience. Swaggering wolves constantly on the prowl seeking to take advantage of the older and weak. Perhaps to some extent he was right. This would do just fine, but he didn't want to kill the old man and leave any dead clues along his trail of escape. A few more moments would be good enough.

214

"You don't want to give us any trouble, bitch." the white boy said waving the knife only inches from the old man's face. The black teen reached down and snatched up the dog and stuck out his tongue while playfully backing away, all the while the dog whimpering and barking.

"You leave my Rocky alone!" the old man started toward him and the Latino reached out and grabbed him by the shoulders from behind. "Don't you hurt him!"

"Calm down, your pooch is fine." the Latino boy told the old man while bringing his muscular arm around for a chokehold. "Now let's have a look at the inventory."

"Cash, credit, jewelry, cell-phones." the black teen grinned while petting the wriggling dog. "Anything will do just fine."

"I don't have a cell, take the rest, just leave me and Rocky alone." he breathed breaking free as the Latino let him loose. The white boy grinned as he stepped up and held out his hands while the old man dug in his slacks, coming out with first his flat brown wallet, followed by his gold watch, his wedding ring, which he was going to have fun telling his wife about for sure, and placed them in his hands. "There, you little thieves. Take it and let us be. Plenty of jobs out there for everyone, you know."

"This pays better." the black teen smiled setting the dog down. The old man knelt in the dirt as the dog ran up to him and began licking his face as he took him up in his shaking arms. "That's very fucking touching. Hallmark moment, boys."

"And me without a fucking camera." the white boy smiled passing the goods around between his two friends. "Maybe we will see you again sometime?"

"Same time next week?" the Latino grinned kicking a cloud of dust at both man and tiny beast. "Give you some time to save up for us." he laughed and his friends joined in as they started to walk away.

"Bastards." he whispered to himself and kept Rocky in his arms as he slowly rose to his feet and turned to go back they way he came. The way home. He turned to the fence where the young boy stood, that creepy smile still present on his pale face. "You little prick. You were a part of this, weren't you? How much are you getting out of this, huh? What's your cut? How much?"

"A comic and a soda." the man-child lied with a laugh. *"It was worth it."*

"I know your face, young man. Marty something?" the old man said hurrying away with his heart still racing. "I know your mother. You can bet she will get a call. They will find those thugs."

Alan Woods smiled at the retreat of the elderly man and his whimpering dog. Marty Fitzgerald's mom just might get a call one day and Marty would remember none of it. The three teens that did not exist in the first place would never be found. And the cops, or some lucky passerby, would find a wallet along with a watch and wedding ring, right there in a neat pile on home plate. Alan Woods had no need for them.

The rest of the walk was peaceful. Alan was feeling chipper again as he saw the edge of the creek come into view. Sure there had been a few hitches in the game plan, but that was okay. Just made him that more anxious, that much more excited. Things were going just fine. He just had to come up with a better plan. Had to find a weak link in the chain, a chink in the armor his son now wore so bravely.

Down past the tall weeds and cat tails, over rocks and muddy waters, past broken beer bottles and abandoned shopping carts, to where he saw the secret hiding place of the weak boy Marty Fitzgerald who had once pissed his pants when, of all people, Alan's own daughter Amy, had scared him one night at a sleep over. This still haunted the boy.

"What a little bitch I am today." Alan laughed heading towards the dark sewer tunnel opening. Not very big, but just enough room for a small child or pissy pants here. He climbed up into the cool darkness and kept crawling through the smelly wet until the morning sun was no longer able to reach him. There he sat and pulled his knees up to his chest and let his frail arms rest over each other and nodded his head for a nap. It was time to take inventory. Past the little fears and paranoia's of this child's every day bullied life. Past the insecurities he felt around the pretty girls at school and the family he had back on Larch Street. Alan Woods needed an advantage. He needed some knowledge. Obviously this runt knew his son, perhaps there was something there that could be useful. A smile edged its way over his face.

"Somebody's having a party." he said out loud and gave a soft giggle. *"Somebody very pretty who just happens to have a crush on my son."*

FORTY FOUR

"I'm not getting anything." Ryan said feeling defeated once more. Somehow his father had slipped away from them. While he was busy pulling Father Leary and his mother out of their illusions of fear, his father had taken over Marty and ran off.

"If you feel anything at all let us know." Thomas Leary said still driving. He also felt defeated. They had stopped by the Fitzgerald residence, along with the skeptical Deputy Lambert, and told them they wanted to talk to their son. The story they came up with was that Marty was frightened because he had witnessed the murder of Chief Rollins. It was all the Deputy could assume had happened since he wasn't buying the whole Boogeyman story. "I wonder how close you have to be to pick up on him."

"Not sure." Ryan answered back. "He was pretty close last time. No telling where he is now."

"Or *who* he is." Laura pointed out. "How long would he stay a child? I think he'd have a better advantage being a full-grown man. Someone with access to weapons or a car."

"Very true." Father Leary said. "We just have to figure out what he's up to. I mean we have who he wants with us. But he might not try another direct attack."

"Why wouldn't he?" Laura asked watching the houses pass by as they drove. Normal houses with normal problems like failed math tests or arguments over who gets to watch what on cable or maybe even some date on a Friday night with a boy far too old and odd looking to take out their daughter. Laura Woods missed these common place hassles that now seemed millions of years ago. The very things that used to give her headaches and kept her awake at night seemed so trivial now compared to this horror. She would give anything to have that simple life back now. "He could do like before and just take control of some dogs or maybe a group of people and-"

"Because Ryan is stronger than he expected." Father Leary cut in. "Otherwise he would have stayed and fought this morning. He nearly had me, and I bet you too, but he was never close to having Ryan. The only reason Ryan never got to attack him was because he was busy saving us."

"I'm sorry." Ryan said nodding his head down in the back seat.

"No, Ryan, we should be apologizing to you." the priest went on. "We underestimated him as much as he did you. I had no idea I still held onto my fear of water. We will be better prepared next time."

217

"So what do you think he's doing?" Laura said leaning back and closing her eyes wishing she had an aspirin, or even better a cigarette. "He can't keep running forever."

"He doesn't intend to." Father Leary said as they pulled into the parking lot of Scooters. "We wait to see if he shows up, but in the mean time I think it's time for Ryan to try his trick again." he said parking the jeep and looking back at Ryan. "If he feels up to it?"

"You want me to look for him like I did before with the bird?" Ryan guessed hoping out into the nearly warming daylight. "Where do I start?"

"Anywhere you want. I'm not sure where he's headed. Just look around and see if you can see your friend Marty. I'm sure your gift works the same way through the animals as it does through you. In other words, if you get close enough to him I'm betting you will feel it."

"Hope so." Ryan said standing a bit away from the jeep as he closed his eyes and took in a deep breath and began to focus.

"You know we will never get the police to believe any of this." Laura said stepping close to the priest while they both watched her son slip into some mysterious trance. "Not Wes Lambert. Not any of them."

"Maybe that's for the best." Father Leary said looking around to make sure Ryan didn't attract any unnecessary attention. "They would just end up getting themselves killed like Rollins."

"Deputy Lambert won't stop looking for a murder suspect." Laura warned. "He might keep his eyes on you."

"If he does that's his choice, Laura. He will regret that decision. That I can promise you. We may have to find a way to throw him off since he's not going to listen to the truth."

"I can't blame him, Thomas, the truth is unreal." she whispered back. "He may have to see for himself. We could use all the help we can get."

"And what will he do when he sees, Laura." he asked turning on her. "Shoot and kill an innocent man or woman your husband takes possession of? Be taken over himself so that we have to kill him? There's no good scenario involving more people in this. Everyone who has known of this is now dead. Your old neighbor, that Bates boy, Benjamin Kelly, your daughter's boyfriend, Rollins. Lord knows where this child is at out there and who else is now housing that evil psycho. Where does it end?"

"With him." she said turning to stare at her son. "It ends with him, Thomas. My son. He will be the last one Alan faces no matter what, right? That's what I have to worry about. If Alan gets inside my son it's all over and he will never leave him. Not until he dies."

"And then he will move on to somebody else. We have to stop this with Ryan's help, but we don't need anyone else. We told Lambert and he laughed, so be it. Let him chase cobwebs while we pursue the real threat. Alan has to come out of hiding if he wants to get your son."

"Yes, but come out of hiding with what on his side is what I'm worried about." she said watching her son slowly fade back into their own world. A doubtful look was on his face. A face that now seemed to be growing a little older every day because of all it had seen and all of the pain it had endured.

"Any luck, Champ?" the priest asked.

"He must be hiding really good." Ryan sighed. "I tried jumping from bird to bird." he said and wobbled a bit in their direction. Laura shot out to grab him before he fell over. "Whoa!" he actually laughed as he fell into his mother's arms. "Guess I over did it."

"Good guess." Laura said hugging her son and kneeling with him. "We don't try that stunt again no time soon, okay?"

"But mom, I have to try and see all over Waverly, otherwise-"

"We will find another way." Father Thomas Leary said digging his car keys out.

"What do you have in mind?" Laura asked.

"We need to go back to where it started." he said climbing into the jeep. "That parking lot where he burned and died. He went there for a reason. He knew he was dying of cancer and up until that point, as far as we know, he couldn't switch bodies like he's doing now. He wanted to die on purpose, but why there? Something happened there that night and maybe with Ryan's help we can figure it out."

FORTY FIVE

More dreams. Dreams of the past, of childhood long ago, of summer skies and distant laughter. Alan Woods too had been a boy once. A boy much like his own son, with timid ways and shy doe eyes both curious and imaginative. And now he was so again.

He stood in a boy's room, a typical boy's room, with sports and action heroes plastered over his walls. Terry Bradshaw, who his father said was overrated. Bruce Lee, who his father said was on drugs because no normal man could move that fast. Muhammad Ali, who his father said was a coward for dodging the draft. His father hated all of his heroes.

He stood there and watched the sun set quickly, turning day into darkest of nights and finally he laid down in his bed, hearing his father's old muscle car roar up in the driveway, the door slamming too hard and his father singing some tune as he staggered up the front steps.

His mother would let him in before he started banging on the door or cursing because he dropped his keys. They would talk or argue. They would make their way to the bedroom and then the moaning and cries of passion would become so great that he would have to put his pillow over his head to get some sleep.

"I'm not hurting her, boy. I'm making her feel good like all women like to feel." he would smile at him the next morning over breakfast and Alan would just shy away.

Alan woke from his dream still inside his dream. He was still a boy and his father, Carl Woods, would be sitting there in the corner of his room. Alan knew this because he could always smell the smoke first, then see the dark shape of the old man just sitting there, his head laid back, a cloud of blue shooting out of his mouth, and without looking he knew his son was awake.

"Almost time for you to carry the load, son." he would say. *"Time for me to pass the torch."*

Young Alan had no idea what his father was talking about. He drank a lot, talked even more, and made little or no sense most of the time. He would sit there in the dark and that little orange light from his cigarette sometimes wasn't the only thing glowing there in the corner. Sometimes his eyes would seem to be glowing too, much like a cat's did when the light reflected off it, but only there was no light reflecting off his father's eyes. This glow was coming from inside him.

"I'm getting too old for this shit." he said one night, it was the last night he would ever see his father alive again, but not the last night he would ever hear his voice. *"You're going to have to shoulder the burden some, son. Time to be the man of the house."*

Deep in his heart young Alan Woods thought his father was sitting there confessing his decision to leave them, and that was fine with Alan. He had always heard stories about how some father's drove off to get a pack of smokes or a gallon of milk from the nearest gas station only never to be heard from again. Drive away in that loud black car with the Stone's blasting and never come home drunk again.

But that wasn't the entire plan was it?

"I have to go away. Only in body though, boy, not in spirit. In spirit I will always be with you. Just like my father did with me and his before him and his before him, and well, you get where I'm going with this shit I guess." he said and his father stood then coming to the edge of the bed. Alan froze. He had also heard stories about father's who did things to their sons they ought not to. Bad things.

Alan had a friend once named Kenny West. Kenny's dad had fondled him in places no father should ever touch his son and Kenny didn't tell anyone. Kenny let it happen for years until one day his mother caught his father doing these things to him and then things went bad fast. His parents split, Kenny's dad went to jail, and Kenny started drinking. By the time he was thirteen he had a serious problem. He was drinking too much and he was starting to fondle little boys and girls himself and one day when he was fifteen and started driving well Kenny drove his father's own car straight into a tree doing well over eighty.

Kenny did these things and Alan Woods fed on them because by that time Alan had the gift that his father had passed to him that night in his room and he had no choice. He was hungry and Kenny had so much to offer in pain and fears and regrets. The wolf had found the rabbit and found him exquisite.

"This won't hurt, boy. That I promise." his father said in a deep whisper and Alan laid there still and so scarred as the faint moonlight washed in past curtains over his bed and those glowing eyes that swirled in colors of purple and red and green descended on him and made him feel weak and helpless as years later Kenny and many more would feel. Like easing into a warm blanket being wrapped up in some strange drug that both frightened and relaxed all at once.

His father said other things that night as he leaned over and embraced him. Things Alan Woods to this day as the evil bastard he was could still not remember. But he knew two things then as he did now.

His father did not want to do what he did, he had to, he was commanded to. He could see it on his face, somewhere past the glowing eyes and strange voice was a gentler soul that was out of control and no longer holding onto the wheel of where things were headed. He also knew his father was not alone that night. There were other *things* there with him.

Evil and wicked things just off to the edge of his sight and hiding in the shadows, watching and giggling like school children who had seen something naughty and thought it amusing. Things with no certain faces or form, but felt all the same. Tiny little specks of light for eyes, quick and nimble in movement, first here then there, on the ceiling, below his bed, outside his window pressed up against the glass, always watching and learning and delighted at the spectacle that took place.

The transference of soul to soul.

His father was right, it did not hurt, at least not in the physical way like a shot at the doctor's or a fall from a tree or a sucker punch from a schoolyard bully. But the things that flashed through his mind as his father made contact with him were terrifying. He could see people he did no know dying, all at the hands of his father. He could feel their pains if only for a split second, their fears.

An old woman burning in her cellar, a teen boy drowning in his car, a woman hanging herself with an extension cord in a garage, a little girl slipping and falling in a shower with thousands of bugs all over her and her screams shattering his skull for the briefest second. A man running from things in the woods, large dogs of some kind, another woman trapped in a closet with dozens of rats breaking their way through the doors to devour her.

And then it was over as soon as it had started. In that moment he snapped open his eyes his father was gone and so were those tiny shadows that lurked about him. He heard the monster engine roar to life and peeked out the slits of blinds to see those red taillights fading fast. He would never see his father again in person. He would see him on the news and in the papers. The man who walked into a drug store and robbed it, shooting three people before the local cops surrounded the place and killed him in a bloody shootout that ended in a blaze of fire as the place went up in smoke, his father reportedly laughing the whole time while firing away at officers, telling everyone in one way or another that he would be back.

Then he switched gears in this dream. He saw a farmhouse, with a big red, white and blue barn and horses and a scarecrow out in the middle of a field. There were children there, playing and laughing and having a good time and Alan Woods knew he had never been there, this was not his past, so it must have been his son's present day life. And such a pretty girl standing there dressed up like a witch or some vampire damn thing. Red hair and freckles all over her face and the brightest green hazel eyes.

"Corrigan Farm. Uncle Joey Corrigan."

It was a Halloween party and he had been invited. Two nights away.

"Finch." he whispered at her and she seemed to shiver as if a goose walked over her grave and perhaps one did just do that. *"Anna Finch."* he said again and smiled. She liked his boy and he liked her too, could feel it all the way here inside this dream. She was going to be at this party, and so was Ryan, and so was Marty Fitzgerald, and so most certainly was Alan Woods.

"Sweet." Alan Woods mumbled to himself as he woke from this strange spectacle and realized he was still housed within the young boy, Marty Fitzgerald, here inside the sewer tunnels. It had been years since he thought of his father and how he had gone out the exact same way. It was far past time that things passed from father to son once more to keep the legacy going, whether anyone liked it or not. *"Getting too old for this shit, boy."* he grinned as he rose up and thought about the party.

A farmhouse, somewhere far enough away that walking or biking would not do, so he would he definitely have to improvise. He might need a friendly ride from someone headed his way. Yes, it would not be long before he made sure that he could be young again like his father before him. Things were starting to look up after all.

That's just the way things were when you were a part of the Woods family. You took your ancestors along for the ride, but the part that did the scaring and the feeding, that was a part that had been there all along, since the beginning. Since the wars of old, since the time Christ walked the earth and the Pharaohs before him, and the garden and the dinosaurs, and the twinkling of distant stars before the void and the darkness, and there would always be darkness.

Always.

And it would continue as long as the blood son of the one before him lived to pass it onto the next. He did not have to be willing to take it, he could be forced, but somehow that had changed. Ryan Woods, his only son, was different. He held the gift sooner than most, and held it with control of some sort. That was fine too. A challenge but still doable. Because once Alan Woods and all the bastards before him had finally squirmed their way into the body of Ryan Woods, the strongest so far in the bloodline that he knew of, all Hell was going the break loose.

And that would be when the real fun began. But for now he needed the upper hand again.

"Where the hell are my children?" the man-child called into the sewer tunnel, his smoky voice echoing in the darkness. He could feel some of them close, some of them eager to come, licking their little lips and small feet and smooth scaled bodies hurrying towards his voice. Others he sensed hesitation, a bit of doubt, and why not, they were confused in the serving of two masters. *"There can only be one master, kiddies. Hear my voice and my thoughts. Get the hell out there and find my son!"*

The rats made it first, hordes of them climbing over one another, and he could hear their screams first, their very heartbeats, then the undeniable stench of their presence. Large black birds formed small clouds outside as they came down and landed on the naked tree limbs. They sat in remarkable silence while waiting for their dark masters instructions. Snakes of various length and sizes slithered out of weeds and from behind rocks. More than a few cats made their way along fences and brush to join the late meeting, a few possum, and even some stray dogs of rather pleasing size and strength. The boy smiled as he felt them all near, waiting for his commands.

"Search everywhere!" he screamed to them from the darkness. *"Find my boy. Follow him and let me know where they are sleeping tonight. We're gonna catch 'em with their guard down."*

He laughed as the rats headed back into the sewers, the dogs and cats and other small mammals headed out into the streets and the birds took flight into the sky. He knew his son was probably doing the same thing, using those who he could control to find him. A race to the finish. A dark version of hide-and-seek.

"Ready or not, here I come." he smiled leaning back into the darkness.

FORTY SIX

"Last time I was here I didn't feel so good." Ryan said feeling the tingling start as they pulled into the strip mall.

"When was this?" his mother asked back.

"First time I went to see him." he said pointing to Father Leary while leaning up over the seat. He could feel the presence of evil here, and it wasn't just his father. "I think this is more than just where he died."

"It's where he was reborn." Father Leary finished for him as the found a spot near the middle of the lot. "Something happened that night that we need to understand. Something very special to your father, besides his death."

"Let me out." Ryan said almost in a panicked whisper. "I need some air."

"Are you okay?" Laura said exiting. "You feel sick?"

"Not sick, just . . . Different." he said looking around the lot. It was the same parking lot he had passed a few days ago, more cars and people, but it felt strange now.

"Try to concentrate in on it, Ryan." Father Leary said coming around the Jeep. "Close your eyes and focus. Work your way through this."

"Thomas, if this is going to make him sick-"

"I'm fine, mom." Ryan said and breathed deep while closing his eyes, trying his best to block out the car horns and distant voices. All of it evaporated away into silence as his heart seemed to slow and his mind took him far away without leaving this place. Far into the past.

***

He opened his eyes and saw the darkness of the night, although he knew it was day, and instantly knew he was in the past. Far past the time when his father died. Far past the time when the first brick or wood plank was set into place in this town of Waverly. Far past the time when human lungs breathed air on a dark patch of land before it was called America.

"Where am I?" he called to the darkness and the darkness smiled at him. He could not see this intangible smile, it held no visible teeth, but he felt it, cold and slippery across his skin. He could see the stars across the night sky looming over the land which held little shape other than blackness. And among those stars one shined brighter than the rest. It twinkled, shimmered with rage, and grew larger as it came closer, shooting towards the earth with no force Ryan Woods virgin eyes had yet seen.

It smashed into the earth with the roar of a train, shaking the grounds and lighting the sky for only a second, long enough for Ryan to see misshapen trees and large hulking stones of a time he never read about in books or internet sites. After the flash the star faded away and only its prisoner lay there in the damp dark earth naked and still. It was a man, Ryan noted, or at least it resembled one, large with burgundy smooth skin that was well toned. He lay in the fetal position and seemed to have steam coming off every part of his body as the burning embers around him lit up his tall frame in a circle of fire.

"Who are you?" Ryan asked.

A purple eye opened and shed a violet tear. A mouth opened to a set of teeth that Ryan thought would have shamed a snake. The frame rolled over on its back and the man stretched out those long roped muscular arms to the heavens and that mouth opened wider and emitted a scream so loud that Ryan fell to his knees from the pain.

"WHYYYYYYYYYY???" the thing roared, its head lolling about as the eyes went wide with both physical and spiritual pains. **"I LOVED YOU FIRST!!!"** it hissed and flung itself upright on its bare feet. It stood there, this blood hued man, nearly as tall as a house and steam still pouring off its naked skin, and seemed to hurt to breath the air. **"CAST ME DOWN, WILL YOU? I'M NOT DONE."**

And then there were many more stars falling. Ryan couldn't count them all but he was sure they numbered in the thousands. Each one split open and spawned a new man, not quite as bright or large as the first man, but still of the same breed all the same.

"I know you." Ryan said to the first giant and the thing turned to him and this time he did see a smile. A smile that while wide and bright, held no joy or beauty or love at all, but the very absence of these things. It was pure evil. It was horror in living form.

"THE BEGINNING OF FEAR." the man thing said as he stood over the steaming form of another fallen one, another shape. Ryan could see this one was not a man, but clearly a female of sorts.

226

The hair long and flowing, the almond shaped eyes, the huge bare breasts and perfect shaped buttocks that Ryan could not seem to tear his eyes away from. She smiled too and stepped away from the bright circles and fell into the arms of her large lover into a steamy embrace. They shared wicked laughter.

"My lover and my lord." she hissed pressing up against him. "Lucifer."

"LILLITH, MY LOVER AND SOULMATE." the large man said holding her face gently up to his as he lowered himself upon her there on the bare rocks. **"WHAT ARE YOU AFRAID OF? TELL ME SO WE MAY SPAWN IT THROUGHOUT THE EARTH AND THE MEN TO FOLLOW ME WILL LIVE IN FEAR AND DARKNESS AND WE SHALL RULE THEM WITH IT."**

The ground around them shook and fell and formed a deep pit. *"Like a basement."* his young mind thought while watching the two giants crawl towards each other. The inhuman lovers quickly found each other in the debris and flames and embraced once more in a kiss. Ryan's young eyes took in the spectacle with both curious wonder and sickening rage. He had never seen sex before, not live and in person anyways, so it was hard to look away. Once Jeff Bates, his now dead best friend, had taken a Hustler magazine from his father's sock drawer out to the footbridge by the ball park and they had looked at it with great interest and Ryan could see pretty much those sexual situations happening here, but he knew what they were spawning.

This was not making love. The very absence of love was felt here. There was only sexual desire, lust and even above those things, a wicked plot to spread this evil and fear all across the face of the earth. As the large figures joined and the man thing entered the woman and her cries echoed through Ryan's ears, he could see the ground around them swelling up and bubbling with life. New evil lives were forming.

Creatures of living darkness sprang forth from the shadows. Spidery things with way too many legs, long snaking slick beasts with nearly human faces, squirming black masses of tangled flesh of all colors coiled around the lovers as they continued their heinous act, and soon the ground was alive with all forms of nightmares coming to life and making their way out of the pit, across the dark grounds, and heading out all across the land, swimming out to the water, and on dark leathery wings finding their way to the skies, the oceans, the hills, and to the very ends of the earth.

"This is how it all began." Ryan thought. "This is where fear came from. Where evil came from." he swallowed hard with a tear rolling down his face. "Where I came from."

227

The scene that followed was blurred away and time sped forward through desserts and hills and flames of wars. Ryan reached out to hold onto something to keep from falling but only the darkness was there. He watched those who he knew belonged to his bloodline, his family, surge past in quick forms of one or another. Killers and madmen and tyrants all of them. Pirates and knights and soldiers and serial killers. Each one passing the dark gift onto the son, who in turn passed it onto his as well. And on it went as from the beginning until the end.

Then he saw another man, a man much like his own father, but not quite. He was big, with the tattoo's and long hair and the black car. He was in the drug store. Gunfire was exchanged and he laughed much like his son would years later inside a car burning on this same lot.

"I'm not done yet." he yelled as the cops shot him down at the doorway of a drugstore and Ryan knew he was watching his own grandfather die in a pool of blood. But not really dead and gone.

In what seemed like years, only seconds passed, and soon he was back to the night his father died. He could see his father's large black car on the parking lot, the police encircled around him with guns drawn, the girl screaming inside, and the smile on his father's face.

"Tell me what you're afraid of." he could hear the voice of the man he barely knew or remembered until just the past few days. He could see the dark shapes around his father then, all around the car, in the glass of the windows, in the mirrors, and dancing around unseen by the cops on the parking lot.

"Sacred ground." Ryan said out loud and could feel this was the same place that the stars had fallen all of those years ago. Where fear was born in the darkest night after the Father of Lies had been thrown free from Heaven in the first war of all wars. This is where they all returned. This is where his father's father had come and died, and the one before his, and the one before his . . .

"If they die here, they can come back. If they come here to die, they can keep living through others and keep living off fears." Ryan gasped and felt himself being pulled free of his trance by an outside source. The darkness swirled away and the light came shining through.

***

"Ryan!" his mother called shaking him. "Honey, are you okay?"

228

"Yeah, Mom." he said blinking away the images and finally seeing Father Leary's face alongside his mothers. "It's sacred ground. This place." he said waving his small hand from edge to edge.

"Maybe sacred is the wrong word." Father Leary pointed.

"This is where it all started." Ryan continued. "This is where Lucifer fell to earth and spawned evil. This is where they come to die and if they die here they come back even more powerful in others."

"So he died here on purpose five years ago." Father Leary said. "And now he needs you to keep going. He can possess these other people, but only for awhile. He needs his son."

"He won't have him." Laura warned hugging him tighter. "I won't let him. I will die first."

"We can't let him keep hurting everybody else, Mom." Ryan said up to his mother's tearing eyes. "I have to face him again. I have to stop my father."

"He's right." Father Leary said kneeling down. "Alan inherited what his bloodline gave him, as did your son. He knew he had to come here after he found out he had cancer so he could die and then come back. But it seems that coming back has its limits, he needs a permanent housing, so to speak. He needs a host to inhabit for their entire life, and what better host than his own son who already has that power in him. What he didn't count on was Ryan's desire for good over evil. I have a feeling that up until now that the son next in line has always been on the willing side, or eventually gave in."

"Neither one of those is me." Ryan said. "I'm not going to accept it and I'm not giving in."

"Good. That's what I want to hear." the priest said standing again. "Now that we know what he is and who you are and what you come from and how he got here and why, now all that remains is how in the hell do we stop him?"

"We give him what he wants." Ryan said to both adults backing away. "We give him me."

FORTY SEVEN

The second search went about as well as the first. Ryan wasn't sure where his father was but he was hidden well. Hiding and waiting. So now they were back at the motel, Father Leary seated in front of the television with the volume turned down low, although Ryan could still hear. The top story of the day was of course still Chief Rollins murdered body found in the boys' bathroom up at the school. There was some mention of another cop being found in Father Leary's basement, and that the priest had no comment as he was not there at the time, and he was not being considered a suspect. How nice.

His mother sat in the far corner on her cell phone, first talking to her sister, Aunt Cheryl, and then Amy, who was doing better and sleeping pretty good but still did not want to come home, which was also good, and then she talked to Aunt Cheryl some more. Then finally, to the soft sounds of his mother's sobbing and some old Twilight Zone rerun, Ryan Woods fell into a deep sleep.

***

Back into the blue of summer, bright skies and soft warm breezes, butterflies stirring at the fields edge among tall flowers and Ryan could see he was seated at the head of a long wooden table, not quite the traditional picnic table, more like something from a conference room in some fancy office building, long and polished deep black with five tall backed chairs of velvet on either side and one for each end. Only this table was smack dab in the middle of some park. He was also not alone.

To his immediate right was his mother, dressed in a pretty dress of blue and white, hair done up fine the way she used to wear it to church. Next to her was Amy, also in a traditional dress, something unheard of in real life, with long braids past her slender shoulders. Next to her was Brandon Lowe, also clean cut out of character in a nice dark suit with no signs of tattoos or bits of jewelry poked through ears or lips or eyebrows. Mister Clark sat tall and smiling next to him and chubby best friend Jeff Bates next to him.

On Ryan's left running up the five guests were, of course, Father Leary, decked out in full priest garb, white collar and silver cross and all, next to him was Mister Benjamin "My friends call me Scooter"

Kelly, and then Mister Darby, who Ryan was shocked to see clean shaven and in nice fitting gray suit and tie with bright white shirt and teeth to match. Madame Bulvaria seated herself next to him, the bright and colorful garments replaced by a simple blue skirt with pink blouse and the make up gone except for small shading around her eyes. The skinny cop, Brunswick, was next to her, his head bowed as if ready for prayer, and at the head of the table opposite his own seat was the once mighty and now fallen Chief Rollins.

Ryan barely recognized him, not only because of his fancy suit and well groomed appearance, but because the man was smiling. A wide and glowing smile, even when he made contact with Ryan, it was almost heart warming. As if all were forgiven.

"Let us pray." Father Leary said and all present, excluding Ryan who was still in a state or shock, bowed their heads and closed their eyes as hands extended out and grasped one another around the massive table and the display of food before them. Ryan could see and smell the plates of various meats dripping with barbecue sauces, bowls of steaming buttered corn, green beans and mashed potatoes, cornbread and gravy, pies of all flavors from his end of the table up to the very sleeves of Chief Rollins. "Dear Father in Heaven, we thank you for this joyous bounty before us, please bless it and those who are gathered here in your name-"

"Hey now!" came his father's voice from above and Ryan shot back off the chair, nearly falling in the process, as he looked up at the dark figure that hovered above them. It was his father, but so much more. Dressed in dark robes of black swirling around him as if the cloth were alive, his face seeming even darker, his hair longer, his eyes on fire with tiny embers of red, and he smiled as he came down to stand just to the left of Chief Rollins. *"What's this table of twelve crap. Thirteen is a much better number. What this last supper needs is a Judas."* he said reaching into his pockets and digging out several silver coins. He laughed as he tossed them onto the table watching them splash applesauce and gravy on those nearby. *"Nobody touch that. It's for the waiter. Always leave a good tip. Hey, I thought a father's place was at the head of the table?"* he grinned and with one swift motion whipped out a long blade and beheaded the older cop, sending his head bouncing past a plate of cranberry sauce. He shoved the remaining corpse over and took the chair for himself while clearing his throat. *"There now, that's much better."*

"Not afraid of you." Ryan said in a choked whisper.

"That's my boy." his father grinned back slicing away at Brunswick throat and sent the skinny cop flailing to the ground like a fish out of water grasping at his wounds. *"Never cared much for pig meat."*

"You won't win this." Ryan said coldly.

"That a fact." he replied while yanking a chicken wing out of Jeff Bates mouth. *"I do believe you've had enough to eat, fat boy. Leave some room for dessert."*

He backhanded Jeff then, the boy fell back and a large black snake too big to be real emerged from the soft wet grass and began to swallow him whole. Ryan noticed but kept his gaze focused on his father.

"Not real." he told him forcing a grin to his face. "They're already dead."

"One guess who killed the fuckers." Alan Woods said pointing a thumb as his chest. *"This guy."*

"But not me." Ryan shot back.

"Of course not, I need you, boy. And you need me." he said waving a hand to his right and both Madame Bulvaria and Mister Darby burst into flames and screamed as they fell backward off their bench. *"Now that's a fucking barbecue right there. Just fat and bone mostly though."*

"I will never be like you no matter what you try." Ryan said waving away the smoke that drifted across the table now obscuring his view somewhat as his father rose up to his full height, which seemed to be more than he remembered. "Never."

"You already are, little man." Alan Woods laughed and waved to the left this time, sending an army of tiny mice climbing over, into and out of every opening they could find on old Mister Clark's body. The old man cried out for help, choking on the tiny creatures that quickly found his mouth and began chewing their way into his eyes and skin. Seconds after he collapsed, Brandon Lowe's skin burst outward on his arms, neck and face with tiny spiders resulting in much the same condition as his elderly companion, which sent Amy up and screaming as she ran for some unseen horizon. *"Women. What the hell do they want from a guy? You bring 'em flowers, chocolates, jewelry, spiders and mice. Just can't make a bitch happy."*

"You will never hurt her." Ryan warned and promised all at once.

"Don't want her, boy." Alan said throwing a tiny jar at Mister Kelly that burst into a swarming cloud of bees. The large black man shot up, tried brushing them away without success and Ryan had to

avert his eyes for a moment while the buzzing insects consumed him once more, his swollen body falling over into the still smoking bodies next to him. *"Thought maybe the barbecue could use some honey."* he laughed rising up and stepping onto the table, kicking plates and glasses out of the way as he did. He took long but slow strides towards his son, but Ryan did not move.

"You will not have them." Ryan reminded him again.

"Would you like to see how they're going to die, boy?" he said squatting down and using one long bony finger to motion to both his mother and Father Leary. *"It's not pretty."*

"You don't know the future. You don't know they will die. I won't let you-"

"Let me!" Alan Woods screamed and reached out so fast Ryan could not see his hand, but felt it grip his tender exposed throat as he was lifted up into the air when his father stood once more there on the table before him. *"You little shit! I am your father, like it or not. You don't **let** me do anything. How well have you protected the rest of these worthless husks of skin, huh? Take a good look around you."* he said still holding Ryan by his throat, who was now having trouble breathing as he felt himself spin in all directions on the table while looking down at the aftermath of his father's evil. Eight bodies to be exact, God only knew how many more they didn't know of, maybe more cops, maybe Marty Fitzgerald.

"Go to hell." Ryan managed to squeak out as he reached up to grab his father's thick hairy wrist and the man just laughed at him.

"Already been, boy. Had so much fun they threw me out of that motherfucker." he said and dropped the child's body to the ground. *"Okay, party's over for now."* he said reaching down and grabbing both his mother and Father Leary by their throats and lifting them effortlessly into the air. *"Say goodbye to the happy couple."*

"Nooooo!" Ryan screamed and shot up, finding himself now floating in this dream, hands reached out and the sky growling under his rage. Alan Woods stood there, half in awe and half in fear and watched the skies fill with seemingly thousands of birds. "Get away!" he yelled and the thunder itself clapped hard and a bolt of bright lightning struck down to the table sending Alan Woods flying back to the ground with a dazed expression on his face. For the briefest second, Ryan Woods detected fear there on that aged and worn face. Only for a second. It was quickly masked by a wink and a smile along with a taunting thumbs up sign.

233

"There you go. That's how the hell you do it." he breathed as he started to rise up. *"Seem to have a handle on things in here too, don't we? Do you realize how special you are, Ryan? Don't you know you were born for this? All of that power?"*

"Get lost." Ryan said finally having composed himself once he saw his mother and Father Leary break free and run off behind him. "We will find you soon enough. I will find you. I will beat you."

"Not even in your dreams, boy." Alan Woods grinned and his body fell apart into a million tiny bugs which scattered, crawling and flying away, until only the dark robe remained lying there in a pile where he had once been. *"See you soon."* his voice echoed in promise, and Ryan Woods woke then, slowly as if being pulled through water or sand, until he opened his eyes to the bright sunlight of a Thursday morning.

FORTY EIGHT

"Little shit!" Alan said within Marty Fitzgerald's body as it jerked awake. *"How in the hell did he do that?"*

Alan Woods had acquired the ability to communicate with creatures of darkness at a young age and somewhat control his dreams but nothing like what his son had just done. Ryan was exceeding all of his expectations which was good in the sense that once Alan had him he could have so much fun with all of those skills. The bad part was that Ryan was mastering them too fast. Which meant Alan needed to move faster.

"Well if you can't fuck with somebody directly, I guess you just do it indirectly." he grinned crawling from the damp darkness of the sewer tunnel he'd been napping in out into the bright sunlight. It was Thursday, the day before Halloween, and Alan inside the little boy he was currently hosting, had a party to go to tomorrow night. Only Alan was going to get there early. All he needed was a ride.

It did not take long for the boy to find one. This was, after all, a small town and small town folk were just accommodating that way. One big nice and friendly Mayberry family. Once the boy reached the side of the road he'd barely gotten thirty yards before he heard the old green pickup puttering over the hill behind him. Marty, with a dark smiling Alan inside him, stuck out his thumb and smiled.

The big man in denim overalls behind the wheel smiled as he slowed and pulled over to the narrow shoulder and waved. Marty stood there grinning and finding the man's eyes, hoping to find something there, trying to get a feel for him. Maybe he was some lonely pervert out preying on little boys. One could always hope.

"Where you headed, son?" the man said turning down Tim McGraw on his radio.

"Corrigan farm." Alan's heavy voice came out of the boy and the man gave him a quizzical look.

"I know where that is." he said leaning over and giving the passenger door a hard shove open and Marty bounded up into the seat. "Have you there in a jiffy. That's a mighty long walk for a boy. Name is Teddy Coleman. Jack of all trades and master of none." he grinned. "And you are?"

"Marty." the boy smiled and grasped the man's hand tight. Alan was hoping for a transfer of souls but instead got quick flashes of the man's life. A buried wife seven years gone. A son somewhere

out on the West Coast. A granddaughter dressed like a princess. A black dog on a porch. Friends shooting pool in a local bar. And a church steeple. It was enough to make him want to vomit. So much goodness in this man's life, even through the pains, and his faith in God. He could see the man singing in the church choir, their voices, especially his, so strong and true. It was just too much.

Marty shook his hand free and let out a yelp.

"You okay?" Teddy Coleman asked. "I give you a carpet shock, son?"

"Must be it." the boy said with nausea leaning into the door. He felt even worse looking up and seeing a stain-glassed cross hanging from the review mirror and a dove magnet representing the Holy Spirit on the glove compartment. Of all the people he could have gotten picked up by, he had to go and get one from freakin' Billy Graham.

"You don't sound too healthy, son. You might want your mother to get you to a doctor. Sounds like your coming down with something."

"Yep." he mumbled while staring out the windows at the fields speeding by. He could only think about his troublesome son and drunken whore wife and that half faith priest out there somewhere hunting him down, planning and thinking of ways to stop him. This thought made him chuckle. The ride only lasted a short fifteen minutes, which was about five too many honky-tonk songs for him, and then the looming red, white and blue silo came into sight. The truck rolled to a stop and the radio went down once more so Teddy Coleman could speak.

"Here we are young man. Hope they are expecting you."

"Kind of a surprise." Alan said from inside the boy as he eased his way down out of the truck. His stomach actually hurt from being around this Good Samaritan. *"Thanks for the ride."* he said slamming the door shut and walking away as fast as he could from the truck and the sun catching rays of that cross.

"You take care, son." the man waved starting away. "Get that cold looked at."

"Screw off." the boy whispered making his way out of sight and falling to his knees and let loose with a spewing of many fluids. There was way too much faith in that truck. *"What the hell?"* he said and vomited some more. He thought how if that lousy priest had that old farmer's faith he would have been screwed long ago. Then the boy stood and took in his surroundings.

"Barn must be this way." he said heading off into the dying field of corn with most of it still far above his head. He hummed to himself as he moved along, feeling better already, and thought about his son and that cute little red head he liked so much. Soon they would all be reunited in a very special way that only he would truly enjoy. Perhaps Anna Finch would grow up a lot faster than she wanted.

Then he froze in his tracks at the sight of a figure up ahead. It was a big man, whoever he was, dressed in overalls and straw hat and Alan Woods, inside the body of Marty Fitzgerald, was about to take cover when he realized the man was not moving at all. He just stood there with arms outstretched.

"I'll be damned." the boy laughed. It was not a man at all. *"How about that shit."* he said realizing just what it was with the body stretched out across some tall pole. *"You're the first thing to give me a fight in years, and you're just a scarecrow."* he said kicking the thing as he walked past.

He made his way free of the cornfields, walked past a nice-sized lake with blue and red paddleboats tied to a wooden dock and finally came the barn and farmer's home. He stood there with a bit of caution, his young eyes darting about for any signs of life. No people. No Uncle or Aunt. No workers. No cats or dogs, but something was in the barn. Something alive, but not human. Not a threat, but something that could be *turned* into a threat.

"Bigger than a breadbox." he said and crept into the cool shadows of the barn. The smell of hay and shit assaulted his nose. Some large animal in the back. Whatever it was it knew he was here as well. He could hear it stirring around in the back, hear it breathing, wanting to run away but not able to for being locked in. *"Hey, boy."* Alan inside of Marty said to the tall black horse with a white diamond on its forehead. The small sign on the gate read out THUNDER. The beautiful creature's name.

He watched the horses eyes grow wider as he came near, sensing the danger not from the boy, but what was inside him. Animals had that sense, he guessed, and it caused him slight amusement. *"You don't have to be afraid of me."* he lied watching the horse back up. *"You and I will be close friends tomorrow. We will have lots of fun."*

He walked away from the stable, eyes finding the other side of the barn open and seeing the farmer's house. No cars in the drive. He smiled as he stepped out and made his way to the porch, whistling all the way. *"Somebody will be home soon."* he said kicking a few stray rocks in his path. *"Somebody will want to help this poor lost boy."* He thought out loud while taking hold of one of the many pumpkins on the picnic table. They had all been carved out of the big party, no doubt. He found the long shiny

butcher knife there on newspaper covered in pumpkin guts and seeds and held it up for inspection.

"Somebody will be coming home soon to a big surprise." he smiled and sat on the back steps.

FORTY NINE

Ryan sat up from his dream, gasping for air and eyes searching the room around him. The first thing he noticed was daylight breaking through the curtains spilling over his mother's dreaming face on the pillow beside him. She was smiling, he noticed, her dreams more peaceful then his own. Maybe, Ryan thought, she was remembering the way things were before all of this.

The second thing he noticed was that Father Leary was not in the room. The television was still on, some goofy carton with talking cars, but no priest in the chair. Just the remote and that big damn gun he had been carrying on him since the dog attack. Ryan slipped quietly out of bed and peeked out the window. He only saw the light morning traffic but he *felt* something out there. Something not so nice.

"It's him." Ryan whispered tugging on his jeans and then heading out into the sun covered lot. Nothing at first that he could see, but still that feeling, that chill that ran all through him. Goosebumps, his Grandmother used to call them. But he saw no threat. A few passing cars, an old man in a fishing hat gassing his car up at the pumps, and the morning bird song. But something else.

"Holy Mother of God!" the old man suddenly cried out and Ryan looked back at the old man who was looking in Ryan's direction, but not at him, but over him. Ryan cringed as he slowly made a half circle to view the motel behind him, his eyes creeping up to the roof. It was covered entirely in living, moving blackness.

"Crows." he breathed watching them, hundreds if not more, all sitting there staring at him, every tiny eye. His father's soldiers. He could feel their thoughts, the reason they were sent here. "I won't let you have them." he said to them.

"Ryan!" he heard Father Leary call from behind him. Ryan gave a half glance at the priest headed his way with a big white bag from the diner in one hand and two cups of coffee palmed in the other. "What's wrong? Why are you out here in-" his voice faded away as he lifted his eyes up and saw what both the child and old man had seen already. "Jesus."

"Must be a hell of a lot of bugs up there or something." the old man guessed coming up beside the priest. "It's not mating season, is it? Name's Warner. Bill Warner. Never seen that many birds gathered together before."

"Excuse me, Mister Warner, maybe you better get back in your car." Father Leary said carefully setting both bag and coffee down. "Ryan, are any of them yours?"

"Maybe some." Ryan said scanning from left to right. "They're confused. They have to obey him and they want to obey me, but they are not sure."

"What's all this about?" Mister Warner asked and the birds began to get a bit louder.

"I think you better go." Father Leary said gently pushing the old man. "Move slow."

"Shucks, Mister, they're just crows and blackbirds far as I can se." he gave a soft chuckle. "They won't hurt you unless you hurt them, and even then not that much."

"What about them?" Ryan pointed to the far corner of the motel where three dogs stood shoulder to shoulder. Ryan could tell from here two of them were German Shepherds, and the last was a Rottweiller. "Those can hurt us."

"Oh shit." The old man breathed.

"More dogs." Father Leary said slowly guiding the old man. "Get to your car now."

"Sure, you got it." the old man said easing back while digging in his pockets for his keys. "You want to come with me? You and the boy?"

"We will be fine, please go." Father Leary said leaving him and coming up close to Ryan while reaching inside his jacket. Ryan knew what he was looking for and caught the man's eyes with his own.

"Your gun is inside on the table." Ryan told him watching the dogs creep up along side the motel.

"Fat lot of good it does me there." the priest said back. "I didn't want to take a chance of getting caught with it in the diner. Any chance of controlling those?"

"I'm already trying." Ryan said afraid to close his eyes all the way. "Hard to focus with so many of his all around us."

"Well it's pretty much the dogs I am worried about."

"Yeah I was thinking that too." Ryan said.

"Move slow." Father Leary said only a few yards from the jeep. He was sure it was locked. A habit of his that he had considered a good one until now. He found his keys and allowed himself to look away from the dogs long enough to find the one for the car door.

"I think I got one." Ryan said freezing up. "Hold on."

"Which one?"

"Wait." Ryan whispered and Father Leary watched as the child raise up one small arm that began to tremble all over as if cold and then his eyes popped open and the boy grinned. "Stop them!" he yelled and one German Shepherd suddenly latched out onto the other's throat while the Rottweiller came for them.

"Damn!" Father Leary said while mentally apologizing to God, who he was sure understood his outrage, and grabbed hold of Ryan and headed for the jeep, key at the ready. "Get in! Get in!" he said taking a few stabs at the lock before sending the silver key home into the passenger side door. As he shoved Ryan in he saw the Rottweiller already leaping onto the hood. He shoved the boy over to the driver's side as the dogs' mouth found his sweater sleeve. Father Leary drew back and gave a hard left-hand punch and the big black dog fell back to the pavement with a yelp. Ryan scooted out of his way as he launched himself inside and closed the door behind him.

"They're not giving up easy." Ryan said. "I got that one but I can't get the other two."

Just then the Rottweiller leapt up onto the hood and stared down the pair with low growls emitting from his throat. Then it shifted over to Father Leary and began clawing at the glass.

"Relax and focus." Father Leary told him. "Or we may have to leave."

"Not without mom." Ryan said.

"Okay. I will call her." the priest said taking out his cell phone. "I hope she's awake in there."

Ryan looked over and saw the two German Shepherds going at it, blood spilling at their feet and he felt bad about it, but there was not other way. Then the Rottweiller on the hood looked at the priest on the phone and then back to Ryan, an almost eerie smile creeping across the dogs face, and it bounded off the hood and headed for the motel room.

"He's going for mom!" Ryan panicked.

"Pick up, pick up." Father Leary breathed hearing the phone starting to ring. They watched the dog slam into the door and it sounded as if it actually gave a little under its weight. Ryan was wondering to himself if he remembered to lock the door, and doubting that he did. "Answer Laura."

"She's still asleep." Ryan said reaching for the car horn. "We have to warn her."

"No Ryan, if you do that she will-"

But it was too late. Ryan blared the horn for all it was worth. The huge Rottweiller backed away, lowering itself onto its haunches, waiting for what Father Leary was trying to avoid. Laura Woods answered the door

"Crap!" Father Leary said reaching in the back for the small umbrella, the only weapon he could find in the jeep and opened the door. "Stay here!" he yelled to Ryan exiting the car and as soon as he did, every bird on the roof swooped down for him. The bright morning was suddenly pitch black as hundreds of birds began their attack.

"No!" Ryan screamed and then focused despite the screams of both human and birds and tried to reach all the feathered attackers that he could. *"Stop this! Those of you who are on my side, stop the other birds! Obey me now!"*

Ryan opened his eyes in time to see his mother open the door and the Rottweiller smash up into her, sending both woman and dog into the darkness of the room past the swirling birds. Father Leary was close behind the fallen pair. Ryan sat and waited, the birds screaming and some smashing into the jeep like large black chunks of hail. Then finally a pair of gunshots that made him jump. Then both gun toting priest and mother came running out of the room as Ryan leapt into the back seat while the adults entered the jeep fighting off the birds as they did.

"Ryan, are you okay!" his mother called back to him as the jeep started up.

"I'm good, mom." Ryan said closing his eyes looking out the back window. "Let me get some of these birds off us."

"Let's get far away from here." Father Leary said watching one dog finish off the other as they roared backwards away from the motel. The birds were now attacking each other instead of the jeep and the windshield got a much clearer view as he turned back towards the road. As they did they could see a small crowd at the gas station and diner standing there with wide eyes and dropped jaws. "I think we given more than a few people in this town some stories for tonight. I guess your husband knows where we are now. We have to keep moving."

"Ex-husband. I wish you could remember that." she corrected him. "They didn't even go for Ryan, did they?" Laura asked watching the birds thin out in the rear view mirror. "That attack was about us. You and me."

"Yes, I'm afraid so." Father Leary said heading for the highway. "I guess he figures Ryan might be easier to approach if you and I are out of the way."

"He figured wrong." Ryan spoke up. "All he did was piss me off. We have to find him somehow, Father Leary. I have to stop him."

"We'll think of something." the priest said driving into the morning sun. "He has to come out of hiding sometime."

FIFTY

Joe Corrigan had decided to take his wife Doris out to dinner that night. Nothing special about it, no fancy clothing needed, just a local steak house. They had spent most of the day at his sister's house, and his sister was quite the talker so she deserved a night off from the kitchen and he had been craving a Porterhouse all week. They both got what they wanted. All said and done it was a nice evening. Doris had talked too much about her sister Kathy from Wentzville, and he had eaten way too many onions, and by the time they pulled into the driveway of their farmhouse after a long day out, Joey was ready for a beer and some television.

They exited the old Chevy, his wife still talking and he himself still belching like thunder, when they noticed the small boy seated on the steps. He looked at them with the look of a lost puppy. His wife took in a deep breath while he himself simply froze and glanced around the yard to make sure there were no other unwanted visitors. Sometimes when folks decided to rob your house, or so he had heard from cable news, they used a pretty young girl or a child to distract you.

"Well now." Joey started scratching his balding head and stifling a yawn. "Who have we here?"

"Are you okay, child?" his wife asked stepping closer to inspect the timid boy.

The skinny kid simply gave them a quick grin before returning to confusion behind his large glasses and shivering arms. He remained silent while staring at the dirt at his feet.

"What are you doing out here, boy?" Joey asked patting his large belly coming to a stop by the railings. "I hope you're lost cause if you're selling something, we already got it or don't want it."

"Hush, Joe." his wife waved him away. "Can't you tell when a boy is frightened? Maybe he ran away. Is that what happened, son? Is somebody bothering you?"

The child merely shook his head with his eyes still glued to the ground.

"Did you come out here all by yourself, sweetie?" Doris Corrigan asked gently reaching out and touching the boy's weeping face. "If you're here for the party, I'm afraid you're one night early."

"Party." Joe huffed to himself squeezing past both of them up to the porch. "That was your brilliant idea, dear heart. Bunch of juvenile delinquents running around destroying our property. They will have my place a mess come morning after next."

"Nonsense, Joe, they are just children." she said focusing on the boy. "You pay him no never mind, child. His bark is worse than his bite. Are you hungry? Would you like something to eat?" she said taking hold of the child's hand while bringing him to his feet. "Your parents must be worried sick."

"Let his parents feed him then." Joe said fiddling with his keys and finally opening the back door. "God, Doris you would take in every stray cat, dog, and child if not for me. Damn place would be a shelter by now."

"Most likely you're right." she said following close behind him into the brightness of the yellow and green kitchen that smelled of cinnamon and coffee. "Just cookies and milk and then a phone call."

"Suit yourself." Joe said keeping his pace until he reached a large green chair that practically swallowed him whole as he reached for the remote. "Just as long as he's not spending the night. If you can't reach his folks, call the cops. I'm sure Rollins ain't got nothing better to do tonight, so let him come take the kid off our hands."

"Joseph Corrigan!" he heard his wife shout from the kitchen and then realized his error while flipping past some nature show where some cheetah was chasing a gazelle. "What a thing to say, and in front of this boy. You know that man was killed this morning."

"Sorry, forgot." he mumbled back half-hearted. He never did like the old fart. The man would pull you over in a heartbeat for a ticket just going five miles over the limit. "Not like I was a huge fan."

"Regardless. Show some respect for the dead. He was an officer of the law." she sighed and he could hear her pouring the lost little lamb some of his milk and most assuredly a few of his favorite peanut butter cookies would go down the brats throat as well.

"Yeah, yeah." he said flipping to some repeat of a college game he was sure he missed. "Just be sure you call his folks and call that freak Lambert, the one with the messed up neck. He will come get him for sure. And save some of those cookies for me."

"Yes, dear." she almost sang to him and he rolled his eyes back to the television. A few drawers banged about, a child's laughter, then a glass dropped to the floor, glass shattering so loud it made Joe jump from his place in the chair.

"Hey, what the hell?" he called to the kitchen. More laughter. "Don't go breaking all of our dishes filling that brat up."

Joe Corrigan failed to notice the lack of response from his wife and watched his game. He lit a smoke, he watched a few beer commercials, then his eyes went back to the kitchen where there was nothing but silence. No movement. He thought he heard something being drug slowly across the floor, like a large bag of trash, but it stopped before he could determine if that was the case.

"Think I could get a beer out here?" he called. Some young blond cheerleader was dancing about on the screen long enough to distract him from the kitchen. Nice smile on this one, bright blue eyes and a body to die for. When her little routine was finished, along with several middle-aged fantasies, Joe glanced back at the kitchen again. It was dark now. "You call that kid's folks yet?" he asked. No response. Darkness and silence. "We out of beer?" he tried again. Nothing. "What the shit?" he huffed raising himself out of his comfortable chair and headed off to the darkness.

He clicked on the kitchen light and noticed first the shattered glass of spilled milk bordered by a pile of peanut butter cookie crumbs. And a few drops of blood. His head turned to the right to the adjoining hall that led down to the bathroom and bedroom. Nothing there either. Just a thin strip of light at the bottom of the closed bathroom door.

"What happened in here?" he asked headed towards the bathroom light. "That kid get sick or something? Are you okay, Doris?" he called out as his pace quickened. "Doris? Answer me dammit! Where's that fucking . . .?"

He froze. His voice trailed off and he forgot all about the boy. His wife was slumped down by the tub, a look of emptiness in her lifeless eyes, a steak knife in her throat, blood pooling out over the bright white porcelain and her pretty dress. Joe collapsed beside her without realizing it, embracing her as tears rolled down his face before he realized they were even there. His whole body was shaking.

"Oh, God, oh my sweet Lord, Doris." he choked grabbing hold of the knife and shaking his head in confusion. "How did this-"

"Hey ya, Joe, waddaya know?" the deep voice came from behind him. Joe Corrigan's red face turned to see the small shy boy lunge at him, grabbing him tight and hugging him like a grandchild who has just found his long lost grandfather. It would have looked sweet and innocent to a bystander if not for the bloody corpse in Joe Corrigan's arms. *"I couldn't get inside her."* the child said in his ear in a cold whisper as Joe felt the flesh on his body grow chilled. *"But I bet you and I are going to be real close."*

The child grabbed the older man's face in a tight grip and Joe felt his world go black around him. He felt his body slip away into darkness, some dark fluid spewing into his mouth, and something even darker slipping into his very heart and soul. His brain was tingling and his heart was racing as all of his breath left his body.

Alan Woods let loose with a deep hellish laughter. This man he was taking over now was about fifty, kind of big but he would do for now. He loved his wife, but not so much as he didn't mind getting a little stray ass here and there, although it had been years since he last cheated. Some lonely housewife he met at a bar. He drank, he smoked, he liked naked young ladies and had the DVD's and magazines out in the barn's loft to prove it. And he really had no deep love for children, which is why he and Doris never had any and it was his wife's idea to have this Halloween party tomorrow night, not his. Alan Woods agreed with all of Joe's viewpoints except for the party. The party was a wonderful idea. The party most definitely would go on as planned. It would just have to go on without Aunt Doris in attendance.

"Where am I?" Marty Fitzgerald said falling back on his butt as the large man rose above him. The child shivered and quickly scooted away from the man and the bloody woman he had dropped to the floor. He looked up and saw the heavy man smiling down at him in much the same way that the janitor, Chip, had done earlier.

"Hey there, squirt." Joe Corrigan said in Alan Woods voice bending down and snatching the child up in both arms. *"Let's you and I make a deal. You stay nice and quiet and I will make sure that you stay alive long enough to see that party tomorrow night. We got a deal?"*

Marty shook his head quickly, his tear filled eyes scanning his surroundings. He had no idea where he was. A moment ago he had been at the school, then Chip the janitor had come in talking in the same funny voice as this big man was now, and held him and the lunch lady hostage. Now he was in a strange house with a strange man with that same strange voice and he was pissing himself again.

"Crap, do you do this a lot or what?" Corrigan said holding the boy out from him as he felt the wet on the front of his jeans. He sat the shivering child down on the bed and lifted one huge hand in the boy's face as a warning while he spoke. *"Okay, no funny stuff. I know you have no idea what's going on here and it really don't matter, boy. You stay good I will let you live. After all, you can't catch much fish with dead bait."* he grinned at the boy.

Marty Fitzgerald tried to fight the large man who grabbed him by the arm and drug him towards the kitchen. He screamed, he hit the man with his tiny balled fist, but he was also drained and tired for reasons he did not understand. He had been possessed and what little strength he had was gone. He watched the wide hairy hand take hold of a butcher knife and then fell silent as he was then drug towards the basement door.

"Gonna find you a nice cool, quiet place, Marty. " the man said with that same creepy voice. He took him down the dark stairs, past baskets of laundry, rusty pipes and shadows of things unseen. After finding a small pantry with a strong wooden door, and leaving a bag of Lay's chips and a bottle of diet Sprite, Joe Corrigan, with Alan Woods residing within, returned to the bloody scene in the bathroom. *"Guess I got some work to do. Should be plenty of places to hide a body on a farm I guess."* he smiled and went to find some bed sheets and a shovel. He stopped once at the kitchen.

"First thing's first though." he said heading for the table. *"Peanut butter cookies."*

FIFTY ONE

There's no place like home, except when it's not really home anymore.

This is where they ended up after a day of searching for Alan Woods. The place she had called home now for almost eighteen years, only it wasn't the same. It didn't even look the same to her anymore as they pulled up into the driveway and Laura felt that fear rising up in her again. The whole aurora of the place just seemed wrong. This was a place where evil had been born and returned after death. It was *his*.

"This is where it all started." she told the priest.

"I remember, I was there." he told her shutting the engine off. "A very bad day."

"No, I mean long ago. Years, in fact. I never told you this, but Ryan looked up some stuff on the Internet before he came and saw you. He found out some things even I didn't know. He said Alan was actually born in this house. *Our* house. His whole family died here and he moved away and then came back and got this house for us to live in after he married me. He wanted this to be the place where we lived again, where he had a new family, a family of his own. He planned this from the beginning."

"And none of that is your fault, Laura." the priest reassured her. "You had no idea what you were marrying into. No idea what you were conceiving children with. He hid it well."

"I still wouldn't know if Ryan hadn't found out on that website."

"Ryan is very thorough for a boy his age." the priest smiled back at the boy who was spread out on the back seat with his eyes closed. "And very brave."

"He is." she agreed. "It just doesn't feel like my home anymore. It's just four walls and a roof and a bunch of bad memories. It was bad enough when it was just memories of a failed marriage, all of the cheating and drinking, but now it's more. Now it's about the birth of my ex-husband, the murder of his family, all of the lies he told me and covered up. The evil he planned. The tormenting of my son and the death of my daughter's boyfriend. It's not home anymore, Thomas."

"It is whatever you decide it is, Laura." he said exiting the car into the night air. "I can understand you not wanting to be here, but I'm running out of motel money and I think we should stop hiding from him. Sooner or later we are going to have to face him. Unavoidable really. We're as safe here as anywhere."

"I know." she said leaning in to grab hold of Ryan and Father Leary sprinted around the car to help her with the boy. "But after this is over, no matter what happens . . ." she said letting the large man take her son from her into his much stronger arms. " . . . I will be ready to start over somewhere else. A new home, a change of scenery. Let somebody else live here if they choose to. I'm done with it."

"As I said, your choice." Thomas Leary said following her up to the door with the boy cradled in his arms. "But you do have to deal with this. You can't run from yourself, Laura. No matter how far you go, you can never escape your memories or your past unless it's dealt with."

"I know." she said sliding the key home and closing her eyes before giving the door a gentle nudge. She was expecting to see things the way they left them. The nightmare creatures from just a few days ago. She was expecting to see things waiting for them darkness. Large snakes and spiders, talking rats and thousands of bugs of all kinds. Laura reached over with her left hand and clicked on the lights, bracing herself for the worst. The soft glow of corner lamps barely lit the room. There was nothing. Nothing more than an eerie silence and shadows.

"Better than what I expected." came the priests voice from behind her mimicking her own thoughts. "I guess whatever was here followed him out."

"I guess." Laura said moving aside and allowing the man to place Ryan on the couch. She crept boldly towards the hallway, eyes darting each way in search of any movement, and saw nothing. "I guess the coast it clear. This doesn't change my mind though. I still want out of this place."

"I can't fault you for that." he said covering Ryan with the blanket stretched out across the back of the couch, draping it over his body slow as not to wake him, and he stood there for a moment in silence looking down at him. The face of a brave young soul, a man's son, an evil man's son, and for the briefest second in time he wished it was his own son. Something he knew he would never have. "That's a decision for later. Right now we deal with your ex-husband."

"You think he knows we're here?" she asked still slowly turning in the hall.

"Not sure." he said coming to her. "It doesn't feel like his presence is still here. If he was why wouldn't he attack us now why Ryan is asleep?" he said taking hold of her shoulders and letting his eyes meet up with her doubting ones. "You know, I actually think he's getting weaker. He needs your son and it probably never took this long before for the father to become one with the son. Your son is resisting and he's getting tired of jumping around from host to host." Father Leary told her looking back at the boy on the couch. "He's going to have to make a move soon."

"And when he does we will be ready. We will stop him."

"No." the priest corrected nodding towards the couch. "He will."

"I pray you're right. Would you like some coffee?" Laura asked heading towards the kitchen.

"Please and thank you." the priest said remaining where he was. "We may need it."

He sat in the soft shadows of the room while listening to Laura start the coffee. He closed his eyes and mostly prayed and somewhat reflected on the past few days until he could smell the coffee brewing. When he opened his eyes again she was walking towards him with two steaming mugs.

"Wasn't sure how you took it. It's been awhile since I brought a man a cup of coffee." she said sitting his cup before him on the corner table. "So I gave you two creams and one sugar like mine."

"That's fine, thank you." he said letting it sit for the moment while his eyes drifted to the window. "I guess I just hate waiting. I'd rather get this last round over with. Finish things."

"You mind if I ask you something?" she asked after a long sip and the priest shrugged in response while still staring out at the darkness, wondering what was lurking out there watching them. How many creatures did Alan Woods have at his disposal on this night? What would attack them next? Laura's words broke his thoughts. "Back at the school, when Alan stepped into my mind or whatever, I faced a fear of bugs." she said with a nervous grin. "Sounds silly I know after all that we have been through. I guess as a kid I just hated them and it stuck with me all of these years."

"Understandable." the priest said still distant. "A lot of people have that fear."

"What about you?" she asked. "I mean, when he was with you, what happened?"

Father Leary sighed and reached over for his own coffee, took a taste, then leaned back and let his tired eyes find hers. "Water. I was in a lake, at least in my mind, and I was drowning." he said with a silly smirk and another shrug of his shoulders. "I never learned how to swim. I almost drowned when I was a child. I've been afraid ever since."

"I'm so sorry." she said sitting still. "That must have been horrible."

"No big deal." he said back. "I wasn't even aware of it until this morning. I'd forgotten all about it. I mean I still don't swim, I don't go near the water other than to bathe in it or drink it, but that whole

251

childhood experience was forgotten. That's how he fights, your Alan Woods, by creeping inside our subconscious mind and prying loose the things we are afraid of. Unless he can control us directly by possessing us, he feeds off our fears."

"He had me once, he won't have me again." she mostly promised herself.

"He knows that." Father Leary reminded her. "He knows he can't use you again or me at all, so he will keep trying to find another way. I'm just worried about who he is going to use. Somebody innocent, somebody your son knows. He may use a friend maybe, like that Fitzgerald boy, or another cop."

"I know, I just hate waiting." Laura said moving to her son's side. Father Leary watched the woman gently stroke her son's hair with so much love in her eyes. "Like you said, that's the worst part."

"I guess we have to be patient." he said watching the boy dream, and praying they were good dreams. The dreams a boy his age should have. Dreams of flying to the moon, riding horses or hitting home runs in front of cheering crowds or flying through the sky like some comic book hero, or maybe even his first kiss from a pretty girl. Anything besides what he was going through now. "They say patience is the art of hoping. And I believe hope is all we have left."

FIFTY TWO

So much to do in one afternoon. Joe Corrigan was a busy man with Alan Woods inhabiting his body. After all he had a party to prepare for tonight. A Halloween party. Even though Halloween wasn't until next week the late Miss Corrigan, God rest her kind but useless soul, wanted the young folks to enjoy it on the weekend. So they would. The festivities would commence without her.

He had been busy overnight while the world around him slept. He buried the woman in the cornfield, far away from young prying eyes, and he enjoyed the hard work under the bright hunter's moon. He knew that the next time the moon rose up he would face his son once again, for the last time. He would use everything he had, all of the disciples at his disposal and all of the bodies he had, in order to make sure that his son gave in to the inevitable. He would surrender himself to dear old dad.

He had the sniveling brat, Marty Fitzgerald, as bait in the basement pantry with food and water and a bucket to piss in. Marty seemed to prefer his own pants for that. There was no need for a lock on the door. Alan had contacted one of his night children, a rather large and ill-tempered Doberman Pincher, to sit and watch guard over the boy. Every time Marty cracked the door the large black dog would snarl a warning and the boy would close himself back in again. Once his son showed up with his ex-bitch and the holy man, he would let him decide. Let Alan enter his body or he would take the boy's life, along with all the other children in attendance. It would be that simple. His son would make the right choice if he was as noble as he claimed.

So he finished carving the pumpkins in all sorts of grinning and menacing faces and decorated the house with orange and black crape paper. Cardboard ghosts and witches covered the windows and rubber bats and spiders hung from the ceiling. He set up the outside with folding tables for refreshments that were kept in the kitchen until party time. Snack food, fruit punch, and bowls of candy. Outside he had stacks of hay bordered by pumpkins and corncobs. Just to the south he saw his good old friend the scarecrow on his pole watching the activities with lifeless black eyes that somehow seemed approving none the less. Past that was the small lake with the bright paddle boats. Beyond that he sensed a few of his own followers coming closer from the woods and the streets. They were staying just close enough to serve him if needed without being seen by human eyes.

He headed inside to find the list of guests there on the fridge under a flower magnet. He called them all, with the exception of his son, making sure to let everybody know that Doris would not be attending the party because she was away to see her sister who was ill in Wentzville, and made an excuse of a sore throat for his odd voice. No, no, there was no need to cancel the party. It wasn't contagious, the kids had to have their fun. He assured everybody they were welcome to attend. Especially Anna Finch.

By the time he was done it was nearly four o'clock in the afternoon. The party would begin in about two hours. Alan, inside Joe, took a nice stroll out to the barn. He smiled again as he felt the fear build up in the horse as he neared. It still knew who he was despite the change of appearance.

"Hello there, Thunder." Woods said stuffing hands to pockets and taking in the full beauty of the large powerful animal. *"You know who I am, don't you?"* he grinned watching the horse back up a few steps in its small stall. *"Same psycho, different asylum. Presto Change-o."* he said letting his hand gently move across his face in curtain form. *"We are going to have us a real nice shindig tonight, boy."*

The horse only grunted and stomped in response as it pushed itself back against the far wall, shaking its head and trying its best to avert its eyes to the horror it sensed before it. Alan Woods inside Joe Corrigan only laughed at the animal's discomfort and turned to walk away back into the cool air.

"We'll talk later, boy." he promised the horse as he exited the barn. *"Gotta make a run into town for some ice. And I got me an invitation to deliver. That is if I can find the guests in time."*

FIFTY THREE

Pirate Jack's Pizzeria on a Friday evening. Hunting monsters, after all, could cause one to work up quite an appetite. Father Leary sat between mother and son, taking in all of the décor of the fast food establishment. Hard wood floors with rum barrel trashcans. Pirate flags with grinning skulls, only these skulls had pizza slices sticking out of their mouths. Ship wheels and crossed plastic swords on the wall and colorful parrots in every corner. Two young teen girls, one a bright red head with freckles, the other with shorter jet black hair and cold eyes, both wearing cute little pirate scarves on their heads and skirts way too short and tight with shameless cleavage showing while they served up greasy slices of pizza. And on the far wall was Pirate Jack himself smiling down on them with a full braided beard and eye patch, one hand holding a slice of pizza, the other hand raised up holding his mighty breadstick sword. Father Leary made a mental note to never return.

It was not as busy as he had feared it would be, but more than enough for the three of them to blend in. They almost seemed to be a family out for dinner. At least to the casual eye it appeared to be father, mother and son sitting at the corner table instead of a priest, a widow and a boy with supernatural powers. All the while, Soundgarden screamed overhead through the ceiling speakers.

"Not bad." Father Leary said breaking the silence commenting on the sausage and pepperoni mix. It was actually a bit too greasy for his taste but why go there now. "Been awhile since I had pizza. Reminds me of my college days. Weekends with the guys or some date I lucked my way into."

Laura nodded in mute agreement, her worried eyes finding his while her mouth offered a weak smile in between bites. Those worried eyes drifted back to her son and casually out the windows of the darkening day. Ryan himself seemed lost in thought while swirling his soda ice about with his straw, his eyes focused on the streets as well. It was as if at any moment he expected some monster to go strolling by and in fact, Father Leary thought, that might just happen.

"I used to work in a place like this." he said. "Grady's Burger Shack, over on Delaware and Third." he reminisced while Pearl Jam sang out. "Three-twenty-five an hour and we had to wear these horrible polyester orange and brown uniforms." he said noticing their silence. "They shut it down years ago. I think they made it a Starbucks." he finished taking inventory of the crowd. "For the best really."

The booth across from them held four teens, two girls and two boys, all so distant in their

language and dress codes yet painfully familiar to his own past. The girls were almost identical. Both had

dyed hair, one with burgundy streaks, the other bright neon blue. Both had way too many metal objects in

their lips and ears, and tattoos of butterflies and thorns on their arms and legs. They wore half shirts that

showed off toned bellies and sparkling navel rings and way too much cleavage, more tats there as well, paw

prints on one and roses on the other. He wondered if anyone ever thought how these tats would look by the

time they turned forty. Both had on tight ripped jeans with bright bracelets and shoes. It was as if they

came out of the same box.

The boys wore clothing typical of today's youth. Their shirts hung off them three times too big,

pants baggy enough for a circus clown. One had a black Mohawk streaked with red, the other a backward

ball cap and a black flame tattooed on his neck, both similar inked markings on their forearms. They

seemed to cry for attention although they clearly wanted to be left alone by the older generation. They tried

so hard to be unique, yet somehow they copied each other constantly.

"Not much has changed about the teen scene." Father Leary said watching them bop their own

heads to Nickelback while listening to them speak. They spoke loud and laughed louder, the girls using

way too much profanity, but such was a sign of the times. There was no respect for those around them,

much less for themselves. The younger crowd seemed to thrive on the fact that they could be as vulgar as

possible. They called each other bitches and whores, talked mostly of sex and party plans. Not one of

them looked old enough to vote, yet they were clearly already familiar with drugs, alcohol and getting

naked to have a good time. Where the hell were the parents unless they were doing the same damn thing?

"Pretty much the same circus, different clowns. They hate everyone except their own kind, sometimes

even that."

"I was like them once." Laura said catching the direction of his stare. "God, my parents hated the

way I dressed. Painted on Levi jeans and low cut blouses. And the guys I dated. Bikers and bad boys. I

had a rebellious phase as soon as I hit fifteen. Then it caused me to marry one. I would love to tell those

girls to go put some clothes on and run away from those maroons as fast as they can, but it wouldn't do any

good. Nobody could tell me shit back then. I thought I knew every damn thing." she said eyeing the one

girl with the bluish streaks running through her raven dark hair. Her eyes looked glazed over like she was already high, her hand kept creeping over to her boyfriends crotch, the laughter high and droning. "She will find out the hard way when lover boy there get's her pregnant and then dumps her ass."

"Very optimistic." the priest smirked at her from across the table while tapping his fingers to The Fugees playing above. "I'd like to think there's still hope for them. I don't believe in a lost generation. That's what prayer is for."

"So you see hope? Are you a good judge of character? Are you what is considered a people person?" she asked with a wicked challenging grin. "Because when I look over there I see more arrests then redemptions."

"I am a priest." he said puffing out his chest with false bravado and she gave a short laugh. "My life is built around hope and I think I can read people pretty well, yes."

"What about him?" Laura nodded to the tall spectacled man wearing the gray work shirt with the name DONNY stitched into a patch. He was seated alone. He leaned over his pizza as if in deep prayer, his eyes lost in a Stephen King paperback, *Cujo*, his fingers rapping lightly on the table. His face was covered in stubble, his sighs a bit louder than they should have been, his right leg bouncing to match his fingers. He looked somewhere between tears and mad laughter while scanning the pages. He was softly mumbling to himself, or maybe just reading out loud.

"Having a bad day, I guess." Father Leary speculated. "A bit lonely maybe. Probably hates his job, most people do. He could use a good woman or a friend." he said checking Laura for a reaction of agreement. "Then again he is reading Stephen King so he might shoot up the joint any second."

"You're terrible." Laura laughed. "I've read all of King's novels, I've yet to take a life."

"I have to confess I have too, so let's just say he's lonely and leave it at that."

"Holy psyche-classes, bat-man. That was very in depth." Laura joked. "What about the family affair over there?" she nodded to the foursome in the corner. Thomas Leary turned sideways in his chair and took in the family she spoke of and began to size them up. "Brady Bunch, Waltons or Huxtables?"

The father was a burly and bearded man in dress shirt and slacks. He sat there next to his blond haired son who colored on some placemat with rapid speed. The wife, clearly younger and a bit more casual in her jeans and Cardinals shirt, sat opposite holding what appeared to be a four or five month old girl with hair as equally blond and eyes as blue as her own.

"Not sure of any of those fit." he said taking in the details. "Late twenties, middle class, he works in an office, she probably stays at home with the kids or works at a market. They like being parents but are desperately trying to hold onto their youth. They are probably wondering if they can afford a real vacation, a new washer and dryer, stuff like that. They probably hate their in-laws, go to the movies a lot and places like this for the kids sake. They sacrifice a lot. They go to P.T.A. meetings and bible classes and backyard barbecues and . . . I don't know." he said smiling over at her. "I'm guessing they love each other very much. Maybe they even have a dog."

"Sounds like some corny ass television family to me, only more boring with out all of the sub plots."

"Boring sounds good right now." he said finding her eyes as Death Cab for Cutie sang out. "I would love boring right now."

"Me too." she offered back finding the street again. "Making breakfast, worrying about report cards, my daughter wanting to borrow the car, trips to the dentist." she said and took a few seconds of silence before speaking again. "What the hell is he doing out there? What is he waiting for?"

"A moment of weakness?" the priest guessed. "For us to tire of waiting or loose control. I don't know, Laura. This isn't something I frequently deal with, you know."

"I'm sorry, I just-"

"Don't apologize, please. You have the right to be concerned. For yourself and for your son. Maybe he's having trouble finding us like we are him."

"No." Ryan said breaking free from his silence taking in a deep breath. He could feel the room growing cooler, the outside world seemed to grow a shade darker as if some clouds were passing before the evening sun. "He's close."

"How close?" Laura asked stopping mid sip on her drink.

"Here." a chilling voice whispered over the intercom as the music died away. *"Right here."*

"Alan?" Laura said with her head whipping around.

"He's close." Ryan said searching the windows.

"This is it." Father Leary said pushing his chair back and standing, ready for battle. Laura joined him but Ryan remained seated while watching the patrons around them. "Are you ready, Ryan?"

"I'm ready, but he's not in here yet. Something else is going on." Ryan said turning to see the middle aged man with the DONNY name patch slam his hands down hard on the table. Everyone in the place jumped. "That guy."

"Is this as far as I go?" the man spoke out looking first at Ryan then the two adults hovering over him. "Cleaning fucking toilets and taking out trash?!" he screamed and the four young teens across from him were shocked into silent stares before they started to laugh. "Sweeping the damn floor every night! Is that fucking it?"

"Old dude is flipping out." one of the punks said while his blue haired girl giggled softly into his side. "Pressures of the job, yo."

"I can barely pay my fucking rent!" he said swiping his arms out and sending his soda over to the next booth in an explosion of ice. "My car is a complete piece of shit! I can't get a girlfriend to save my fucking life!"

"He needs to get laid." Mohawk sneered grabbing his girls right breast and causing her to squeal. "Here you go, dude. I'll let you bang my bitch for one hundred. How bout it, Jess?"

"Crow, you prick!" the burgundy-streaked girl cursed smacking his muscled tatted arm.

"Do you folks mind, some of us have children here." the heavy set father said in polite tone while his son dropped his crayon and watched as the man shoved his entire tray off the table.

"Eat my cock!" the man said tossing off his glasses. "I live in a fucking shack! I don't even have cable or the internet. I'm going to be homeless soon, you fat bastard!"

"Are you sure he's just having a bad day?" Laura asked as Father Leary crept closer with hands out in surrender.

"I think it's more than the paperback too." the priest said watching the manager come from around the front counter. He looked all of twenty one with his forced robotic grin and fresh cut crop of blond hair and blue vest with matching blue bow-tie over his bright yellow dress shirt. His gold name badge read Philip in black capital letters. Philip had no idea what he was getting into. "Excuse me Sir, if there's a problem, you are going to have to-"

"Have to?!" Donny said and shot up to take hold of the young man. Philip's eyes went wide as he held out his hands in surrender while the tall janitor stared him down. "I don't have to do any damn thing I don't feel like doing, you little shit! Who the fuck are you anyway? Did your daddy get you this job?

Whose cock did you suck to wear this pussy outfit and make more money that I do?"

"Hey bro, I just need to-"

"I'm not your fucking *bro*." the tall man sneered gripping the young man's collar tighter. "When

did we become related? I missed you at the last family reunion, pussy boy!"

"Yeah, smack his ass, yo!" the ball capped punk at the table of teens cheered and his friends joined

him. "Show him what's up, pops."

"Sir, why don't you just calm yourself down for a minute?" Father Leary tried inching closer to

the wild-eyed man.

"This is enough!" the mother said with the tiny girl in her arms. "We have children here. Please

take this outside. You're scaring my family."

"I agree." Father Leary said coming up on the two men, the young man trying to still break free of

the older man's grip. "Let's just go outside and relax and get some air and I'm sure we can work this-"

"You'd like that, Father?" the man said shoving the manager backwards so hard he slipped in the

spilled soda and fell into one of the empty booths with a loud smack, hitting his head on the table's edge.

The teens cracked up once more.

"You know me?" Thomas Leary said carefully studying the man's eyes for any signs of

possession. "Is that you, Alan?"

"Not quite, Padre." the voice came over the loud speakers again. *"Merely a puppet for your*

amusement. I hope you enjoy the show."

"What show?" Father Leary said backing away. The place fell silent all at once. Then a new

song came on the speakers, but it was not one he recognized, something far older. It wasn't some alternate

rock group or R&B song as they had been playing. It was something much colder. Soft piano keys and

scratchy violin strings, almost haunting in nature, with female voices that breathed sighs and whispers more

than sang lyrics, and then he felt a chill pass through the place all at once. Like a cold winter wind

shooting through his bones.

"What's wrong with *them*?" was all Ryan said and both priest and mother turned to follow the

young boy's gaze across the room. Everybody in the restaurant seemed to be having one big synchronized seizure. They all shook and backed away from the places at their tables, even the two teen girls at the front serving counter and their injured supervisor seemed infected.

"It's him." Father Leary said. "We have to get these people out of here."

"What is he doing to them?" Laura asked making her way towards the woman who was holding the tiny baby girl who was starting to softly cry. She was rocking back and forth with a lost look in her blank eyes and holding the baby tighter and tighter with each approaching step Laura made. "Is this some kind of hypnosis or what?"

"He's scaring the hell out of them." Ryan said watching the man called Donny turn and run out of the place, screaming his list of failures while doing so. For a moment the priest, mother, and child were distracted from the others shaking around them as they watched the man run across the parking lot, tears running down his face, as he made his way into oncoming traffic. A large pick-up came screeching to a halt but not before slamming into him at the intersection and sending his body tumbling a good twenty feet before rolling to a bloody stop.

"Jesus, Thomas!" Laura cried out watching the car doors open and a crowd form around the fallen man. The priest grabbed her back to reality, noticing her own tears start to well up and turned her to face the current situation at hand.

"I need you here, Laura." he whispered. "We will have plenty of time for mourning later."

"Get them the fuck off me!" the punk with the ball cap screamed. He was on his back now flailing away at unseen things on his chest and arms.

"See if that manager's okay over there." Thomas pointed to where the young man fell into the booth. "I got this one here." he said kneeling. "There's nothing there, son. Nothing at all. It's just your imagination. Do you hear me?"

"They fucking hurt, man." the tattooed teen said trying to break free. "Get them off me!"

"Are you okay?" Laura said kneeling down as the blond manager tried getting to his feet.

"Why is it so dark in here?" he said looking up at her with wide frightened eyes. She could feel him shaking while talking hold of his arm. "What's going on? Did somebody shut the power off?" he asked looking out the windows at the suffocating darkness there. "What happened out there? An eclipse or something. What happened to the light?"

"It's going to be okay, young man." Laura told him helping him up, but he shoved his way free and made his way in a swift walk back towards the cooking area of the restaurant. "You need to get outside. Everybody needs to get out of here!"

"Screw that, I can't stand the dark. I have to get the power back on." he told her and broke past the dark haired pirate girl. "Move, whore." he screamed as she slammed into the wall, a dazed look on her face. She gave Laura a desperate glance and then darted off into the back office, slamming the door shut behind her. Laura was about to go after her when she noticed the mother who was embracing her child rocking back and forth in the booth again. She was crying and speaking in gibberish.

"We're going to crash, we're going to crash." she chanted over and over while holding her crying baby to her breast tightly. "Please let us land safely. Please let us land over water, my God, the lightning, it hit the wing. I know it hit the plane." she said over to Laura. "We're going to die, aren't we?"

"We're not in a plane, miss, look at me." Laura said. "We're on the ground now, okay?"

"I don't want to die this way, not with my baby." the lady begged and Laura reached in for the child. "Please save my baby."

***

"No, no, no!" came the voice of one of the teen girls. The one with the burgundy streaks, Jess, was scooting backwards across the floor while holding her stomach. "I can't be pregnant, not now." she cried and shook her head in disbelief as she watched her belly grow larger. "I can't me a mom now. No fucking way! Crow, you bastard, you said you pulled out!"

"You're not pregnant, young lady." Laura called to her while trying to pry the baby free from the crying woman. "This is all a hallucination. You're going to be fine."

"You fucking nuts, look at this!" the teen said ripping her clothing away to expose a smooth flat stomach with a belly ring that matched her hair. Laura was sure that in her mind, the young girl saw something far worse. "I'm huge! Nine months already! My life is fucking over!"

"Thomas, we can't help them all." she said trying to take the baby away from the weeping woman who still thought she was in a plane crashing in a storm.

262

"Help who you can." he said grabbing the young man and looking into his eyes. "Son, there is nothing on you, do you hear me?" he shook the teen and gave him a light smack on the face. To him maybe it was as if on some bad drug trip, something he might have already been rather familiar with. "I need you to help me, Sir." he yelled to the heavy set man with the dress shirt who stood staring out the windows now while his young son hid in the corner away from the screaming mother and child.

"The Boogeyman is coming." the boy whispered and Ryan cast a worried glance back at him while the boy hid himself behind the trash can. Ryan looked around the room at the building chaos before finding the smaller boy's own eyes again. "Isn't he?"

"He's already here." Ryan said back watching the outside world grow darker still.

***

"Who's going to help us?" the big man said slowly turning on the priest. "Look around you, man." he continued with a crazed look in his eyes that Thomas did not want or need to see right now. The eerie music with strings and keys was still playing, those voices still doing their unholy chorus. God, how could it be effecting all of them? Was the human will truly so weak?

"I know, I see, that's why I need you to help me. It's going to be fine, it's-"

"No, you don't see at all!" the man yelled at the top of his lungs. "The sun is giving us all cancer, man. The freaking ozone layer is paper fucking thin and nobody is doing anything about it. The water you are drinking is poison, bottled or not, can't you taste it? We are polluting ourselves to death with car and plane exhaust and factory fumes. Supermarkets are selling us food soaked in chemicals that are eating away at us from the inside out! White sugar, man! The North Pole is melting away, global warming is destroying us and you say everything is fine?"

Father Leary leapt up, leaving the boy who seemed to be coming out of his daze, and walked over to the plump man and grabbed him by the collar, shaking him hard. "Look, Al Gore, I need you to help me and then we can protest later, you understand! Get some of these kids out of here, now!"

The fat man stood there, the look of fear and anger sliding away as he gave a quick nod and then blinked many times while looking around at what was going on.

263

"But the oil spills and the plastic bottles and flu shots that have little bits of-?"

"Not right now." the priest shook him again. "Help me with these people first."

"Jesus, what's going on here? What is all of this?" he said breathing deep and stepping away. "My wife, my kids?"

"They are fine." Father Leary said leading him over to the teen boy who was sitting up now at least and still brushing unseen things off his clothing and the sobbing girl with the ripped shirt. "Help me get these two outside, please."

"She's going to be fine too." Laura said guiding the woman towards the door behind the man and two teens while carrying the baby herself. "There are three in the back, Thomas. One girl went inside the office and locked the door, the manager is worried about the dark, I don't know where the other girl is."

"I will be back as soon as I get them situated outside safely away from this place." Father Leary said taking the baby from her arms. "Grab anybody you can and get them out of here."

***

"Help me, please." a soft voice came from somewhere out of sight and Laura stopped short of the door. "I'm dying, please somebody!" the girls voice called.

Laura was cautious in her approach. She rounded the far table and saw the other teen girl, the one with the blue streaks, kneeling on the floor, staring at herself in her own mirror. She held one hand to her face and tears were smearing the dark mascara over her pale cheeks. When she noticed Laura she held up the tiny mirror to show her, as if Laura would see what she saw.

"I'm getting old so fast." she whimpered. "How did this happen? My hair, my face . . ." she said reaching up and running her hands over her self. "God, I'm eighty, I'm ninety, look at my hair! It's falling out! What the shit is happening to me?"

"Ssshhh." Laura shushed her kneeling down at her side. "It's a trick, young lady, okay. You're still a teenager. You need to go outside with the others."

"No, it's real, can't you see?" the girl said looking again for herself and seeing the ancient wrinkled skin that was covered in spots, her hair gray and hanging in strands over her scarred scalp. She leaned back and opened her mouth, seeing most of her teeth gone and the gums rotting and black. "I'm a damn corpse! Look at me!"

"Yeah, bitch, you are a corpse." the one called Crow said rising up behind them both. Laura turned to see him coming at them both, a large knife in his right hand and an evil grin on his face. The teen with the muscles and Mohawk smacked Laura Woods out of the way and grabbed hold of the teen girl by her throat. He pulled her up in one swift motion and slammed the knife straight into her chest. The girl gave out a short scream and then choked out her last breath and collapsed to her knees drenched in her own blood. "And you're staying that way. Who's next? How about you, Laura? I got orders to cancel your ass right now if I can."

"No!" Laura said back paddling across the floor as the punk turned on her. "Alan, you fucking coward. Thomas, help!"

"No one can save you bitch." Crow smiled lifting the bloody blade to his pierced tongue and licking a few drops of blood. "I am a servant of the dark master. This is my true calling. Can't you hear them calling me over the music? Sacrifices have to be made. Blood must be spilled."

"Stay away from my mother!" Ryan called out and the large boy with the Mohawk paused long enough to look him over and cut loose with a laugh.

"Who's going to make me, junior?" Crow laughed looming over him and twisting the sharp jagged edged knife in the air for him to see.

"I am." Ryan said and stepped forward, both arms shooting out in rage and he could feel the familiar tingle shoot through his entire body, his arms feeling wet and slippery as dozens of snakes shot out of his sleeves like some mad magicians trick. It scared him nearly as much as it did Crow. "Back off!"

"Fuck!" the knife wielding teen cried stumbling backwards as the black snakes slithered across the floor, up his jeans, some inside of them, and over his chest and arms with lightning speed. "Lucifer, save me! Help me, Dark Father!" Crow screamed while swinging the knife wildly, cutting a few snakes along with himself, and fell back through the exit door with the serpents still intact. They continued their attack and his screams became muffled as the door closed behind him.

"Now that's my boy." his father's voice chimed in across the speakers. *"You have to love how they call out to Satan for help, like he gives a fuck."*

265

"How did you do that?" came the voice of the small boy still peeking out from behind the trash barrel. He regarded Ryan with both fear and amazement. "You got magic powers like the comics. You made snakes come from nowhere."

"I'm the Boogeyman's son." Ryan stated simply and looked towards the kitchen. "Mom, there's more back there.

"I know, I'm on it." she said heading in that direction and glad to see Thomas returning just in time to help her. "Get that boy out of here now, Ryan. We will be right behind you."

"We have to go, come on." Ryan said coming over to the boy. "My name's Ryan. Ryan Woods." he said holding out his hand and the boy reluctantly took it, checking first for snakes.

"My name is Alex Parker." the boy said. "My mom and dad were acting kinda strange so-"

"They will b okay, Alex. Promise. But we have to go, okay?"

The small boy nodded and together they ran hand in hand out of the dark place of blood and snakes and into the parking lot with the other adults who were coming out of their trances and fears.

***

"What did I miss?" Thomas Leary said casting a worried glance back at the dining room while following her back behind the stainless steel of the kitchen. He saw a girl's body and some remaining snakes sliding about under the tables. "Are those his or ours?"

"Ours, thanks to Ryan. That Mohawk punk killed a girl, and Ryan got rid of him." she said forcing the words out and trying to blank out the images from her mind. "He stabbed her."

"Maybe we can help her, she might-"

"She's dead." Laura assured him finding the office door and knocking hard. "He got her right in the heart. I saw a girl go in here earlier, Thomas. She looked pretty frightened. Young lady, open up! It's going to be okay."

"Step aside." Father Leary told her and when she did he gave the door two good tries with his shoulder before it smacked open, shattering glass and causing the lights to flicker on automatically. The dark haired pirate girl sat sprawled back in the rolling chair, her head tilted back with lifeless eyes staring at the ceiling, both of her wrists slit vertically in long red lines and pools of blood in her lap. "Jesus, help us please." he breathed stepping in going for her neck to find a pulse he knew would not be there. "She's gone."

"Two more." Laura said running into the storeroom where the other girl, the red head with freckles, started throwing canned goods and boxes at her. She was in a wild frenzy, there were packets of ketchup and mustard everywhere. Boxes and canned goods and glass littered the floor. "We can help you out of here." Laura said dodging a large jar of mayonnaise that exploded on the wall behind her. "Stop fighting me! I'm here to help!"

"It's not you, it's them!" she screamed tossing a jar of pickles past Laura, missing her head only by inches. "Get them the hell out of here!" the red haired girl screamed while trying to actually climb the shelves behind her. "I can't stand cats. How did so many get in here? God, there's hundreds!"

"They're not there." Laura said dodging one more can but catching the next one in the shoulder as she charged in to grab the girl. Once upon her she thought she might be in a better position since she was much larger than the girl, whose name tag read Christine, but the tiny teen was quite strong, probably from her fear of felines, and wrestled her against the shelves. "It's not real. Let me get you out of here. We can take the back door. Just listen to me, girl!"

"You can't save them all, darlin'." her husbands voice taunted from the speakers. *"Best get out while you still can. I think our boy, Philip, is about to make things get real hot in here."*

His laughter that followed was not human at all and seemed to be joined by other dark things laughing with him. Laura smacked the teen girl hard, causing her head to bang into the floor and then drug her up to a kneeling position before turning her around and dragging her towards the exit sign.

"Thomas, get that manager now!" she said. "He's getting ready to do something bad!"

***

"Where the hell is all of the light?" Philip said with teeth actually starting to chatter as he rubbed his arms while loading more chemicals on top of the fryers and grills. "It's getting so fucking cold. Gotta do something before it gets worse. We are going to get this puppy nice and toasty in here, yes sir."

"What are you doing?" Father Leary said rounding the corner and catching the young man starting to twist all of the dials up to maximum settings.

"I . . . will not . . . freeze to death in this pitch black shit." he said watching a cool frosty mist spray out of his own mouth. He could hear the walls cracking from the ice, the ceiling starting to cave in at certain points from the weight of the snow. The temperature must have dropped at least fifty degrees in the last five minutes. "Why didn't they warn us about this shit, man?" he asked the priest while rapidly flipping switches. "How could they not know? Don't you see what's happening, bro? It's pitch black out there, the power's out, it's getting colder by the minute. This is our only chance."

"Just let me get you out of here, son." Father Leary said approaching with caution. "I promise this is not what you think it is. It's not real, focus on me, not the darkness around you."

"You nuts or something?" he said, eyes still wide and wild as he continued to stack boxes and plastic jugs on the flat sizzling fryers. "I'm fucking freezing, man! How is that not real?"

"Screw it." the priest said taking only a second to size the young man up and realizing he shouldn't be too much to handle. He grabbed the skinny young man from behind and drug him towards the back exit, the young manager flailing out with arms and legs knocking various things over while Father Leary watched flames leap up from the assortment of chemicals and cardboard on the fryers all the while. "I guess we might make it out before the place blows." he grunted as his back smacked into the door, sounding off a shrill alarm as they broke into the sunlight of the back parking lot.

"You got him in time." Laura said running to him out of breath. The young dark haired girl she had saved sat on the far curb of the lot with the others, her hands shooing away unseen things, and the young manager, Phil, was still struggling with his obvious fear of the dark. Meanwhile, inside, things were starting to crackle and pop.

"Is everybody out?" Father Leary gasped struggling to get the young man to calm down who was now on his knees shaking uncontrollably. "From the front dining room, I mean? Everybody?"

"Yes, I'm sure of it, why?" Laura's face turned to horror as she helped him lift the manager back up to his feet. "You got him, right? Before he could do anything?"

"Get as far away from here as you can!" he yelled to her and the others. "He piled a bunch of flammables on the grill and it's getting ready to blow."

The three of them together made it another ten yards or so when the place blew. The back part of the roof went up hard in a big ball of fire. They fell to the parking lot, scrambling in separate directions while others screamed as the windows exploded next, sending debris across the lot and into the streets around them. Cars stopped and people got out to come and aid if they could, which mildly surprised Father Leary, but he was grateful for it. Some huge trucker lifted him back up while a black man in suit and tie helped Laura away from a flaming piles of shingles. Philip was in the grass now, shaking free of his delusions, and staring in horror as he watched his so-called career literally go up in flames.

"Thank you." Father Leary told the trucker and caught up with Laura who was scanning the lot for Ryan. "Are you okay?" he said taking hold of her to see her eyes. "Are you hurt at all?"

"I'm okay." she said brushing past him and running to where Ryan stood alone by the bright entrance arrow on the lot's edge. "Ryan, baby, are you okay?"

Ryan stood motionless amidst the chaos ensuing around him. He paid no attention to the screams and alarms and distant sirens growing closer. He stood staring up at the phone wire where a single large crow sat staring back at him. In its beak was a long white envelope.

"I think we have a visitor." he said watching the bird swoop down and land on the sign, its dark eyes fixed on him, the white envelope tucked neatly in its bill, Ryan seeing the writing from where he stood. He was about to reach out and take it when Father Leary's larger hand beat him to it.

"Get lost!" the priest said waving the bird away once he had the envelope and the bird cawed loudly at him and took flight. Ryan watched it until it vanished while the priest ripped open the envelope, letting it fall to the parking lot once he had the letter inside. Ryan's eyes drifted down and saw the one word written on it. It was for him.

"SON"

"What is it?" Laura asked leaning in.

"An invitation." the priest responded and Ryan's mind turned back to the comic store once run by his friend Scooter. He could see Anna Finch standing there next to the chips and soda with her pretty red hair and freckles on her nose. He could see her smile and those pretty green eyes. She was going to wear something scary but sexy, she had said. She wanted to dance with him. She might even want to be his girlfriend someday. Now his father was ready to stop all of that.

"Tonight." Ryan mouthed before the priest could continue. "The party Anna invited me to is tonight out at the farm. That's where he will be."

"Seven o'clock. No sooner or later or the boy dies." Father Leary read aloud. "Now we know where Marty Fitzgerald is. He's going to take the whole party hostage in exchange for-"

"Me." Ryan finished and turned to face the two adults.

FIFTY FOUR

Message received. Now all he had to do was wait.

His little bird let him know that Ryan got the letter, even though the priest had to be the one to read it, and that he now understood how this would play out. He knew where to be and when to be here. He knew that tonight it was all coming to an unavoidable end.

The party had already started and it was now a quarter of seven. He could see everybody was having a good time, and why not, it wasn't that often that the Boogeyman himself got to host a Halloween party. The kiddies and the few sappy parents who decided to hang around were all having fun with the creepy dance music, the party games, the candy and punch, and all the rest of the festivities. Alan Woods, still inside the tiring body of Joe Corrigan, stood on the porch watching the events unfold around him. The dancing, the running about to and from the barn, the children playing their games. They would all die if he couldn't get his son to cooperate tonight.

So he waited.

Mostly he stood there watching the lake on the edge of the property. Not so much the lake but the pair of girls who were out there in a bright red paddle boat. One girl in particular, Anna Finch, who was dressed like a sexy little witch. All dolled up just for his son. If he cared for her the way Alan thought he did, then he would behave himself and he might just get Anna Finch in more ways than one once Alan Woods was in there with him. So many ways.

"Great party, Joe." some asshole dressed as a king said while sipping on some punch. Joe slash Alan nodded back and smiled, wishing he could just taste the man's fear a bit right now, finish him off even, but he had bigger fish to fry and he needed to save all of his strength. The priest and his ex-wife would surely try to save the night and Alan needed to be strong for that.

"Sorry Doris couldn't make it." a skinny woman dressed like a vampire said from the snack table. She was scoffing the cookies down pretty fast and hard for a slim bitch. "Tell her I will see her next week at the yard sale."

Alan nodded and smiled again thinking that, *"No, I doubt very much you will see Doris at any yard sale next week unless somebody digs her ass up and drags her over there."*, and then looked back to

271

the lake where the two girls were laughing and singing while racing against two boys in a blue paddle boat.

They were having a good time for now.

For now.

The waiting was almost over.

FIFTY FIVE

"That's it up ahead." Ryan said. "I feel him. He's there."

"Okay, this is it." Thomas Leary said veering the jeep off to the edge of the road with the farm in sight. "We can sneak up on him from here and-"

"No." Ryan whispered coming up between them as the jeep rolled to a stop. "He already knows we're here. Just like I can sense him, he can sense me too."

"So much for the element of surprise." Laura said exiting.

"That was never gonna happen." Ryan said back. "He's expecting us, remember?"

"This is your show, Ryan." the priest said once they were all out on the shoulder of the narrow road. "How do we play this? It's you that has to face your father."

"Give your gun to mom." Ryan said walking past them and keeping his eyes focused on the farmhouse, and the barn and the fields of corn. He could hear music, the children's laughter as well. "She will need it." he said letting his eyes close and he focused through the darkness around him. "He's still got Marty inside. He's being guarded by something. Father Leary, you just save as many kids as you can. I think there are adults here too. Help them to clear out I guess. I will take care of my dad."

"Ryan, I-" his mother said kneeling next to him and hugging him tight. He gave her a small hug back, still focusing on what was going on beyond what his eyes could see.

"I'll be okay." he told her and actually reached out and wiped away a few tears from her face. "Gotta do this, mom. It's the only way and too many people have died."

"I know." she said letting go and looking him over and seeing how quickly he had grown in just the past few weeks, at least on the inside. "I love you. Be careful."

"If you don't mind me asking, Ryan." Father Leary said bringing up the rear as the three of them headed down the road's edge. "Just how do you plan on beating him? How are you going to kill something that's already dead, son?"

"You can't." he gulped and clinched his fists as if ready for battle. "I just need to send him back to where he was before. Back to hell." he looked back and gave a small grin and the priest returned it.

"But how?" his mother asked as they all entered into the tall grassy fields.

"By using his own powers against him." Ryan said. "And besides, he can't hurt me anymore."

"How's that?" the priest asked watching the boy's long strides out distance his own.

"Because I'm not afraid of anything anymore." the child said with an evil grin of his own.

***

"Here we go." Alan Woods voice came from the old body of Joe Corrigan. He could sense his son approaching from the northwest corner of the field. That meant his bitch of a wife and the holy bastard were with him or possibly coming from other directions. They didn't matter. They were simply here for search and rescue. They might save a few kiddies and themselves but that was fine. No huge loss. All Alan cared about was the main prize. Winning the war, not a few battles. As long as he had Ryan at the end of the night the rest was minor details.

He stepped down from the porch, his eyes cast in the direction he knew he son was coming from, a smile coming across the old man's face, and he headed for the barn. There was a new friend he had waiting there for such an occasion and he couldn't wait to switch bodies. This one had served its purpose but it was getting tired and weak.

He slipped past the children playing games and dancing and found the darkness of the stalls. The last one, which was the only one occupied, was where he stopped and turned to greet his new host.

"Hey, Thunder." Alan whispered and the horse backed away. It recognized it's masters appearance, but not the voice or the smell and chilled feeling coming from him now. This was not the same man that had cared for him these past few years. *"Time for a lil' horseplay, wouldn't you say?"* Alan grinned unlocking the stall gate and the horse snorted and backed away as far as it could, it's eyes wide with fear. *"Don't worry boy. You won't feel a thing."*

Alan reached out with old Joe Corrigan's shaking hands and latched onto the bare shoulder of the horse, sending a shockwave of awareness through the animal that it could not possibly understand. Images of evil and suffering that caused it to go into a frenzy. Alan grabbed the horse by the large head and spun the creature to face him, opening wide as a powerful spray of black inky darkness shot out and latched onto the horse's muzzle and drowned out any further sounds of protests.

"Just looking a gift horse in the mouth." Thunder snorted as Alan took over his new powerful frame and the old man slumped down to the straw covered stall in a daze. Alan blinked his huge eyes and focused in on the man who was coming around a bit more quickly than he thought he would and the horse actually smiled. This was the first thing Joe Corrigan saw when he looked up and he thought he had been dreaming.

"What in the name of-" he said rolling over to his side and taking in his dark surroundings. "How did I get out here? What's happening to-"

"You're no longer needed, old timer." Alan said and raised himself up on his powerful hindquarters and let those massive legs and hooves come smashing down on Joe Corrigan's skull with a loud crack. It sounded a bit like a walnut to Alan so he did it three more times to be sure and did a slow walk out of the stall. *"Let's find out who wants a pony ride."* the horse smiled again and galloped towards the open end of the barn.

***

The three of them heard the screaming as soon as the house came into view.

"That's not party screaming." Laura said bringing up the gun. "Those kids are in trouble."

"Get into the house like Ryan said. Save Marty if he's still there." Thomas said breaking into a sprint for the field of glowing lights and pumpkins and running children. "I will get who I can out of here. Ryan, deal with your father wherever the hell he is."

Laura watched her son and the handsome priest run for the panicking crowd while she made her way into the dark house from the back. Surprisingly, the back door was wide open. Country folk, she guessed, had no fears of intruders or crime, although these days maybe they should, especially in Waverly. She braced herself cop-style and burst in, one hand flicking the lights to life and the other waving the gun in all directions for movement.

"Marty?" she called out and there was a small laugh from the hallway to the left. She crept past the fridge and rounded the corner. The long hall was dark save for the bathroom light. "Marty? You in there, Honey? It's me. Ryan's mom."

A single splash and some more mumbling that she couldn't make out. She kept her head moving, not wanting any of these guards her son spoke of to sneak up on her, and made her way to the bathroom door. Another splash.

"Marty?" she said knocking, eyes still looking up and down the hall, and she reached out for the knob. What if he was tied up in there, drowning maybe, and she did nothing? "I'm coming in." she stood back with her weapon aimed and kicked hard, sending the door smashing open and the bright bathroom light bathing her in the hall, nearly blinding her it was so bright. "Marty? Are you okay? Where the hell are you?"

"Hi, sweetie." came an older female voice somewhere from within the bright yellow room. "Care to join me. Come on in, the water's fine."

Laura blinked and saw an older woman, naked and bloody rising up from the crimson waters of the tub and lurching forward to grab her in a death embrace.

"Shit!" she yelled leaping back and nearly tripping over her own feet as the bloody corpse smiled at her while dragging its bloated skin across the wet tiles towards her in the hall.

"Don't be afraid, Laura." the thing spoke over its own gurgling blood that dripped over cracked lips. "We all have to go sometime, sweetie. Would you like a cookie? They're fresh from the oven."

"Stay away!" Laura said backing down the hall with the gun aimed at the dead woman who was now on the carpet and using her elbows to still pursue her. "Where's Marty?"

"Such a tasty little boy." the thing cackled and now did little frog hops trying to catch up to Laura who was nearly back in the kitchen. "He's tucked away for later. A midnight snack, sweetie."

"Fuck you, you're not real." Laura said and calmly leveled off the gun and fired. Her first shot caught the thing in the shoulder and a black hole formed which released an ocean of green goop onto the carpet. The naked body still kept coming and smiling. "Fuck you, you're dead." she fired again, this time right in the forehead. Another hole and this time the entire face was soaked with the dark liquid, but the smile remained all the same.

"Can't kill what's already dead, bitch." the voice of her late husband sounded through the corpse that crawled faster. *"This woman isn't even here. She's buried out in the corn, but please feel free to waste all of your bullets."*

Just then as Laura entered the kitchen, the dead woman with her husband's voice still pursuing her, she heard another noise from behind her. This one was alive. A low growl. She turned just in time to see a large black Doberman leap from the linoleum towards her throat.

***

"Father Leary? It's the horse! It's going nuts!" some man dressed up like a wizard told him as he came into the middle of the chaos. Father Leary thought he recognized him as a high school teacher or something, he wasn't sure. He saw another woman and man also herding the children in his general direction.

"Don't suppose anybody has a gun?" he asked the wizard who was trying to gather a few kids to safety. "A rifle maybe in their truck?"

"Joe might have a few, but I don't know where he got off too. We could check in the house-"

"No!" Father Leary warned. "Stay away from the house. Get these kids out of here. Head that way if you can." he said pointing to the direction he has just came from. And then he took off for the large black horse. Alan had spooked it somehow, he knew, and Joe Corrigan was probably dead by now, maybe Marty too. He had heard gunshots in the house. Two so far. He hoped Laura got past whatever traps Alan had set for her and saved the boy, but right now he had to worry about the rest of these children.

Some poor man dressed up like a king tried to grab the horse but was throw clear across the fence into a stack of pumpkins. The horse whirled on the priest as he and Ryan drew near and once Thomas Leary looked into those eyes he knew what had happened.

"Alan." he said coming to a dead stop.

"Father." the large horse acknowledged him for only a second as it shifted its gaze over to the boy. *"And son. My son. Let's finish this. Give me what I want, boy, or all these people die."*

"Let's find out, dad." Ryan said and raised his arms up, a tiny snarl on his lips, and turned back to Father Leary. "Go help them." he told the priest who jetted past the horse. "Okay, then." Ryan said and for the first time Alan Woods saw that same glow in his son's eyes that he himself had.

"That's my boy." the horse replied with its own eyes growing equally bright as well.

"Tear him apart!" Ryan screamed and a rush of wind swept past him and the large animal. Over his shoulder there was now a huge flock of birds of every dark color and size coming up from the cornfields around them, so many they nearly blocked out the rising moon in the darkening skies, and Ryan was commanding them. "Send him back to hell!"

***

"What's all the screaming about you think?" Anna Finch asked from her shotgun position in the paddleboat. Donna turned the boat in that direction and saw only the flickering party lights and some kids running about in circles.

"Playing some kind of game, I guess." Donna answered back steering closer. "It does sound kind of creepy."

"Awww, are the little girls afraid?" came the voice of the older boy in the blue paddleboat, Tony Pryor. "It is a Halloween party." he said lighting his smoke while steering the boat closer to the girls.

Anna peered over at the two teens that had crashed the party. Both freshman in high school, but losers by her book. Tony with his beady eyes and slick black hair that was always flirting with younger girls. Scott Campbell who ate everything in sight and still thought he was hot because he hung out with Tony, his weight nearly tipping the paddle boat in his own direction.

"So why aren't you guys wearing costumes?" Donna said. "I'm a nurse and Anna's a witch. What are you two supposed to be?"

"Horny and drunk." the chubby boy, Scott Campbell, smiled at them. "Guess which one I am."

"A virgin." Anna chimed in and both Donna and even Tony laughed.

"Not what your mom says." Scott tried but got little response.

"My mom said she couldn't find your tiny pecker, even with a magnifying glass." Donna shot back and the girls broke into laughter once more.

"Why so mean?" Tony tried coming close with his boat. "We're being nice."

"You two shouldn't even be here." Donna snapped back. "You're in high school. Can't you find girls your own age."

"Had 'em." Tony said back blowing a smoke ring in her direction and grinned. "Maybe I like jailbait, you never know."

"So gross." Donna said back over the boy's laughter, but Anna kept her eyes on the other side of the wide lake. The screaming had not stopped and now something else was going on. A huge flock of birds was there. Maybe they were attacking.

"Look at that!" Anna said pointing. "By the barn!"

"Careful, don't fall." Donna warned and followed her friends stare. "What's going on?"

"Just some birds. Maybe they want to party." Tony grinned.

"Who cares, they're birds, big freaking deal." Scott said back. "So how about let's race you girls again and see what you got."

"Don't know when to give up do you, Scott." Donna grinned. "You lost the last two races. I think it's because your weight is slowing the boat down."

"So let's put a wager on this one." Tony chimed in. "We race from east to west, longest part of the lake, and if we win, Scotty here gets to kiss the hot nurse, and I get the witch."

Anna flung her head around and met his eyes with a hard glare. He gave her a wink.

"Screw you, Tony."

"Well, I'd settle for a kiss, but if that's what you got in mind-"

"Eeewwww. You are a complete perv." Donna shot at him and turned the paddleboat away.

"What are you afraid of?" Scott taunted as Tony paddled after them. "Like you said, you beat us twice already, what's the big deal? Name your prize if you win."

"If we win, you both have to kiss each other." Donna said and Anna couldn't help but burst out laughing at that one and nearly forgot all about the birds.

"Now who's a perv?" Tony chuckled while paddling faster. "Besides, I let you girls win the last two races. It was the gentlemanly thing to do."

"You, Tony Pryor, are not a gentleman." Donna sneered and turned away.

"Agreed." he said back. "But come on, what are you afraid of?"

"She's afraid of the dark." Scott said over. "Or the birds."

"Maybe she's just afraid of the Boogeyman." Tony said in his best spooky voice.

"Not afraid of you." Donna said tapping Anna on the shoulder. "Hey, help me out. These guys are verbally assaulting me."

"Sorry." Anna's eyes were fixed on the other side of the lake again. She could have sworn she had seen the horse running around by itself with no rider. And for an instant she thought she saw . . . Ryan.

"Let's just race them already and shut them up."

"Are you crazy." she said looking back at the grinning duo. "I am not kissing the horny fat toad back there."

"Hey, who are you calling a toad?" Scott grinned.

"Let's just race them and then get back to your Uncle's house. I want to see what's going on there." Anna said and Donna let her stare fall on the far banks.

"They're just playing and dancing." Donna said but sounded doubtful.

"Now you ladies won't punk out if you lose, right?" Tony smiled brightly as they came up close.

"No, but you guys probably will." Donna sighed and started to paddle for the east part of the lake. "We see any cheating, all bets are off."

"Won't be any need for that." Scott said as the boats slid near the shore of branches and tall grass, both turning at the same time to face the west and the now thin red line where the sun once was.

"It's so dark." Anna said at once.

"There's nothing in the way out here." Tony reminded her. "Don't get scary ass now."

"She's right, this could be dangerous." Donna said watching the water rippling around the boat. She imagined what it would be like to be on the ocean this late at night, and all the scary things in those waters that might come after her. Sharks, jellyfish and the much dreaded octopus. "There could be snakes out here."

"Come on, one quick race across the lake." Tony tried again, nearly begging. "We won't let anything bother you."

"Yeah, this is fucking farmland in Missouri." Scotty said rising up to his knees to look in the black waters before them all. "What do you think it the scariest thing in this water, besides me that is."

Something shot out of the water with such speed that nobody saw what it was until it had hold of Scott Campbell, and even then the two girls did not see it clearly. Whatever it was it had wrapped itself around Scott's plump waist twice with lightning speed, causing him to cry out in both shock and pain. Tony fell back in the boat, his cigarette flying away in the dark, the girls both cut loose with a high pitched scream, holding each other and rocking the boat from side to side as the fat boy struggled with the long dark slippery thing that was squeezing tighter around his belly. Then something else reached up and grabbed his arm, and another dark slimy something shot out of the water, slithered across the boat and latched itself onto his legs.

"Snakes! Snakes!" Donna cried out reaching for the wheel of the paddleboat. But Tony Pryor, now that he had gotten a good look at the waters behind his own boat and Scott, saw that it was not snakes. Not at all. Tony let his eyes drift past his friend and over the edge of the boat where five more long slimy tentacles were working their way up the edge of the blue paddleboat. His friend was being killed by an octopus.

***

"Not another dog." Laura said and raised up the gun, the first shot catching it square in the chest. The Doberman exploded in a spray of blood, made a short whimper and fell with a thud to the floor. Laura turned and closed the bedroom door as well, the cackling dead woman with her husbands voice sliding up to it and pounding as she herself grabbed onto the basement door and swung it open.

"Marty?" she called down the steps. She clicked the switch but no light came. Great. Complete darkness. "If you can hear me, answer me."

"Down here." came a tiny boy's voice and Laura scrambled down the steps as fast as she could with her eyes darting about and gun switching directions every few seconds.

"Where at?" she called and a thud came from her right. There beside the shadows of a hulking furnace was a closet door. She ran to the wooden door, hearing now noises scuffling along in the blackness, and tried the silver knob. It was locked. "Sweetie, can you open it from the inside?"

"No, it's stuck." came the weak voice. "Help me please. Are you the police?"

"No, honey, it's Ryan's mom." she said tugging harder and then heard those noises getting closer. She turned, barely able to make out shapes with some of the outdoor party lights flickering in now through the four small basement windows. Those shadows were moving. Across the floor, on the walls, even up on the ceiling. Whatever they were there were lots of them and they were almost on her.

"Shit! Stand back, Marty! Get out of the way of the door!"

She gave him a few seconds to move and then aimed the gun at the handle. She squeezed off two shots to play it safe and watched the knob and door splinter into pieces. Laura yanked the door open and Marty came out, dressed only in his underwear and glasses looking sicklier than he usually did. He started to speak, so many questions on his mind she was sure, but she pulled him back towards the steps where the shadows were already gathering in heavy forms.

"We have to go right now, sweetie.." she said but froze when they reached the foot of the steps. "Oh God." she breathed with a shivering child pressed into her leg as she watched the creatures flooding down the steps. Spiders of all sizes, snakes, rats, roaches and only God knew what else pouring down the steps at her with tiny glowing eyes.

"No way out, bitch." her husbands voice laughed from somewhere above them in the kitchen.

***

The horse was actually breathing fire. Ryan Woods stood there with outstretched arms watching the birds that he controlled getting roasted by some strange power he didn't know his father possessed. It must have been one of the kids fears close by. His father was drawing on everyone's fears to fight him and with this many kids around, Ryan figured he had plenty to choose from.

"It won't be that easy, son." his father warned him rearing up and blasting a flock of crows from the sky with a ball of fire. *"I have too many weapons to choose from here. And your mother and that cute little red head bitch you like . . . They are all in danger. How can you save them and fight me? Not exactly the multi-tasker, are you son?"*

"They will be fine." Ryan said calling to more of his own minions with his mind. He had them appearing out of nowhere now, as he did at the schoolyard. He balled up a fist and suddenly a pile of rats and mice poured from the barn and ran up to attack the flaming steed. From his left he called up a hole in the ground and snakes and centipedes sprang into action and attacked as well. "Rip him to pieces!"

The horse that was now his father roared as it shook off the attacks, kicking away the rats and snakes while stomping the rest with fiery hooves. Ryan's eyes glowed brighter still and the skies filled with a dark spinning circle of bats and ravens all descending on the horse. It shook its large mane about and sprayed more cones of fire about, setting the yard, the barn and a few trees ablaze.

"Parlor tricks." his father chuckled through the horses mouth. *"That the best you got, boy. You think you can hurt me with things I'm not even afraid of."*

"No." Ryan grinned backing up. "Just wanted those children and parents to get to safety so I distracted you long enough for that to happen."

The horse looked around and saw there was nobody left now except him and his son and let loose with a roar as he charged forward. *"Sneaky little bastard!"*

"You're not going to kill me." Ryan said boldly standing his ground. "You kill me you're all done here. You have to jump bodies the rest of your life." he said watching the large horse come skidding to a stop right before him, the heat from its flaming nostrils nearly singeing Ryan's hair. "You need me a hell of a lot more than I need you."

"Maybe I just knock you the hell out and take what I want." the huge head said shooting down and taking hold of Ryan with those large white teeth and lifting him up into the air. Ryan gasped as he felt himself being thrown several yards away, his little body striking the ground hard, knocking the breath from him as he rolled closer to the flaming barn. *"I'm not going back to hell because of you, boy. No chance. So maybe I just force you to take my gift."* the horse said coming closer now, but slowly enough to let the boy gain his composure.

"It won't work that way either." Ryan said holding his right arm that he landed on and scooting away from the heat of the burning hay and wood. "I have to accept it, like you did with your dad. You took what he had before he left you, right? If you could force yourself on me you would have done that by now. You know it."

"Stubborn little shit, ain't ya." the large horse said coming closer. *"Give in to me now and I will call off those about to devour your mother and your precious little Anna Finch."*

"If I did give in." Ryan said looking the horse right in its red glowing eyes. "You would kill them anyway. You always intended to kill Anna and Mom and Father Leary. That's all you will do when you pass that evil inside you onto me. But I don't have to be evil just because I'm your son. You're nothing but a liar and a coward." Ryan said raising himself to his feet again. "And now I know what you're afraid of. Let's see if I can make it work."

"I ain't afraid of shit, boy." his father's voice came from all around him in the dark. *"I don't fear things, son. I AM FEAR!"*

The horse roared as it came forward again, rearing up once more and blasting a spray of flames across the path, blocking himself off from Ryan and turning to trot away full speed towards the lake, leaving Ryan entrapped within a circle of fire.

Ryan raised up his hands again, blocking the fire from his view, closed his eyes and simply began walking forward. There was some heat to be sure, and a few bites of pain, but he walked right through that fire without so much as browning one item of clothing much less his own skin. He was actually impressed with himself.

"If you're not afraid, where are you going?" he called after his father and then looked past the running horse and he could see two paddle boats out there in the lake. Anna Finch was in one of them, and something deadly was already out there with her. "God, no . . ."

***

Father Leary heard the screams from the cornfield. He was not blessed with the eyes of Alan or Ryan Woods, but the good Lord had given him excellent hearing. He knew the screams came from the lake, the east side to be exact, and once he had cleared past the corn at a full run, he could see the young people in the paddleboat by the edge of the lake. He was just in time to see one boy pulled into the water by something long and slick like a huge serpent or . . . Tentacle? There were more of them as well and they were attacking both boats.

"Really, an octopus?" his mind echoed as he ran along the slippery path leading around the lake. It had to be one of the girls or boys he saw struggling to get away with that particular fear. He forced himself to run faster although he wasn't exactly sure what he could do once he got there. Laura had the gun. He had nothing but his faith and two fists.

284

"Help us!" the dark haired girl with the glasses cried out, a fat gray tentacle was wrapped around her thigh squeezing tight and had her half way in the water struggling. Anna Finch was already covered in three more lashing arms that had drug her into the water up to her waist. She beat effortlessly on them with her tiny fists that did no damage. Thomas Leary leapt into the boat, nearly tipping it over in doing so, and grabbed hold of the slimy thing squeezing on Donna's leg.

"It got Scotty!" the other teen was yelling and he was working his way free by himself with some Bowie knife he had, the thing bleeding green into the water as he sliced his way loose. "It fucking killed him!"

"Help this young lady to shore and get out of here!" Father Leary called to the boy as he pried the tentacle loose from young Donna Corrigan's leg, passing her over to the boy who jumped boats. While Tony Pryor helped the girl away, Father Leary leapt into the water and lifted Anna Finch up and started to pull. "Let her go you bastard!"

"Here, man!" the teen behind him yelled and Father Leary took the knife the boy tossed into the boat close to him just as the beast yanked both him and Anna under. "Oh, shit! They're gone."

***

"How do we get out of here?" Marty asked as the creatures made their way down the stairs.

"We use the window. Get up there now, I will follow!" Laura said jerking him over to the corner to the washer and dryer. "Get up there!" she said boosting him up as spiders had already made their way to her legs. "Shit! Get off me!" she said brushing them away as the fell from the ceiling on her shirt. A few large rats came at her and she fired off some shots, blowing them away into bloody splotches against the basement walls.

"They're biting me!" Marty called out and she took a towel from a basket of folded clothing and began to swat the ones on the small boy's legs and arms. She leapt up to join him on the washer and wiped the window clear of spiders and bugs and found the biggest bottle of bleach on the shelf next to her.

"Cover your eyes, Marty." she said and hauled back and slammed the plastic bottle into the window three times, breaking away the glass and ripping back the screen.

A small group of rats and mice attacked her legs as she forced herself through the small window and she screamed, all the while Marty crying for her, kicking and slapping away the rodents with her legs while crawling out across the broken glass, adding further injury to her body.

"Run, Marty! Just get out of here!" she called to the boy while retrieving her gun, but the boy waited and helped her limp away from the house that was now crawling with all kinds of creatures and bugs. "We have a car close by." she breathed as they rounded the house and she saw for the first time all of the fire that was consuming the place. "Jesus, what's going on? Everything's burning. Ryan! Thomas!"

"Laura?" came a deep voice from behind her and she whirled around with her gun aimed high. "Whoa! Whoa! Easy with that thing. What the hell's going on out here?"

"Wes?" she asked covering her eyes at the flashing lights of a police car and a fire truck and looked up into the deputy's face.

"Deputy Lambert." Marty said running over to the big man and embracing his side.

"Walker Farm down the road spotted the fire. Said he heard some shots and screaming. Figured it must be more than a party going on here."

Laura forced herself to stand and fell into his chest as the fire fighters rushed past with hoses aimed at the barn and the trees nearby. "My son, Wes." she said up to the cop. "He's still out there somewhere, and he's in danger."

***

Father Leary was not only facing his greatest fear again, which was water, but now he was fighting an octopus which was trying to kill a little girl in that dark cold water as well.

Only it wasn't really an octopus, it was Alan Woods, or one of his minions doing his bidding, or some fear created by these young kids out here tonight. Either way he was running out of strength and air and the red headed girl he was trying to help seemed to be slipping away, her eyes closed for the last time a few seconds ago and she had gone limp. All Thomas Leary could keep doing was praying in his mind and stabbing until his hand cramped up.

Finally, one or the other, or possibly both, seemed to work. The thing after having taken enough blows from the Bowie knife let loose and gave up the ghost as Father Leary surfaced with the unconscious girl in his arms, letting out a long gasp for breath and backing away from the floating dead thing before him.

"Pass her over, man." Tony Pryor said coming into the water and Father Leary gladly did so, collapsing into the brush by the lake right after.

"Is she alive?" Donna asked rushing up to Tony's side.

"I don't know. Let me look at her." Tony replied laying the girls body down gently in the wet grass. He leaned his head into her chest and a small grin appeared on his face. "I can hear her heartbeat. She's breathing. She's alive."

"Not for long." came the voice above both of them and they looked up to see the second impossible thing in their life in one night. An octopus that should not exist and had come from nowhere had killed their friend only moments ago. Now a huge fire breathing horse towered over them and was actually speaking in human voice. *"Party's over."*

***

Ryan gave chase after the horse that was now his father but as he saw the creature gaining distance on him was distracted by something. Something he saw from the corner of his eye. He cut left away from the lake, despite the fact that Anna was in danger, and headed towards the tall pole. It hung above him watching over the nights festivities, its lifeless eyes and stuffed body looking like some crucified piece of sackcloth. It was a scarecrow. Designed to install fear. Just like his father. Just like him.

"Hey!" Ryan said staring up at the tattered clothing. "I need you! Wake the hell up!"

Something stirred in the night air. Ryan felt that familiar chill running through him just like at the playground and the junkyard. He looked up and the scarecrow shimmered as well, its hollow black eyes lit up in tiny orange flames and a wide grin spread across its sewn burlap face. Ryan reached out with both hands buzzing with jolts of tingling electricity and took hold of the thing by the legs and ripped it off the pole down to his level, still holding its glowing gaze within his own.

"Time to use one of his own gifts against him." Ryan said gripping the thing by the head. His own boyish eyes lit up in brilliance to match that of the scarecrows and a bright purple mist floated from his mouth and entered the face of the scarecrow. "I'm your master now. Let's finish this."

***

"You kids get out of here!" Father Leary shouted over to the two teens, especially the young man holding the limp body of Anna Finch, and came closer to the black steed with smoke still drifting from its nostrils trying to distract it away from them. "This creature is mine." he said reaching up to touch his dangling crucifix.

"You think that cross can save you, padre? I ain't no freakin vampire."

"I know what you are." the priest said standing waist deep in water. "I know who you are and where you are from, your entire history. About your father and his before him. I know it will end tonight with your son defeating you."

"Pretty damn sure about that, aren't you?" the horse said ignoring the fleeing youth as he stepped down into the lake, flames leaping to life. *"Right or wrong, too bad you won't live to see it."*

A blast of fire and wicked laughter and Thomas Leary was diving back underwater, the one place in the whole world he hated to be, but surmised in an instant it was better than being flame broiled. The large hooves sought him out next and he had to dodge them as the demon stallion came further into the water to search for him. He waited until the flames died away into darkness above him before he surfaced for air.

"I think I'm getting over my fears, Woods." he grinned staying neck high in case the fire returned.

"Maybe there's something else in the water we can work with." the horse grinned and suddenly in a blur Father Leary witnessed the horse transform before him. The soft black fur fell away to reveal harder gray wet skin. The legs fell away and the head expanded to an enormous size as the mouth ripped open and revealed row after row of sharp jagged teeth. *"How do you feel about sharks?"*

"Same way I feel about any other living thing, Woods." the priest smiled looking past him to the shore where two new arrivals were standing. "If it breathes and bleeds, it can be killed. Shoot it!"

Alan Woods felt the bullets hitting his shark hide even before the priest finished his statement. He thrashed about, turning to view his attacker, and saw the big burnt cop and his ex wife standing there on the shore behind him.

"Tell me this isn't happening." Sergeant Lambert said still firing at what appeared to be a fifteen-foot great white shark. "How the hell did a shark get into this lake? I hate sharks, scare me to death."

"He's feeding off your fear. Just kill it, Wes." Laura said trying to find a safe place to enter and help Thomas Leary, a man who in her eyes had sacrificed so much for them both.

"I remember you, cop." Woods spoke and Wes Lambert actually stopped firing and froze watching this huge shark actually *speak* to him. *"I should have finished your worthless ass years ago. What else are you afraid of, besides sharks? I bet I know. I remember that night what hurt you so much."*

"Christ in Heaven above." Lambert breathed and squeezed the trigger some more as flames leapt out of the sharks mouth and surrounded him. "No! Get it off me!" he said falling to his knees.

"Here, you bastard!" Thomas Leary shouted grabbing hold of the sharks tale. "Turn and face me you coward!"

"Don't be in such a hurry to die, holy man." the shark answered and smacked the priest back into deeper waters with a single swipe of its tail. The priest reached out for the edge of the paddle boat as he watched the big cop on the shore rolling about and screaming, nothing in sight to his own eyes as to what was happening to him, so he figured it must have been inside his own mind.

"Die, Alan! Once and for all would you just fucking die!" Laura said picking up the gun and taking over where Wes Lambert had left off. The shark just turned on her, coming closer to shore, and once its massive jaws were open, a spray of bugs of every kind swarmed from its mouth, quickly covering Laura Woods as she fell to her knees.

"Already did that, sweetness, remember? Don't worry I haven't forgotten your fears, darlin." the shark grinned as it turned back to the waters for the priest who was pulling himself up into the paddleboat. *"Plenty of bugs for you to scream over. Plenty of fear for everyone. Now then, Father, where were we?"*

"Ryan, where are you?" Laura said swatting the large creatures off her arms and legs as she turned to see the paramedics who were now attending to Anna Finch and the others. And then something else caught her eye. Somebody else was coming, and coming fast, leaping and hopping about through the tall corn, blending in with the shadows. Somebody big and lanky, dressed in dirty clothing and straw hat, and eyes of fire blazing bright in the darkness. "Ryan?"

"DAD!" the voice came from the dark figure moving faster now. "FACE ME NOW!"

"Ryan." the priest grinned from his place on the boat looking to the shore. The shark that was Alan Woods swimming in for the kill of the priest turned to see for himself as well. The dark scarecrow darted past the fallen cop and his ex-wife, leaping across the surface of the water, arms outstretched and eyes blazing.

"Somebody learned a new trick." the shark grinned as the scarecrow landed with a splash.

"I know what you're afraid of." the scarecrow smiled and stretched out its hands to either side and the creatures of the night responded once more. "I know all that you know, *Dad*." he said with a smirk on his burlap face. "Let's see what you really got."

"Sounds like a challenge, my boy." the shark said rising up and in those black lifeless eyes Ryan Woods could see for the first time the human eyes of his father Alan Woods. The eyes he remembered as a boy. *"Winner take all."*

Laura ran to where Deputy Wes Lambert was rolling around on the grass screaming and holding his face and took hold of him. "Wes, there's nothing there!" Laura said shaking the strange bugs loose from her own body and shaking the large cop who was rolling on the ground. "It's not real! It's a trick, can you hear me?"

"I hear you." he mumbled removing his own hands from his face and reaching out for hers now. "I was on fire." he breathed looking back towards the lake. "My God, what's happening?"

"The end." Laura said helping him up to a kneeling position. "The end of a nightmare."

***

The night air was alive again with its children. A swirling dark circle over the lake had formed in a matter of minutes with all kinds of crows, ravens, owls, bats and other birds that the human eyes on the ground could not make out. Just like it was back at the parking lot all of those years ago.

"Attack him! Attack all of them!" the shark thing cried out.

290

"There not yours anymore, Dad." the scarecrow grinned moving in closer to the shark while using its limp arms to point to the edges of the lake where eyes lit up on its dark borders. "They all are mine. And they are here to watch you finally die once and for all."

Alan Woods in his shark form looked around himself, seeing all beasts of the field, the snakes and lizards make their way into the water's edge, the rats and cats and dogs standing guard on the shores of the lake among other creatures, the fowl of the air above him, and he reached out with his mind and found none of them responding to him.

"What have you done!" he screamed lunging for the scarecrow.

"They like me better." Ryan inside the straw body replied grabbing hold of the massive jaws that opened wide for him. "Just because I come from you doesn't mean I have to be evil. I came from *her* too." he said looking back at his mother next to the big cop as they made their way closer to where Father Leary sat in the paddleboat. "And like I said, I *know* what you're afraid of."

"You know jack shit." the shark said opening wide and breaking free of the scarecrow's grip. It lurched forward some more and bit into the limp legs of the man-sized thing his son inhabited. *"I don't want to kill you, but I will before I let you kill me, boy."* the shark laughed ripping into him. *"I will just have to keep switching bodies. Maybe little Anna Finch would be a good host."*

"You can't have her or anyone else!" Ryan cried out smashing his fists into the side of the sharks body. "Tonight is the last night you walk the earth." Ryan said in his child voice. "Nobody else dies because of you!"

***

"Why aren't they helping him?" Laura asked the priest as both her and Lambert came out into the one boat to help him exit the other next to it. All three sets of adult eyes studied the edges of the lake to see the seemingly hundreds of glowing eyes there and then up to the still steady flowing circle above them.

"Maybe they're waiting for a winner." Thomas Leary suggested watching the spectacle in the water before him. "I don't know how Ryan did it, but he's inside that scarecrow, and he's losing his form. He's going to need another host. Something alive, not made of straw and burlap."

"Please tell me what's going on." Lambert said from his place at the edge of the boat. "Who is that guy in there fighting that shark? How is it even possible for a shark to be-"

"I'll explain later." she hushed him searching the edge of the lake. "Maybe he could enter one of them." Laura said pointing to some of the larger dogs not far away. "Or all of them?"

"Or me." Thomas Leary breathed to himself. "I'm sorry, Laura." Father Leary said and took Laura's face in both hands and kissed her softly on the forehead. Then he dove into the lake.

"No, Thomas!" Laura started after him but the strong arms of Wes Lambert held her back.

"You can't go in there, Laura!" the big cop struggled with her wresting her back into the boat. "Not with those things in there. What the hell is he doing?"

Father Thomas Leary did not have to really swim. The water was only chest high at this point. He just kept moving towards the battle only twenty yards away from him, watching Ryan's scarecrow frame being shredded apart while hammering away at the tough hide of the sharks skin.

"Ryan!" he called out moving faster nearly in reach of the thing's tail. "Take me, Ryan! Switch with me!"

"What? No!" Ryan called out and shoved the large thing back just as it devoured him from the waist down and the scarecrow bobbed about like some clothed buoy. "Get out of here, Father! I will deal with him!"

"You're losing son." Father Leary breathed struggling to keep his balance on the slippery mud beneath him. "Alone in that form your can't take him." he said keeping a wide breadth from the shark and circling to join the wounded scarecrow that actually had Ryan's eyes beneath the burlap. It almost looked human. "But together, with your powers and my faith, we can beat him."

"Father Leary." the scarecrow sighed turning to view the shark moving in closer again. "Do you know what you're doing? If I enter you, he's going to attack you, and you're still human."

"Just do it now!" Leary said standing so still and the scarecrow reached out with both arms and took hold of the priest face.

"Open your mouth." Ryan's voice whispered. "You won't feel a thing."

"No greater gift is there than for a man to lay down his own life." the priest said and watched as a brilliant purple mist floated out of the scarecrows. "And we're not dead yet, Ryan."

292

"*I can remedy that shit, Padre.*" the shark said coming full speed at him with mouth open wide, revealing hundreds of teeth, all seemingly made of steel sparkling in the moonlight.

"Eat this!" the priest cried out and shoved what was left of the scarecrow into the sharks mouth, then shoving the beast away from him after. "You're done!"

"Thomas, no!" Laura cried from the boat while Lambert still held her. "My son was-"

"It's me, mom." the priest said in her son's voice. "Father Leary is in here too, but right now its pretty much just me." he said looking at first his large hands and then his own reflection in the waters from the bright moon and fires around them. "So this is what it feels like to be a full grown man."

"*Don't get used to it, boy.*" the shark grinned. "*You won't be in there for long.*"

"Let's find out." the priest said, eyes glowing bright, even his cross dangling from his neck over his chest was glowing like hot fire and for the first time when both strong hands reached out and took hold of the shark by the sides of its massive head, Alan Woods knew fear as well. "WHAT ARE YOU AFRAID OF?"

"*Nothing! I don't know fear, I am fear.*" Alan tried, but knew better, and now so did his son inside this priest.

"LIAR!" both the priest and his son's voices called out at the same time. "You've been someplace bad, Woods. A place I'm very familiar with. A place you don't want to go back to."

"*You think you know where I've been, Padre?*" Alan called to him struggling to free himself. "*Your precious faith barely scratches the surface of what waits. You have no idea!*"

"I know it's a place where you were all alone." Ryan's voice halfway came out of the priests body while touching the dark mind of his father. "A place of torment. A place where angels fear to tread. And I can send you back there."

"*If I go I'm taking you with me!*" the shark cried out and pushed forward to attack the holy man standing before him. A cry of agony echoed across the lake as those teeth sunk deep into the man as he fell to his knees in pooling blood.

"No!" Laura cried breaking free of Wes Lambert who went into the water after her. "Thomas! Ryan?"

"Laura, stay back, there's nothing we can do now." the big cop said taking hold of her again.

"We're not done yet, mom." Ryan's voice sounded and stood again, taking hold of the shark and forcing its mouth open and back away from his own bleeding body. "You're going home, father. Show me your fears! Show me!" his son's voice taunted and Alan Woods felt a tickle somewhere in the back of his mind. He looked about him while struggling with the priest and saw the waters of the lake begin to bubble and boil with steam, hissing out as it burned his thick skin. "Show me what's coming, dad! Show me Hell!"

Alan Woods in that shark's body did look around and saw the flames, smelled the sulfur, could hear the screams of torment from all around him as he saw others suffering there. He was in hell once more. He screamed as both priest and boy, mother and cop, watched as the shark skin and teeth fell away to a less massive form. The skin went pale, the body narrow and aged, the hair wet and tangled over a near skull face with scars and bony arms of tattoos and within one minute it revealed the man who was truly Alan Woods in all his unholy glory. *"I can't go back there."* the thing choked up at him. *"Please."*

"Begging now?" the man looked down with a boyish grin. "Who's giving you a choice?" Ryan said lifting up his father's near skin and bone form, even less so than the scarecrow he had devoured moments ago, and held it high to the bright moon as if some dark sacrifice. "Take him! He's yours! Rip his soul apart!"

With one last thrust before collapsing into the waters, the body of Father Thomas Leary threw the weak frail body of his father up into the night and the children that had obeyed his commands against their will for so long descended upon him and had their feast.

"Nooooooooooooo! I can't die!" Alan Woods cried watching the world spin around him.

"Maybe not, but you can go back to Hell." Laura breathed unable to look away.

Everyone below froze in horror as they watched that dark circle of birds swoop down and attack. Alan Woods body was ripped into pieces in seconds by every creature that could fly, and his bloody remains that fell to both water and land were eaten by those dark creatures as well, until there was nothing left but tattered clothing. Then, as quickly as they came, they left, all glowing eyes blending back into the darkness of the woods or waters or dark skies, taking their cries of freedom with them. Sergeant Wesley Lambert watched in both horror and fascination for the second time in his life knowing that he must have been witnessing the beginning five years ago, and praying to himself he was now witnessing the end.

"Thomas! Ryan!" Laura cried out and this time she did break free as she made her way across the lake to where the body of the priest floated face down in the water. She waded through the blood, her shaking hands reaching out and taking hold of the man and turning him over to see his face, his wide blinking eyes, and he gasped for breath as those eyes found hers.

"Did we beat him?" the priest asked shaking in her arms.

"You did." she knelt down and kissed his forehead. "You and my son. Thank you, Thomas."

"No problem." he said and coughed up blood letting his hand reach up and take hold on hers. "Take care of that . . . son of yours." he finished and Laura felt him go then, all at once, and she sobbed while falling to her knees in those dark waters while Sergeant Lambert took the limp body from her and headed for the shore. Father Thomas Leary had died a hero.

"I will." she promised looking up at the bright moon. Then her thoughts went to her son. "Ryan?" she said and leapt to her feet. "Ryan!"

"Here!" came the boy running from out of the cornfields and Laura cried tears of joy this time, running through the waters and past the cop and fallen priest and finally kneeling down into the embrace of her son. "Mom!"

"You're alive." she breathed into his neck and hugging him. "You and Father Leary did it. You sent him away. But I don't understand. How are you still alive?"

"I did what he did." Ryan said. "I switched into the scarecrow, while my body was sleeping back there." he said pointing to the cornfield. "Then I went into Father Leary." he said finding the shore where the big cop leaned over the fallen priest. "He's dead, ain't he?"

"Yes, baby." Laura sniffed turning with him as they both watched the paramedics coming too late. "He knew what he was doing. He knew what had to be done."

"So do I." Ryan breathed and turned to see the remains of the war around them. "Anna?"

"She's going to be fine, they are treating her. Honey, things can back to being normal again."

"Not sure about that." Ryan said watching them cover the body of Father Leary and carrying him away. He had lost a good friend today. A brave one. A man who had sacrificed everything to save him and his mother and all of these people. "Not with me. Not ever again."

"It is what you want it to be, sweetie." his mother said guiding him away from the lake. "You don't have to use those powers if you don't want to, right?"

"We'll see, mom." he told her watching the moon look down upon him, it's new master of the night. "I guess we'll see."

EPILOGUE

My name is Ryan Woods.

It's been twenty years since I sent my father back to Hell. A lot has happened since. My mother lives in Texas now. She owns her own gift shop and eventually married Wes Lambert, who is a Sheriff down there with her in a small town called Red Rook. She is happy. I call and write often.

My sister became a veterinarian and moved to Colorado where she married a dentist and had two daughters. No sons. Thank God.

Father Leary was buried at Saint Michael's and I visit his grave a few times a year. He sacrificed so much. People here think he drowned in that lake saving the life of a little girl. I guess he did. That and so much more. I miss him.

Anna Finch grew up to be even more beautiful and went to college out east somewhere. She dropped out and married a drummer in a rock band, and got her heart broken. He beat on her some, they divorced and she moved out west with friends and eventually got herself back on track and became a teacher. She eventually married again, another teacher, and they had kids. She is happy.

I miss her but she deserves so much better than me. She got it. She survived. Her ex-husband, the drummer, did not.

I paid him a visit one night and found out he had a fear of water, much like the good Father Leary did, and the band found him dead in his hotel room. He drowned in the tub. They would blame it on drugs. That was fine with me.

People usually believe what they are told or read.

I moved back to Waverly after graduating high school in Texas. It's my home, my birthplace of those ancestors before me, and I protect it. I even live in the same house. Got it at a cheap price too. It does not hold bad memories for me anymore. I worked hard and eventually bought a bar. The Cubby Hole. It helps me keep an eye on things. It allows me to do what I was born to do. Only this time it will be different. This time I will do what's right.

I'm meeting an old friend here tonight. Steven Butler. He used to bully me years ago. Now he's been in jail for drugs and car theft. Nothing that much mattered until just a few weeks ago when he came

297

back through town and beat up some girl who refused to have sex with him. Cops couldn't pin it on him so he got off.

At least he thinks he did.

So here he is sitting in my bar on a Monday night, a slow night. I find a reason to get rid of my waitress, Sara. I tell her I have friends coming for a late night of poker and that she can have the night off with pay, and then I wait. I wait until the old duff who used to deliver mail gets up and leaves and Steven is sitting there tossing a few back watching the football highlights on the news before I lock the place up.

"Closing early?" he asks more aggravated than curious. "It ain't but ten-thirty."

"Nope, just wanted a minute of your time." I tell him rounding the table. "Thought maybe we could catch up."

"Catch up?" he asked eyeing me. "I know you, pal?"

I stand in silence while watching his eyes scan me up and down for any familiar trace and then I move towards him with a grin.

"Ryan Woods." I tell him directly as I sit before him filling my own mug and then topping his off. "Daniel Boone Elementary."

"Holy shit!" he cries and his face looks like he can't decide anger or joy. "Damn, son. It's been years." he says lifting his mug to toast me. "Last time I saw you I was just a kid."

"Me too." I smile reaching out and tickling his tiny brain. So much there to snack on. One thing in particular strikes my fancy. "Just passing through?"

"Yeah, I guess. On my way to Chi-town." he grins and seems nervous we are alone. "Got some things lined up. A job and a place, you know. Times are hard."

"Yes, they are." I tell him and can hear them coming from outside, from the corners, from the darkness and shadows around us.

"You own this place?" he grins looking around.

"You bet." I smile back. "Not much but it pays the bills."

"I hear that. What else matters? My old man used to drink here."

"Mine too." I grin back and his smile fades at the mention of my father. "Heard you been busy since you been back in Waverly."

"Not sure what you mean." he squirms a bit and sips his beer. "Only been here a few days so-"

"Amber Carson." I say her name directly to see if he even knows the name of the woman he attacked and his eyes find me, first rage, then fear and denial. "Dark hair. Dark eyes. Cashier at the market down the road a ways. Twenty-three. Ring a bell?"

"Hell no, man. What are you talking about?" he slides his chair back. "Look, nice seeing you again, Woods, but I got to hit the road, you know. The new gig and all."

"What makes you think you're leaving?" I ask him and stand myself, in much better shape from all the working out I do and running, and Steven sizes me up some. Steven looks like maybe he's been eating all of his meals in fast food joints and the drugs and booze have done nothing in his favor either. He's got a gut and no muscle tone in his arms. I figure I could take him without help from my friends but that would be letting him off too easy.

Besides . . . I'm hungry.

"Look, man." he warns me taking out his cell phone. "You want me to call the cops? Open this fucking door, shit head, or your psycho ass is in huge trouble!"

"Call them." I grin coming around the table and now I can smell them as well. Steven Butler's greatest fear coming to greet him, a long time missing him and wanting to get reacquainted. "I'm not going anywhere."

"Your ass, pal." he dialed 911 smiling the whole time while reaching for the door. I could hear the phone ring three times, and then a soft female voice on the other side. I take over a bit from there. "Yes, this is Steven Butler, I'm over at the Cubby Hold on Truman Road and the owner, one mister Ryan Woods, is refusing to let me leave so I think maybe you should get over here and-"

"You're not going anywhere, sweetheart." the female voice said coldly and laughed and Steven held the phone back from his ear, staring at it and then up to me and he could see my glowing eyes. *"We can't help you. Nobody can. Bye-bye, Mister Butler."*

"What the fuck is this shit?" he said snapping the phone shut and pulling out a hunting knife from his jacket. I smile. "You got these fucking cops on your side, Woods? Is that what's going on? You want some of this?" he waves the knife at me.

"I don't need the police and your welcome to try." I smile eyeing the knife and stretch out my arms as the room grew darker still. "Take him now!"

Steven Butler saw them then. Along the walls coming in such great numbers they were climbing over each other. His hidden fears. Long and fat, black and gray, all screaming as they came for him with such hunger. Rats. Hundreds of them.

"Woods, you sick fuck!" Steven Butler cried out and with a mighty kick of his work boot he shattered the door open a few inches and ripped it aside only to realize it was all for nothing. Outside, covering the entire parking lot, even his truck and the streets, were thousands of rats with glowing eyes and sharp teeth just waiting for him. "God, no." he breathed and tears were actually dripping over his face as he began to fight and scream his way through them with the knife. "Help me somebody!"

"Rip him apart." I tell them casually and sit to finish my beer. "Don't leave anything."

They don't take long. They never do. Justice has been served once more. It is my purpose. I will only punish the guilty, you see. Not like my father. Those who do evil, will face evil. At least in Waverly.

I am Ryan Woods.

I am the Boogeyman.

THE END